THE HILLINGDON FILES

PAUL A COOPER

authorHOUSE®

AuthorHouse™ UK
1663 Liberty Drive
Bloomington, IN 47403 USA
www.authorhouse.co.uk
Phone: UK TFN: 0800 0148641 (Toll Free inside the UK)
*   UK Local: 02036 956322 (+44 20 3695 6322 from outside the UK)*

Published by AuthorHouse 07/05/2021

ISBN: 978-1-6655-9081-5 (sc)
ISBN: 978-1-6655-9082-2 (hc)
ISBN: 978-1-6655-9080-8 (e)

PREFACE

◇◇◇◇◇◇◇◇◇◇◇◇◇◇

This is my first book, and I can honestly say it came from nowhere. Its initial title was *The Tithe Cottage*—the starting point for an adventure about which I had no idea regarding its direction, storyline, or conclusion. The Tithe was based loosely on a cottage in Graffton Flyford, Worcestershire, England. Honeysuckle Cottage belonged to a great-great-aunt of mine that I don't believe I ever met, but where my parents spent their honeymoon.

The story as it is today grew page by page, character by character, and I was as excited to see each chapter develop into a proper novel, as if *I* were reading it for the first time. Most of the settings are real, and I have tried to stick to as true a representation of them as possible, but with some embellishments to help with the storyline.

I can only offer apologies to those with any real knowledge of CID, sailing craft, business skills, or corporate funding, as these items are presented based on my knowledge at best gained from detective stories that I have seen or read, or at worst completely made up.

I have no idea why the base for the story is in Bournemouth; I've been there a number of times and visited Poole and surrounding districts, and I can only assume it has struck a chord somewhere in my subconscious. But I have enjoyed exploring it, and the many other places within the book, through the magic of Google.

This story will continue and, at the time of writing, is called *The Follow-On*. Doubtless this will change into something, with any luck, a little more inspiring. I hope you enjoy the book if you are reading this segment first, or that you haven't been too disappointed if you have just finished it.

Until we meet again, many thanks for your time.
Paul A. Cooper

ACKNOWLEDGEMENTS

◇◇◇◇◇◇◇◇◇◇◇◇◇

I need to thank my wife, Caroline, for her patience and understanding while I was writing this book, and for her many hours of assistance correcting my appalling grammar and spelling. I also offer thanks to our sons, Nick, Mark, and Ben, for technical help with IT, police protocol, and money laundering references. Not that any of them have actual experience of money laundering, you understand.

I need to acknowledge Google and my thesaurus, as without them I would still probably be on chapter 7.

I must also acknowledge our daughters, Joanne and Nicola, for inspiration on all things female.

In addition, I would like to thank AuthorHouse UK for making my first venture into publishing a far less daunting task than I may have expected. Their support and guidance have been helpful, making the transition from draft manuscript to finished product relatively painless.

CHAPTER 1

◇◇◇◇◇◇◇◇◇◇◇◇◇◇

Seven in the morning was early for me to get a call from Aleysha, but not unheard of. However, her tone of voice was, to say the least, very much out of the ordinary. At first I wasn't sure whether it was fear or anger I detected, but as I had no reason to suspect she should be angry with me, I went with fear.

'Are you at home?' she asked, with no 'Hi, Greg, you okay?' as normal. 'If you are, can you come to the Tithe cottage *now*?'

The line went dead before I could say, 'Sure, what's up?' Aleysha could be brief and to the point, but she would never leave something this open-ended without explanation. I rang her mobile, but it immediately went to voicemail.

I got dressed without a shower and raced to the kitchen with a mixture of unease and concern. I stumbled over Jet, my collie cross, grabbed my keys, and headed down to the car.

We were scheduled in court today to give preliminary evidence in a hit-and-run from the weekend—just two of many other witnesses to this event. *Maybe it's a family thing*, I thought. The Tithe cottage used to belong to her uncle and aunt, who had both died along with a myriad of others caught up in the 2011 tsunami in Japan. Aleysha had been long-term letting the cottage to professionals. I didn't know how she had ended up with a business interest on such an impressive property, but I was aware that she had declared it. I had been there only once, to help clear out a few things during a crossover between one set of tenants leaving and another's arrival. I was somewhat in admiration of the property and gardens but more in awe at the time at its upkeep and maintenance than its relationship to Aleysha.

Catching the lift down from the third floor of my flat, for some reason I always habitually look up at the security cameras and wonder whether there is ever anyone watching or even checking them out, and if so, why. The air was chilled as I dropped on to the leather seats of the Ford Focus. They felt cold, almost damp, but strangely I remember reading somewhere that we have touch, smell, hearing, motion, and sight receptors but no wetness sensors. We can only detect wetness via its temperature in relation to our skin, so if a wet seat were the same temperature as my body, I would likely not detect it at all.

I drove left out of the parking complex onto the Boscombe road with the magnetic blue light stuck to the roof flashing, allowing me to push the speed limits.

From my flat in Bournemouth to the old Tithe cottage could be an hour and a half at the height of summer without blues and twos, but it was about thirty-five minutes this time of year, late October. Still, that left plenty of time for me to mull over a number of imponderable scenarios. Aleysha was a good DI, one of the best I'd had working for me, but she'd had a number of run-ins with other force members who didn't appreciate being told that they were crap detectives and should find another career, and with criminals who didn't appreciate being put behind bars.

A gentle rain fell as I drove across the moor, and on my approach to Thorney Hill the tension in my chest grew tangibly. I passed Bramble Lodge on the left to turn right into Pound Lane and thought of the last time Aleysha and I were here. We were staking out the lodge, trying to run down a pair of drug couriers. That was a very long night with nothing to show for it, as it appeared that they were fully aware we were on to them; they skipped over the fence at the back of the lodge and caught an Uber back to Bristol.

The Tithe should have been about half a mile up Pound Lane on the left, and for a minute I was concerned that I hadn't recognized the entrance. Then there it was: the open gateway to the drive and gardens in front of the property, just as impeccably manicured as they were two years ago.

As I pulled in, my heart was racing. All my senses were on high alert. But there were no cars; Aleysha's dirty blue Honda was nowhere to be seen. I eased myself out of the car quietly, listening; nevertheless my feet crunched on the gravel driveway as I walked up towards the cottage. I looked into the open ivy-clad garage: an unused bench, a couple of bikes hung up on hooks, an old canoe on the floor.

I tried to take in every detail just in case I was looking at a crime scene, which right now I had no reason to suspect it was, as I saw nothing out of the ordinary—except, that is, for the open garage door, which was seemingly incongruous, as it spoiled the picture-book look of the cottage.

'Aleysha!' I called out, but there was no response. I walked towards the front entrance, an ornate mahogany door encased in a traditional brick-and-slate cottage porch. The light rain seemed to have muted even the birdsong, and the stillness was eerie. I called out again, even the sound of my voice sucked away by the heavy damp air, and still received no answer.

The front door was locked; I rattled it and called out once more, looking in through the front windows. There was nothing obviously out of place, and while such cottages are always dark even in bright sunlight, the rear windows overlooking the moor illuminated the rooms sufficiently to see in. Nothing seemed wrong; nothing was moving. *No sound, no sign of life.* That last thought sent a shiver of fear through me. What was I expecting? I'd thought she would be here—maybe upset, maybe angry or irate about something, but never *not here*.

I had known Aleysha for some six years. We were very similar in many ways—our approach to life, what is right, what is wrong—but she could hold a grudge, and I have come to accept this in my experience as quite a typical female trait. We had no emotional ties to each other, and though I had no siblings, I thought of her as I imagined I would a sister. We had genuine concern for each other's well-being. I knew she had my back, as I had hers, and not just in our professional life but also socially and practically. And right now, my anxiety levels were heightened to the point that I started to feel a darkness settling in.

I moved right, across the front of the property towards the garage, which is set back slightly—an early sixties addition, I would guess. It was more than adequate for a Hillman Imp or Mini but completely inappropriate for the BMW 5 Series, which most of the residents I passed on the way seemed to prefer. I passed the garden shed with the tools that the occupants were expected to use to keep the garden tidy—just the simple stuff, like keeping the patios clear of leaves and looking after the hanging baskets. The real gardening and maintenance were done by a local who came once a week for however long it took.

I recalled that a door at the back of the garage led into a utility room, another late addition to the two-hundred-year-old cottage. I went in under the hardwood up-and-over door and tried the rear door, but it too was locked. Nothing appeared out of place, other than the canoe on the floor that should have been in its rack, hanging from the roof.

I called Aleysha on my mobile, and again it went to voicemail. This time I left a message, trying not to sound too concerned. 'Hi, Aley. Just arrived at the Tithe. Where are you?'

Back outside and making my way to the rear of the cottage, I was immediately drawn to the conservatory door, which was slightly open. I went inside and called out, 'Anyone home?' Nothing.

There's a very specific smell to these old cottages, and it hit me the minute I walked in, like opening an old china cabinet. I have never been able to establish its cause; it's not nice and it's not nasty—just a very individual, recognizable smell.

The cottage, for its type, is unusually large, with five bedrooms and two reception rooms in an L shape. The lounge forms the upright of the L, and the kitchen is snuggled between it and the second reception room, which has been given over to a large dining area. All are well-equipped in typical period furniture of the Victorian era, dark and heavy. I spent the next ten minutes going from room to room, stopping every few seconds to listen for anything, looking at, into, or on top of every cupboard, shelf, worktop, and drawer. Looking for what? Clues, inspiration—anything that would enlighten me as to why I was there and Aleysha was not. There were a lot of personal effects around the cottage, so it was obviously under tenancy; but there was little sign, other than the open conservatory door, that anyone had been in the house recently—no cups left in the sink, shoes in the hall, or coats over chairs. Everything was just as one might leave it when going away on holiday.

The phone in the hallway was a high-end landline with a control panel and display, even a joystick. *A combined phone and security system*, I mused, but certainly I lacked the capability to figure out how to recall messages if there were any. I assumed the security system was switched off. I looked at it blankly, hoping for it to come to life. I didn't know what to do next.

4

I got a feeling of nausea the likes of which I hadn't felt since childhood when I was left to do something really important, had absolutely no idea how to do it, and was too embarrassed to ask.

I defaulted to my mobile and decided to call the office—something I should probably have done earlier. I talked to Chris Bowden, the governor, and filled him in. He was equally troubled but said she had probably gone chasing a lead on the MEMS case and couldn't wait for me. 'You know what she's like,' he said.

The MEMS case related to an organized syndicate known for low-level illegal drug distribution and now suspected people trafficking. The thought of Aley going off on this on her own didn't diminish my anxiety one little bit. Bowden said I might as well head back and he would coordinate things from there. I didn't feel I should leave just yet, as she had been quite definite about me being here. Chris said, 'Someone just might want you out of the way for a while; have you thought of that?' I hadn't, but I couldn't make any sense of that either. Why would anyone have a reason to want me on the Dorset moor as opposed to Bournemouth, which is hardly the crime capital of the south of England?

With the lack of anything more constructive to do, I revisited each room with what I considered my best forensic approach, looking for anything that might suggest Aleysha's presence or anything she may have left as a clue as to her whereabouts. It wasn't like we had any secret code or a history whereby we had a pact that in certain circumstances we would have a special meeting place.

I became increasingly aware that I was snooping around someone else's property without either their agreement or a warrant, or really any way of explaining myself should they return. After another ten or fifteen minutes, I decided, as there was obviously nothing here that was going to assist me in finding Aleysha, I should leave. As I was closing the door to the conservatory, my phone buzzed. It was a text reminder from the court: 'Bournemouth Crown Court—Densleigh Road Bournemouth—10.30 court-room 3—Judge Kilburn—Crown/Hillingdon V Hunter - End message.'

I called the office, and it seemed to ring forever. 'Hello, Jackie speaking ... Oh, good morning, Greg, any joy with Aleysha?'

'No,' I said, probably a little too abruptly. 'Can you put me through to the super please?'

'Sure.' Jackie's voice was replaced with some inane message about burglaries in the Bournemouth area and how we all need to be more vigilant to protect our property and, almost as an afterthought, that we should keep a watchful eye out for the elderly as well.

Chris came on the line. 'Any news, Greg?'

'No, nothing. You?'

'Well, only that John Graham, the Crown's solicitor in the Hillingdon–Hunter case just emailed to say that the other three witnesses have decided that they no longer wish to appear for the Crown.'

'What? You're kidding me, right? That's way too coincidental. What reason are they giving, and do they all give the same one?'

'We don't have that information right now, but we're still digging. In the meantime, I think you should head to the courthouse and see what you can get out of Graham.'

'Okay, guv, I think we should look a little closer at Hunter.' John Hunter was the perpetrator of the hit-and-run and had been heavily shielded from us by his brief.

I walked past the shed, between it and the garage, and realized that I hadn't checked inside. There was what looked like an expensive combination lock through the rather simple hasp and staple, which seemed a massive overkill, as I could flick the hasp off with a reasonable screwdriver. As it turns out, that wasn't necessary, as the lock was open. I slipped it out of the staple and pulled the shed door slightly. As I did so, it caught on something, I glimpsed through the opening and saw inside what looked like a row of butane gas canisters. I heard a mechanical click as the door opened a little further, followed by that arcing sound you get when trying to ignite a gas cooker ring. My mind went into overdrive as I heard the unambiguous *wumph* of gas igniting and realized that what would follow was likely to be the canisters shredding into a million pieces as they exploded from the inside. I dived backward, heading for the outer back corner of the garage as the first heatwave and deafening blow hit me. The heavy padlock in my hand was propelled upwards and smacked me in the chin. By now I was on my backside, kicking frantically to get around the back corner of the garage as the second and third canister ripped through what was left of the shed and a good portion of the side and back wall of the garage, that being the only thing that was now protecting me from any further blasts. I was aware of being surrounded by an immense heat ball which thankfully faded almost as fast as it emerged. Dazed, left flat on my back, but very conscious of the overriding smell of butane gas, burning wood, and brick dust, I tried to get a hold on my senses and establish whether I was damaged. Having rubbed myself down and verified that all limbs were working, I got up and looked around at the carnage. I was mindful of a gash on my chin and was visibly shaking. At this stage, I had no idea whether all the canisters were exhausted, but my immediate thought was for the ensuing fire.

Tinged with a mix of fear, deafness, and adrenalin, I was torn between just getting the hell out of here and trying to dampen down the fire to protect the Tithe.

I called Chris on speed dial. I was sure he could probably hear the tension in my voice as I filled him in while trying to unravel the hose located on the other side of the conservatory to douse the flames emerging from the garage. He said he would get the emergency services at once.

'Are you okay?' he asked.

'I'll be fine. Just do whatever you can to locate Aley,' I said. 'Get a tracking lock on her phone.'

'Already run that, it's switched off,' Chris said.

I called Aleysha's number again; it was now unobtainable.

I worried about the smoke and flames billowing from the now exposed side of garage and what looked like liquid smoke pouring from under the utility door, made worse because the up-and-over was open and fanning from the other side. I was frantically playing an inadequate stream of water at an ever-increasing inferno for what seemed like an inordinate amount of time in an effort to stop the blaze getting a hold on the rest of the cottage. Finally, I heard the very welcome sound of sirens just as I consumed the last remnants of adrenalin and collapsed on the patio steps. My forty-two years were probably showing on my face.

Over the next twenty minutes, I was prodded by paramedics and questioned by members of my own force, which was a strange experience thankfully brought to a close when Chris arrived. With obvious concern, he drew me to one side. 'This sort of thing doesn't happen out here,' he said.

It was also obvious that Aleysha's safety was the cause of as much anxiety for him as it most definitely was for me. Though far from thinking straight, I was aware that it was important right now that we pool all resources in a concerted effort to locate her.

The fire brigade did a good job of smothering the blaze and kept the real damage to the shed, which was spread all over the garden in smouldering heaps; the sidewall of the garage, which other than its pitch roof was not supportive to the house; and some blackening of the door, walls, and windows in the utility. A good portion of the garage and its roof would have to be demolished and rebuilt, but the fire chief said that thankfully the door to the utility was a good quality fire door and probably saved significantly more damage to the rest of the cottage. They thanked me for my probably feeble efforts with the hose, but I appreciated it anyway.

A small crowd of locals had gathered at the end of the drive and were being processed by our officers as to what, if anything, they had seen over the last few days. The paramedics reluctantly let me go, as other than looking as if I had spent a couple of hours up a chimney and having what felt like severe sunburn on my left cheek and a gash on my chin, I was remarkably unscathed. I would need a haircut; I'd let it grow a little longer than normal of late, which I felt might turn out to be a blessing, as there was probably enough, mostly dark with the odd sliver of grey peppered in, to match the right-hand section of my mop to the singed left. My ears were still ringing, and my head was a little fuzzy, but I considered myself exceptionally lucky. At the same time, I had the sense of what can only be described as a sickening feeling in the pit of my stomach that there was an element out there prepared to kill me, though for what reason I had no idea. I wondered whether, having failed once, they would try again.

Chris said that he had been in touch with the court and asked for an adjournment to the Hillingdon hearing, so I said I would head home, get showered and changed, and meet up back in the incident room.

Driving back to the flat was, to say the least, traumatic. I found it very difficult to concentrate on the road and on a couple of occasions headed way too fast into bends and had to rely on my automated senses to take over. My mind was trying hard to focus on how we were to find Aley and why I hadn't been wiped out in the side passageway of the Tithe. When

I did arrive at the flat in Enfields and parked up, I had no recollection of the journey at all.

I put the key in the door, expecting Jet to be scrabbling on the hardwood floor of the entrance hall, his tail wagging and waiting for his customary rub-down and tickle. The silence hit me, and for a moment I thought this was something else in the morning's events that had been sent to upset it. I quickly realized that it was now gone ten o'clock and Lucy would have Jet. She comes in every morning when I'm working to do a little clearing up—puts the dishes away from the sink, hangs any coats or shoes I've left around, and the like. She also loves taking Jet for a walk; it gives her thinking time, she says.

I quickly got showered, forgetting the burn on the side of my face, still covered in gel from the paramedics, until it felt as though I had just poured boiling water over it. I wound the knob down to warm, and then further to cool, before I could put my face in and finally feel the water's soothing effect. I changed into fresh clothes. The plaster on my chin was already starting to peel back, so I pulled it off. It wasn't bleeding and didn't look that bad, so I left it, threw everything I'd just taken off into the washing machine, tossed in a tab, and set it to extended wash at forty degrees, hoping the black wouldn't run into the white—least of my worries. After the shower, my head started to clear, and I soon felt as though I was starting to take control again. I needed to get to the incident room and see whether there was any news. I quickly scribbled a note to Lucy before leaving, to ask whether she would mind popping in on Jet later just in case I didn't get back for his six o'clock feed.

On the way back to the car, I checked my phone. No messages, no missed calls. The disappointment was physical. I felt the need to try to lay my emotions to one side so I could think clearly, but I seemed to be able to achieve this for only a matter of seconds before the dread of what Aleysha may be going through built up inside me again.

CHAPTER 2

<><><><><><><><><><><><>

The Dorset police station on Madeira Road is a five-minute drive from my flat, and thankfully I had no time to conjure up any more what-ifs before I pulled in through the front gates. The now heavier rain made the blue facade and green copper roof of the station look almost majestic. I drove around the back to the officer parking section, perfunctorily showing my ID card to Lee Weatherly, who lifted the barrier. 'You okay, mate?' he shouted as I drove past with my window down.

'Had better starts to the week,' I said in return.

There was a space close to the rear entrance, so I coerced the Ford Focus in front-first. It was not the best of landings, and whoever was in the car to the left-hand side was going to struggle to get in, but frankly, right now I had more pressing things to attend to.

I signed in as usual, nodding to Janis on reception, who had a questioning look on her face.

'Don't ask,' I said with an attempt at a smile. After taking the stairs two at a time to the first floor, I paced along the corridor and burst through the double doors. The incident room was already in process; all old cases had been moved to the back, and two large whiteboards had been set up centre stage. There were only three officers, Phil Green, James Powell, and Joanne Dawson, along with Chris, milling around taking pages from the fax machine and printer, and downloading photographs and attaching them to the whiteboards. We were all very used to seeing a case build in this way, and the first few hours are the most frenetic, but it is an unnerving experience to see faces of not only your colleagues but also yourself on display along with photographs of a scene you were heavily immersed in and almost part of.

Chris came over and put an arm around me and said, 'You okay doing this?'

'Like what else do you think I could be doing?'

Phil Green, a genuinely nice guy, came over. 'James says her phone signal was last located in Poole; he has triangulated it out to between the Travel Lodge and the Dolphin Shopping centre.' He pointed to an enlarged map on the second of the whiteboards. 'Sometime just before seven this morning.'

'I know the area,' I said, but it meant nothing specific. 'Her sister lives in Poole, fairly close to there.'

'I'll get HR on it,' Chris said. 'They should have records on the family.'

'That would have been the call she made to me. Nothing after that?'

'No,' Phil said. 'Apparently there was an active blip up until around eight thirty; after that it was fully switched off. But James is still monitoring it. He's not getting any radio or phone chatter from his special box of tricks that's giving us any assistance, I'm afraid.'

'Thanks,' I said.

'We are also looking into the background on the Hillingdon hit-and-run victim' Phil said.

'Is he out of hospital yet?'

'Not sure that's happening anytime soon; he has been put in an induced coma.'

I suggested that in light of all this, we should get some protection at the hospital for him. Chris agreed.

'How accurate is the last location of Aley's phone?' I asked Phil.

'Well, the masts are at Parkstone golf course, Nuffield Industrial Estate, and the RNLI College, so they are well split. It should be within a few metres.'

'Can you pinpoint it on an OS for me? I'm going to see if anything clicks.'

I grabbed a cup of coffee and parked at my desk for a moment, trying to gather my thoughts and put some sense to this morning's events. They keep coming back to something Chris said earlier—that maybe Aley was following up on the MEMS case. Were these guys even up to this level of hostility? All our intelligence so far suggested that they were unsavoury, low life career criminals, but nowhere had there been any hint that they had, in the past, resorted to physical harm. Even what we have on the people-trafficking front wasn't along the lines of shipping them in containers or lorries. It was more associated with locating illegals that were already here and giving them false identities so they could work. There had been no hint of violence—certainly nothing about kidnapping or explosives.

Joanne shouted, 'Her phone's on!'

We all raced over to her monitor and were joined by Doug Rimmer from HR, who was holding a Manila folder. I saw and guessed what it was, but my attention was fully on the red blip on Dawson's screen. It was on the peninsula of Sandbanks where Panorama Road meets Banks Road. 'It could be Haven Cafe,' I said.

Chris was immediately on the intercom, using his override code to all units. 'Possible location for Aleysha Coombs at, or around, the Haven cafe.'

Chris got PC Roger Morgan and PC Jeff Hill back almost immediately. Morgan was in Cranford Cliffs, and Hill was just leaving Tesco Express on the Sandbanks Road, both about five minutes out and on their way. I saw the blip on the screen move slightly left before it disappeared. Though it was a good twenty minutes from where I was, I grabbed my coat and ran for the door. I shouted to no one in particular, 'Keep me informed!' I heard Chris say he wanted an armed response at the scene as soon as possible as I took the stairs three at a time.

I gestured across to Lee to lift the barrier as I dropped into the Focus. Because the car park was now full and very tight on space, I chose to reverse out the same way I came in, around the side of the building and in front of reception. I got some startled looks from a bunch of smokers, and some smart arse amongst them retorted, 'Go get 'em, Starsky.' For sure my Ford Focus was never going to be mistaken for a Ford Torino, but I flicked both dashboard switches to light her up and set the sirens off, to cheers from the small audience. I made my way out turning right onto Lansdown Road and took Oxford Road at the island, which fortunately for me was now clear of any rush hour traffic. Making my way onto the ring road, I was able to open up, and with everything flashing I got a clear run to Cranford Cliffs Road before it started to snarl up. I heard Roger Morgan calling in. He was outside Haven Café but saw no sign of Aleysha. I pressed the button on my radio.

'Is the ferry in? Over.'

'It's just docking on the other side. Over.'

Jeff came on to say that he had blocked Banks Road so nothing could get back that way and Chris was arranging other patrol cars to block Ferry Road on Hartlands before it meets Studland. He also redirected the armed response team to the Corfe Castle area. But he knew that if they were not in place within the next five or six minutes, there were any number of routes around Corfe Castle that one could get lost in, and right now we had no idea what we were looking for. I felt completely deflated, realizing I was in no position now to get anywhere useful, being ten minutes from Sandbanks and probably forty from Studland or Corfe. I pulled over into the Penn Hill car park and radioed to Roger.

'Have you got binoculars with you? Over.'

'Already on it. The passengers are being let off the ferry, but I can't say I can see Aleysha. No one struggling or being led away. Over.'

It would have been good if there were a possibility of Aley wearing a red jacket, but that's not her. She would likely be wearing an understated grey or navy waterproof.

'Can we talk to the ferry pilot? Over,' I said.

'Joanne is talking to the ferry operator,' Chris said.

'Apparently Old Joe has a mobile. Nobody there has called him for years, but they are trying to get his number. Over.'

I got a sinking sensation as I felt I was losing the link to my partner. I now no longer needed any confirmation that she was in trouble; I knew, and I felt helpless.

After being lost in my own thoughts for a moment, I was brought back by a crackle of the radio coming to life.

'Morgan here. I can see Aleysha getting into a white van—small, probably Peugeot or VW Caddy. She looks okay; she's got in on the passenger side of her own accord. IC1 male and IC5 male. IC1 driving, IC5 got in through back doors. Over.'

'Chris,' I said, 'can we get a chopper up? Over.'

'It's already up, but unfortunately it's in a pursuit over Southampton. We're on to Weymouth; they are finalizing some safety checks and will be airborne within five minutes, but that's fifteen to twenty away. Over.'

'It's a Caddy,' Morgan said. 'Possible registration DK68, maybe 0 FY something. It's off down Ferry Road. Over.'

'Roger that.'

During the next ten minutes we got messages from patrol cars, three in number. They were through Wareham and heading for Corfe; two others were en route and setting roadblocks on the A351 and the road to Church Knowle. These were obvious routes out, but as I looked at Google Maps on my phone and zoomed in, I was very aware of just how hopeless this seemed.

The head of the armed response team requested a location, and I could detect the hesitation in Chris's voice as to where to deploy. In the end, he resolved to stand them down.

I decided to head over towards Corfe castle anyway.

I called in and ask Chris whether someone could check on Aley's sister. 'She may have talked to her this morning,' I said. They had been very tight over the last couple of days—so much so that I would say that if Aley wasn't working, she would be with her sister. I'd come to know her sister Maya quite well recently and could say they were in many ways very much alike, with Maya being a little less edgy, definitely the younger sibling, and very proud—and, at times, somewhat envious of her sister's police career. I recalled she was in marketing; I think Aley referred to it as some flaky job with lots of perks.

It was gone two thirty when I passed Corfe Castle, by which time we had eight vehicles on the Hartland peninsula. Nothing so far from Studland, Kingston, Harman's Cross, or Woolgarston. The guys were going through each little hamlet as if they were going through a house on a drug bust, clearing each area and calling it in.

I decided I would head for Swanage, as it was the largest town, and the one I would choose if I wanted to lie low for a while. It was also somewhere I could get something to eat and drink; my lone cup of coffee in the office earlier had definitely been expended.

Driving slowly into town while looking up every alley for a white Caddy, of which there were far more than I expected, I saw none with any resemblance to the registration DK68—though every white van sent an electric shock through me.

I eventually pulled up outside the Parade Fish and Chip Bar on the square and grabbed a tray to go with a Coke. I'm sure they were good, but my mind was elsewhere, still trying to make some sense of any of it.

My mobile rang. It was Joanne.

'Hi, Greg. Maya Coombs, Aleysha's sister—twenty-nine years old, number 37 Elizabeth Road Flats, Poole?'

'Yes that sound right; I've always gone with Aleysha never taken any notice of the address,' I said.

'It's a couple of blocks back from the Dolphin Shopping centre.'

I asked, 'Do we have a mobile number listed?'

'No, just a landline, and there's no answer on that.'

'Has anyone been dispatched to the address?'

'I think Chris sent PC Morgan, but I haven't heard back yet.'

'Can we dig a bit more to see if we can get a mobile number please?'

'Sure, I'll see what I can do.'

'Thanks.'

I contacted Roger over the radio. 'No answer at the door an hour ago,' he told me, and he said he was trying to get in touch with the landlord to see whether he would let us check the place out.

Whether they allow this without a warrant is normally down to the landlord–tenant relationship.

'Oh, by the way,' Roger said, 'Aleysha's car is parked outside. I have put a "police aware" sign on for now. We'll see what develops but will probably get it towed back to the pound later and get it checked over.'

'Thanks,' I said, and I asked him to keep me informed.

I continued to drive around Swanage, trying to create a grid in my head and work back from the seafront. As the day wore on, there were more and more patrol cars on the streets doing the same thing. They filtered in having cleared the rest of the Hartland villages with unfortunately the same result.

At five fifteen I got a message that one of the patrols checking the Ferry drop found two mobile phones in a waste bin; one was Aleysha's. I had trouble with this. If you wanted to dispose of mobile phones, why use a waste bin when you have only just crossed a stretch of water?

I called PC Morgan.

'Hi, Roger. How sure are you it was Aleysha getting in the van?'

'Ninety-five per cent. Why?'

'They've just found Aleysha's phone in a waste bin the Hartland side of the ferry stop. Just seems strange to me.'

'I agree,' said Roger 'Why not drop it overboard?'

My phone buzzed. 'Got to go,' I said, 'I have another call.'

I cleared down and tapped the green accept button. 'Hello.'

'PC Dawson.'

'Hi, Joanne. What have you got?'

'Maya's mobile number, but when I called it, PC Tate picked up. It's the other phone from the waste bin.'

I had a scenario going around my head that whoever had Aley—and now it looked like it might include Maya as well—wasn't expecting us to get on to them as quickly as we did. Planting the phones on Hartland's, leaving them live, would lead us in that direction. My greatest fear now was that we were on a wild goose chase and that Aleysha and Maya were probably never on the ferry or even on Sandbanks, but just their phones and a decoy mule.

I decided I would head back to the incident room, letting Chris know on the way what I suspected.

Halfway back, I heard a radio message that they had found the van in the old railway car park. It had an all-day ticket, and we had an unmarked car with it providing surveillance.

While all vehicles were now being scrutinized leaving the area, other than one white and one Asian male and a woman, who were very unlikely to still be together, with the Asian male being the only one that might be seen as a minority on Sandbanks, the odds on turning anything up were now slim to none.

It had gone seven when I got back to the office, and there'd been a changeover of staff, but Joanne, Phil, and Chris were still around and busy on the phones. There had been another three officers assigned to the investigation, which I saw from the top of the left-hand whiteboard was now called 'Blue Rabbit'. I hoped we didn't pay people to come up with these project names. I quickly called Lucy just to check she was okay with Jet, which, as always, she was.

I don't think, in the last six years that I had worked with Aleysha, there had been a day gone by that we hadn't been in contact over something or another, until today. I felt as though a part of me had been surgically removed, and I wasn't sure I had appreciated just how important that part was.

Since lunchtime, Phil had been monitoring all movement of boats in and out of Poole Harbour. Virtually all craft were registered and recognized. Probably fewer than fifty boats a week were new to Poole, and today there were eight; six had registrations that tied them to the Southampton area, and the other two were unknown. One left the harbour at three o'clock and headed down to Weymouth, where it moored offshore, and it was still there. We had a patrol in the vicinity checking that out now. The other left the Port of Poole Marina about six and headed out to the English Channel in the general direction of Guernsey. I looked over at Phil's screen and asked whether we knew the name and ownership of the one in the English Channel. He flicked through a few screens, and an image of a small, and what I would call nice, personal fishing boat came up. It was a Proline 26 with a single outboard motor; the owner was Don Lewins, and it was registered at Portsmouth.

'Do we know anything about this Don Lewins?' I asked. A few minutes later, Phil had the full registration documents and Lewins's ID. He was forty-eight years old, with a registered address at Portchester Road, Portsmouth. He'd been an accountant for Banfield for three years. Before that, he had been an accounts manager for HSBC Mexico. 'Thanks,' I said.

Why did the name 'Banfield' register with me? There was something in the back of my mind, but I couldn't drag it out; it was probably not relevant, but I hated not being able to pigeonhole it.

I went over to where the guv'nor was discussing one of the other live cases with another crew. I heard one of the guys talking about a shot being fired on the pier. *Nothing new there.* I asked Chris whether he could spare me a minute.

'Sure, what is it?'

'I want to do a check on a boat that left Poole just over an hour ago.' I knew the local coast guard was limited to a three-mile offshore zone, but we did have access to the UK Coast Guard, who work primarily with drug enforcement and immigration. I took him over to Phil's screen, and Phil ran through his shipping monitor and focused on the Proline 26 as the only boat out of the harbour that looked suspicious. He looked at me and said, 'You do know we can't set these guys off on what just might be another wild goose chase? They need solid intelligence to launch, and I just don't think this is it, Greg.'

'Could we just try?' I asked, not wanting it to sound like a plea, though in reality, it was.

'I'll make a call,' he said.

'Thanks … Look, I'm going to pop home, get freshened up, and have a bite to eat; I'll get back shortly.'

Driving back to the flat, I felt as though I was abandoning Aley and her sister to some fate I had no conception of, and I was still no further forward in establishing any rhyme or reason for the predicament they found themselves in. But I knew it wasn't good.

Pulling into Enfields, there was a radio message informing of an incident at Alderney Hospital: 'Officer on-site requests response.' Within seconds, two patrols called in saying that they were only a couple minutes away. This was where Neville Hillingdon was. I was ten minutes out, but with the sirens I was able to do the trip in six.

Two PCs were talking to the registrar as I ran in through reception. I recognized one of them but couldn't remember his name so had to resort to rank. He looked up, a little surprised, and said, 'Hi, Greg. What brings you here? Wow, you've been through the wars!'

That's awkward! I carried on, hoping it would come to me.

'Yeah, got caught up in an incident of my own. I heard the call on the radio and wasn't far; I just wonder what the incident was? We have a hit-and-run victim here in a coma.'

'Yes,' said the other officer—obviously the one on guard duty. 'PC Colin Taylor, sir.' We shook hands. 'We had a woman on the first floor in a nurse's uniform, but she got called out by one of the doctors. This is a small hospital, and just about everybody knows everybody else, and when the doctor approached, she lashed out with a knife drawn from under her uniform. She only caught the doctor's arm, and he had the wherewithal to sprint down the corridor to the nearest alarm call button. The assailant must have considered continuing too risky and fled via the fire escape. When I heard the alarm, I stayed put with Mr. Hillingdon and locked the door. I spoke shortly after with security, who filled me in, and I thought I should call it.'

Wow, well that was concisely presented, I thought. 'Thanks,' I said. 'Has anyone spoken to the doctor?'

'Yes,' he said, gesturing to the forgotten named officer.

'Graham's partner Jilly is with him now.'

Graham—half a result anyway! 'Where are they?'

'In room twelve.'

'Anything else from security?'

'They found a discarded uniform at the bottom of the fire escape, but no sign of where she went.'

'Make sure you bag the uniform; it may have DNA.'

'Should we get forensics in?' Graham asked.

'I'll talk to my guv'nor. In the meantime, if you could, restrict access to the fire escape until I get confirmation. Unless there's a fire, of course. Where's room twelve?'

'Down there on the left.'

I head in that direction. 'Make sure Hillingdon stays safe, Colin,' I called back, effectively suggesting that he get back on duty.

'Sir,' he replied.

I knocked on door twelve and peered in. 'DCI Greg Richards, CID,' I said, introducing myself.

Jilly stood and extended a hand. 'Evening sir, PC Jilly Smith, and this is Dr Ball.'

'How is it?' I asked, looking at the bandage on his left upper arm.

'I'll live. It's just a scratch—not at all deep, thanks to my suit jacket. That's not so good. Is this to do with Mr. Hillingdon?'

'I suspect so,' I said 'There's something bigger going on here than just a hit-and-run, we think. Did you get a look at the woman?'

'I already have a statement from Dr Ball' Jilly said, handing it over.

'Thanks.' I look over the description given.

> 5'2" to 5'4"—Woman of colour—black hair, natural, tied up—slim build—25–30 years old—perfect teeth— possible scar left side under the chin—black chinos and trainers.

'Woman of colour?' I said. 'Very PC. Any ideas?'

'That's inbuilt in our profession,' he said. 'Not Indian or African. Possibly Asian, Arabic, or a mix. Attractive though.'

'Perfect teeth? That's an unusual observation,' I said.

'When she pulled the knife, she screamed like a trapped animal as she lashed out. That's when I noticed her teeth, and as she pulled her head back for the second slash, just before I high-tailed it, I caught a glimpse of what looked like an old scar under her chin, about this long.' He spread his forefinger and thumb to about ten centimetres. 'Longer but similar to the one you'll have in a couple of months,' he said with a smile. 'As I said, I ducked and ran at that point. Oh, and my daughter's a hairdresser; it wasn't dyed.'

I added the doctor's additional comments to the statement, countersigned it, and handed it back to Jilly.

'Thanks,' I said to them both; then, looking at the doctor, I added, 'Anything else you may remember or think of later, please contact me.' I handed him my card, he nodded, and I left.

The registrar was still passing the time of day with PC Graham, and I enquired as to whether there had been any change to Hillingdon's condition.

'His vitals are more stable today; they are talking about bringing him out of the coma in a couple of days.'

'Thanks,' I said, and I nodded to Graham, whose surname still was not coming to me, and exited through the swing door.

I called Chris on his mobile. I could hear cutlery chinking. He was obviously at home now. I brought him up to date on events at the hospital. He already had an outline report but thanked me anyway and said he had requested SOCO to attend the scene in the morning. He has also arranged for forensics to be at both Alesha's and Maya's flats first thing tomorrow.

I fired up the Focus.

CHAPTER 3

◇◇◇◇◇◇◇◇◇◇◇◇◇◇◇

Five days earlier

Neville was seated at his desk in the large, mainly open plan office, when he received an email marked 'URGENT' from the head of IT Security Omnicamp.

> Omnicamp is an international marketing organization with its head office just off Savoy Place in London. It is run by a brother and sister who are majority shareholders with a 46 per cent stake of the business. Omnicamp Group has a registered combined worth of $3.4 billion and a recorded turnover of $295 million in 2018.
>
> The brother acquired other businesses in the UK equating to an estimated £100 million, always paying over the odds to guarantee purchase. That being said, they now contribute some 25 per cent of the Omnicamp turnover, at just over £70 million, and a gross profit of £19 million. They all show a remarkable turnaround from a gross loss to the multimillion-pound gross profit when last registered.
>
> It apparently has several other such subsidiaries, primarily in Europe and the old Soviet states, employing several hundred staff purportedly on marketing and allied activities. It has banking facilities in the Caymans and other offshore tax-free locations and a not insubstantial number of high-profile media marketing clients.

It was a request to upgrade the firewall on the top-level systems account network server before 6.30 am on the coming Monday and stated that there was a software patch he would send via secure protocol this Friday lunchtime. 'Please do not close the network down until after 7.30 pm the same day.' At that, the email concluded. Neville noted there was no 'please' or 'thank you'. *Have a great weekend ... Ha, what weekend?* he thought. The last time he'd had to upgrade the network over the weekend, it was to incorporate a new version of the Linux operating system, which took from nine o'clock Saturday morning through to four thirty Sunday afternoon, and then three very late nights after that debugging.

The email had been copied to Jess, his line manager, so he wandered over to her office, knocked, and went in.

'I've seen it,' she said. 'Do you want Gary to lend a hand?'

'No, I'm sure I'll cope, but I know just how many down-line computers I'll need to verify, so it's going to be a long one. Could I wrap up lunchtime today and come in tomorrow, say, five pm?' he said.

'Have you sorted Pam out?'

'Not yet, but I'll close that before I go.'

'Make sure you do; you know she has the ear of JC.'

'Will do. Thanks, Jess.'

No one really knew whether Pam was just a very diligent PA for Jeremy Caine, the CEO, but she was rarely in the office when he was not, and it did appear that everyone jumped rather too high at her requests. She had a file that she couldn't open, that she insisted was very important, the contents of which must not be lost as there is no backup, blah blah. He suspected it was corrupted, and if it were that important, it was a schoolboy error not to have a backup.

He looked down at his keyboard and mentally sent a note to himself: 'Must clean.' he clicked on the properties of Pam's file, and an information box appeared in the centre of his screen. The details looked okay, but under security, all levels of access were denied. Even at the most senior level, including Admin, access was restricted. Quite how this could happen he had no idea. Fortunately he had the wherewithal to de-restrict. He called her up and ran through how she could get access, assuming her password would allow it, and while on the phone, he heard keystrokes and then a sigh of relief. 'Thanks, Neville, you're a star.'

'Whatever,' he said with a smile, and he put the phone down.

He cleared his desk, threw his sandwich box, still full, into his rucksack, unplugged the works tablet from the iPad lead and slid it into the special compartment of the bag, threw the lead and plug into the zip pocket at the front, and plugged the tablet into a remote battery pack in the side pocket. The iPad battery would last only about a half hour now, so it was permanently plugged. He needed to put in a request for a new one.

He left the office and walked about sixty yards to the George, an unimposing—no, dingy—pub purporting to be a hotel and bar, though Neville had never seen anyone there sporting anything remotely like a suitcase. The faded brass door handles on the double swing doors were sticky, as though they had been wiped down with a beer-soaked rag, and the left-hand door squeaked like an old saloon door should. However, any authenticity was lost on him. He raised his hand to Gale; she acknowledged him with a smile while pulling a pint for one of Poole's unkempt. 'You're early. Lost your job again?'

'No, got a couple of all-nighters coming up, so going to chill until tomorrow evening.'

'Usual?'

'Please.'

'I'll bring it over.'

'Thanks.' He took a seat in what used to be labelled 'the snug', a term he never really understood, which overlooked Barclays Bank, probably the tallest structure in Poole. Gale came over with his London Pride and asked whether he was eating.

'I have sandwiches if that's okay?'

'The boss is at the Cockleshell today, so no worries. You seen Maya?'

'Not for a couple of days. I think she's in London until tomorrow. I'm just going to text her.'

'Send her my love.'

'Will do.'

He didn't expect Maya to answer. She rarely did during the day; she was always too busy organizing presentations, arranging venues for foreign clients, or putting together virtual marketing campaigns for the website. They both worked in the same building but rarely came in contact with each other at work. They met for the first time about six months prior here at the George when the top floor was celebrating a major overseas campaign sponsor. The actual party was at some swanky hotel in Bournemouth. IT, accounts, and processing never get invited to such events. Maya had been there until around eight o'clock and decided she had had enough Champagne and craved a pint of lager. Neville was there with a group of his IT friends when Maya popped in on her way home with a couple of other top-floor marketeers. All of them were a little worse for wear and a little too loud for the George. They ended up on a table alongside Neville's group and eventually pulled the two tables together. Neville and Maya talked easily; though they had little in common professionally, they seemed to enjoy similar music and social activities. Both had been to the recent Beach Riot concert at the Sixty Million Postcards venue, though neither knew the other was there. Neville rummaged in his wallet and pulled out his entry ticket, which for some reason he'd hung on to, and Maya flipped the same from her purse. 'Snap,' she said.

They saw each other originally only when they both ended up at the George, either after work or on their way back from some other event. Their first proper date was probably two months later, when Neville plucked up the courage to ask Maya whether she would accompany him to an open mic night at the Buffalo Bar in Bournemouth. She agreed, and they had a great evening and had been doing so at least once a month ever since.

As expected, Maya didn't answer his text; she would probably reply later that evening.

He ate his ham and tomato sandwich, checked his emails and messages, and had another beer before leaving the George.

So Neville arrived back at the office at 5.30 p.m. on the Friday, just in time to see most of his colleagues wrapping up for the weekend. He sent a group email to everyone, letting them know that the network would be unavailable from 7.30 this evening until 6.30 a.m. Monday and that he would appreciate it if everyone could log off completely but leave the computers switched on. Otherwise he would have to do a force close on any computers left open, and unsaved information would be lost. *Always good to throw in a threat*, he thought.

He opened the patch folder sent by Doug, the head of IT, which contained eight files. All were encrypted, but a text file identified each one and listed the order in which they were to be run.

He got himself organized with a coffee and logged on to the network's over-screen, which gave him a view of all the network computers and their current statuses. Virtually all were still operative. He scanned across the stats panel and opened up the network usage graph, which was still showing 77.9 per cent. Normal operating level was 83 percent, and he just hoped that would drop to zero in the next couple of hours.

In the meantime, there were some computers used by staff who were on leave or off sick that he could make preparations on. He rang round to the various office team leaders to confirm their identities and the serial numbers of their individual computers. He got twelve hits—a good start—and proceeded to key in a close and restart routine on each of them. He then dropped in a file that displayed on each monitor that the computer was being upgraded and should not be turned off. He loaded the access file from the patch list to each computer, which opened a gateway to the CPU, and waited for each one to respond.

Eventually he got the full list of twelve computers on his screen, indicating in red that they were 'openaccess.'

When in full swing, he would prefer to work on a complete screen of thirty-two computers, but making a start on the twelve may highlight any glitches, which could save time later.

He loaded the next file from the patch to each computer in sequence, and after about twenty-five minutes, some of the red 'openaccess' indications turned amber and displayed 'uploadinprogress.' Some machines took much longer than others, depending on how well the systems were maintained. Very few employees ran regular updates, file cleaning, and defragmentation programmes, which can make a significant difference to operating speeds. Neville had long campaigned to have a default programme run over the weekend to ensure all computers operated optimally but had always been overruled, either by security or by key individuals who needed twenty-four-seven access. Having said that, some machines are just slow. He grabbed another coffee, and over the next hour and a half, all twelve turned amber. *So far so good*, he thought, loading the final patch routine, which consisted of six individual files, combining a full system check with project authentication. He opened the final file in the patch, named 'ident11877', which is where he must then enter the serial numbers of the computers accessed.

As seven thirty approached, he was watching his screen as the twelve amber signals turned to green and flashed 'end11877.' He operated a remote close and rerestart on each as they all went solid green. This operation automatically took him to his ident file, where he electronically signed his initials to complete the process. He felt he'd had a good start clearing twelve computers before he was scheduled to begin.

There were a total of 194 computers on the account network of Omnicamp, and the usage graph now showed 3.61 per cent, which equated to seven terminals that were still live. He loaded a full screen with inactive computers and started the process, and he then rang the seven operators with live ones. Only one answered; she apologized and logged off immediately. He had to assume the others had left for the weekend, and he remotely shut the machines down, noting that only a couple of files had actually been left open; these he could drop in an archive file for recovery later if required.

At eight thirty, while waiting on files to process, he texted Maya just to see what she was up to and to let her know that he was ensconced at the office in solitary.

She came back saying that there was nothing much going on and asking whether he wanted her to bring in a takeaway.

It was very much against regulations for more than one person to be present when these updates were being performed—not from a security viewpoint, as everything was encrypted, but more for fear of the IT worker losing concentration and forgetting where he or she was in the process. If anything was missed, one couldn't simply go back to the last stage; one had to uninstall all previous files and start all over again, which in the case of one computer could take upwards of an hour. A page full didn't bear thinking about.

Neville thought for a moment, looking at his cheese and pickle sandwiches. He texted back, 'Okay, but you can only stay for a while.'

Neville could see she was responding and hoped he hadn't offended her.

'Who said I wanted to stay? I only offered to bring in a takeaway. 😬'

Phew, he thought. *Thumbs back on the screen.* 'Have you got your access key with you? I can come and let you in if you haven't.'

'I have it. What do you fancy?'

'Whatever you want will be fine with me; it has to be better than cheese and pickle.'

'Oh, I'm staying to eat now, am I?'

'As long as you don't get it all over my keypad.' He added a smiley face with a bib on.

'Okay, will get a couple of lamb pasandas with naan and stuff. I'll text when I'm on my way. Should be about an hour.'

'Thanks, see you then.'

Neville felt good when he was around Maya and was pleased she was coming over.

By the time she arrived, he was just starting his second full screen, and so far all had gone better than expected. At this rate, he could be back in his bed before breakfast.

Neville had set up an empty desk alongside his so as not to have any spillage problems, and they sat, ate, and chatted while Neville kept getting up to move another computer on to the next stage or complete one and sign it off.

At ten thirty they had finished with their curry, and he noticed a computer line flashing amber, which generally indicated a low-level incompatibility somewhere. It meant delving into the operating system of terminal 1027. Having done so, Neville immediately saw that the computer clock was an hour out. This should have been an easy fix, but for some reason every time he corrected it and went back to the systems menu it was still the same. He decided he would get back to this at some other time; he didn't want to disrupt his flow, and he could input a sixty-minute offset, which would enable the process to continue.

It was gone eleven when they kissed and Maya headed home.

In the stillness that was present after she had departed, Neville realized just how quiet it was and how strangely alone he now felt.

At 23.13, a flashing red warning lit up on terminal 1027, the same one as before, but red is a completely different kettle of fish. The indication was that there was a mismatched file with a theoretical potential to break through the coding of the new firewall. After just a few minutes, he identified the file and immediately recognized it as file 10:2277:84.sce, the one Pam Cole had had the security access problems with on Thursday. On checking, he found that terminal 1027 was, in fact, Pam Cole's computer.

While the file name was the same, the extension was different; this file extension was listed in the company manual as a coded file requiring special access.

Knowing his way around these folders from previous experience, he quickly found the old coded file poorly hidden in the previous firewall backup directory. He knew he really should seek approval to use such a code, but as this was quite obviously an oversight and it had potential to impact his ability to upload the new firewall on all the Omnicamp accounts, he went ahead and implemented it anyway. He continued to justify himself, in his mind, by wagering that it was too late to contact anyone for approval, and he didn't want to be held up anyway. Terminal 1027 went from red to amber, and while this was an improvement, the same single file kept dropping out when he ran the upgrade. After several failed attempts and having satisfied himself that it had nothing to do with the sixty-minute offset, he looked a little closer at the file extension, which was in the correct format but used a different font. Fonts aren't something that are even changeable with respect to file names or extensions, and he had never come across this before.

Neville simply wanted to include this file within the new firewall and was concerned that if it were to be left out, it could be at risk from a virus or used as an entry point for a Trojan. According to Pam, this was an important file, so he didn't want to take the risk. He took out the extension, retyped it, and hit enter.

The file inexplicably opened up, which should never happen with an encrypted file, and what he subsequently saw, and realized he shouldn't have, filled him with dread.

CHAPTER 4

◇◇◇◇◇◇◇◇◇◇◇◇◇◇

Six weeks earlier

Joe Riley was a twenty-six-year-old insurance salesman who had lost his job at Allied & Co. some weeks earlier. He applied for a position advertised in the *Bournemouth Echo* for an enthusiastic senior loan advisor. He had no idea what that was, but they were offering an eighteen-thousand-pound salary with benefits, which far outweighed the ten thousand plus commission he had been on at Allied.

There was a thorough online application form to fill out, but nothing too exhaustive. It listed the company as IN-Need, and he was invited to the next stage, an interview, within minutes of completing the form.

Four days later, the interview was conducted in the Royal Bath Hotel, and he appeared to be the only candidate. The plaque on the occasional table in the conservatory read 'IN-Need - Miss J. Turner'. He saw the funny side of that but let it slide.

He introduced himself, and the J. turned out to stand for 'Julia'.

She offered a coffee from the machine, which Joe accepted, and they settled down to a relaxed conversation in which Julia learned a lot about Joe and Joe got virtually nothing back about Julia.

The job was effectively to run a high street loan shop called IN-Need, which offered personal loans, house loans, car loans, payday loans and so forth. He thought that this was all done online these days, but apparently IN-Need had built up an impressive following of clients in other areas that preferred the face-to-face approach. It did turn out that a good proportion of the transaction would, in fact, be set up online, but as part of the contract, all IN-Need clients had to agree to a consultation, either up front or at least in the early stages of their loan period, whereby an IN-Need adviser would spend some time evaluating their financial circumstances to help prevent the necessity in the future for unscheduled loans. This seemed to Joe to be self-defeating in the long run, but he assumed they knew what they were doing, as they had been doing it for over nine years. The job included being the IN-Need adviser, and extensive training would be provided. The premises were currently being renovated, and the position would need to be in place within six weeks. Julia said that she could see from the on-line application that Joe's availability was immediate, which was most definitely in his favour, and that all the other signs were equally good. Were there any questions he had?

Joe asked about the benefits that the ad referred to and was shown a bonus chart, relating to the number of clients signed, and the value of their portfolio. This was not too dissimilar to the commission structure at Allied, except the figures seemed to be higher, but that's all relative, and until you get some idea of the potential, you can only have a vague inkling of actual returns. Either way, Joe wasn't so uneasy about that, as the baseline was more than acceptable.

Joe spent a portion of his increasingly extensive free time either catching up with friends or going through every page of the IN-Need website, which was professionally put together and made a big thing about the financial advice offered to all clients.

Three days later, he got a job offer in the post as a senior loan advisor, grade E, at fifteen hundred pounds per calendar month, in association with an attached benefit chart—a copy of the one shown to him by Julia. There was a workplace pension scheme operational, and other schemes could be discussed if he chose to take up the offer. Enclosed was a return letter for him to sign as acceptance, and a stamped, addressed envelope.

He had a phone call a couple of days later informing him that the start date was in five days' time and he should report to the conference room back at the Royal Bath Hotel, room 433, where a one-week business management course would take place, followed by a three-week financial advisor course.

With nothing else on the horizon or any likelihood of a better offer, it was a no-brainer.

Joe had walked past the In-Need shop front several times over the preceding weeks, but it was nice to see it complete. He was formally introduced to the new premises by a head office official, Billy. There was quite a large open area to the front of the shop, with three sizable kidney-shaped desks, an office for Joe in the right-hand corner, and a back office for files and refectory.

Billy was quite officious, with no sense of humour and a personality bypass. He just wanted to get through all the handover material as quickly as possible. That was fine by Joe; he had covered all the operational stuff on the training course and was quite looking forward to getting stuck in. He had been given a contact list as a start point to get networks going, and once he had settled himself, he would make a start there.

Billy said he would be visiting a couple of times a week to make sure everything was in order and to hopefully introduce some new clients to the Bournemouth branch. With that he passed his card to Joe and suggested that if he had any problems he could call the mobile number on the back. He then smiled for the first time, grabbed his briefcase, and left.

Joe examined the card, which read, "William Conro, financial and credit consultant, IN-Need."

By his third week, Joe was getting in the swing of things, and barring the visits from Billy, which were too frequent for his liking, it seemed to be going well. Head office had sent over an assistant before the end of the first week, which helped no end. Stephanie Clarke was a twenty-five-year-old postgraduate from Plymouth uni who had a very agreeable personality, was easy to get along with, was quick to learn, and preferred to be called 'Steph'.

He was pleasantly surprised at just how busy the office was, and he had a portfolio in excess of £50,000 in its second week and well on the way this week to £75,000. This excluded Billy's clients, as they were considered corporate, whatever that meant. But anything over £200,000 on his account for the month put Joe on the bonus chart.

He also actually quite enjoyed the client meetings he'd had, and so far, in all cases, he had been able to offer advice that would make a positive difference to these people's lives. This gave him a sense that he was doing some good in an industry that had experienced years of very bad press.

At the end of a busy Thursday, after Billy had taken his leave for the second time that week, Joe asked Steph if she fancied a drink on the way home. He'd discovered she didn't have a regular boyfriend, and he felt comfortable about asking, and she responded quite enthusiastically. They went to the Shamrock Bar, which was just a ten-minute walk from the office. It was unexpectedly full, and they struggled to get a table but eventually found an alcove towards the back of the pub.

Steph was uncomplicated and had a relaxed, easy demeanour, and they talked comfortably about themselves for several hours, which passed in the blink of an eye. By eight thirty, the previously manic bar had, unknowingly to them, cleared, and Joe was feeling hungry.

'Do you fancy something to eat?' Joe asked.

'Why not.'

'Here, or do you want to try somewhere else?'

'Let's look at the menu,' Steph said.

Steph settled on a veggie burger, which began a completely new dialogue, as Joe had not for one moment appreciated that she might be veggie. In fact, it turned out she was vegan and had been so for the last two years. Ironically, this was something that Joe had been looking into since he lost his job at Allied. He put it down to too much time to watch too many documentaries on Netflix, but he couldn't completely dismiss it, and after another hour with Steph, he had reinforced a commitment to at least cut down on meat, even if not necessarily to cut it out. Either way, he ordered lamb cutlets and decided to reconsider tomorrow.

They had thoroughly enjoyed each other's company, and as ten o'clock approached, Joe offered to walk Steph home. She agreed for him to accompany her to the top of the high street, where they would go in opposite directions to their respective flats. There was a difficult moment when neither new whether to kiss or shake hands, so they settled on a man hug and headed off.

The next day seemed a little awkward at first, a bit like their parting the previous evening. But after a coffee, Steph brought some biscuits into Joe's office, they sat down to discuss the day's clients, and their working relationship returned to normal. Joe had four appointments, and Steph set to work getting all the documentation together in preparation. They could expect up to ten walk-ins a day. Steph would normally handle the introductions and products that they could offer before handing the clients over to Joe, assuming he wasn't in a consultation, in which case she would organize a date and time when she knew he would be available.

There was no Billy due today, which always lightened the atmosphere, and by lunchtime their customary banter had returned, and noises about how they had enjoyed last night were made. Joe even ventured to suggest they might do it again, and Stephanie, far from declining, gave what Joe saw as a positive nod.

At three thirty, however, Billy burst in with a face like thunder and a mood to match.

He marched straight into Joe's office, and Joe looked up a little surprised and said, 'I wasn't expecting you today, Billy.'

'I can see that,' he said. 'What's with client documents being left on Miss Clarke's desk in full view?'

'She's working on them, Billy,' Joe said.

'Well, they shouldn't be left unattended. Very unprofessional.'

At this point, Steph came back from the outer office, where the coffee machine and sink were located, with two cups of tea. She made eye contact with Joe before realizing Billy was in the office, and she immediately about-turned, put the teas on the drainer, and returned to her desk.

Joe called Steph over and said, 'Stephanie, Billy here is concerned about the client's paperwork being left unattended. If you could just drop them in your drawer if you are leaving your desk.' Billy turned around to face Steph and looked a little sheepish, Joe felt. He wasn't sure he had expected him to deal with it immediately. As he did so, Joe gave Steph a wink, suggesting he was working under instructions.

'Okay, err ... sorry,' Steph said sheepishly.

'Anyway,' Billy said, turning back, 'I have some work to do on the accounts, and I need your computer for a while.'

'No problem,' Joe said. 'But I do have a client consultation in'—he looked at his watch—'twenty minutes.'

'Should be fine,' Billy said, 'but if not, you'll have to conduct it in the main office area.'

Is that very professional? Joe ventured to think, but he thought better of voicing it. He gathered his client's paperwork and took it to the desk in front of Steph's and carried on with his preparations.

Steph, having finished with her client information, filed it and asked Billy and Joe whether they wanted tea or coffee. Billy waved it away impatiently, and Joe accepted. She popped the previously poured teas into the microwave for two minutes and brought them out.

'What was that all about?' she said under her breath.

'Beats me,' Joe said. 'Got a bee in his bonnet about something.'

Joe's clients did, in fact, arrive before Billy was complete, and he apologized that the office had been double-booked. He told them that if they were unhappy about conducting the meeting in the open office, he would be happy to rearrange. They said that they would be fine and sat down around the desk. All went well with the proposal, and they appreciated Joe's advice about restructuring their other commitments. They concluded, and Joe signed them up before Billy was done.

When Billy finally wound up, his mood seemed a little lighter. It was difficult to tell really, but at least he wasn't barking at either of them, so that was to be seen as a good sign. He hurriedly made his way out of Joe's office, always seemingly in a rush to get away, with his briefcase tucked under his arm. He achieved a semi-wave and a nod as he went out through the front door.

'Well, that was odd,' Joe said, looking at Steph as he returned to his office.

He noted that Billy had shut his computer down, and given that it was now ten minutes to closing time, he decided not to bother reopening again tonight.

Joe said to Steph, 'Are you up for an early-doors?'

'I have yoga at seven, but yes, we could catch a quick drink, if that's what you mean.'

'Great. Let's shut up shop and get out of here.'

As he was tidying his desk, Joe noted that Billy, in his haste to leave, had left his notepad. He dropped it in his drawer with a reminder to himself to give it back when Billy next made an appearance.

CHAPTER 5

◇◇◇◇◇◇◇◇◇◇◇◇◇

Jeremy had called for an ad-hoc board meeting at Omnicamp at 10.30 Sunday morning between himself, Bryant, and Anni Rizvy. It had not gone well; neither Bryant nor Anni were impressed by weekend meetings that they had not called.

The atmosphere became even more toxic after Jeremy said, 'He knows!'

'Are you sure?' Anni asked.

CHAPTER 6

◇◇◇◇◇◇◇◇◇◇◇◇◇

The clock in the Focus console read ten thirty as I pulled up in front of the Rhaj. Having realized on the way back from the hospital I was hungry but also completely unprepared and quite honestly ill-equipped to create anything edible, I'd made the decision to go for a takeaway. The chicken dhansak took about fifteen minutes—just enough time for me to catch up on emails. Fortunately, there were very few that needed my attention, just one from Phil confirming that the Proline 26 had, in fact, docked on Guernsey. The local bobby had been asked to watch out for anything suspicious; the UK Coast Guard didn't materialize, and the Weymouth chopper got called to a pileup on the Exeter bypass. And there was a bit about SOCO going to the girls' flats in the morning. He'd signed off with 'Sorry, Greg.'

I closed the iPhone as my takeaway was despatched on the counter. I paid, left the Rhaj, and drove back to the flat.

Jet was ecstatic to see me as usual—at least that's what I convince myself of, as he is the only sane thing in my personal life at this moment. I grabbed a dog biscuit from the cupboard, and Jet took it gently. I then parked myself on the sofa and picked at the dhansak. The dread in my heart for Aleysha and Maya boiled up again. I couldn't recall ever feeling so desolate and strangely alone.

I woke up on the sofa, empty takeaway tray on the floor, with the hope I finished it and not Jet. The digital clock on the surround sound showed three forty-five, so I made my way to bed to grab another couple of hours, but that really wasn't going to happen. After what seemed like an age of tossing and turning, I got up, had some toast which I shared with Jet, and left for work.

I was in the office by 6.00 am. Chris, already there, was on his third Nespresso.

'What have we got?' I said.

'Quite a lot. We had a report from the Port of Poole Marina from one of our patrols asking questions of yacht owners as to whether they had seen anything suspicious yesterday evening. A Mr. Amid, the owner of the *White Angel,* a PF-MY40 yacht, said that two women had been taken aboard a small vessel about six thirty to seven last night. He thought it a little strange, as the light was fading and it was, as he said, a small vessel.

'However, the Proline 26 has been impounded on Guernsey, and its occupants are in the nick—one Janet Frasier and her cousin Rosalind Poldine. Apparently they were over for a few days sightseeing. I say "apparently" because they have no accommodation booked and one overnight bag between them. I have asked the UK Coast Guard to pick them up and bring them back here. I had my work cut out to persuade them, but when you mention that one of our own is in jeopardy and these two may have information as to their whereabouts, it tends to sway things a little. They left at 5.30 a.m., should be back in Poole before eight thirty.'

'Mr. Amid …' I said. 'Did he specifically say two women had been taken on board? Because that's very different to two women taking a boat out.'

Chris looked at the scan of the report. 'PC Matt Day has written "Two women taken on board a lite vessel at 18.30 to 19.00".'

'Is the *White Angel* still in dock?' I asked.

'I don't know; let me get on to port authorities.'

'What do we have on this Janet and Ros combo?'

'Nothing right now; I've left a note for Joanne to get on it when she gets in.'

James Powell, our IT and communications expert, came into the office from his comms cell in the basement, grabbed a cup of coffee, and called out, 'You guys want one?'

I nodded and said 'Thanks.' Chris put his hand up to say no.

James is the quiet one of the team. I have a lot of time for him, but he is also one of the detectives that Aleysha had a run-in with a few years ago, when he should have called something in and left it just that little too late. I can still hear James through my earpiece saying, 'Greg, I think

Rigley might have gone in ahead of you; I've just rewound the live feed, and someone like him walked in about five minutes ago.' We were, by then, across the floor of the launderette, and Aleysha was already opening the back door of the office when we came face-to-face with Rigley, a convicted serial killer that Aleysha had helped to send down, who was on the loose, having been busted from a holding cell in Southampton two weeks earlier, and now aiming a gun directly at Aleysha's head. You get a real narrowing of vision under these circumstances, and the only thing I could focus on was the barrel of that Beretta 92.

'Rigley,' I said, hoping it would confirm to the rest of the response team that Powell's suspicions were correct, 'Put the gun down; we're not alone.'

'You should have thought about that before you walked in here.'

I saw the hammer pull back on the Beretta as I ploughed into Aleysha's midsection, heard the discharge, and felt the ringing in my ears and shattering of splintered wood from the door frame behind. This was a one-time charge in an effort to move her head away from the line of fire. I had no backup plan, and Rigley would still have the gun and be on his feet, and we were sprawling on the office floor. The next thing I became aware of was the outside door, which would be directly behind Rigley, being smashed off its hinges and one of the officers bursting in and announcing, 'Armed officer, put your weapon down!' at which point, apparently, as I was face down over Ali and wasn't looking, Rigley spun round and was shot. The ringing from the gunfire was immediately followed by a violent yelp, the last sound to emit from the serial killer. Once the resonance died away, the office fell into a deep silence for a few seconds. We recovered ourselves from the floor, and Aleysha got up. Her first response was 'Where the fuck is Powell?' She turned and left the launderette.

I later learned that she drove straight to the control centre and bawled James out and had to be restrained by Dave Wilkins, the then superintendent. While the incident didn't go any further, there is a note in her records, which is something else she has never forgiven James for.

James, for his part, was devastated, and things have never been the same since between them.

He came over with my coffee. 'Cheers,' I said.

'I'm going to Maya's flat in a bit to tie up with forensics,' he said. Chris looked at me and said, 'You should go to Aleys, they will be there around seven thirty.'

Powell arrived at Maya's just after SOCO was getting robed up, and Sarah, the head of the team, was insisting he do the same if he wished to pass over the threshold.

'And,' she said, 'as observer only; please don't touch anything until my officers have cleared it down.'

'No problem,' James said, and he proceeded to fight his way into a clown suit, plastic overshoes, and hair cap.

It was at least another half an hour before the whole squad was fully prepared and Sarah called the team together to agree who would focus on what rooms, that there were no agendas as to what they were looking for, and that nothing should be left uncovered. 'This is the sister of a missing police officer, so anything we uncover may be the fragment that leads to her whereabouts,' she said. At that, the team of five, with James following up the rear, strolled in single file from the hallway into Maya's flat.

I pulled up at Aley's flat just after nine o'clock and saw the forensic party already in full flow.

This was a surreal situation. I had been through this routine a lot, but always with Aley; it felt like an intrusion into her private space without her being here. I knew the SOCO head well, we knew the routine, and we'd both been here too many times before.

Nathan Blake turned around and scrutinized my face.

'Hey, Greg, how you doing? Unusual make-up. Have I missed Halloween this year?' he said.

'Funny guy,' I replied. 'Stand-up not working for you then?'

We smiled and shook hands.

'Sorry about Aley, mate. Let's see what we can find.'

I robed up, and we proceeded into, for me, very familiar surroundings.

There followed lots of dusting and bagging of personal items, ferreting through drawers and cupboards. It was not unlike my experience at the Tithe twenty-four hours ago, but a lot more methodical, and with a much greater level of purpose now. I watched in awe as these five guys tackled every inch of Aley's flat as if their own lives depended on finding something significant.

On the fridge was a picture of the sisters taken at a SeaWorld centre somewhere—not that long ago, I would suspect—both smiling naturally. Though I have never looked at them this way, they are really both very attractive. I looked closely and could see the similarities; there was no doubt that they came from the same gene pool. I was pulled back by my phone buzzing. It was James. 'Maya's flat is bugged—audio,' he said. 'Lounge, kitchen, and bedroom. Check pictures and mirrors. They are very sophisticated devices, Greg; they were found by chance. They must be emitting a very high or low frequency, as they were not picked up electronically.'

'Thanks,' I said. 'Anything else coming to light?'

'Lots of different prints. they are just logging these at present. No obvious break-in, but there is possible evidence of a struggle. According to Sarah, the SOCO head here, the kitchen table has been disturbed, and a cabinet door, when opened, partially hangs off its hinges. No way of knowing if this is associated or not.'

'James,' I said, 'I've been there recently, to fix a broken window latch; I'm sure she would have mentioned a cupboard door problem.'

'Okay, Greg, I'll pass that on.'

I called over to Nathan and filled him in on the findings at Maya's. He quickly redirected one of the operatives to search for bugging devices, and within minutes they unearthed one taped to the back of the clock in the lounge, disguised as a CE quality label. It got loaded into a metalized bag to eliminate both reception and transmission, and the search for others continued.

I needed no further evidence that there were some big fish at play here and that it had nothing to do with the MEMS case. I nodded to Nat as I left and made my way across Bournemouth to the station.

Back in the incident room, I scanned the boards for anything positive. There was a stock photograph of a PF-MY40 yacht marked up as the *White Angel*. Underneath is a Post-it note: 'The *White Angel* sailed at six o'clock 23 October.' I knew this to be impossible, as the report of the women leaving was logged by PC Day at eight thirty.

I called across to Joanne, 'Any intel on the two women? And where's Chris?'

'Chris has gone to the Port of Poole Marina to check on the *White Angel*. Janet Frasier is in the system; she has been up on possession twice,

2016 and 2017, nothing since. Nothing on Rosalind Poldine, but it would appear that she *is* the cousin.'

'Thanks.' I called Chris on the mobile, it went to voicemail, and I punched the red button.

'Do you have PC Day's mobile?' I asked Joanne.

'Hold on; give me a minute,' she said.

She found it, and I dialled. 'Hi, is that Matt?'

'Who's that?'

'DCI Greg Richards. Is Chris with you?'

'He's on the yacht, sir.'

'I thought it had already sailed?'

'Yes, it has. Apparently the *White Angel* is not an MY40; this vessel is the *Life Line*, is unoccupied, and looks as if its nameplates were switched.'

'Do we know the *White Angel*'s scheduled destination?'

'I don't, sir; Chris might.'

'Thanks.'

This conveyor belt the girls were on kept slipping away faster than I could catch up with it.

My mobile lit up; it was Chris. 'Hi, guv.'

'Sorry, I was on to the port authorities. I guess you know the actual *White Angel* left last night; it had documents logged that put its destination as Doca de Pedroucos, Lisbon. According to the manifest it hasn't docked there and went off radar at twenty-three hundred last night. It is officially listed as missing, along with god knows how many others.'

At nine thirty, Janet Frasier and Rosalind Poldine were escorted in to interview rooms 4 and 5, already cuffed. Phil and Joanne were assigned to head up the initial interview, and they had detectives Ryan and Peterson assisting. Chris arrived back from the port, and we both watched on from the glass cage. Janet was the cocky one, while Ros was completely out of her depth and looked like a rabbit in the headlights. Joanne had Ros, and we were in communication from the cage. She was the one likely to spill the beans first, and we concentrated on how that interview progresses. Joanne is good; she has a very disarming manner, which after about ten minutes put Ros more at ease. The two girls had a well-rehearsed script and stuck to it until Joanne mentioned that their actions had put a detective's life at risk. That was another stab in the chest for me, and I immediately had the picture of the smiling pair at SeaWorld explode in my mind's eye—another time, another place.

As expected, Ros was the one to crumble. In tears, she said, 'We just had to take the boat to Guernsey; Janet had done it a hundred times before. And we would get the money.'

'How much?' Joanne asked.

'Ten thousand each up front and another ten when we bring the boat back.'

'From whom?'

'I never knew, and I don't know if Janet does … Oh shit, shit, shit.'

I held the mic button and said to Joanne, 'Wind it up for now; we'll come back to her later.'

She did, and we moved our attention to Janet.

I told Phil over the headset what Ros has said, and he adjusted his line of questioning. Joanne joined us in the cage, and I congratulated her on a job well done.

Within the hour, we had an email address and a phone number, none of which I expected to be active, but at least our IT guys had something to work with.

After another couple of interview sessions, both women were charged with attempting to pervert the course of justice and remanded in police custody pending further investigation, or the arrival of their brief, whichever came first.

Later, and realizing it was somewhat unethical, I called Alderney hospital and asked to speak to Dr Ball. I could normally circumvent the usually impossible access to a doctor by introducing myself as DCI Richards investigating a probable murder. The receptionist listened to my request, and the line went quiet.

'Dr Ball speaking, how can I help?' I introduced myself. 'Sorry, detective; wasn't sure it was you.'

'How's your arm?' I enquired.

'It's fine, but thanks for asking. What can I do for you?'

'How is Mr. Hillingdon?' I asked.

'Well, I spoke to his consultant this morning, and his signs are encouraging but we are keeping the induced procedure in place for a few more days.'

'Oh,' I said. I'm sure the doctor heard my disappointment.

'Why?' he asked.

'It's just that I think he has vital information concerning a double kidnapping.'

'You do realize that he is very likely to have amnesia when he does come around and that there is no way of knowing when, or even if, his memory will fully restore? Look, I have your mobile now; I'll keep you informed if there is any change.'

'Thanks,' I said.

I decided I needed to look into Hillingdon's background. *What does he do, where does he hang out? Does he have any affiliations to a crime syndicate?*

I got Joanne and Phil on the case and let Chris know what I was doing. He told me he'd been in touch with the owners of the *Life Line* to explain the situation and get permission to put a forensic team on board. They were fine with that and were on their way down from Yeovil now. Unfortunately, the team at Maya's was the only one available in the short term, and they were unlikely to be complete there before this evening.

I wasted the rest of the day chasing my tail, running down more dead ends, with nothing to show and no further forward. There was no more forensic evidence unearthed so far at either Maya's or Aleysha's flats, though they were still looking to tie up fingerprints.

I arrived home exhausted at eleven thirty, had a large glass of milk, gave Jet a chew stick, and saw a note from Lucy saying that she had to go to Chippenham tomorrow to see her Mum for a couple of days and she'd sort Jet in the morning but probably wouldn't be back before eight o'clock Wednesday evening.

⟊⟊⟊

I was woken up at two thirty in the morning by my phone ringing. In my head it's Aleysha, but when I answer it's a male voice—not one that I recognize.

'Hi, is this Greg Richards?'

'Can I ask who's calling?' I said.

'It's Kevin, Kevin Goodwin. I'm Aleysha Coombs's cousin.'

Suddenly I was wide awake. I grabbed a pen and paper from my bedside table.

'This *is* Greg. Go on,' I said.

'I'm sorry to call you out of the blue, and to be honest, I have no idea what time it is where you are, but I had a weird email from Aleysha a couple of days ago asking if there were any problems with the Tithe deal. I know what she meant but had no knowledge of any problem.'

'Hang on, what Tithe deal, and what's your connection to it?' I asked.

'My mum and dad owned the Tithe before their deaths some years ago.'

'I know about that,' I said, 'and I'm very sorry. How did you get my number?'

'She left me a contact list in an email she sent last year; said her job sometimes meant she couldn't always answer her phone straight away and that if it was urgent, well, your name was on the top of the list, as her boss. I hope you don't mind?'

'Not at all; we have been worried about her. What's the Tithe connection'

'Well, they left half to me and the other half to Aleysha and her sister Maya. To be honest, it felt a bit like a millstone, and we struggled for years to get any reasonable tenancy, given that it's out in the sticks. And then a few years back I got approached by Bodican, a leasing agent, to ask if we would be interested in long-term occupancy. They specialize in agreements with international companies, and if we were prepared for them to handle all bookings and we would just look after maintenance and changeovers between tenancies, they would pay a monthly figure regardless of occupancy.'

'How long ago was this?'

'Five or six-years, I guess,' Kevin said.

'And where are you calling from?' I could detect a short delay.

'I'm in Puerto Rico.'

'Wow … and do you have regular contact from Aleysha and Maya?

'Only Aleysha, maybe two or three times a year; and though we threaten to get together, it never really happens. I don't think Maya likes me. Generally; it's just about the bond. We just go over the figures and discuss if there is anything we want to do with it. There is currently only one regular payment to a Mr. Kemp, who I understand to be the gardener and handyman at the Tithe. To be honest, I don't think we have ever drawn more than a few thousand, and I believe that was for some car—a Honda, I think—that Aleysha wanted in the early days.

'Was that the extent of the email she sent?'

'Yes, and I emailed straight back—well, to be fair, about six hours later, when I got up—to ask why. She never came back. Are *you* in contact with her?' he asked.

'Every day until two days ago, and we fear she has been kidnapped along with Maya.'

'Shit.' Kevin was taken aback. There was silence on the line. In an effort to break it, I said, 'Why Puerto Rico?'

He said that it was a long story, and so it turned out to be—one that right now I didn't have either the time or the inclination to absorb. Cutting him short, I asked about the bond and what it was worth.

'Currently around five hundred fifty thousand dollars.'

'That's not enough to warrant kidnapping to this scale,' I said.

'What do you mean, "to this scale"?'

'Well, currently it looks like they have been whisked away on a yacht worth a couple of mil—' I pulled myself up, realizing I was divulging crime information to a complete stranger.

'Look,' I said, 'we need to sit down and talk, but I'm uncomfortable doing this over the phone. Is there any chance you are likely to be coming to the UK? I'm going to find it very difficult get out to the Caribbean on my expenses.'

There was a short silence.

'Greg, right now I need a good excuse to get off my arse, and this seems to me as good a reason as any. Let me see what I can do. Can I call you back later?'

'Sure,' I said, and I thanked him for calling.

Putting my mobile down, I finally felt I had something tangible to focus on—and, of course, something else to prevent sleep.

CHAPTER 7

◇◇◇◇◇◇◇◇◇◇◇◇◇◇◇

The atmosphere around the board table was intense.

'How can you be so sure he knows?' Anni asked.

Jeremy shifted awkwardly in his chair and referred to a computer printout. 'The log shows that it was open for forty-five minutes.'

'Does the log register whether it was copied?'

'Yes, it does, and it wasn't.'

'So as long as we destroy the file, it's his word against ours.'

'Maybe, but do we really want that level of exposure? This could lead to a deep investigation, which we most definitely could do without.'

Bryant, silent up till then, got up from the table and walked across to the picture window facing out over the Thames. He contemplated the slow but inexorable movement of the London Eye and talked to the window. 'We have put a lot of things in place to avoid such circumstances, paid a lot of money to software experts on your say-so.' He turned around and faced Jeremy full-on. 'Not that this is a discussion for now, but you might like to start thinking about how this has happened and who is responsible.'

Jeremy felt uncomfortably hot with the gaze of both of them on him. He gathered his printouts, stuffed them in his briefcase, got up, and left the boardroom. They watched him go and closed the door behind him. The room was silent for a while as they both mulled things over in their heads. Finally Bryant said, 'Leaving this in the hope that nothing transpires is not an option.'

'I agree,' Anni replied. 'I'll sort it.'

'Fine, but keep it clean,' Bryant said. 'In the meantime, we also need to put checks and balances in place at the other divisions. I'll talk to Maris in Riga and Kozlov in Kiev.'

Anni got up and grabbed her handbag. 'I'll contact Filip in Prague.

Call you later. They both leave the boardroom and enter different elevators. Bryant heads up to his office, Anni down to reception.

On her way down, she pulled her mobile from her bag and speed dialled 'Janek'. It went to voicemail, and after the usual non-personalized message, she said, 'Call me; I have a job for you and Tia.'

CHAPTER 8

◇◇◇◇◇◇◇◇◇◇◇◇◇◇

Kevin rang at nine thirty as I arrived in the station. I made my way to an unoccupied conference room and shut the door. 'Any news?' he asked.

'Nothing yet, how about you?'

'I'm heading out to Antonio Juarbe Airport shortly. I have a flight to Heathrow at eleven our time that gets me via Atlanta into Heathrow at twenty-one hundred your time. Any chance of a pickup?'

'I'm sure I can organize something. Can you text me your flight details? Oh, and thanks; I appreciate you doing this,' I said.

'Yeah, well, they're my cousins. We'll talk later.'

I phoned Chris and relayed the conversation I'd had with Kevin Goodwin. He was as staggered as I was as to where this was going and where it would end, but he was also pleased that I hadn't agreed to travel to Puerto Rico.

Back at the incident room and checking on the whiteboards, I could see that we had no unidentified prints at either flat, and three bugs in each, manufacturer unknown. There was nothing from the hospital except a potential footprint at the bottom of the fire escape. A photograph was clipped alongside the printout from forensics. The print in concrete dust looked like the tread of a trainer of sorts.

Joanne came over with a mug of coffee. 'We have an outline on Hillingdon,' she said, leading me back to her desk. 'Neville Hillingdon, 23 Palmer Road, Poole; works for Banfield Marketing as an IT specialist. No known hobbies but is connected, not sure if romantically, to Maya Coombs. We have receipts from restaurants, bars, and concert venues that they have both attended.'

'My god, they are all linked, and Banfield, that's another connection.

Maya works for Banfield, and something else …' I rack my brain. 'The Proline owner—he was a former Banfield employee.'

'How did we not know that Maya had an attachment to Hillingdon? I'm sure Aleysha never mentioned it, though why I should have taken note I don't really know.'

We finally had a lot of information: pictures, photographs, and annotations on the whiteboard with links. The common denominator was Banfield.

Chris headed up a meeting of the team, which was eleven strong now, outlining who was to do what. I reminded him that I had to pick Kevin up from Heathrow this evening and asked whether there was any chance anyone could be passing Enfields around six o'clock just to pop in and feed Jet. Pat, a new member of the team, said she would do it on her way home.

Chris put half the team on running down everything we could find about Banfield, current and former employees, all aspects of their business, other subsidiaries, and so on. 'You know what we need?' he said. 'More intel on this Don Lewins. Somehow, he has to be intrinsically connected. And the *White Angel*.' He slaps the picture on the board with his fist. 'We need to know everything there is to know about her. She has to pop up somewhere. Phil, can you open an international call alert at all ports? Let's see what we get.'

I caught up with Pat after the meeting and gave her a spare key from my desk drawer, thanked her, and said, 'Behind the flat is a dog-walking green. It's close and small; if you wouldn't mind just letting him off in there for five minutes, he'll be fine. Also, there are some biscuits in a tin by the microwave; if you could leave him with one, that would be brilliant. And thank you again.'

CHAPTER 9

◇◇◇◇◇◇◇◇◇◇◇◇◇◇

Jeremy caught the 6.34 a.m. out of Bournemouth. He knew it was a slow train, but his anger was such that he needed to confront Bryant head-on. And he hoped his rage would subside to some extent during the journey. Instead, it just made him focus even more on the sheer arrogance and greed by which the company seemed to be being directed of late.

The office block on Savoy Place is expansive; the reception is made out to dark bronze marble with subtle amber floor lighting and large ornamental glass chandeliers hanging the full height of three floors. There are three screens showing CNN, BBC, and Sky News channels. He took the first lift up to the fifteenth floor and tried unsuccessfully to compose himself. He burst into Bryant's office uninvited. He had never had the nerve to do this before, but this development is hellish.

'Our IT guy, Hillingdon, is in hospital. Tell me you didn't have anything to do with that!' he said with a raised voice that he didn't even recognize himself.

'Sit down,' Bryant said without even looking up, 'and don't ever blunder in here like that again. Who the hell do you think you are? It was an accident, it's been dealt with, and it's none of your concern.'

'He is one of the best individuals we have—dedicated, accurate—and he's in a coma.'

'We *had*,' Bryant said.

'What do you mean, "we had"?'

'Like I say, it's been dealt with. Have you cleaned up your act? Are there any other revelations you would like to impart?'

'Look, I brought this to your attention because I was concerned for the business.'

'Bollocks,' Bryant said. 'You brought this up to protect your own back, your own little love nest. Well let me tell you, your sweet Miss Cole will wish she had never got entangled with you if you hold anything else back, believe me.'

Jeremy sat down, the wind taken out of his sails. 'What do you mean?'

'Let's start with this Hillingdon character. If he was to pass any information on, who would he go to?'

Jeremey noticeably deflated in front of Bryant, and he saw it.

'Okay, so it's worse than I thought,' said Bryant. 'How bad?'

'According to Pam—'

'Miss Cole,' Bryant interrupted harshly.

'According to Miss Cole, he's been seeing someone from the office—Coombs, one of the marketing girls. And the building log shows she entered the office at nine thirty the evening Hillingdon was doing the updates and left just after eleven. There was a problem with terminal 1027.'

'Miss Cole's terminal, I believe,' said Bryant pointedly.

'Correct.' Jeremy shook his head.

'You failed to mention this before.'

'Anyway, she was there when this terminal exposed the classified file.'

'Bloody hell. Anything else?'

'Her sister's a detective—Bournemouth CID.'

'Jesus fucking Christ.'

There was deathly silence for what seemed like an age.

Bryant, a small Malayan man, suddenly stood up. His chair went flying, and for a moment he looked like a giant fit to burst. He screamed, 'I need everything you have on Coombs, her sister, any associates, and anything else that is remotely connected to this fucked-up catastrophe! And I need it *now!* Get the hell out of here, get it sorted, and report back to me tomorrow, latest.'

Jeremy got up, physically shaking, and made his way to the door.

Anni was waiting outside as he crossed the hall to the elevators, and she gave him a look that could freeze hell over. He waited for one of the elevators; both were down at the ground floor, fifteen levels below.

Anni slammed the door to Bryant's office.

He could hear raised voices, but they were both shouting at the same time and he couldn't make anything out. After a few moments, he did hear Bryant yell, 'What! Where is he?' And something smashed against the door or the wall immediately adjacent to it. He was able to hear Anni saying something along the lines of 'Not to worry, he will be out of commission for at least a week even if he does survive,' and she had it covered.

Jeremy left the building less than forty minutes after entering it, walked less than ten minutes to Charing Cross, and caught the 11.37 back to Bournemouth. He had well over two hours to contemplate his future, which right now looked bleak. He was sure that his relationship with Pam would have to be terminated, as indeed would her employment at Banfield, being the only way to safeguard his own position.

A dreadful thought then occurred to him: *Pam knows what Hillingdon knew and what I know.* If Bryant was prepared to eliminate Hillingdon, presumably he would have no qualms about doing the same to them.

Did he truly want to be part of this any more? Maybe there was a way out; maybe he could find a route to salvaging something from this. After all, the stress of late had taken its toll on him and his life in general.

It was 2.30 p.m. by the time Jeremy got back and called Pam. He'd made a point of not mentioning the file to her before, in an attempt to keep her away from any backlash, which was now quite clearly unavoidable. She picked up on the fourth ring. 'Hi, I wasn't expecting to hear from you today; to what do I owe the pleasure?'

'Hi, Pam. We have a problem.'

'Houston—you missed Houston,' Pam said.

'What!—oh right.'

'Sorry, what problem?'

'File 102277. It's been accessed by a third party; someone in IT managed to open it during the firewall update.'

'Neville?'

'Yes,' Jeremy said.

'How? It's supposed to be encrypted—your encryption.'

'We don't know, but you and I are being put in the firing line.'

There was a pause, and Pam said, 'Neville's in hospital, been there since Monday. Is that connected?'

'Possibly,' he lied. 'Definitely' should have been his response.

'How much trouble am I in?' she asked.

'I think we are both in way over our heads.' He paused. 'How seriously do you feel about us?'

'What do you mean, "us"?' Pam asked.

'How would you feel if I said we should cut and run? Leave the country. Start our own life together.'

The phone went quiet.

'Pam?'

'Is it really that bad?' she said.

This wasn't quite the response Jeremy was hoping for.

'I don't have that sort of money, Jeremy.'

'Look,' Jeremy said, 'I was instrumental in setting up this scam in the first place. For the last three years, I have had my own independent IT guys employed skimming an incidental amount off each top line. Went down as software support costs. I ... have at least six mil in a Caymans account.'

'Dollars?'

'Sterling.'

'Shit, Jeremy, you're scaring me. I don't know; I need some time to think.'

'Not sure how much time we have, love; it took less than twenty-four hours for them to get to Hillingdon.'

'Bloody hell, so he was hit as a consequence.'

''Fraid so.'

'If they, whoever they are, are that switched-on, we shouldn't be having this conversation over the phone,' Pam said.

'You're right. Can we meet?'

'Yes, I'll see you in the Reef Cafe on the pier in two hours.'

With that the phone went dead.

Jeremy opened his laptop. After logging on, he clicked on the icon labelled 'CY Account' and entered his details and twin passwords. A code was sent to his mobile almost immediately. He keyed in the number, and his profile details were displayed on the screen for him to verify, which he did, and he then proceeded to his accounts screen.

Bottom line $8,675,232.33. That's £6.5 mil, he thought.

Over the next hour, he opened three new accounts at different banks and transferred £300,000 to each, and another £100,000 to an existing current account in the name of Brian Campbell, requesting cards and any correspondence to be directed to a PO box in Port of Casablanca that he had set up three years ago for just such an eventuality.

He made three phone calls; changed out of his suit and into casual slacks and jumper; picked up his keys, wallet, and mobiles; grabbed a coat; and left, having decided to walk to avoid the necessity to search for a parking space.

He was unaware of a grey Toyota RAV4 parked fifty yards up the hill on the other side of the road, which contained one passenger and a pair of binoculars.

CHAPTER 10

◇◇◇◇◇◇◇◇◇◇◇◇◇◇

Neville was astounded at the contents of the file: seven pages of transactions, each transaction with nothing less than two hundred thousand sterling in the right-hand column. This document alone equated to well over ten million pounds. It was quite obvious that this was not being declared, and there were links to other documents which presumably would reveal the same.

He sat and stared for quite some time in disbelief.

He could, by coding one of these links into a file routine he had pulled off the Dark Web some months ago, be able to open it on his iPad through the VPN without it registering in the log.

This is madness, he thought as he pulled out his iPad from his rucksack and opened it up. It came to life, but the low battery symbol made him aware that it had only 7 per cent battery left. After clearing the message, he checked to see whether it was still plugged to the battery pack, and it was, which meant it, too, was also drained. He searched in the front zip for the iPad lead and plug, only to realize he'd left them at home. 'Shit,' he said to himself. 'Low Battery' came up again on the screen. He quickly scanned the office in-case anyone had left an Apple lightning charger around. No one had. The tension in his chest was physical and intense. He was aware that he was breathing heavily and his fingers were quivering. A battery at 7 per cent was probably enough to find his file and run the routine. He hunted the file down in his very well organized structure, used it to remotely connect to the Omnicamp network, and typed in one of the links. Sure enough, his tablet, with 4 per cent battery, showed an almost identical file with four pages, with transactions each equating to another five or six million. He quickly scanned down to see if there were any company names he recognized; there were none. The recipient's name, in the top left-hand corner of the statement on the screen, was, in this case, a company called IN-Need. He now looked at the document on his desktop; the recipient was Banfield.

He was about to run a remote copy of both files to his iPad when the screen went dead and was replaced with an empty battery symbol. 'Shit,' he repeated.

He was very aware that while his activities via his Dark Web file should be invisible, the fact that this file had been opened outside encryption would not. He'd have to blag it if anyone asked, saying that he hadn't taken any notice of it being open but was only interested in getting it processed.

He quickly photographed each of the seven pages with his mobile, sat back, and wondered what sort of hornets' nest he had just poked his finger into. He closed the file and reran the routine. After four minutes, the amber text went green.

Getting back into the throes of the job in hand was now difficult; his level of mental distraction was off the scale. Several times he had to scrap and restart terminal upgrades. At 3.00 a.m., after three such restarts, he decided he needed a break. This resulted in him crashing on a sofa in the rest room. He came around just after eight in the morning and carried on. This meant he did not complete the installation of the new firewall until nine thirty Saturday evening.

He arrived home, and though his head was buzzing, he really wanted to catch up with Maya, but it was too late; he knew he might mention something about the files that he shouldn't. He needed a clear head for that, and besides, he was not going to be good company tonight. He fell into bed and quickly dropped into a deep sleep.

After what seemed like minutes, he was woken by a familiar droning noise; it was a text message from Maya asking whether he was done, how it had gone, and whether he wanted to come over this evening. She had a couple of their friends, Mike and Jenna, coming around to watch a film.

The horrors of the previous twenty-four hours suddenly roused within him, and the tension again returned to grip his chest. What should he do with what he knew? Whom, if anyone, should he tell? Should he just play dumb and find another job?

He decided that he would broach the subject with Maya later if they got a chance to be alone.

He texted back, 'All done, went okay and would very much like to catch up later. What film?'

She came back: 'The Blackcoat's Daughter, a bit of a psycho, horror drama, I think.'

'Cool, what time?'

'Say sevenish.'

He replied with a thumbs up and a smiley face.

He checked his watch; it was twelve fifteen. He'd slept for over twelve hours but was far from feeling refreshed. The sun was shining through the slits in the curtains. He rolled over and tried to catch another hour, but eventually the bathroom called, so he got up and showered.

Neville was on edge, counting down the time until he could leave for Maya's. He knew she had a spinning class on a Sunday afternoon, so she wouldn't appreciate him being too early. He both busied and stressed himself out, downloading the images from his phone to a couple of memory sticks, and similarly copying one to a hidden file on his PC. He also made sure his iPad and remote charger were plugged in, albeit a little late to be of any use now.

He called in at the off-licence on his way, to pick up a bottle of Pinot Grigio, and arrived at Maya's flat at around seven. There was no sign of Mike and Jenna's car, so he thought it safe to assume they had yet to arrive. *Good*, he thought, *might broach the subject of the file before they get here.*

However, they had caught the bus over and already made a start on a bottle of wine. Maya opened the door, grabbed his hand, kissed him on the cheek, and pulled him in. 'We started without you,' she said.

'So I can see. Hiya,' he said, walking into the kitchen while waving at Mike, who was sitting in the lounge. Jenna came over and pecked him on the other cheek.

Maya was making chilli with rice, and Jenna had brought some nibbly bits in the way of tacos and various dips, which they all tucked into while the rice was cooking. There were two bottles of red and the Pinot, and as one of the reds was open, Neville helped himself and put the Pinot in the fridge.

Maya's flat was quite small but very comfortable, with a dining table at one end of the living area and two large sofas facing the fifty-two-inch flat-screen. Movies were her passion, and Neville was similarly getting hooked.

She also had an exercise bike, folded away in the alcove alongside the chimney breast, that she wheeled in front of the TV to run her spinning classes when she couldn't get to the gym.

They finally settled down with a hearty helping of chilli con carne on trays on their laps in front of the TV.

Maya sorted the DVD, and the film kicked off.

It opened with the two protagonists: Rose, in her senior year, who feared she was pregnant, and Kate, an awkward and disturbing freshman who is being haunted by a dark spirit. Neither was picked up by her parents at the end of term as expected, and both were left behind in the care of two nuns.

It *was* dark and satanic, but it struggled to hold Neville's attention. He was still pondering whether to involve Maya or not, debating in his mind the pros and cons. At one point he said out loud, 'God, I don't know.' It was an unfortunately quiet part of the film; otherwise he might have gotten away with it. As it was, they all turned and looked at him.

'Sorry, miles away,' he said.

'You don't know what?' Maya said.

'Oh nothing, just an algorithm going through my head.'

'Really! you need to switch off more, mate,' Mike said.

'Yes, I know; it's been a long weekend'

The film wound up around ten o'clock, with comments made about how good and bad it was, the general consensus being that it was okay. However, all agreed it wasn't one that required a rewatch. Everyone chipped in to help clear up before Mike and Jenna set off home.

Maya and Neville sat back down on the sofa with what was left of the Pinot. The extra features from the film were running, and the director's vision on how the film had been put together was playing out. Neville was still chewing over the fraudulent files as they nestled together and relaxed on the longer of the two sofas.

Maya looked up at Neville and said, 'Do you want to stay?'

All thoughts of the files vanished.

CHAPTER 11

Every time the phone rang, I thought it was going to be Aleysha; and every time, I was disappointed.

'Hi, Greg; it's James. How are you doing?'

'Fine. I'm on the M3 at Longcross, some hold-up ahead, and I'm avoiding my blue light; I'm sure the motorway boys won't appreciate my involvement. What you got?'

'Forensic have a fingerprint match on the *Life Line*—Lewins's,' he said. 'He was suspected of fraud when he was at HSBC, which is why he was fired. Low level in the UK and why he was never convicted, but the fraud squad suspected he had his finger in a much bigger pie in Mexico. Known associates are Kim Ta, suspected of drug involvement—he is the subject of an active undercover operation in Southend and Basildon— Janek Dvorak, previous for aggravated assault leading to the death of a Mr Kamid Hussain in Canary Wharf, Greater London 2017, and other related crimes on the Interpol list. The London conviction fell over due to lack of evidence. Current whereabouts unknown, but last recorded address was 32 Middle Street, Croydon.

'Lack of evidence,' I said. 'Could that mean lack of witness statements, by chance? Any others?'

'Well, we're still working on it. On the witness statements, by the way, all three witnesses in the Hillingdon case won't talk to us; they just don't want to get involved. One of them, Mr Felcroft, says his family was threatened and is not prepared under any circumstances to discuss anything. No news on the whereabouts of the *White Angel* other than that we now know what sort of yacht it is—a fifty-five-metre Amels listed as a superyacht. That's a long way from the PF MY40; if you wanted to hire one, it would cost you around two hundred ninety thousand pounds a week'

My phone buzzed with another call. I had the option to accept or decline. I told James I had another call and hit accept.

'Greg?'

My throat constricted. 'Aleysha?'

'Yes. I haven't got long. I've managed to grab a phone that got left behind, but they'll be back. It's a burner, so don't waste time trying to track it. I'm with Maya. We're okay, but I have probably put you in danger.'

'Where are you?'

'I don't know, other than on a boat—a big one. Now shut up. There's a file that Maya's boyfriend acquired that these guys need, which is why he is in hospital. I have told them that we only know of the file, not of its contents, and that it was sent to your flat on a pen drive. They obviously didn't believe that we hadn't seen the contents. The file has photographs of Benfield accounts, but I guess by now you will have seen them. I just wanted it kept safe, which is why I left it with you. Sorry. All I know is that there is serious money involved. I suspect drugs, which makes these people very dangerous. I haven't figured out yet why we are still alive; we have nothing to offer.'

I heard Maya's panicked voice in the background. 'Someone's coming,' Aleysha said, and the line went dead.

Oh my God! So many questions. What did she mean, 'left it with you';—that I would know about its contents? The traffic was moving now, and all I wanted to do was get off the motorway and gather my thoughts.

She's alive; that is at least something I can be thankful for. But other than confirming that, what does it give me? I searched my brain for answers and got nothing.

It was emotional to hear her voice, and as usual, she was calm and collected, unflustered and professional.

I followed the slip road onto the M25 and realized I was unlikely to be able to pull over now much before I got to the airport. And satnav was telling me I was only seventeen minutes from my destination. I decided to carry on. However, it might be seventeen minutes anywhere other than London. It was over thirty minutes before I pulled into security parking alongside the arrivals. I was immediately approached by one of our finest, armed to the teeth; he walked around to my open window; thoroughly examined my warrant card that I held out, before handing it back; and directed me to a parking space on the concourse, marked 'Security'. 'Leave your key at the gate over there, sir.' I parked and went to the security window, filled in a form, flashed my warrant card, and handed over my key. A cheery guard looked over the form; checked that it tallied with my card; said, 'Thanks, sir'; and passed me a ticket.

Walking in the general direction of arrivals, I interrogated my phone. No last number, no new messages. No further forward.

I rang Chris. I didn't think he was going to answer, but he finally picked up. 'Hi, Greg, how's it going?'

'I had a call from Aleysha—she *is* being held on a large boat—I suspect the White Angel. They are together and are okay. It seems this is about a missing file that they think the girls know about. Aleysha has told them that they know of the file but not its contents, and that a memory stick has been sent to my flat. She was hoping we would get a chance to intercept them. That was all she said before she got cut off.'

'Christ. Any trace of the phone on yours?'

'No, just checked.'

'Did she say where they were?'

'She didn't know; she also said they were dangerous and didn't know why she and Maya were still alive.'

'Is there a memory stick being sent?'

'No idea. She just said that's what she told them and that she had left it with me. I know nothing of it though.'

'Okay, look, I'll get a patrol car over to yours.'

'Cheers, we should be back around 2.30 a.m.; Kevin is staying with me tonight,' I said.

'Thanks for letting me know; we'll talk tomorrow.'

I walked into the arrivals area and went to the Virgin lounge, which is where Kevin said we would meet. I was greeted at the desk by what looked like an attractive flight attendant. 'Good evening, sir, do you have a Virgin Flights card?'

'No,' I said. 'I'm meeting someone who does.'

She had a tablet attached to the desk, which she looked down at.

'Mr. Richards'?'

'That's right,' I said. *I could be anyone agreeing to that; you need to tighten your security,* I thought, but I didn't pursue it.

Checking the flight times, I could see Kevin's was still on schedule. I had half an hour before it landed. Taking a table at the window overlooking one of the runways, Miss Virgin came over and offered me the drinks and snack menu. I didn't feel hungry, but I felt I probably needed something. I skipped the Champagne snack menu and ordered from the lite bite section, a smoked ham and salad hoagie—I guessed at a posh BLT—and a tonic water.

My phone buzzed to tell me I had only 3 per cent battery. *I must put it on charge when I get back to the car*, I thought.

Tiredness and fatigue suddenly came over me. I settled back in the luxurious seats of the first-class lounge.

ᏇᎷᎡᎩ

I was rudely awoken by a voice I now recognized as Kevin's. 'Hi, buddy—long day?' As he rolled his case to the end of the table and sat in the seat alongside me, I was conscious of the family resemblance. The voice, although male, had familiarity; the piercing eyes, a quiet confidence that I had admired in Aleysha on many occasions. He was tall with long fair hair and a natural tan.

'Sorry,' I said, turning around to shake his hand. 'It most definitely has been a long and emotional day. How was your flight?'

'As they go, not bad. You look like you've been through the wars.'

'You could say. Aleysha rang earlier,' I said, and I went through the same conversation I'd had with Chris beforehand.

'Wow, I'm lost for words, Greg; this must be a nightmare for you. Perhaps you can fill me in on all the details later. Where are we staying?'

'I'll take you back to mine. If you don't mind slumming it a bit, it'll only take a couple of hours?'

'I don't at all mind, and I don't imagine it would be slumming, but why don't we crash at the Novotel here? You're knackered, I could do with a shower, and I have a premier card.'

'I'm not sure my boss is going to agree my expenses this month as it is.'

Kevin put his hand up. 'It's a company premier card, and I own the company.'

'That does sound tempting,' I said. 'Okay, if you're sure.'

'I'm sure. Now let's have a drink while I make the arrangements, and you can have a go at that sandwich, which is starting to curl.'

He called Miss Virgin over, who was waiting to be called, and ordered a long Glenmorangie with ice for himself and looked at me. Not having thought about it, I said, 'Same, please.'

He chatted easily about the flight while thumbing his mobile and finally said, 'Done, we're in. We have adjoining rooms on the sixteenth floor and a priority parking space. Where's your car?'

It was odd for someone else to be taking charge. But right now, it was quite welcome. 'Just out on the concourse,' I said.

Our drinks arrived, and we went through some details of the investigation that I felt comfortable about discussing at this stage. I needed to fill in some background on Kevin before I could fully open up.

The drink left a very warm glow, and I was glad I'd had the sandwich and that the concourse to the hotel would only be a matter of yards and not miles away.

We headed back to the car; I showed my warrant card to security, swapped the ticket for my keys, grabbed one of Kevin's bags, popped the boot, and dropped it in. As Kevin lifted his case in, he said, 'Where do I get one of those?'

'My warrant card? You have to sell your soul for that,' I said.

The hotel turned out to be as plush as the Virgin lounge; check-in was slick.

I helped him out of the lift with his bags and walked up the hall to 1615. He swiped his pass and walked in. I followed, probably with an open mouth, and dropped his bag by the writing desk. He turned and said, 'Yours should be the same. I'll have a quick shower, and I'll join you for a nightcap in your room. Is that okay? I'll be about fifteen minutes.'

'Sure,' I said, thinking it would give me some time to formulate a few questions.

I swiped 1616 and I entered, leaving the door on the latch, and dropped my keys on the dresser. Both rooms—or, more appropriately, suites—were, in fact, the same, but a mirror image of each other.

The tiredness had thankfully subsided, and I texted Chris to let him know what I was doing, though I knew he would probably be in bed by now.

This is all very well, I thought, *but I have no change of clothes, toothbrush, or anything.*

Fortunately the bathroom was very well equipped with a personal hygiene bag including a shaving kit, toothbrush and paste, and the like.

I investigated the mini bar, which was less mini and more maxi, and grabbed a bottle of Peroni. It seemed to be loaded in order of value, with champagnes at the top, wines in the middle, and beers and soft drinks at the bottom. I popped the cap with the bottle opener attached to the wall alongside the minibar and picked out a pack of dry roasted peanuts from the door compartment.

Sitting down in front of the large solid-oak writing desk and looking out across the runways, I noticed that there was virtually no noise other than a low rumbling of aircraft engines penetrating the triple-glazed picture windows. I gazed out across the floodlit scene with its myriad small coloured lights, animated every thirty seconds or so by a plane landing or taking off, and wondered what the hell Aley and Maya were doing right now. I quickly tried to erase it before the thought engulfed me.

Opening the complementary writing pad, I tried jotting down some notes about Aleysha, Maya, and the Tithe, but I struggled to focus on any one thing for more than a few seconds.

Then there came the not unexpected knock at the door.

Kevin, in T-shirt and jeans, walked in and looked up at me while typing something into his phone. 'Everything okay?' he said.

I nodded. He sat in the easy chair, and I offered him a drink from the mini bar.

'Is there a small bottle of red?'

Looking through the glass door of the drinks fridge, I asked, 'Merlot okay?'

'Sure.'

I poured his drink into a crystal wine glass from the cabinet, passed it over, grabbed what was left of my beer, and sat on the sofa.

'Right,' I said. 'I hope you understand, but before I can talk frankly about the investigation, I need to fully appreciate and verify your relationship with Aleysha and Maya.

'Of course,' he said.

We spent the next half an hour with Kevin going through the horrors of the news about the tsunami, knowing that it hit an area in Japan where his parents were staying, and not being able to get any information about the extent of the disaster or the whereabouts of his parents. He was able to arrange a flight out there but on arrival could get nowhere near, and there was a virtual news blackout.

On day three, he flew Aleysha out, more for moral support than anything else, but she had been ringing him every few hours, chasing news which he didn't have. It was day five before limited information trickled down from the aid organizations. The Red Cross was by far the most well organized, issuing lists of patients and hospitals where they could be found. By the seventh day, there were lists of known dead, and by that list they knew just how severe a catastrophe this was. There seemed little likelihood that Kevin's parents had survived. He and Aleysha finally got to see the devastation for themselves and appreciated the utter terror that the individuals must have suffered during the initial onslaught of the thirty-foot-high wave bursting through the town, taking and destroying everything as it went, only to find if they had survived that the lake of water that had been driven inland was set to return with even more destructive power, as on its reappearance it was crammed with shattered building materials, glass, and vehicles.

On 19 March at seven-thirty in the morning, Aleysha, going through the now exhaustive lists online, found a Joe Goodwins admitted to Mayako Hospital on the thirteenth with severe head trauma.

They got dressed, gathered some supplies, and called a taxi.

When the driver arrived half an hour later, he said the hospital was about forty minutes away from the Fugane Hotel, where they had been staying. However, the roads were very congested, and it could take longer. It did, forty minutes longer, and then they had to walk the last half mile.

The hospital was both depressing and distressing, and on the face of it, it appeared to be in organized chaos, with the sheer scale of the problems and numbers involved, the severity of the injuries, and the volume of dead that were having to be transported constantly away to who knows where, as well as the obviously too few, overstressed staff racing around making life-and-death decisions on the hoof.

Though at this point I had extreme empathy for Kevin and the situation he found himself in, it wasn't, other than circumstantially, tying him to Aleysha and Maya.

'Can you tell me about the Tithe?' I said.

'Well,' he replied, and he continued his narrative as if I hadn't spoken.

'When we eventually found my dad at the hospital, he was in a very bad way and asleep. Whether this was drug-induced there was no way of knowing. Despite the reported head injury being the prime cause for concern, he was bandaged from the hip down on the left side, and blood had seeped through just below the knee to the ankle.

'Trying to find anyone to assist was near impossible, but eventually Aleysha found a nurse who agreed to change the dressings.'

That sounds like Aleysha, I thought.

'The sight and smell when the dressings were removed was gut-wrenching. It was as much of a shock to the nurse as it was to us.

'She cleaned the leg up as much as possible, but the wounds were deep and black. After she had redressed it, she looked at his notes and established that my dad had had an intensive level of antibiotics, and she didn't feel she could increase them without a consultant's say-so.'

I wanted to move things along, but I could see Kevin needed to go through this process with me, so I let him continue.

'We spent the next two days at his bedside, with him coming in and out of consciousness,' Kevin said. 'But he was never really lucid. He did appear to be trying to express something, but we couldn't make it out.

'When he was asleep, every now and then, one or the other of us would go to a small bar just a few minutes' walk from the hospital, where they had Wi-Fi and were happy for us to plug in our mobile phone chargers for a small fee. We would go through the latest lists, where eventually I found my mum, under that day's deceased column. Even though I was expecting it, it still hit hard.

'When I told Aleysha, she sobbed for the first time. I think she had been holding it in on my account.

'That night, in one of Dad's more coherent moments, we realized that what he was trying to say was, "Where's Jilly?" I spoke as unemotionally as I could to say that everything was okay and that he should just concentrate on getting better. I think we both knew this to be an unlikely outcome.

'At one o'clock in the morning, he awoke and all but sat up. And far from articulate, he said quite clearly, "She gone hasn't she?" looking directly at me. I had to say yes.

'Then, looking at Aleysha probably for the first time, he said, "Please see Dr Bates at B and G."

'That must have been an extreme effort, as he slumped back on his pillow, closed his eyes, and fell asleep. He passed away at eight fifteen the following morning. Cause of death was listed as septicaemia brought on by extreme trauma, and I think this was probably correct.

'Over the next few days, we arranged to get my mum and dad back home, which was harrowing and frustrating in equal measure.

'On our way back, Aleysha asked about Dr. Bates, and what that was likely to be about. I was able to tell her that he is the family solicitor at B&G in Bristol. Other than that, I didn't know, but we gave a commitment to go and see him together before I headed home.

'I stayed at Aleysha's flat for a couple of nights, and we arranged to see Lee, Dr Bates, on the Tuesday morning. After informal introductions and his very heartfelt condolences for our loss, he said he had heard a lot about Aleysha and Maya from my parents over the years and that B&G were the keepers of my parents' "last will," but, after reviewing the document, he concluded that Maya would also need to be present before the reading.'

Though I was desperate to hear the rest of this story, it was by now 2.00 a.m. and I was struggling to stay awake. I said, 'Can we continue this tomorrow? It's important, and I want to give it my full attention.'

'Sure,' Kevin said. 'Sorry; I was probably getting carried away.'

'No, not at all,' I said. He finished his wine and we both got up. Kevin bade me goodnight and headed for the door. 'Shall we say eight thirty for breakfast in the restaurant? It's on the second floor.' he said.

'Sounds good.'

I doubt it took more than five minutes for me to hit the sack and fall asleep.

⚭

I was woken by a knock on the door. Suddenly aware that I hadn't set an alarm, and thinking I was late and Kevin was chasing me, I looked at my watch. it was 7.50 a.m. Throwing on the dressing gown from the back of the glass wall of the shower room and noticing myself in the mirror for the first time since the Tithe, I was shocked. I opened the door to see what appeared to be a porter with a bag.

'Compliments of 1615,' he said. He handed me the bag, turned, and left.

Back in the room, I opened the Novotel bag to find a new white shirt, grey trousers, and underwear. All were well within my size tolerance and over and above my normal quality standards.

Returning to the mirror and using a pair of nail scissors from the shaving kit, I attempted to level up my hair to reduce the scary affect of the guy looking back at me. Eyeing the cut on my chin and the surrounding bruising, I decided that I would be sporting a beard for a while.

I showered, changed, and went down to the restaurant. The waiter at the front desk showed me to a window seat where Kevin was reading a broadsheet. He immediately put it down and stood up to welcome me. 'Good night?' he asked.

'Very good, under the circumstances,' I said. 'And thanks for my new outfit.'

'You're very welcome. You look a little more human this morning. Hungry?'

'For the first time in days, I feel ravenous,' I said.

'Good. Let's order.'

We had the full English XL with breakfast tea and fruit juice. We chatted about the weather, which was thankfully brightening up somewhat, British politics, police, and the state of the health service. The latter lead on to an account of the do-it-yourself medical care that existed in Puerto Rico. It also turned out that Kevin was employed, on an ad-hoc basis, by the Puerto Rican police authorities. As a prominent individual there, and a member of a number of societies—in his words, 'to meet ladies and curb boredom'—he had become recognized as bit of an analyst and had helped out with several investigations. I wasn't sure if this was bullshit for my benefit or not.

By nine thirty we had checked out and were in the car on the way back to Bournemouth. I asked Kevin whether he would mind continuing his account from the previous evening.

'Okay, where were we? So the three of us rock up at B&G two days later, having delayed my return home, Me and Aleysha reliving some of the horrors of the previous week, with Maya following up behind, a little awkward. I do remember Aleysha saying that she intended to apply for a position in CID, now having all the qualifications she needed.'

I thought, *At least this is something I can verify back at base.*

'At the time,' Kevin continued, 'Maya was still in college, studying business and economics, but was quite a sulky sort; although according to Aleysha, this was only around me.

'Lee met us in reception and led us to a conference room where we had coffee and biscuits. After the pleasantries were out of the way, Lee started. "Right, there are two parts to the will: one that affects all of you, and one that is directed specifically at you, Kevin. Let's start with the compound one first, as the second stage is to be conducted in private between B&G and Kevin, so"—he looked at me—"you and I will deal with that later, Kevin. The first part relates entirely to the Tithe cottage near Thorney Hill in Dorset.

'"The will states that the cottage should not be sold, but is to be let on long-term lease. This arrangement is to stay in place for at least the next ten years. Value wise, it is a simple 50-50 split: 50 per cent to Kevin, the other 50 per cent to be divided equally between Miss A. and Miss M. Coombs, the deceased's nieces.

'"If any party wishes to take the value in cash and not get involved with letting, this will have to come out of the estate, and that portion of the Tithe will remain as a living part of the estate, wholly owned by Kevin. Not quite sure how we would deal with that, but we can cross that bridge if we have to.

'"I have had the property valued at nine hundred fifty thousand pounds. We would have to allocate about twenty thousand to expenses, so you can work the figures out."

'Lee went silent for a moment waiting for a response.

'I remember seeing what could almost be akin to shock on both Aleysha's and Maya's faces, and I could sense the question—Why them, and how did I feel about that?

'The fact was, the estate aside, Mum and Dad had set me up quite comfortably with a working business in Puerto Rico some years earlier, which provides for me very well, so I had no problem with it at all.

'I think Maya would have probably liked to have taken the money, but after taking themselves off for a few minutes to another conference room,

I think Aleysha convinced her that in the long run they would have an income for life and a pension. Which is what was decided.

'I had my private meeting with Lee to conclude the other half of the will, which effectively left the rest of their estate in my hands to do with as I pleased. In the end, this equated to nearly four million pounds, of which three point nine is still in place today.

'And that', he said, 'is what I can tell you of the Tithe.'

'That's a vast sum,' I said, 'and I don't feel so bad about the Novotel any more.'

'It is, and I live very comfortably off the business and occasionally dip into the interest if I want to splash out.'

It suddenly occurred to me that I hadn't checked my phone, likely because I had been so wrapped up in Kevin's story,. At the same time, I realized that I also hadn't put it on charge. I asked Kevin whether he could pass it over from the inside pocket of my jacket on the back of the seat. He did so, and I plugged it into the charger in the armrest. After a few seconds, and after the apple logo faded away, it pinged and buzzed. Kevin looked down and said, 'You have a mountain of emails, messages, and missed calls.'

I glanced down to see calls missed from Chris, Joanne, and the office switchboard.

'I'd better pull over,' I said.

As I was looking for somewhere convenient, my eyes were drawn to my rear-view mirror, which was filling up with very recognizable flashing blue lights as there came a short blast of siren. I moved as far to the left as I could to allow them to pass. As the first patrol car came along side, the passenger signalled for me to pull over. *Well, this is a new experience,* I thought.

'Was I speeding?' I asked Kevin.

'Does it matter?' he said.

'Not really, but it can go on my record.'

There seemed some urgency, and the lead car pulled across my front. Before we stopped, the passenger was out and heading to my side. I buzzed the window down.

'DCI Greg Richards?' he asked.

'Yes, that's right.'

'You need to follow us back to Bournemouth; we will escort you.'

'What's this all about, sergeant?' I asked.

'There's been a problem, and I have been told to get you back quickly and safely.'

'Is that it?'

'Yes,' he said, and he headed back to his car. I noted that the other patrol car was parked very close behind.

I punched the hands-free button on my steering wheel, and after going through about three different menu messages and realizing why I normally just pick up the phone and hit speed dial, I got through to Chris.

'What's going on?' I asked.

My escort pulled away with everything flashing and sirens blaring. I followed.

'Your flat was broken into last night.'

'Shit, did we get anyone?'

'No. Let's talk about it when you get back, Greg.'

'Okay but ...' The line went dead.

'What the fuck.'

I called straight back, but it went to voicemail.

By now we were doing sixty-five going through Egham High Street and I was aware that Kevin was plastered to the back of his seat and holding on to both armrests for dear life.

'Sorry about this, Kevin,' I said.

'It's okay,' he replied without moving his mouth.

I flicked the radio button but realized I was well out of range of our control centre.

Feeling somewhat troubled, I was less concerned about my flat than I was about Jet. *Oh Christ!*, I thought. *Pat—I hope she didn't get caught up in anything.* I tried Chris, but the call again went to voicemail. 'Bloody hell, Chris, what are you playing at.'

Kevin took his eyes off the road for a second as we pulled onto the M3, and I could visibly detect him relax a little, as we would no longer be weaving in and out of traffic on the right, and quite often the wrong, side of the road. Well, at least for twenty minutes anyway.

He said, 'I thought landing at Juarbe Pol airport was traumatic.'

'Sorry,' I said again.

For the rest of the journey, I had to focus fully on the driving to keep in touch with my escorts, who were most definitely pushing the limits of safety. At 130 plus miles per hour, if you are not on high alert, it can be like watching a video game—except the other road users don't bounce out of the way.

We got back to the station without any real incident, but I'm sure we were both still high on adrenalin. I left the car in a visitor's space in front of reception and bowled out. I called back to Kevin to follow me up; I would clear him en route. Running into the foyer and heading towards the stairs, I noted that Helen was on reception and called across to her to sign in the tall, fair-haired guy following me and send him to a vacant conference room, adding that I'd be with him as soon as possible.

There were several people in the incident room, but not Chris, Joanne, or Phil. I passed conference room one; Phil and Joanne were in there with three other officers. I continued on to Chris's office. His door was open, and he was seated at his desk.

'Come in, Greg; shut the door.'

'What's going on, guv?'

'Your flat was ransacked last night, mate. According to the CCTV in the hallway, they entered shortly after Pat arrived and knocked on the door, and as Pat opened up, they barged in.'

'Is she all right?'

'I'm afraid not; she's just being moved from the Royal to Alderney as we speak. She suffered a blow to the head and a gunshot wound to the upper chest. She lost a lot of blood. Your neighbour in the next flat was lucky; he raised the alarm when he thought he heard a blast of some sort—thought it was an explosion. He called 999 and went to investigate just as they were leaving. One of them swung at him with a baseball bat but hit the wall instead and ran off.

'Greg, Jet's in a bad way too. We have him at Aniwell Veterinary Clinic. His pelvis is shattered; he wasn't so lucky with the bat. You may well have to make a call on that one I'm afraid. Sorry, mate.'

I sat down and felt as though I'd taken a gut thump. 'Will Pat be okay?' I asked.

'Too early to tell. They think the gunshot caught an artery, hence the blood loss, but they are more concerned about her head. She had a bleed, which they have managed to drain, but they have no idea what, if any, damage had already been done.'

'Anything useful on the CCTV?'

'Masks and gloves, so no, though the one without the bat was quite slight—could have been a woman.'

'Is there anything else we can gain from the footage?'

'The recordings from that and the camera in the lobby have been sent to the forensic lab. We don't have anything yet.'

I got up, still feeling dazed. 'Can you arrange a hotel for Kevin Goodwin, guv? I need to talk to him, but it will have to wait until I've been to the hospital and the vet.'

'There's nothing you can do at the hospital right now, Greg. Go and see Jet; I'll deal with Kevin, and we'll catch up later.'

'Thanks, boss.'

I called in on Kevin on my way out just to explain the situation. He was very understanding and said not to worry about him, as he was used to occupying himself.

'Though I would like to know a little more about my cousin's predicament,' he said.

'I know,' I replied. 'We will get back to that as soon as I can. In the meantime, Chris Bowden, my super, will look after you.'

'I can assure you I don't need looking after. Head me in the direction of the coffee machine and a mobile charger and I'm sorted.'

'Thanks,' I said. 'The coffee machine is in the mess at the end of the hallway. Chris will sort out a charger for you.' With that, I left.

I knew the Aniwell; Jet was there a couple of years back after swallowing a Koosh ball that expanded in his gut and had to be surgically removed.

The receptionist, an attractive young Asian girl who was new and looked as though she should still be in school, was expecting me and showed me into a side room where she explained Jet's known injuries. She was not only very professional but also knowledgeable, belying her youthful looks.

'I'm very sorry, Mr. Richards,' she said, 'but other than keeping him comfortable, we can't proceed with any work until we have your say-so. We are aware that you have insurance, but looking at the state of his injuries, I doubt it will cover, and there is no guarantee of success, I'm afraid.'

'I understand that—and it's Greg, by the way—but I need you to do whatever you can.' I felt a lump in the back of my throat as the thought of losing him overcame me.

'Do you want to see him? He is sedated at the moment,' she said.

'Yes please … sorry, I didn't get your name?'

'It's Jaz,' she said as she got up and escorted me out.

She led the way into a clinical room at the back of the practice. The light was quite dim, and there were several cages holding a menagerie of animals from mice to a miniature goat.

I saw Jet immediately, looking so small and bedraggled, as though he had just been pulled out of the lake. His tongue was drooping from the side of his mouth, and he had a tube taped to his upper jaw.

'He's been wiped down in antiseptic, and the bandages are temporary, just trying to hold things together,' Jaz said.

She grabbed an X-ray plate from the side of the cage and stuck it up on a lightbox. Even I could see just how bad this was. The hip was separated on the left-hand side, and his upper right leg was broken at the thigh.

'The breaks are worrying, Greg,' Jaz said, 'but'—she pointed to a vertebra in the middle of his back—'there is no way of knowing if the damage here has severed the spinal cord. It is something that we can confirm as soon as we have the go-ahead. We can bring him back to semi-consciousness and do a pin test to check for a reaction.'

'Okay,' I said. 'How soon can you make a start?'

'I have an appointment with a border collie at two o'clock, but I can prep Jet after that. My assistant will be back at three thirty, so we should be able to make a good start today.' I was even more staggered that Jaz herself was the veterinary surgeon. 'We can work on a daily costing if that suits you, and we'll sort out just what we can claim from your insurance later.'

'Fine,' I said. 'Do you need anything up front?'

'No, let's see where it's going first.'

'Thanks, Jaz,' I said, and I left.

I was torn as to whether to go to Alderney but decided that my time would be better spent trying to get a handle on my partner and her sister's whereabouts. On the way, I took a slight detour to my flat, which had a squad car parked outside with Graham, no surname, in the passenger seat.

'Hi, Graham,' I said.

'Boy has someone got it in for you, sir. Anything I can do, please don't hesitate.'

'Thanks,' I said. 'Anyone inside?'

'PC Smith is having a wander up there now; SOCO left about an hour ago.'

There was crime scene tape across the stairwell, though the lift was still open for business. I took it while sending a text to Joanne to ask whether she could check when Aleysha would have passed her CID exam.

Jilly was in the hall outside my door and turned to acknowledge me.

'Sir ... quite a mess I understand ... inside.'

'Really. Forensics have finished, I believe?'

'Yes sir; you can go in.'

Looking around, I found there was not too much damage, just everything all over the floor. It was obvious that they were looking for the pen drive, and given that it was never here, it was a fruitless task. *Christ, I wish I did know where it was and what it contained; it just might give us a clue as to what we are up against.* Moving towards the kitchen, I was suddenly struck and sickened by the smudged dark patches covering most of the tiled floor and kitchen cabinets.

Nothing for me to do here right now, I thought. *Get on to it later.* I *would* have to sort out a hotel for tonight, at least.

Back in the car, I was again alone with my thoughts, not a good place, and I was relieved when I eventually pulled into a parking slot behind the station.

Inside headquarters, Kevin had taken himself off to sort out somewhere to stay. Chris had gone out but left me a message to take care and call Kevin when I got a minute, and that he had arranged a clean-up team for the flat in the morning.

In the incident room, there were now four whiteboards, with many way-too-familiar photographs pinned up, showing my living room, kitchen, and bedrooms. Joanne was at her terminal, and she turned to ask whether I was okay.

'Nothing getting any better,' I said.

'No, I know. How's your dog?'

'Not good. Might know a little more tomorrow. Thanks for asking. Have we had any news from the hospital?'

'Nothing on Pat yet, but they are looking to attempt to bring Hillingdon around later today. Anything useful from Mr. Goodwin?'

'All I can say right now is that I think he is genuinely the cousin of both Aley and Maya. Hopefully I can tie up with him this evening.'

James walked over to one of the whiteboards and stuck a note on the new stock picture of the *White Angel*.

'Greg,' he called across. 'We have a report from Refshaleøen in Copenhagen that a craft identified as the *White Angel* docked there last night after registering an issue with their navigation transponder. It sailed again at nine this morning with a planned destination of Rostock. However, ninety minutes out the signal was again lost.'

I looked at the new picture associated with the *White Angel*. *A playboy yacht*, I thought.

'Why was it not impounded?' I asked.

'Copenhagen didn't receive notification of interest in the *White Angel* until nine thirty this morning. Apparently they have an ongoing backlog of vessel investigations due to them being an international hub for drug trafficking.'

'A dubious honour,' I said.

My phone buzzed in my pocket. It was a message from Kevin.

'I've booked us both in at the Derby Manor. I'm assuming your place will be out of bounds for a while.'

I looked at James. 'Have we informed Rostock?' I asked.

'They have, and they have a watching brief on it, but without a signal they can only let us know if and when it arrives. We have issued a warrant for its impoundment, but if it doesn't arrive, we're stuffed. Also, when its signal was live, it showed it heading out across the Baltic Sea in the general direction of Rostock. But it was fully re-fuelled at Refshaleøen, so by now it could be anywhere. Have you heard anything more from Aleysha?'

'No.' I shook my head. 'I'm guessing satellite is not an option?'

'The sort we have access to couldn't locate a vessel without reasonably accurate coordinates.'

I grabbed a coffee and sat in front of the whiteboards, hoping for inspiration.

CHAPTER 12

Neville was aware of an alarm going off—one he was not familiar with. It took a few seconds for him to realize where he was. He turned over and came face to face with Maya. *How can someone look so good first thing in the morning?* he thought. Memories of a joyously wonderful night were suddenly shattered as the thought of the predicament he was in flooded back into his consciousness.

Maya turned over and smacked the top of the clock, and all was silent again. She turned back and wrapped her arms around him. Though they were both still naked, the passion that should probably have been present was dulled in Neville.

'Maya,' Neville said 'I need to talk to you about something, and I'm not sure I should.' She looked up at him curiously, giving him the sort of look one might get from someone expecting bad news—like, "I'm not sure this is working" news. She pulled back in anticipation.

'Friday night, just after you left,' Neville said, 'I had a problem with a file that wouldn't process. I had to do some technical jiggery-pokery, and I inadvertently opened one of the encrypted files from Pam Coles's computer.'

'Oh, okay?' Her shoulders expressed relief that her concerns were ill founded.

'No, not okay—*really* not okay.' He pulled himself up and leant back against the headboard.

'Wow, you look worried; what is it?' she said, sitting up and pulling the covers around her.

'I think our company is heavily involved in fraud—like big-time fraud. This file was a list of accounts with deposits in the hundreds of millions— way over what our turnover would be for the last ten years—and there are loads of them.' He got up, pulled on his shorts, and sat back on the bed. 'And I don't know if I'm putting you in danger by even mentioning this, so if you just want to pretend I never said anything, that's fine by me.'

'God, Neville, no. Did you download the files?'

'Not exactly; I was trying to avoid a trail, so I photographed the files on my phone, but the fact that it was accessed will be registered, and though you weren't there at the time, your access to the building will also be logged.'

'Look,' Maya said, 'we need to get sorted for work now; let's go through it later this evening when I have a bit more time to fully grasp the gravity of what we are dealing with.'

'Okay,' Neville said. 'I have a memory stick in my jacket with the photographs on. I have others, but would you mind keeping this one safe for me?'

'Of course,' Maya said.

As he got off the bed and began to get dressed, he felt a degree of relief in sharing his problem and at her reaction to it. It seemed true to him that a problem shared is, in fact, a problem halved.

He went around the bed and pulled Maya into his arms. He thanked her, and they kissed passionately.

She headed for the shower while Neville collected his things, dropped the memory stick on the bedside table, and shouted through the bathroom door, 'Goodbye! The stick is by the bed. See you later!' He then made his way home. He thought about getting a taxi, but it was a nice morning for a walk. It would only take half an hour; he had plenty of time, as Jess wouldn't expect him to be in early today.

His flat was cold and empty, and his mind was already looking forward to seeing Maya later, in a way he had never felt for anyone before. He showered, changed, and grabbed a bag of sausage rolls from the fridge. *That will have to do for lunch,* he thought, and he left for work.

The walk allowed him plenty of time to reflect on events of the last two days, along with a lot of confusion as to what to do next. It was going to be difficult to roll up to work as though nothing had happened. Should he just mention to Jess that he'd had a problem with one of the files not updating automatically but had adopted a workaround which seemed to have been successful?

He walked along Sheldown Road and through the alley on to Mount Pleasant Avenue. Checking the road both ways, he walked out to cross Mount Pleasant. There was nothing coming, but he was immediately aware of a high-revving engine and the squeal of tyres. He looked around again to see a white car pulling out of a parking space just a few cars down from where he was. His immediate thought was that it was just someone in a hurry or angry at something or other, but he was very mindful it was heading straight for him. He dashed for the footpath on the other side of the road and was about to wave some two-fingered abuse as the car mounted the pavement.

CHAPTER 13

◇◇◇◇◇◇◇◇◇◇◇◇◇

The Shamrock was typically packed with like-minded office workers grabbing a beer on their way home for the start of the weekend.

Joe and Steph managed to perch on a couple of stools at the end of one of the long tables.

They got to talking about hobbies, and Joe asked about Steph's interest in yoga and where it had emanated from.

'I went out with a chap from Weymouth some time ago now,' she said, 'and he was into mindfulness, meditation—that sort of thing—and yoga. He took me along to a yoga session, and I found it very calming, both physically and emotionally. I've kept it up ever since. You should come.'

Not wishing to sound dismissive, Joe ventured an 'Um, yes, maybe.'

'That's a no if ever I heard one,' Steph said.

'No, I really have never considered it; that's all.' *Not good at not sounding dismissive*, he thought.

They were just getting on to talk about families, brothers, sisters, and the like when Joe's mobile rang. It was not a number he recognized or an acquaintance from his contact list, so he pressed mute and let it run. 'They'll leave a message if it's important,' he said.

Steph, it turned out, had an older brother, Harry, whom she was very close to and who was in the navy, currently posted to HMS *Dragon*, the MOD's latest type-45 destroyer, which was undergoing trials at Portsmouth. He was a lieutenant, recently promoted from midshipman, which is a double jump avoiding sub lieutenant by means of graduating from Britannia Royal Naval College Dartmouth six months ago. She was obviously very proud of him and had attended his graduation ceremony, and she proceeded to show photographs of the day, which included a lot of pomp and ceremony that she was really chuffed to have been invited to be part of. Their mum and dad, also navy and currently living in Cyprus, where they had been for the last three years, similarly attended the graduation. Photographs showed a very attractive middle-aged couple, both dressed in civvies, which surprised Joe, but Steph explained that Dad didn't want, in any way, to upstage Harry.

Joe's phone buzzed. It was a text telling him he had a missed call and a voice message.

'It's probably a sales call or something,' he said. 'Excuse me; I will just check.'

He tapped the voicemail icon and placed the phone to his ear.

He felt the blood drain from his face and his body tense.

'What is it?' she said.

'My sister has been taken to hospital; I have to go right away.'

'What's happened? Which hospital?' Steph asked.

'The Royal. I need to get my car.'

'Can I come with you?'

'What about yoga?' Joe said.

'It'll be there next week. Why don't we get a taxi?' Steph said. 'It might be quicker?'

They checked Uber; there was one two minutes away, which would be at least ten minutes quicker than getting the car. They booked it, and sure enough it was there within the allotted time.

'Did the message say anything about what had happened?' Steph repeated.

'No, just that I should get there, and if I couldn't they would arrange for someone to pick me up.'

'That sounds official.'

'She's a police officer, so I guess it has come through formal channels.'

'How old is your sister ... sorry, what's her name?'

'Pat, and she's two years older than me. Twenty-eight.'

'What about your parents?'

'They are on holiday in Greece. I'll get more information before I contact them.'

It took twelve agonizing minutes to reach the hospital and a further eight before anybody knew what they were asking about. Eventually something must have come up on the monitor, and they were ushered into a small office to the side of the reception desk by one of the clerks and asked to wait while she located Dr James.

Finally a doctor, accompanied by a police officer, PC Willoughby, made his way into the office.

'Hello, you must be Joseph Riley.' The doctor shook Joe's hand. 'My name is Dr James, and'—he looked towards Steph—'this is?'

'Steph—Stephanie Clarke,' Joe said

'And is Stephanie a relation?'

'No,' Joe said, 'a friend of mine.'

'Oh, that's good. Would you mind stepping outside just for a moment, Stephanie, while I have a quick word with Joseph? Thanks.' He opened the door and steered Steph out.

'Can you tell me what's going on?' Joe asked, anxiety building up at the subterfuge.

'Certainly. Sorry. Your sister was involved in an incident. She has been hit over the head and suffered a gunshot wound to the upper chest. She was brought here by ambulance'—he looked at his watch—'an hour and a half ago, but we are going to transfer her to Alderney as soon as we can. She's in surgery at the moment to stabilize the wound, which I understand is going to plan. But Alderney have a very sophisticated head trauma unit, and we need them on the case as soon as possible.'

Joe went cold and gritted his teeth. 'Gunshot?' he said. 'Can I see her?'

'When she gets out of surgery,' the doctor said.

'Hello, Joe, I'm PC Gail Willoughby. Your sister got caught up in a rather violent burglary, I'm afraid.'

'No shit, Sherlock. Was she on her own?'

'It wasn't an operation; she was doing a favour for a fellow officer, looking in on his dog after her shift.'

'What!'

'I know; it was just unfortunate that she was there at the wrong time.'

Joe felt sick and wasn't sure he was going to keep the pint of Amstel down. 'I need the gents',' he said.

'No problem.' The doctor led him out, and he passed an alarmed Steph and crossed the hallway.

He dived into the fist cubicle and sat on the toilet with his head on his arm, leaning on the sink for what seemed like an age, hearing only the thump of his heartbeat in his ears. His head was struggling to come to terms with the reality of his sister's plight and what exactly to tell their parents.

'Joe? you okay?' It was Steph outside the cubicle door. 'What's going on, Joe?'

Hearing Steph and moving focus away from his physical condition seemed to reduce the nausea.

He stood up and opened the door.

'She's been shot, Steph,' he said.

'Oh my god! How bad?'

'Not sure. She's in surgery, and they are going to send her to Alderney as soon as they have finished, because she also has a head injury.'

'Oh Joe, Christ, I'm so sorry; what can I do?'

'I'd appreciate your company right now if you don't mind waiting with me until I get a chance to see her.'

'Of course.' She put her arm around his shoulders and pulled him towards her.

Joe was close to tears, and Steph guided him out of the toilet and back into the hall to a chair.

The doctor came over and asked whether he was okay and whether he needed a nurse, to which he shook his head.

Joe looked up at the doctor. 'Just let me know what's happening, please.'

'Will do. As soon as I know anything, I will be down.'

PC Willowby couldn't really add anything, as her information was sketchy at best, and it was another forty-five minutes before the doctor came back, by which time Joe had had several attempts at contacting his mum and dad, but to no avail. He left message after message, each one slightly more desperate than the one before.

Dr James sat on the chair next to him.

'Okay Joseph?'

'Joe, please.'

'Right, Joe. The surgery on the gunshot wound has gone well. No organs have been damaged, but the subclavian artery was partially severed.'

'What does that mean?' Joe asked.

It's the main artery feeding the right arm. She may lose a little movement in her hand and wrist, but it should recover after a short period of rest followed by physio. She is just being prepared for transfer to Alderney, and as a precaution she will go with a life support unit, but I don't want this to alarm you. It is just in case there's an issue en route. She has had a bleed in the temporal lobe, and a drain has been established and the pressure is now under control. All subconscious motor functions are working fine, and hopefully that will be true for everything else. The next few days are critical, and she will need as much undisturbed rest as possible. They will bring her through to the ambulance bay in the next few minutes. You are welcome to see her there, but I really don't want to delay getting her to Alderney.

'What are the likely effects of the head injury?'

'Best not to worry about that at this stage; they can range from none to major, but I think we got to her in time, and she is in the best possible hands.'

'Thank you, Doctor,' Joe said, still dazed and still in shock.

He stood up and shook the doctor's hand, and Steph got up and grabbed Joe's.

'Come on; let's wait at the bay,' she said.

The lift doors opened as they arrived, and a bed appeared with so much equipment strapped to it and around it that it took four nurses and two porters to escort it.

Joe was shocked to glimpse what little he could see of his sister in such a vulnerable state. She was always the tough one—the one in control. To see her wiped out like this was shocking.

He managed to grab her left hand, which was just about the only part of her that wasn't connected to apparatus, as she passed, and he squeezed it. There was no reaction.

84

CHAPTER 14

◇◇◇◇◇◇◇◇◇◇◇◇◇

4 days earlier

Maya was just getting her things together when her mobile buzzed. It was a message from Neville. She couldn't quite make it out, but as she was running very late, she decided she would check it when she got to work. It was a few minutes after nine by the time she left for the office, and as she walked along the back of her block to the parking area, she was aware of an array of sirens a little way off.

As she drove her Peugeot 205 out of her road, two police cars with lights and sirens flashed past the end of the street. At the junction, she turned in the same direction. The police cars vanished, and she carried on for another five minutes before her road forked. She wanted the left-hand road to Bournemouth, but it was blocked with, she was guessing, one of the patrol cars that just raced through. 'Bugger,' she said under her breath. 'Five minutes earlier I would have got through.' As it was, this would add another ten minutes to her journey time. She had a budget meeting at ten thirty with some prep work to do beforehand.

By the time she arrived, she was flustered and edgy. She took her phone out to check Neville's message, which just read 'dilbert.'

Maybe a film he wants us to watch, she thought. She closed her phone and ran up to her office.

Two of her team were already in and getting to grips with what was needed for the meeting, and she thanked them, saying she had got held up by an accident.

The meeting went well, and budget figures for the next quarter were surprisingly easily approved, which would open up some new opportunities for Maya and her team.

It was lunchtime when she got back to her office and rang Neville on his mobile. He didn't answer, so she rang his office number on the third floor.

'Hello—Jess Parker.'

'Oh, hi Jess, it's Maya; I was hoping to speak to Neville?'

'He hasn't turned in yet Maya; I'm guessing he had a late one updating the firewall. He'll probably be in after lunch.'

'Right, yes, sure. Thanks.'

She tried his mobile again, but there was no answer. She left a message. 'Hey, what you up to? How come you're not at work? Call me please?'

Her screen showed a voice message and three missed calls from Aleysha. She tapped the icon and put the phone to her ear. Aleysha was always straightforward, no-nonsense, and practical, but there was an air of hesitation in her voice.

'Hi, sis. Do you know a Neville Hillingdon? Well, I'm guessing you do, as the last message on his phone is to you. He's been involved in an accident; could do with having a word. Love you.'

Shit, what sort of accident? she thought as she rang Aleysha.

It rang out, as usual. She checked the log; it was two and a half hours ago. She left a message saying that she was sorry she had been in a meeting and asking for her to call back when she got the message. For her sister to get in touch when she was working was very unusual, which made her feel uneasy about just how serious an accident Neville had been involved in. Maya called her sister three times over lunch and eventually got through just after two o'clock.

'Aleysha, what's happened?'

'Hi, babe, who is Neville Hillingdon?'

'He's a colleague here at Benfield … well, we've been seeing each other for the past few weeks. What's happened, Aleysha?'

'Sweetie, he's in a bad way. Got the wrong side of a hit-and-run this morning.'

'How bad?'

'It's critical, Maya. He's in Alderney.'

'Shit. I'm on my way over to the hospital.'

'I'll see you there. I need to talk to you,' Aleysha said.

'Yes, I think I need to talk to you too.'

Aleysha arrived at the hospital ahead of Maya and was told by the registrar that Mr. Hillingdon was still in surgery and was unlikely to be able to see visitors today. Aleysha showed her warrant card, but the registrar looked up at her and said, 'It's still unlikely that he will be seeing visitors until tomorrow.'

'Fair enough,' Aleysha said. 'Can I get an update on his condition?'

'I will get the consultant to talk to you as soon as he is free. There's a waiting area with a coffee machine just around the corner.'

'Thanks. I'm expecting my sister, a Miss Coombs; could you let her know where I am when she arrives?'

'Certainly.'

She got herself a black coffee and sat facing the entrance. It was a light, relaxing space with a small fountain in the centre and screens around the outer walls showing tasteful marketing videos of the various procedures offered at this and other hospitals in the group. She became absorbed by one on rehabilitation after an acquired brain injury, ABI. It typically featured children undergoing water therapy and cognitive exercises.

Maya walked in about ten minutes later and sat next to her, and they put their arms around each other.

'What's going on, Aley?'

'I don't know much; he was in a bad way when he came in, but I haven't had an update yet as to his condition. Who is he to you?'

'He's a colleague at Banfield, in IT, but we have got close recently. He's really nice; you would like him.'

'We don't think this was an accident, Maya. He messaged you, right? this morning?'

'Yes … well, sort of. Just a single word.' Maya got her phone out.

'Dilbert,' Aleysha said.

'That's right—why?'

'His phone was in his hand at the scene. We think he was trying to type "deliberate".'

'Shit, really? Why?'

'Because the car, a white Volkswagen, mounted the pavement, hit him, and drove off. We have several witnesses who confirm this, and Greg and I managed to pull the guy over after a chase on the A35 at Stanley Green. He's in custody, denying everything.

Maya looked dazed. 'He might have got himself mixed up with something he didn't intend to.'

Aleysha looked quizzical. 'What do you mean, 'mixed up with'?'

'He had work to do over the weekend in the office, updating the network firewall. He came across something in the company files that could have suggested that Banfield and its subsidiaries may be involved with something fraudulent. I didn't take too much notice, as he mentioned this before we set out for work this morning and I said we would look at it this evening.'

'This morning before work?' Aleysha tilted her head.

'Yes, okay, he stayed over.'

'Right, so *that* sort of getting a little close.'

Maya looked at her big sister with a 'Yes, *and* …?' expression.

'He left me a memory stick with, apparently, some screenshots on.'

'Where is that?' Aleysha asked.

'It's in my jewellery box.'

'Fine, but that's not a great place for it if it *is* that important.'

Aleysha looked at her watch. 'I have a conference call back at the station with our lawyers on this case at three o'clock. I'll go via yours and pick up this stick. I'll call you later. Let me know what comes up about Hillingdon.' She kissed her sister and got up to leave.

'Have you got a key? And it's Neville,' Maya said.

'Sorry, yes I have.'

On her way out, she asked the registrar to direct the consultant to her sister on the condition of the patient. She nodded, which Aleysha took as agreement.

At Maya's flat, she went to the bedroom and recovered the memory stick from her jewellery box, tucked it into her breast pocket, and made her way back out. She locked her sister's flat and went down the two flights of stairs.

She failed to see the white Transit with a loop aerial on the roof parked a few spaces further up the road, as indeed she would also miss the same Transit parked outside her own flat later that evening.

◇◇◇◇

A doctor in a white coat entered the waiting area and called out for a Miss Coombs.

Maya got up and walked towards him.

'Miss Coombs—Gary Hollis. I'm Neville's consultant. Let's talk in my office.'

Maya followed him in, and he directed her to a chair. He pulled his up in front of her.

They went through the formalities of establishing that she was not a relative and that she didn't think he had any relations close by. His family was, she believed, in Norfolk, and she didn't have contact details.

'Not to worry; we will sort that out later. Now I guess you know that the police are involved, so there is little I can tell you about the events leading up to Mr. Hillingdon's injuries, but they are severe, I'm afraid. He has several broken ribs, and serious facial and head injuries; we have decided that his survival will be best served in an induced coma for the time being.'

'Survival,' Maya repeated.

'Sorry, not a good choice of words, but how he responds over the next few days will give us a better idea of just how bad, or not, it is. He's in ICU on the second floor, and you are welcome to come up and see him through the glass, but you can't enter at this time. 'Would you like to?'

'Please.'

Maya didn't really know what to expect, but she was shocked to see the state he was in. The part of his face and neck that wasn't either bandaged or covered by his breathing apparatus was heavily bruised and swollen. To think that less than seven hours ago he'd walked out of her flat, cheerily saying goodbye to her.

꩜

Later that day, Maya was in her kitchen with the window open, smoking a B&H from a packet she'd picked up on her way home. She hadn't smoked for years, but the thought of Neville in hospital, and not by accident, had created the urge for a cigarette. The urge turned out to be greater than any relief it offered. After the third drag, which caught the back of her throat just as badly as the first, she stubbed it out and threw the pack in the bin. She felt her phone vibrate in her pocket; she must have put it on silent when she was in hospital. It was Aleysha.

'Hi, sis. How was he?' Aleysha asked.

'They've put him in an induced coma to give him a chance of survival.' Just saying the words hit her so hard she broke down. 'Aley, he looked awful,' she cried.

'I know. Listen; let's go and get a drink. I'll see you in the George?'

'Can we make it the Dolphin; I don't feel like bumping into anyone I know.'

'Okay, I'll be there in thirty minutes.'

Maya pulled herself together and repaired her face with wet wipes and some foundation.

It was a twenty-minute walk to the Dolphin, and she thought the fresh air might do her good. Though she couldn't get the image of Neville on that trolley out of her mind, she was determined to stay strong. She was always the one to show emotion, while her sister was the one with resolve. She still found herself fighting back tears.

The cool air of Poole was in stark contrast to the heated, airless vents that greeted her at the entrance to the Dolphin. It was thankfully desolate and was greeted by a young, and quite obviously inexperienced, barman. She ordered two Amstel's, going for something simple that wouldn't tax him, paid, and sat at a table in the corner to wait for her sister, who arrived within minutes carrying her laptop bag. They hugged, which brought Maya near to tears again.

'Have you seen any of these?' Aleysha asked, holding the stick in her right hand as she opened up her laptop.

'No, as I said, we were going to go over them this evening.'

'They do look to be active files, like live transactional statements.'

She plugged in the USB and opened up the first jpeg.

'The problem with it being linked to and activated by another computer is that a simple algorithm or accounting error could have added a number of zeros to each entry, but if not, they are staggering figures. And if you look at the "from and to" dates at the top, you can see this is a biannual statement, April to September.'

Maya stared in disbelief at the screen.

'They are just wrong, Aleysha,' she said.

'And there are seven pages,' her sister said, pointing to the screen. 'These underlined links here could possibly give some explanation, but we may never know.'

They looked at the other pages, Aleysha saving each one to the laptop.

'Look, I'm going to put this somewhere safe, and I'll come back and stay at yours tonight.'

They finished their beers, and Aleysha dropped Maya back at the flat and drove on to Greg's with a view to discussing how to proceed in the light of this information.

Lucy had just arrived at Enfield and was about to go up in the lift as Aleysha walked into the lobby. 'Hey Luce.'

'Oh, hi Aleysha, Greg isn't back yet,' she said, putting her hand on the lift door to stop it from shutting.

'Shit. I should have called him first.'

'He probably won't be long. He said he wouldn't be late tonight, but I wanted to see Jet anyway.'

'Would you be able to give him this? Ask him to keep it safe, and I'll talk to him about it in the morning.'

'Sure, no problem.' Lucy took the stick and put it in her pocket.

'Thanks, Luce. I'll see you soon.'

Aleysha left. The lift door closed, and Lucy went up.

That evening, having viewed all Neville's images on Aleysha's laptop, they were both stressed as to what to do next. Aleysha said she would talk to Greg and Chris in the morning and see what they thought. They ordered a Chinese takeaway that arrived forty minutes later, which they both picked at, but most of it ended up in the bin. Even the wine had no appeal, and eventually they both fell asleep in front of the TV on the sofas.

They were roused by a loud knock at the door. Aleysha tapped her phone; it was 1.30 a.m.

CHAPTER 15

◇◇◇◇◇◇◇◇◇◇◇◇◇

James's concern for Aleysha was palpable. I didn't think he had had any more sleep over the past few days than I had. He had relentlessly followed every clue, no matter how dubious or doubtful its origins.

We both sat staring at the whiteboards, cold coffee and curled up canteen sandwiches on the table in front of us.

Chris came in and took off his coat and threw a pod in the coffee machine. He hung his coat on the rack while the machine buzzed and gurgled his coffee into a mug, which he grabbed before sitting between James and me.

'Where have you been?' I asked.

'Trying to talk to any of the three witnesses that have gone silent.'

'Any joy?' I ventured.

'None, even when I threatened them with contempt of court if they didn't show when asked. They are genuinely frightened. They didn't even want to be in my company—couldn't get rid of me quick enough.'

'What about offering protective custody?' James asked.

'Hmm … maybe. Not sure even that would work, if I'm honest.'

Joanne came over and dropped a document in front of me. It was a copy of Aleysha's CID exam pass certificate dated 12 August 2011. *Okay that tallies*, I thought.

'What's that about?' Chris asked.

'Just some verification that Kevin is who he says he is.'

'What can we do to track down the *White Angel*?' James asked.

'Well, after our conversation earlier, James,' Chris said, 'I contacted the home office and filled in a Mr Roger Horrobin, MP, on the investigation so far and the fact that it definitely now has international connotations, with the suspected vessel entering European waters. He said he would get back to me this evening when he had had a chance to speak to the security services.'

'Right,' I said. 'I'm going to tie up with Kevin and see if there's a line of enquiry there worth following. I'll be at the Derby Manor if you need me.'

'Pushing out the boat, aren't we?' Chris asked as I strode for the door.

'Just the one night while my place gets cleared up. I doubt Kevin will let me pay anyway.'

'No problem either way.'

'Are you okay with me sharing investigation details with Kevin?' I asked.

'I trust your judgement, Greg. Whatever you think. And if you want my input, just call.'

'Thanks, I will.'

'I'm going to contact all the marinas and harbours in and around the Baltic with an image of the *White Angel* and see what comes back,' James said as he left the table.

The sun was now quite low but warm as I walked out of reception and down the steps to the car. The past few days of rain had left everything looking bright and smelling fresh, with just a hint of sea and salt.

I drove out of town towards Boscombe on the Bath Road for about twenty minutes and turned left through slow-moving traffic onto Derby Road, which I stayed on for another couple of minutes before hitting the roundabout, where the Derby Manor was sited directly opposite. The display plaque on the wall outside stated it to be a boutique guest house, whatever that meant.

I pulled onto the shale driveway; it was most definitely more a guest house than a manor. I parked up and went into reception. Looking around, I saw Kevin sitting on a lounger in the conservatory with a laptop open, thumbing something into his phone. He looked up as I entered, walked over, and shook my hand.

'Hi, how's it going, buddy?' he said.

'Nothing that's leading us anywhere, unfortunately. I'm sorry about earlier, leaving you back at the station.'

'No problem.'

I scanned around the expansive glass-covered conservatory; there were just a few others engaged in conversation. 'We need to sit down and talk, pool what we have. There is a connection to you and Aleysha and the Tithe that I have yet to get a handle on.'

'Has my security clearance been sanctioned?'

'I'm happy, and the guv'nor seem fine about it,' I said.

'I have a room on the first floor,' Kevin said. 'It will be more private.'

'Okay, that sounds good.'

He collected his laptop, and we made our way up to room 107. It wasn't the Novotel but was still very pleasant and, by current hotel room standards, spacious, with a couple of easy chairs and a coffee table, along with all the other usual, but luxury, facilities.

I took off my jacket and laid it on the bed. Kevin poured a couple of coffees from the jug on the heated stand and placed them on the table, and we both sat.

'Right,' I said. 'What I have so far …' I went on to cover the Hillingdon hit-and-run, the abduction of his cousins, the existence of a file with potentially incriminating fraud evidence, my flat being vandalized because of it, and that his cousins were probably on an opulent yacht, which I think I mentioned over the phone, that was now, we believed, somewhere in the Baltic—and a great deal more of a luxury yacht than we first thought.

'What I need to know is what you can tell me about the Tithe deal with the leasing agent you mentioned. Aleysha must have had a reason for calling you over it.'

'Bodican,' Kevin offered. 'Yes, I have been thinking the same. Well, here's the thing, while I was kicking my heels waiting for flight details out of AJ airport, I did some searching of my own. I had dug out and brought with me all the paperwork on the leasing of the Tithe. I've had little communication with them since the contract was written up five years ago.'

'Did you bring any of that with you?' I asked.

'Sure, I have it all, but it took some investigation work to figure out who is who and what is what. Bodican is now West-Line Investments and, as far as I can tell, has little to do with property leasing, though the transfer each month into our secured bond is still from Bodican.'

'What were the circumstances surrounding this co-opt between you and Bodican?' I asked.

'Well, I was approached by a guy.' He got up and walked across the room and grabbed his briefcase from beside the Georgian dressing table.

He laid it on the coffee table and pulled out a large Manila folder. He leafed through it and withdrew an A4 letter with a business card attached. 'John Grant,' he said, passing over the document.

It was an introductory letter summarizing their interest in leasing high-end or specialist properties to international customers.

'And how did he get on to you?'

'Well, it turns out that this John Grant did some property consultancy work for Mum and Dad in Japan, and I'm guessing that at some point the Tithe came up in conversation. I remember thinking he seemed to know a lot about it. He knew about Mr. Kemp, the gardener and handyman, saying of course that they would expect everything to be maintained as per normal and would include an amount to cover such costs, as well as that they vet their clients extensively to ensure they will be very respectful to both property, goods, and chattels.'

'And did they?' I asked.

'Handsomely,' Kevin said. 'After several meetings with me in Puerto Rico and one at London Gatwick with Aleysha, we signed a contract operating from 31 December 2014, to be reviewed after seven years.' He pulled another folder from his briefcase and extracted a very official document with an embossed Bodican logo. 'This is the contract.' He handed it over.

While I scanned the document, I asked, 'What exactly did your parents do?'

'They set up a clothing line, FXI, branded in Japan but manufactured in other parts of Asia. To be fair, I think they did all the promotional work, taking it to Europe and the US. I know they employed some rapper and his girlfriend in the early days to do all the design work. They were very progressive for the time; I was really impressed—even more so when they decided to set up a manufacturing arm in the Caribbean, to support the American market, and asked me to run it. My background was in electronic manufacture, so I was a bit out of my comfort zone with textiles, and it was a massive culture shock, but the benefits soon outweighed any concerns I had. And they had control of the order book. They made it a policy to underproduce, focusing on quality and repeatability, not volume. There were, and still are, far more customers for the products than we attempted to manufacture for. The policy is to set manufacturing volume twenty per cent below known requirement. That known requirement, in the US anyway, has remained virtually stable over the last five years, allowing us a natural, steady growth pattern, and sensible investment to ensure we stay ahead on both cost and retail price.

'I see from this contract that they reserve the rights over the telecommunications equipment to be fitted.'

'This was explained to us as a necessity to ensure the property had the latest phone and Wi-Fi. Their international guests would expect to be able to communicate to anywhere in the world. As such, they would provide and install all the necessary kit. I believe it also has a satellite phone with a dish in the loft.'

That would explain the overcomplicated phone and joystick in the hall of the Tithe, I thought.

'Sounds a bit MI5-ish,' I said.

'Yes, they're very strict on security, although this was a later amendment and came with an embellished fee and new contract about three months after we took on the original one. We—actually, when I say "we", I mean "Aleysha"—gets a message via email and text five days in advance of an occupancy. The message will have a list of things that will need to be in place, which is normally food stuff, but on occasion, clothing and prayer mats have been included. It is expected that everything will be completed a minimum of twenty-four hours in advance of their expected arrival just in case they are early for whatever reason. There will be an end date, and again Aleysha is not to enter the property until at least twenty-four hours after this time.'

'Who sends the emails and texts?'

'Well, I've always assumed it to be a member of the Bodican staff; right now I'm not sure.'

'And how many tenancies a year do you get, and for how long?' I asked, thinking we were probably getting way off track here.

'Five to ten a year, and they range from just a few days to … I think five weeks was the longest.'

'And they pay a full-time retainer?'

'Correct.'

'That's a lot of money for what—less than six months' occupancy?

'We were not complaining.'

'No, I'm sure, and I don't blame you.'

'Look,' I said, 'I need to pop back to the flat to get some things. I'll also call in on the vet to see if there's any news. I'll be back later.'

'Shall I book a table for dinner?' Kevin said.

I glanced at my watch. 'If you can wait till around seven, that would be good.'

'Seven it is. I'm going to do a bit more surfing to see if I can unearth anything on West-Line Investments and their link to Bodican.'

'Okay. Did you say you have already booked a room for me?'

'Yes, 202. It's on the top floor, and you are my guest for as long as it takes.'

'Thanks, Kevin. I'll see you later.'

CHAPTER 16

◇◇◇◇◇◇◇◇◇◇◇◇◇

Bryant had not left the office after Jeremy departed; he'd had a phone call from Central Office in North Korea that made resolving this shitstorm even more complicated to deal with. He sat with a mixture of emotions ranging from livid anger to fear of total loss.

He buzzed up to Anni, but she had gone out. He rang her mobile, and she picked up.

'Hey.'

'You still in touch with Janek?' Bryant asked.

'I'm seeing him in about an hour.'

'Where?'

'The Pepper Saint Ontiod, Canary Warf. Why?'

'I'll see you both there.'

୧ﬗﬗ୨

The Pepper Saint Ontiod had an outside space with tables and benches facing onto Millwall Inner Dock. They were both smoking, and the atmosphere between Anni and Janek was intense when Bryant arrived. And what he brought to the party only made it worse.

Three beers, which Anni had ordered earlier, were brought out by a waiter.

After a discussion that went on for some time, Janek got up and said, 'This isn't something I can handle on my own, Bry, which is going to make it costly.'

'I realize that,' Bryant said, handing him a slip of paper from his pocket with a number scrawled on it.

'What's this?'

'It's a contact. They have all the details of what can and what can't be done, and the resources to carry it off.'

'So why are you involving me?'

'Because if the "can't be done" becomes an issue, I can rely on you to tidy up.'

As they left, Anni grabbed Janek by the hand. 'I've transferred twenty grand from the offshore account. Be careful.'

They held on to each other for a little too long, Bryant thought, as they all took different paths out across the Isle of Dogs.

CHAPTER 17

Jeremy arrived early at the Reef Cafe—or, as it now preferred to call itself, Coffee Reef. The sun was disappearing around the Heartland peninsula, and the air had become decidedly chilled, which was a shame because Jeremy was hoping they could sit more privately outside. He checked the opening times as he walked in. *Open until 7.00 p.m.* He looked at his watch. It was 5.15 p.m. *Plenty of time*, he thought.

Barring a family at the far end with three children, it was empty. He made his way through countless randomly placed tables and chairs to the counter and ordered an Americano and sat at a table to the right of the front door, looking back to the main promenade. This way he would see Pam arrive. She did shortly before half past five. He stood up as she entered and hugged her but felt some resistance. She was clearly uncomfortable. 'Hi, what would you like?' Jeremy asked.

'Oh, I'll have a cappuccino.'

The guy behind the counter called across. 'Got it; I'll bring it over.'

Right, not so private, Jeremy thought.

He looked at Pam. 'You okay?'

'Hardly,' she said, 'it's bad enough worrying about losing my job, but now it appears my whole life is under threat.

The guy from the RAV4 was now seated on an outside table at Hot Rocks overlooking the Coffee Reef, with his hands cupped around a large, hot black coffee, glad he'd put his fully lined parka on. He could see Caine and his lady friend sat just inside. Their body language when she arrived was awkward, but that was just about all he could record.

He drank half his coffee, got up, and walked back to the RAV4, which was parked illegally on yellow lines behind the Hot Rocks Cafe.

⁕

'Pam, listen. Look, we neither of us have any real commitment to staying here other than a very lucrative job. If we take that away, what do we have? Nothing but each other. My wife is most definitely ex; fortunately we don't have children. My parents are self-sufficient and wouldn't raise an eyebrow if they never saw me again. Yours are in Newcastle, and for sure we would have to avoid them for maybe a year, but you only see them at Christmas and maybe birthdays. I'm sure we can work around that.

'Wow, it's that simple for you?'

He paused. 'I guess it's that simple because I love you. Maybe that's why it's not so simple for you?'

'I'm not saying that; I'm actually very scared, and quite honestly I can't see beyond scared.'

Jeremy took Pam's hands in his; they were trembling. She didn't pull away.

'Do you have a plan?' she asked.

'I always have a plan,' he said, 'but it normally just includes me. Any plan I have now—if you want—has to suit both of us. I have invested over the past few years, not only in the Banfield skim but also in a dual identity that has been operational now for two years. My other self has a fully formed life, albeit a retired one, which helps with keeping things simple. Say hello to Brian Campbell.'

'Really?' Pam said with scepticism.

'Really,' Jeremey replied, pulling out a driving licence with his picture and details.

Pam sat back, just looking at him.

'Brian Campbell also has a very nice yacht moored in Poole harbour, from money left to him by his deceased father.'

'How come you managed to keep all this from me over the last year?' Pam asked.

'Not something that comes up or would be considered normal in everyday conversation: "Oh, by the way, I have a dual identity with the view to starting a new life when the dodgy business I'm involved with goes tits up. What do you reckon?'"

He saw her stare at him in disbelief and shake her head almost indiscernibly. She turned to look through the window, appearing to gaze out without seeing. There was a muffled ringtone from her handbag and she leaned down to get it just as the front window of the cafe exploded and collapsed to the floor. She fell back off her chair, and they were immediately showered in plaster from a hole the size of a golf ball in the wall directly behind where her head had been. Screams came from the family at the back, the parents and children quickly gathering together in a huddle. Jeremey grabbed Pam's arm, lifted her from the floor, and pulled her back from the window. All he could gather was that the shot, if that's what it was, had come from the left, as it had passed through the wall on the right. He moved himself and Pam to the left of the cafe.

Over the next couple of minutes, a crowd gathered outside, and Jeremy was aware of sirens. Not wishing to get caught up with the police, he grabbed the two coffee cups and Pam's bag from the floor, guided her out behind him, and mingled in the crowd. Making the assumption that the assailant had fled, he edged out onto the wooden walkway in front of the cafe.

'Try to stay calm,' he whispered to Pam.

'What! I think I have just been shot at.'

'Maybe, but we need to get out of here without raising suspicion.'

Given that their attacker was located left of them, as they walked out, they moved casually to the right and tried to blend in with the gathering crowd.

As soon as they were clear of the pier entrance, they picked up pace and headed down the promenade. One of the blue-and-white road trains was trundling down the lower promenade, and Jeremy flagged him down. Pam got on, and Jeremey ran across the road and dumped the coffee cups in one of the large wheelie bins, hoping to leave as little evidence of their presence as possible. He leant into the driver's cab and handed over a twenty-pound note, held up his hands to change, and hopped on beside Pam. She was white and shaking and attracting some attention from other passengers. He put his arm around her and gathered her up. She went limp. He placed her handbag on her lap, aware she was silently sobbing.

Pam and Jeremey got off at the far end of the promenade and walked into Boscombe, constantly looking over their shoulders.

They walked into the first place they came across, the purple-painted Harvester, and took a cubicle towards the back of the lounge area. Pam still had no colour and seemed to go into spasm at the slightest noise. She still had not spoken a word since leaving the Reef.

A waiter came over and asked whether they needed a menu. Jeremy said no but asked whether they could have two large whiskies and ice with one bottle of dry ginger.

'How can you be so calm?' Pam finally said.

'I'm not; I've never been so scared in my life.'

'I think we can safely assume that we are on a hit list, and I'm guessing my Monday morning meeting with Bryant is now cancelled.'

'We can't go home, can we?' she said.

'No.'

CHAPTER 18

◇◇◇◇◇◇◇◇◇◇◇◇

The flat hadn't changed, other than that the crime scene tape had been removed. It was still upside down, but now with fingerprint dust everywhere. I didn't feel the need to touch anything and decided to leave it to the team in the morning. I'd get it back to normal after that. I grabbed a bag and folded a couple of shirts and add stuff I think I might need for a couple of days. There was a knock at the door, a key in the lock. It opened, and Lucy peered around, looking alarmed.

'Christ, what went on here, Greg?' she said.

I suddenly felt thankful that I was here; this would have been a much bigger shock for her had she come in to find it unprepared.

'Hi, Luce. Sorry, I really should have let you know. All a bit up in the air at the moment.' I explained about Aley's abduction and the break in and told her about Jet, which she was as much distraught about as the fact of Aley's kidnapping. I left out the bit about Pat being caught up in it. She asked about the vet and said that if there was anything she could do, she was there for me. I thanked her and told her I was going to see the vet now for an update.

'Oh Greg.' Her expression changed as realization dawned. 'I nearly forgot, Aleysha left me this Monday night. I meant to put it on the side but forgot. I'm so sorry; I'm guessing it's important?'

It was the memory stick.

'Well, I'm hoping it might just throw some light on an otherwise murky subject.'

'I'm sorry, Greg; please let me know how Jet is,' she said.

'Will do,' I replied, somewhat distracted.

I decided I needed to see how Jet was. I saw Lucy out, still apologizing, grabbed my coat and keys, and put the stick in my wallet.

⟨∞⟩

Jaz's assistant was on the front desk when I got to Aniwell.

'You must be Jet's dad,' she said.

I always think this is a strange correlation that as an owner you become 'Dad'.

'I guess I must be.'

'Jaz is just cleaning up; she'll be with you shortly.'

'How is he?'

'Brave' was all she would venture.

Jaz came through a few minutes later and called me into her office.

'How is he?' I asked again.

'Well, Greg, his spinal cord is intact, which is great news, and the damaged vertebra has been pinned to one either side. This may make him walk a little strange, but other than that, I'm happy with this part of the procedure. He has been plastered from the hip down purely to prevent any further damage while we were having to pull him around. The fractures down there will probably have to be broken and reset in a day or so when we feel he has recovered sufficiently from today's routine.'

I felt such relief and almost filled up. In the back of my mind, I'd had the dread I was coming to have him put down.

'Thank you.' I struggled to say anything else.

'They're a tough breed,' Jaz said, 'and he's in good shape other than his injuries. I'm sure he'll be fine.'

'Look,' I finally say, 'I have no idea of costs for these things, but I'm happy to set up a direct debit and for you call off as required.'

'That won't be necessary. Mandy has created an account for you, which you can access online and pay as you go. Today was quite expensive, and the overnights are not cheap, but all of this is shown on the account. Along with a total projected cost of nine hundred seventy-five pounds, assuming we don't get any further complications. As I say, we can spread the overall charge if you prefer.'

'That's very kind,' I said, and she gave me all the details of account access. We went into the recovery room, and I stroked the sad little head that lay on what looked like an enormous hotel-style pillow.

⁂

My next port of call was Alderney. En route I spoke to Chris just to get any updates on the case and tell him I have the memory stick. 'What's on it?'

'Haven't had chance to look at it yet; I'm just on my way to see Jet,' I lied. He didn't need to know I was going to the Alderney, and I didn't feel I could talk about Jet without cracking up.

'The IT guys', he said, 'are getting somewhere with the email address that Janet Frasier had given up.' Not that it was earth-shattering, but it emanated from an Internet cafe, 11 Charing Cross Road, London. There was also a CCTV camera outside the Garrick Theatre facing in the direction of the Western Union cash machine next door to Internet City. This was interesting but, without knowing who we were looking for, useless. There had been no further sighting, or active transmissions, of the White Angel, but they had a lead on Lewins. He came up on the radar of the undercover team in Southend. Apparently an unknown male handed an envelope, suspected to contain cash, to Kim Ta. He was subsequently identified as Don Lewins. At Chris's request, the team now had him on their persons of interest list. 'No sighting since, though. Oh, and we had a report from a neighbour that there was a disturbance at Neville Hillingdon's flat. Turns out it's been ransacked along the same lines as yours.'

'I don't suppose there's any way of establishing what might be missing?'

'Well, given that he's in IT and there was no computer or laptop recovered, I'm guessing they've been made away with.

'Okay, thanks. I'll call you later when I've had a chance to look at the USB stick.'

'I hope Jet's all right.'

'Thanks,' I said.

On arrival at Alderney, I was pleased to see that Pat and Neville Hillingdon were in adjoining rooms and we had a guard on duty covering both. I showed my card to the officer and looked in on Hillingdon.

'He's down in surgery, sir,' the officer said. 'Been there since three o'clock.'

'Thanks,' I said, and I went into the room marked 'Pat Coleridge'.

I walked in and approached the bed. My legs immediately went weak as I hung on to the end rail of the cot to maintain balance.

This could be my wife, eight years ago. It was a different hospital, different ward, but Pat's head was bandaged the same; she had the same pallor, and she was plugged and wired in the same. I took a seat by her bedside, cupping my head, hoping the nausea would pass.

A nurse came in and went directly to the other side of the bed, presumably to read off the monitor or something. She looked over at me.

'Are you okay, sir?'

'Sure, I'm fine.' I swallowed hard. 'how's she doing?'

'She's responding well, I believe. I think you've missed the consultant, but the front desk will have the latest. Are you a relative?'

'No, a work colleague.'

'Police?'

I nodded, preferring not to risk any further conversation until I could get the image of Catherine out of my head.

I lost Catherine the year after I joined CID. It was probably the first year we'd had good quality time together. We both qualified the previous year, me at the police academy and Catherine at med school. We moved to Bournemouth from Bristol because of my CID posting, and Cat got a senior registrar's job at Nuffield Health. Both were a sea change from what we had been used to. She oversaw A & E at the Bristol Royal Infirmary, which, like most NHS hospitals, was underfunded and understaffed, and I was in Bristol Met studying for my CID qualification. We used to cross in the hall of our flat most days of the week. If we were lucky, we might get one morning or one afternoon together a week, which we quite often just spent sleeping. When we moved to Bournemouth, there was time to go out walking in the evenings, with Jet, who was then just a pup. We visited pubs and restaurants for pleasure rather than picking up the pieces after a drunken brawl. Life was special for the first time. We were able to make plans. We bought a flat in Milton Villas on Milton Road, which was a ten-minute walk from the Nuffield—my biggest regret. That walk killed her. On 12 May 2012, at nine thirty in the evening, a black Audi pulled out of Beechley Road on to Lonsdale Road, floored it, and lost the back end, which picked Cat up as she crossed the road. The car dragged her down the bus lane and into the metal-and-fibreglass bus stop. Her neck and head injuries would, in three weeks, prove fatal. Those were three of the very worst weeks of my life. And right now I was looking at Pat, hoping to God her fate wouldn't be the same.

I was pulled to awareness by voices outside the ward. It was the officer talking; his tone suggested he knew who had just arrived. He knocked on the door.

'Sir,' he said, 'the patient's brother is here.'

I got up. 'Okay, I'm just leaving.'

A smart young guy entered the room, holding the hand of a tall, attractive blond girl.

'And you are?' he said, a little defensive, I felt.

'DCI Richards,' I said, holding out a hand, about to say that I was sorry about his sister.

'Your dog, was it?'

'Err, yes,' I replied, realizing where the prickly edge was coming from.

'Pity you couldn't have afforded a dog walker, don't you think?'

Ignoring the fact that if it hadn't been his sister, it would probably have been the dog walker, someone else's sister, I said, 'Yes. I'm very sorry, but we will do everything we can to ensure her recovery.'

'When you say "we", I'm guessing you mean the taxpayer, which is me.'

'Joe?' The girl, whom I presumed to be his girlfriend, gave him a gentle tug.

I realized I was not in the right frame of mind to deal with this and would probably end up saying something I'd regret.

'Look, I understand,' I said. 'I'm very sorry. If there is anything I can do'—I hand him a card—'please get in touch.'

Nearly snatching the card, he walked past me towards Pat, and the young lady looked at me a little apologetically.

I closed the door behind and nodded to the officer as I made my way down the corridor.

Inside the ward, Steph turned Joe towards her and said quietly, 'This is not his fault, Joe.'

'I know,' Joe said reluctantly. He mused for a second and sighed. 'It's just …'

'I know.' Steph squeezed his hand.

He rushed to the door.

'Hey.'

I reached the stairwell. It was Pat's brother, calling from the ward entrance.

'Listen, I'm sorry; I overreacted.'

'It's okay,' I said. 'I get it. I hope she gets better soon.'

I call at reception to ask about Hillingdon, but there is nothing they can offer and no way of knowing how long he will remain in surgery.

On the way back to the Derby Manor, the clock on the Focus was showing seven thirty; I thought I'd probably missed dinner.

As it turned out, Kevin had booked seven thirty for eight, and we walked into the restaurant at five past.

He mentioned what a good team we had back at the station. Chris had gone to the trouble to introduce him as an interested party and said that he was welcome to be involved as long as he didn't interfere.

'Seemed fair to me,' he said.

Kevin is quite the investigator, it turns out. He had unearthed Bodican's registration documents dating back some eleven years with five amendments to its scope over this period.

Three years ago, it got into financial difficulty and was taken over by, and became a backwater to, West-Line Investments. West-Line's ancestry, it would appear, was not quite so transparent. They emerged in 2008 as West-Irui Industries, based in Taipei, Taiwan. They grew quickly and added subsidiaries in Thailand and the Philippines. In 2010 they created a head office in Goseong, South Korea.

A waiter came across and asked whether we wanted to order drinks.

'Shall we crack a bottle of red?' Kevin asked.

'Fine,' I said

Kevin studied the menu for a few moments, and then his eyes lit up.

'Oh, one of those please.' He pointed to the menu.

'Certainly, sir,' the waiter said. 'And are you ready to order?'

'Can you give us a few minutes please?' Kevin asked.

I later found out it to be a Barons de Rothschild Lafite Réserve Spéciale Pauillac—2015, having spied it on his bill. It came in at forty-seven pounds.

He grabbed a sheet of paper from the pile in front of him.

'Now, here's where it gets interesting, and this took some real detective work. You would have been impressed,' Kevin said.

Little did he know, as I leafed through just some of the documents that he had printed via the hotel computer, I was already quite amazed at what he had uncovered in such a short time. I felt perhaps he wasn't a bullshitter after all.

'In 2011,' he continued, 'West-Irui were suspected of involvement in trafficking Columbian drugs through the Philippines via North Korea—while Goseong is in South Korea, it's on the border of North Korea—and from there it forged links into mainland China and Japan. It was also considered that they were looking for routes into Europe and, more specifically, the lucrative UK market.'

'Where did you get all this from?' I asked.

'You'd be surprised what you can get from Wikipedia, Though you do have to do a lot of verification work. There's a news article somewhere.' He rummaged through the paperwork. 'Here we are. "It was revealed today that the Metropolitan Police, in conjunction with other agencies, exposed a fledgling drugs syndicate based in the East End of London, but with ghost cells in Birmingham, Manchester, and Bournemouth ..." Err ... yes, here it is: "It is believed that the consortium is run from a South Korean base and is linked to West-Irui Industries, who are under investigation by the South Koreans for international drug smuggling."'

Kevin looked up at me. 'What do you think?'

'I think you have been very busy. Not sure where this gets us,' I said.

'No neither do I, but it makes me want to look further into the affairs of West-Line and Bodican.'

I agreed and looked up to see the waiter hovering. We both grabbed menus; Kevin swept up the paperwork and slid it into his case. He tasted the wine, and the waiter poured us each a glass.

I ordered the seared pork tenderloin, and Kevin the fillet of gilthead bream.

We sat back and relaxed for a moment, having been completely unaware of the other diners, who had by now pretty much filled the restaurant.

'How's your day gone anyway?' Kevin asked.

'I didn't have to put Jet down.' We both smiled.

'That's great.'

'And I got rightly abused by a colleague's brother.' I explained about Pat and the dog sitting, and it being the reason I had to rush off this morning. Kevin was sympathetic.

'And I have the USB stick that I think all the trouble is about.'

'What's on it?'

'Don't know yet, but if it is IT stuff, I'm hoping it will mean more to you than me.' Our meals arrived. 'Let's look at it after we have eaten,' I said. The wine turned out to be exquisite, and we tucked in, going very quiet for a while.

Afterwards, we moved to the lounge with what was left of the Barons de Rothschild, mulling over what Kevin had discovered and how it may or may not have relevance to Aley and Maya's dilemma. If drugs were involved, that might explain Aleysha's comment about big money and dangerous people. Kevin also ventured that ports around the Baltic are home to a lot of drug movement and this might just be the link.

It also brought home some guilt that *we* were very comfortable and *they* were probably not.

'Let's see what's on this,' I said pulling out my wallet and removing the USB drive.

Kevin slipped his laptop from his briefcase and laid it on the coffee table. It booted up, and he plugged in the stick.

There were just seven jpeg files, and he opened the first.

It looked like a bank statement, headed 'Willow-Genkin Omnicamp/ Banfield account CY255657765111'.

Looking down the right-hand column, the numbers were eye-watering.

'I don't know anything about Omnicamp, but Banfield, as I have discovered recently, is a small- to medium-size marketing organization working out of four floors of an office block in Bournemouth, employing, among others, Hillingdon and Aleysha's sister.'

Any one row of the lines on this statement would have been reasonable for a half-yearly turnover, but the page added up, as Kevin pointed out, to £49 million.

'I'd like to be part of that organization,' Kevin said. 'You say this is a marketing group.'

'Well, Banfield is. Beyond that I don't know.'

I opened the second jpeg file.

Same thing. The header read, 'account CY255657765121'. There was a similar set of accounts, adding up to just £18 million this time.

'What do you think these links are?' Kevin asked, pointing to an underlined statement reading '*InneedAcc2-5*'.

'Maybe more accounts; IN-Need is also in the header; look,' I said, pointing to the top right of the screen.

Kevin pulled the laptop towards him and typed 'In-need accounts' into Google. IN-Need was flagged as an alternative. He clicked on 'filing history', which came up with five divisions and PDFs for each for 2017–18. Turnover for all five was £5,828,513, with a profit after tax of £692,548.

'That's a long way from eighteen million,' he said.

He flicked back to the last account and ran his finger down each row, stopping at the tenth one down.

'And that's the only one they are putting forward to your tax department.'

Sure enough, line ten showed £5,828,513.

'I need to get this registered into evidence back at the office.'

We looked over the other five jpegs, and they all showed the same account format with differing initial company name, account number, and figures. All had equally staggering bottom lines.

We both sat back, not really knowing what to think about what we were looking at.

Kevin asked whether he should save them to his computer, and I agreed.

We finished the last of the wine, and Kevin asked whether I would mind if he joined me at the station in the morning. I said that it seemed Chris was happy, so that was fine with me. We agreed to meet for breakfast at six thirty and retired to our rooms.

I had a couple of hours of online CID administration, emails, and phone calls to make, none of which I found at all constructive, but I appreciated its importance in ensuring all information was correctly logged.

Preparing to turn in, my mobile lit up, which reminded me to put it on charge.

It was a text. The number was unknown; it read just 'Riga AC.'

Could this really be Aleysha, Riga? I recognized that as a place but didn't know where it was. Google Maps identified it as the capital of Latvia, set on the Baltic Sea. That had to be it.

I called the incident room to see who might still be around. Phil was there, about to go off duty.

'Hi, Phil,' I said. 'I think I have just had a text message from Aley. No caller ID, it just said, "Riga AC." Riga is in the Baltic region, and that was where the *White Angel* was last reported.'

'Yeah, I know. When did you get it?'

'Five minutes ago.'

'I'll get on to their port authorities now.'

'Thanks, Phil. Did James get any hits from his email exercise around there?'

'There's nothing on the board, so I'm guessing not. I'll call you back in a bit.'

'Don't bother; I'm coming in. I'll see you in half an hour.'

Any thoughts of sleep had now been abandoned. I left a message at the front desk of the Derby for Kevin, to say I would have to take a rain check on breakfast, and for him to come into the office if he wanted; I would see him there.

CHAPTER 19

◇◇◇◇◇◇◇◇◇◇◇◇◇

Jeremy ordered a taxi from the Harvester and, after moving to a table in the window, waited on its arrival. Pam still had a disengaged look, but her shaking had subsided a little.

'Let me have your phone,' Jeremey said.

'Why?' she asked as she scrabbled in her handbag.

'We need to dispose of them, but I'll get all your contacts off before we do.'

'You're kidding me, right?'

'We have no time to mess about now, Pam. I don't know how they knew we were in that cafe, but I'm going to assume they tracked one of our phones. I walked there, and I didn't see anyone following me. The contacts are all we need to take. And we will have to go through those at some point to decide which we can afford to hang on to.'

'Have you thought that could have been a random act of violence?' she said.

'Really … did you see the hole in the wall? No, Bryant and his associates have decided we offer too great a risk to their organization.'

He could see the reluctance in her face as she looked down at the screen of her mobile. It lit up automatically, showing the missed call that probably saved her life. It was Kerry, her best friend, but no voicemail was showing. 'Can I call, or at least leave a message for, Kerry?' she said, almost pleadingly.

'No, sweetheart. Maybe when we are safe, in a few months.'

He tapped an app on his phone called SMS Group. Pam welled up and reluctantly handed over her phone.

He shared the SMS Group with Pam's phone, loaded all her contacts to it, and sent all to his other prepaid phone. The buzz from inside his jacket verified that they were arriving. He did a factory reset on both and pocketed them. Jeremy put his arm around her, and she sobbed.

They saw the taxi pull up outside, gathered their things, and walked out, cautiously scanning both ways, ready to dive back in if need be.

Jeremy, looking around, held the taxi door for Pam and leant over to assist her with her seat belt.

'Can you hang on just for a second, mate? I've left something inside.'

Pam gave him a startled look.

'It's okay; I won't be a minute.'

Jeremy walked back inside the Harvester and made his way to the gents'. In there he took out both phones, applied a hard close to both, and removed and folded the sim cards until they broke. He then wiped everything down with toilet tissue and dumped it all in the waste bin.

Back in the taxi, he pulled round the seat belt and clipped it in.

'Old Christchurch Road, please—The Coconut Tree?'

There was a nod from the driver, and they set off.

'Where are we going?' Pam asked.

'A phone shop to get you a pay-as-you-go,' he said in a quiet whisper.

They left the taxi outside the Beirut Lounge, opposite the Coconut Tree, and walked down the street to the Smart Shop, a PC and phone repair outfit.

A young, overweight Asian lad was behind the counter, clipping together an Ericsson smart phone. He looked up and said, 'We close in ten minutes.'

'That's fine,' Jeremy said. 'Is Khalid around?'

'He's over the road at Asia's. I can call him if you like?'

'Please, that would be helpful. I need to get another pay-as-you-go anyway. I'll sort that out while I wait.'

The lad picked up another phone, tapped the screen and tucked it between his ear and shoulder, and finished off the Ericsson.

He spoke briefly in his own language, removed the phone from his ear, and said, 'He will be back shortly.'

Jeremy took Pam's hand and led her over to the display of blister-packed phones. He suggested one similar to his, an LG TracFone. She nodded her agreement absently. He unclipped it from the rack and walked over to the counter and handed it to the lad.

'Mr Brian! How are you this evening!' Khalid blustered in and extended his hand, and Jeremy took it enthusiastically.

'Good to see you again,' he said, gently and limply pumping Jeremy's hand. Turning towards Pam, he asked, 'And who is this?'

Pam gave a wilted smile.

'This is Carol,' Jeremey said.

'Pleased to meet you, Carol.' He gave a knowing wink to Jeremy. Turning to the counter, he said, 'Give me that,' and Khalid took the LG from the lad's hand.

'Come in the back,' he said to them both, squeezing his extensive frame between the counter and a rack of phone accessories.

They followed him into a small, cluttered office with a desk, two armchairs that had seen better days, and a stool. Khalid arranged the chairs and stool so they could all sit, and with a bit of shuffling, they did so.

'So you want another one of these? I have a better model now that has much better memory if you like?'

'Actually,' Jeremy said, 'You know you arranged some documents for me quite some time ago now.'

'Ah, that. Yes I do—for the young lady, Carol?'

'Quite.'

'This I can arrange, but my cost has gone up since last time, Mr. Brian.'

'That's not a problem, Khalid. Time is more likely to be the issue.'

'You need in a hurry this time?'

'Yes, we would like to get away as soon as possible'

'Okay, let's see what Khalid can do.' He dialled a number on a mobile retrieved from his sweaty shirt pocket.

He talked in Hindi for a few minutes, shut the phone, and pocketed it again.

'So, assuming we can agree on details now, I can make arrangements for the documents to be finished tomorrow. My cousin is sending through some identities for you to choose from.' He scribbled something on a Post-it-note and handed it to Jeremy.

Jeremy looked at the note. '£5,000.'

'I will throw in the new LG,' he said.

'That's fine.'

His phone pinged, and Khalid opened it up.

116

'You will need to choose from one of these.' He handed the phone to Jeremy.

It was a list of female names; virtually all were foreign.

He scrolled down to a Jennifer Krauss and showed the screen to Pam. She shook her head. Further down he found a Prudence Sutcliffe; this time she shrugged.

'Pru—it's okay, yeah?' he said to Pam.

'Whatever. I really want to get out of here,' she said under her breath.

'I know.' He turned and pointed Prudence Sutcliffe out to Khalid.

'How old is she?' Pam asked.

Khalid flicked the screen across. 'Thirty-five. That close enough?' It was a question to Pam, but again she just shrugged. Pam was thirty-seven.

CHAPTER 20

◇◇◇◇◇◇◇◇◇◇◇◇◇◇

Getting information out of the Riga port authorities was difficult, and Phil finally got some sort of confirmation that an unidentified vessel matching the description of the *White Angel* had moored alongside the White Island pontoon just after midnight, requesting a fuelling station. Apparently they filed the same report as was issued to Copenhagen—that their transponder was faulty—which was good enough proof for me that that was the vessel the girls were, or had been, on. The port police had been sent to investigate, but after numerous phone calls back and forth, there had been nothing official from them.

It had been a frustrating night, but at 6.30 a.m. Chris walked into the incident room flanked by two burly characters in smart suits that I had never seen before. It turned out that we had attracted attention from both MI5 and MI6. Chris introduced a Robin Grant from MI5 and Julian Porterfield from MI6, who, he was at pains to say, were here to help us with our Blue Rabbit investigation.

We spent the next two hours going through every aspect of the investigation so far, with each member of the team joining in as he or she arrived. They were keen to get the memory stick to their forensics to see what could be gleaned.

'We have a team on the border of Lithuania,' Robin said. 'I'm going to see if they can be reassigned. If so, we should be able to get them on the ground in Riga before'—he looked at his watch—'lunch time, hopefully.' He got up with his mobile in hand, tapped the screen, put it to his ear, and walked out into the corridor.

Julian looked at me. 'Can you manage without your phone for a while?' he said.

'Do you need the SIM?' I asked.

'Just for a few hours. If the phone's used to send the text, and the call you received from Miss Coombs had hotspots activated, they can leave a trace, even if it's a burner.'

'But there was nothing showing in my received data,' I said.

'There will be, in the background,' he said.

'Sure, no problem; I'll get a spare from supplies.' I handed it over.

By eight thirty I was registering a replacement phone and was beginning to feel the effects of sleeplessness when Joanne came over and said that Kevin Goodwin was in reception.

I went down to meet him, and he looked refreshed and cheery—just about the opposite to how I felt.

'What's new? You look like shit,' he said, handing me a brown paper bag. 'Breakfast.'

'Thanks,' I said, for both the comment and breakfast.

It was a large bacon and tomato roll, still warm. We grabbed a coffee and sat in my office, and I filled him in on the night's events while chomping my way through breakfast.

'I don't have a good feeling about them; you know that, don't you?' he said.

'We need to keep positive,' I said. 'It forces us to sustain the pressure and hopefully them into making mistakes.'

He looked out of my office to the boards in the incident room.

'The yacht there,' he said.

'It's a stock photo of an Amels superyacht, the same as the *White Angel*.'

'I've seen one before, a couple of years ago. It brought some wealthy clients to the factory in Puerto Rico.'

'Was it the *White Angel*?'

'No idea; I didn't take any notice.'

'Did you take any photographs?'

'There would have been some taken, but I wouldn't have them here.' He thought for a moment 'But I might be able to access the works computer, via a VPN link to the cloud. We have a presentation display in our reception area, and I'm sure there were pictures of the guests as they left to return to Mexico.'

If I'm right, they would have been taken at San Juan. I recall it being moored there, at the La Puntilla. It's impressive in that picture you have over there, but close up it's awesome.'

'Who owned it?' I asked.

'FXI, I assumed.'

I went out to look for Phil but realized he had gone home for some well-deserved shuteye—something *I* would have to consider soon.

Chris was in his office with the two suits. I knocked, and he waved me in.

'Sir, do we know where the *White Angel* was registered?'

'Phil will know.'

'Yeah, he's gone,' I said.

'He will have a file on it, I'm sure. Check on his desk; he won't mind.'

'Why?' Julian asked.

'Kevin Goodwin, the girls' cousin, recognizes it as one that brought visitors to his textile factory in Puerto Rico a few years back. I mean, it could be just the same make and model, but it seems a bit of a coincidence. I think there might be a link. He has joint ownership of the Tithe, as I mentioned earlier in the meeting.'

'Right, the one with the exploding shed and satellite phone.'

'That one,' I said. 'Any news on the reassignment of your team in Lithuania?'

'Still waiting, but it wasn't rejected. That's a good sign.'

'Why don't you get off home for a bit, Greg?' Chris said. 'Or maybe back to the hotel. I haven't had anything back from the clean-up team yet. You look done in.'

'Let me see if I can find Phil's file.' I went to close his door.

'Greg,' he said, calling me back. 'The CCTV from your place. They are looking into the baseball bat. It's quite distinctive, and they are hopeful of establishing its origins. If they can, we may be able to tie down an outlet and a credit card.'

'Thanks.'

Sure enough, there was a file on Phil's desk headed 'Blue Rabbit—White Angel'. It sounded like a new Disney film. The second sheet in was a document showing its original registration—2016 in Yokohama, Japan. *The birthplace of FXI*, I thought.

I showed the file to Kevin, who was examining the whiteboards. I could see the concern written on his face. The impact of this could be far-reaching if our suspicions were anything like correct.

CHAPTER 21

◇◇◇◇◇◇◇◇◇◇◇◇◇

The *Costa Magna* was a ninety-foot vessel, and though she was over thirty years old, she was a magnificent ocean-going luxury yacht. She had been on charter for virtually all of her existence prior to Jeremy's ownership in 2017 under his assumed, soon to be permanent name of Brian Campbell. Since that time, it had undergone a complete refit, and the five state rooms on the middle deck had been converted into a large lounge opening up onto a spacious foredeck, a dining room with an open-plan galley, and three double bedrooms, all with en suites. The upper deck housed the control room and living quarters for up to six crew. When under charter it operated with a minimum of six staff, but this had been reduced to one full-time docking crew member, and the ship was now fully ocean operational with three crew. The one resident crew member was Gary Saunders; the other two, on retainer, were Kip Larkin and Jake Rose. Gary was the skipper of the *Costa* when it was last chartered and was introduced to Jeremy/Brian at the auction in Southampton, where he finally purchased it for two and a half million pounds and agreed to keep Gary on as skipper. Kip and Jake ran an IT business, specializing in software development to highlight and combat business fraud. This was a business that could work both ways, as Jeremy was able to ascertain, and he subsequently employed them both to handle the Omnicamp skim. They were more than prepared, and eminently capable to hack into the Omnicamp black accounts. Owing to the lucrative nature of the contract, they took it on with gusto. All had become firm friends with a single goal to free themselves, through financial independence, from predictable routine. In their spare time over the last two years, they had both worked under Gary to acquire RYA and MCA offshore yacht master qualifications. All three had prepared new IDs and had been on standby to assume them whenever Jeremy hit the go button.

The lower deck of the *Magna*, other than the engine compartment, swimming pool, and gym, had been turned over to Jake and Kip to kit out with whatever electronic equipment they needed to continue to operate their new, fully prepared, and wholly legitimate IT business on the open seas.

So none of them were particularly surprised to receive Jeremy's call to arms. And all, without exception, felt excitement mixed with a little fear of the unknown.

Jake and Kip had the need for very few customers other than Jeremy, to which they sent prepared apologetic letters saying that as a result of unforeseen circumstances, they were going to have to wrap the firm up, but leaving contact details for other IT outfits that would be able to assist.

Gary had plans logged with the navigation authority to dock at Portsmouth at eighteen hundred hours with a view to sail out at midnight, destination Morocco. He made arrangements over the phone to have the *Magna* fully provisioned at Portsmouth through a stocking company he had used when chartering.

Pam and Jeremy arrived on the dock in front of the *Magna* at 8.30 p.m. after a testing private hire from Bournemouth, the driver of which never stopped talking about his time as a black cabbie in London and his relationship with the London Mafia—just what they could have done without.

Pam, still in shock, had at least stopped shaking and was able, and seemed to prefer, to walk without Jeremy's assistance. Looking up at the *Magna* as Gary appeared on the walkway, she turned to Jeremy.

'Seriously?' Jeremy took her hand, which she reluctantly allowed, and walked up the gangplank to Gary and introduced her as Pru, and Gary as Harry. Gary felt happy having a name that wasn't too dissimilar to the one he'd had for thirty-six years.

She nodded, and Gary led the way across the aft deck, down the right-hand corridor, past the bedrooms, and into the extensive lounge.

'Drinks?' Gary asked.

Jeremy looked at Pam. 'Gin and tonic?'

'Please.'

Gary opened the well-stocked drinks cabinet, where all the bottles and glasses had their own specific green cushioned pouches.

Gary's accent was south of Newcastle but still very northern, though clipped by the four years skippering well-heeled clients. 'Hendrick's, Plymouth, or Bombay?'

'Hendricks,' Jeremy said.

'Pru?'

The name took a moment to engage. 'Oh, same. Lots of tonic.'

They all sat on separate, luxurious loungers around a coffee table of glass and dark oak.

Jeremy took a deep draught of his gin.

'We have a slight change of plan,' he said to Harry. 'I have to go back to see Khalid tomorrow afternoon.'

'No problem. We can anchor offshore overnight, and I'll take the dinghy in. What time?'

'He'll call me and let me know,' Jeremy said. 'Do you mind? I would rather not be seen in and around Bournemouth if possible.'

'No problem, I'll get the plan changed.' Gary got up and went up the flight of stairs off the lounge to the control room.

'You okay?' Jeremy said to Pam.

'I have no idea,' she said. 'So is this home from now on?'

'If you want it to be?'

'I feel really short on choices, but I guess it could certainly be worse.' There was the faintest hint of a smile.

He called up to Gary, 'When will Kip and Jake be here?'

'They said it would be around tenish.'

'Kip and Jake?' He got a look from Pam. 'Something else I need to know about?'

'We can't pilot this on our own, more's the pity. Three stroke four is the minimum crew for a vessel of this size. I should say that Kip and Jake will be Nick and Mark when they arrive.'

'How much do they know?' she asked in a lowered voice.

'Other than today's events and Neville Hillingdon, they know everything. They have been with me from the start.'

'And'—she took in her surroundings—'just how much does this cost to run?'

'My dad's estate cleared over five mil. This, all-in, cost me three and a half. I invested half what was left in Bitcoin and pulled out four mil last year, just before it crashed. That alone is invested in a unit trust bond and returns more than enough to keep this afloat, including Gary/Harry.'

'What about the other two?'

'They have been funded so far out of the Omnicamp skim. They intend, from now, to build a legitimate international software business here on board. I'm offering free board and lodgings and business premises until such time as they are completely independent. Then it's up to them.'

'How in God's name have you managed to handle all this while still heading up Banfield?'

'Banfield runs itself. It has some great employees, of which Neville was just one, and I genuinely hope it will be able to work its way through to independence from the Omnicamp corruption once the dust settles and Bryant and Anni have fled, as they will surely have to.'

'Are you not a part of that corruption?'

'I was initially brought in to optimize tax benefits. As time went on, they kept introducing excessive befits for me if I bent the rules a little, showed them how to hide funds. These funds from unknown sources grew into the 102277 file as it is today—the file that will topple their world. It became unsustainable ages ago, but you are as aware of that file and its contents as I.' He drained his glass. 'So we are both tarred with that brush, I'm afraid. The only difference is, I could see the end coming, though I underestimated the lengths to which they would go to protect it.'

'Do you want to eat?' Gary said from up top. 'I have salmon salads prepared, if you like. Take ten minutes.'

'Great, thanks.'

Pam finished her drink and seemed to relax a little.

'Another?'

'Yes please. When will we be safe?'

'As soon as we get out of port, love.'

Kip was the first to arrive, a twenty-six-year-old bundle of energy. Jeremy had always thought that at six foot two, his dark hair and pale complexion, with chiselled facial features, would make him ideal for a catalogue man. However, nothing would appeal to him less. He was bright and energetic, with a lively personality that could lighten any mood, although he might have his work cut out with Pam.

He bounded on board with one large suitcase and an infectious smile, parked his case at the foot of the stairway, and dumped himself on a free lounger. 'Hi, shipmates, to where are we heading?' He then looked at Pam. 'You must be, hmmm, I'm guessing … "Pam" is on the way out?'

'Hi, Kip.' Jeremy walked over and shook his hand. 'This is Pru.' He faced her. 'Meet Nick. Yes, this is all a little confusing and a bit of a shock to her at the moment, isn't it, love?'

'Understatement,' Pam said trying out a smile.

Nick leant over, offering his hand to Pam. 'Pleased to meet you. Welcome aboard our merry pirate ship.'

She took his hand. 'Thanks, I think.'

'Is Jake here yet?' Nick asked.

'Not yet,' Harry said as he emerged from the upper deck with a tray of salmon and assorted salads.

'You okay … Nick?' he asked, trying out the new name.

'All sorted … Harry. What time do we get under way?'

'Around midnight, but we are holding in the channel until tomorrow afternoon. Brian has some paperwork for Pru that needs picking up from Khalid. I've just spoken to him; he's going to call me as soon as they're ready.'

'Great, gives me time to get organized here. I'll have a quick celebratory beer and get to it.'

He helped himself from the fridge behind the bar and sat back down beside Pru and across from Brian.

'So what kicked it off, mate?' Nick said to Brian.

'One of the Benfield IT guys managed to open 102277, and all hell let lose. Bryant, or an associate, put the IT guy in hospital, though I don't think that was their intention. I think the morgue is more what they had in mind.'

'Shit, really.'

'Bloody hell, that's a bit extreme,' Harry said. 'How did he break in?'

'I don't know, mate, but they also had a go at us.' Brian relayed the experience in the cafe on Bournemouth Pier.

'Well, Jeremy, the sooner we get away, the better then,' Nick said.

'*Brian.*'

'Sorry—*Brian.*'

'We need to ditch our old names from now on and develop our new life history with as much detail as possible and as a matter of urgency. We'll have plenty of time over the next week or two—so we should all, and I must include Mark when he gets here—to familiarize ourselves with our own and each other's virtual past as much as possible.

'Okay, skipper,' Nick chimed.

'He's not the skipper; I am,' Harry said. 'And don't you forget it.'

Nick stood up and gave a mock salute, downed his beer, picked up his case, and dragged it up the stairs.

Brian was just about to text Mark on his prepaid as he heard him clattering his suitcase up the gangplank.

'Hi, guys,' he said, appearing from the corridor. 'And new member,' he added, directing his attention to Pru. 'You must be …'

'Yes, Pru,' Brian interjected. 'Glad you could make it.'

'Wouldn't miss it for the world, mate.' They shoulder-hugged.

Like Nick, Mark was over six feet with short dark, almost black, hair and obviously worked out—a lot. He had a kind, approachable face and a forthright manner.

'We sail at midnight,' Brian said, 'so you'd better get prepared. Harry has the plan approved.' He repeated what was said earlier about laying off in the channel to get back for Pru's documents and about them all using their new names and so forth. He also got confirmation from all of them that their phones, iPads, and laptops associated with their old names had been disposed of.

While the crew busied themselves with their allotted tasks in preparation for departure, Brian and Pru had time to reflect on what had been a harrowing day.

'I have no things,' Pru said. 'Nothing.'

'We're okay; I have got basics already loaded here. Let me show you to your room.'

They got up and made their way to the first bedroom. The sign outside the door read 'Juliet'.

'Don't tell me yours is "Romeo".'

'Seemed appropriate.' Brian led the way in and opened a few drawers just to show Pru that she wasn't going to go short—certainly not before they made the next port of call.

He had arranged mostly T-shirts, shorts, trousers, and a selection of blouses and jumpers that he felt would suffice in an uncontrolled evacuation, as this has now turned out to be.

An array of cosmetics and toiletries was arranged in the en suite, and all appeared to meet with Pru's approval.

She grabbed his hand. *The first sign of affection today*, he thought. He pulled her towards him and hugged her tightly.

'I'm sorry,' he said.

'I wished I'd had your insight. It would have made this a lot easier. Preparation is the key to success, and I feel I'm about to crash.'

'That'll change; you'll see.' He kissed her lightly on the forehead.

'My room's just through that adjoining door, and you are welcome anytime.' They both gave guarded smiles and then detached from each other.

'I'm going to have a shower and get changed,' Brian said. 'I'll see you back in the lounge?'

'Sure.'

He closed the door and walked down the corridor.

She flopped down on the super-king-size bed and fell into the luxuriant quilt that almost wrapped itself around her.

She looked up at the ornately carved ceiling panels, her thoughts going wild. Her house, car, money, friends—all gone. This was worse than a bereavement of one's best friend, it was a bereavement of all her friends. All the sentimental things in and around her house and garden. She began to sob but tried to subdue it as much as possible.

CHAPTER 22

◇◇◇◇◇◇◇◇◇◇◇◇◇◇

I needed to go back to the hotel to grab some sleep; any energy I had absorbed from the bacon and tomato batch, and endless cups of coffee, had been exhausted long ago.

As I got up to gather my things, I noticed Robin and Julian leaving Chris's office. They walked over, and Robin said that they were heading back to London to see whether they could lobby to get something moving on Riga. While I appreciated their motivation, to me this was another two to three hours lost.

I checked that Kevin was okay. He waved me off, his head stuck in his laptop. I and the suits left together, and I asked to be kept informed. I wrote my new number on the back of one of my cards and told them to call me at any time if there were any developments. They agreed and asked the same of me.

One of the other CID teams working the incident room called a meeting with Chris, and they collected in Conference Room 2.

DI Mike Collier started by pushing some photographs of the Pier Cafe across the table to Chris. He pointed to the hole in the wall, which was marked up on the photograph as 58mm in diameter and having penetrated 85mm into the brickwork.

The photographs of the bullet showed it totally crushed from the front back, but it had an intact end cap.

'That is a .338 Lapua brass, typically shot from a Savage 112 Magnum sniper rifle.'

'This was no casual gang revenge shooting,' Carl Boothe, another team member, said.

'What else do we have?' Chris asked.

'Well, according to the waiter,' he said flicking through his notepad, 'there were two people, one male and one female. The male came in first and ordered a coffee and sat in the window seat, looking through the window that the shot took out. He was joined a short time after by a woman. According to this waiter guy, she seemed somewhat agitated, as though this was a bad date. The male IC1 ordered her a coffee, and the waiter took it over. A few minutes later, the window crashed in. He said the noise was like an explosion, and he dropped behind the bar.' He began reading from his notes. 'There was screaming from a group to his right of the bar, and when he looked up, the woman by the window was on the floor. The man she was with was helping her up. They seemed unharmed, and they moved back from the window. No one spoke, he said, but he was aware of a crowd gathering outside. That's when he noticed the hole in the wall and realized someone hadn't just smashed the glass.'

'Who were the two at the window?' Chris asked.

'That's just it—they disappeared, completely.'

'Did they leave anything behind?'

'No, the waiter said he didn't touch anything before our guys got there, but there were no coffee cups. All we have is a lady's heeled shoe print in the dust alongside the table, but nothing distinguishing about it.'

'Do you think it could be associated with Blue Rabbit?'

'I don't know, but I think we shouldn't dismiss it,' Chris said. 'Can you add copies of these to the other whiteboards, please.'

'One other thing Chris,' Carl said. 'James asked us to cross-refence with ballistics on the bullet found at the Fairfield crime scene—Pat Riley?'

'Yes?' Chris was quizzical.

'Same weapon that was used to kill'—Carl looked down at his notes again—'a Mr. Kamid Hussain in Canary Wharf, 2017.'

'Stick that up on the board as well, Carl. And thank you.'

At 10.10, James received an email from the Rigan authorities with a video attachment.

'This was recorded at oh five thirty Rigan time, Zunds Dock' was the message.

The video, though of poor quality, clearly showed a vessel that matched the description of the *White Angel* docking to a pontoon.

There was movement on the aft deck; two men, smoking, came out and stood at either corner, quite obviously checking for activity up and down the pontoon. Minutes later one went back in, and he almost immediately came out leading two women. They were either holding hands or, more likely, shackled to each other, with another man following behind, pushing the two women.

'Guv,' James called over to Chris.

They watched it several times and were both convinced that the lead woman was Aleysha.

James immediately emailed back to ask whether there was any further footage relevant to where the four individuals might be heading.

'This was six hours ago,' Chris said. 'Kevin, come and have a look at this.'

Kevin pulled up a chair, and they reran the video.

His breathing becomes deep, and his face hardens. 'That's Maya and Aleysha. We need to get over there.'

Chris said, 'Send that to Robin and Julian and let them know that we have confirmation that the girls in the video are the two we are looking for. Also, send confirmation to Riga that they have a UK officer being held against her will on their soil.'

Kevin got up, closed his laptop, and stuffed it into his bag and called across to James, 'James, can you forward that video to my email address, please. He walked across and handed James a card. 'My email is on the back, @JJC.'

James looked across at Chris for approval, and he nodded his agreement.

'Where are you going, Kevin?' Chris asked.

'I need to check something out; I'll keep in touch with Greg.'

⁂

I felt as though I'd slept for only minutes when I was awakened by a knock on my door. I groggily got myself up and opened it to see Kevin, who burst in.

'We need to get to Riga,' he said. 'Look.'

He had his laptop already open; I noticed the time in the corner and realized I had been out for well over three hours.

The video came up of the *White Angel*, and there they were, both being dragged off along the pontoon to hell only knows where.

I tried to pull myself together. 'I can't just do that,' I said.

'DC Richards can't, but you can,' Kevin said.

'I'll lose my job …' As I said this, I was thinking, *Which is more important?*

'Look,' Kevin said, and he opened another web page on his computer. 'We can get flights from Southampton this afternoon.'

I peered at the timelines. Sure enough, there was a flight at six o'clock this evening. 'That's going to cost over a grand just to get us there and back.'

'Will you stop worrying about money? I have a vested interest in my cousins and an ulterior motive in taking you. You will be able to open doors that will remain permanently shut to me.'

'Not as good old Greg Richards, I won't.'

'We'll work it out. Grab a bag. We will probably have to pick up coats at the airport; it's minus five over there right now.'

'We'll take my hire car; I can leave it at Europcar at the airport and pick one up at Riga International. The airport is less than forty minutes away from the White Islands Pontoon, which is where the *White Angel* was moored.'

'You've been busy again, I see. But "*was* moored" is the operative word.'

'There's something else, but I'll fill you in on that later; it may or may not be connected. I need to do a bit more work.'

'We have time,' I said, looking at my watch. 'I need to check on Jet and Pat, and I can also see if they managed to bring Hillingdon out of his coma.'

'Fair enough, Greg. Can you get a weapon?'

'What? No, no way, not going there. We would never get it through customs anyway. Forget it, Kevin.'

'Customs,' I said, 'shit, I will need to get my passport; it's at the flat.'

'Fine, okay,' he said with resignation in his voice.

'Have you thought for one minute what we do when we get there?'

'We'll work something out, Greg.'

'Looks like we're going to be doing a lot of that.'

'Maybe. Get a bag, and let's get going before we find a reason to change our minds.'

CHAPTER 23

Anni was seated in an alcove of the Tiger-Tiger Club in Chinatown with her girlfriend Tia. It was dark and noisy, and there was a heavy sent of sweat, weed, and alcohol. They were well into their second bottle of sake when her phone lit up on the sticky glass table; it was Janek. She took her arm from around Tia's shoulder and stood up. 'Sorry, I need to get this.'

Hitting the red symbol on her phone and putting it to her ear, she said, 'Hold on, Jan,' making her way to the front lobby and out onto Haymarket.

'You okay?' she said.

'It's a negative on Caine and Cole. But I think they have been scared off.'

'What! Not good enough, Janek. They could bring us all down.' She moved into a doorway next to the club and pulled her scarf up over her mouth. 'You included,' she said in a whisper. 'Where are they now?'

'I'm not sure; I had to get away and back here. There were too many prying eyes. They have obviously ditched their phones.'

'So you have no way to trace them?'

'Don't panic, Anni. There's more than one way to skin a rabbit. I have a hook into CCTV around Bournemouth, and a couple of guys scanning as we speak. His flat and her house are both being watched; they'll show up soon.'

'You'd better hope so, Jan; Bry's going to be incensed. What about the other two?'

'They're safe and locked down in Riga. Maris will take it from there. I'll go over when I have things cleaned up here.'

'By the way,' she said, 'what Bryant said about orders regarding the two girls—and you potentially overriding them … Avoid it at all costs, Janek; those orders came from a very dangerous source with Triad contact here in London and the Far East.'

'What's that about anyway?' Janek asked.

'Not sure, but I think there's a family connection. Where's *here* anyway? Where are you?'

'In the den.'

The den was an extensive basement flat off Primrose Hill with three rooms and every electronic listening, surveillance, and cybernetic computer device packed floor to ceiling into every available space. It was capable of interrogating just about any government, banking, or security system. The ground floor was Janek's apartment, and the top floor and attic rooms were the communications collection hub, with aerials, boosters, and satellite dishes of all types and styles.

The basement was manned by three of Janek's associates from the Ukraine. All four graduated at the same time from Kiev National University of Technology in 2009. They all spent the next four years at Suvorov Military School in Kiev, where they met Bryant, a high-flying cadet with interesting connections in banking and drugs.

CHAPTER 24

◇◇◇◇◇◇◇◇◇◇◇◇◇◇

'Look, Greg, I can't sanction that; you know I can't. That puts you off the grid without backup or support.'

'I know,' I said, 'but I can't sit around here knowing that Aley and Maya are out there on their own, hundreds of miles away, waiting for security services to get clearance, which they may or may not do. I'll keep you informed—if that's okay and doesn't compromise you?'

'I'm not going to be able to stop you, am I?'

'Sorry, guv.'

'Okay, keep in touch. I'll do what I can from here. Your warrant card will be useless—you know that, right?

Chris looked in the direction of the whiteboards and the recently added photographs. Listen, while I've still got you, do you remember that shooting on the pier? It might be connected, and if so, you'll need eyes up your arse. It was a high-velocity round, probably from a sniper rifle.'

'Who was it aimed at?'

'We don't know; we are pulling in security camera footage from the area now.'

'Fuckin' hell, who are these people?'

'I don't know, Greg, but you be careful; we're not trained for this. Oh, and the bullet that Pat took?'

'Yeah?'

'Was shot from the same handgun that took out Kamid Hussain—in London.'

I ended the call and, looking at Kevin driving the hire Mercedes CLA, relayed what Chris had told me.

'You sure you want to do this?' I asked.

'I don't know about you,' he said, 'but I couldn't live with myself if anything happened to those two while I sat here twiddling my digits.'

I agreed and directed him to the Alderney.

When we arrived, Kevin asked whether I wanted him to come in with me. He seemed to be concerned I might be further abused by her brother. I said it wasn't necessary.

I was informed by her consultant that Pat was stable but heavily sedated and that Miss Clarke was sitting with her at the moment and that I was welcome to pop in.

I knocked on the door to her room and walked in. Her brother's girlfriend got up as if to leave, but I held my hand up for her to stay.

'I'm sorry,' I said, 'I just wanted to see how she is.'

'She's just had the dressing on her chest wound changed. Look, I'm sorry about Joe's reaction yesterday; he's still very upset.'

'I really do understand,' I said.

'I have to get back to the office anyway,' she said. 'There are only the two of us running it, and I know Joe's stressing about that too. He's gone to get his parents from the airport; he'll be back shortly.'

'I can sit with her for a while if you want to get off. Where is it you work?'

'Thanks, that would be helpful, if you don't mind. It's a credit shop in town called Indeed, still quite new. Joe has already had a text from the boss asking all sorts of questions about why he is away from the office. Not a nice guy'

'I'm happy to talk to your boss if you like. Unfortunately, I'm going to be out of the country for a couple of days, but I can call him if it helps?'

'I'll ask Joe when I see him, thanks.' She tossed her jacket over her arm, smiled, and said, 'My name's Steph, by the way.'

'Greg,' I said. 'Pleased to meet you.' She nodded and left.

I texted Kevin to say I would be here for a while, if he wanted to get something to eat, and that I'd call when I was leaving.

I looked at Pat's inert body and felt a wave of guilt flowing over me, which developed into a stabbing sensation deep in my chest. I recognized this as deep loss: the loss of my beautiful wife, way too early in our relationship—one I was sure I would never fully recover from. *I need to go and see Jet*, I thought.

The officer on the door knocked, poked his head round, and said, 'Mr. Caine and family are on their way up, sir.'

'Thanks,' I replied. 'I'm off anyway. Do you know whether they have managed to bring Hillingdon round?'

'Apparently he went into a seizure when they tried earlier, so they put him under again. I don't know what the latest is; sorry.'

'No problem. Dr Ball is supposed to keep me informed. I'll contact him in a bit.'

As I walked towards the lift, it opened, and Pat's brother and family emerged. There was an awkward moment, but Mr. Riley held out a hand, which I took, and he introduced himself to me as Joe, and me to his parents as Pat's work partner, which I greatly appreciated.

'Greg,' I said, and I looked at the mother. 'I'm very sorry about your daughter. Apparently everything seems stable.' That was just about all I could think of to say. They nodded and walked on towards the ward.

I rang Kevin on the way down in the lift. He said to walk to the hospital gate and that he would be only a few minutes.

I stopped at reception to ask whether Dr Ball was free. He came out of his office and apologized for not getting in touch and confirmed what the officer told me earlier, and he added that they would try again tomorrow but that it was not something that could be rushed. Seizures of the type he experienced can be physically, as well as psychologically, damaging.

I thanked him and left with him ensuring me he would let me know if there were any changes.

I waited ten minutes at the gate for Kevin to arrive, flicking through my emails. A few days ago, I would have jumped onto any one of these cases requesting assistance with a robbery, a domestic violence issue, or a road traffic incident. They all seemed so trivial right now, which I knew to be wrong; and rather than ignore them, I forwarded them to Chris.

He came back with a 'Thanks a lot. You had better put an out of office on your email.'

The yellow CLA pulled up at the gate. I got in and noticed a Waitrose bag on the back seat. I guessed it was full of supplies for the journey.

'You're like a kid,' I said. 'Can't go on a trip without goodies.'

He smiled and said 'Can you put the airport in the satnav? I've tried, but I'll be buggered if I can work it out.'

'Yes,' I said, 'but I need to see Jet first and pick up my passport.' I directed him to Aniwell.

Jet was in surgery when I arrived, and I could only speak to Mandy, who said that he was doing well under the circumstances.

I left my direct debit details so that she could set it up on the account and organize a weekly payment. I signed a blank debit authorization form, and she promised to do it straight away.

CHAPTER 25

◇◇◇◇◇◇◇◇◇◇◇◇

Harry arrived back on the *Magna* well ahead of schedule. Khalid had called earlier to say everything was in order and ready for pick-up at 9.30 a.m.

By ten thirty they were underway, and within thirty minutes they were in open water with no sign of land.

Finally Pru was able to relax a little. The previous evening had been difficult after she emerged from her cabin a little red-eyed, but the crew turned out to be quite endearing—not at all how she expected criminals to be. And Jeremy—she hadn't quite come to terms with 'Brian' yet—had been charming and attentive.

She turned in soon after they left the marina around one o'clock, after a few more gin and tonics, each of which seemed to get stronger every time Harry produced one. Jeremy saw her to her cabin, and he proceeded on to his.

It was probably because of the gentle rocking motion of the yacht, along with the stress of the day, but she fell asleep almost the minute her head hit the pillow. She was awoken by the crash of seawater on the hull and the steady sway. She was staggered when she looked at her Gucci Dive cat watch, just about the only thing of any value she now possessed, to see it was nearly eleven o'clock. She sat up and looked around her. Peering through her long, narrow window, she saw that it was a little cloudy but mostly clear as she looked out on the open sea. Apprehension was still very present, and she couldn't quite escape from the idea that she would never return to her home in Bournemouth. Planning to do this was something one could give oneself time to come to terms with. Doing it overnight with no forethought was scary.

What if she and Jeremy didn't work out? Where would she be then? *Jeremy*, she thought. For all their sakes, she had to start thinking of him as Brian. She pulled on a sloppy jumper and slacks from one of the wardrobes and made her way to the lounge. Everything looked so different in the daylight. It was a magnificent craft, and just for a moment she felt privileged and fortunate to be in the company in which she found herself. Brian was sitting on the large lounger facing the front deck, on his laptop.

'Anybody looking for us yet?' Pru asked.

'Oh hi, how are you? Did you sleep okay?'

'Surprisingly sound,' she said. 'Well, are we on the news yet?'

'Not really. There was a reported incident on the pier, but no casualties. So I would guess no interest.'

'Where are the others?' she asked.

'Up top, in control. Do you want to see your papers?'

'Not sure, do I?'

'They're good,' Brian said, picking up the box file from the coffee table and handing it to Pru.

She opened the box and took the first Manila folder and sat down beside Brian. There was a surprising number of documents and folders in the box. All were a little authentically creased and worn. In the first folder was her new driving licence, both paper and credit card type. In another was a passport and national insurance documents. There were utility bills for a place in Weymouth, and two credit cards with letters attached affirming that they had been closed several days ago. Also attached were closing statements for the same accounts, showing a zero balance. There were at least ten wage slips for Prudence Sutcliffe from a company called Asspire, where apparently she earned £1,537.44 per month as a part-time tax advisor. One very large bundle, which she wasn't expecting, was a set of divorce papers, complete with a copy of the decree nisi.

She looked at Brian. 'What happened to her?' she asked.

'We don't ask those questions,' he said. 'Best not to think about it; just try to absorb what is there and take on board your new identity. Not too many people get the chance to wipe out previous mistakes and start with a clean sheet. This is ours.'

Nick came down the stairway with some charts.

'Bit of a storm coming up off the north-western tip of France. We are going to head away from the coast and let it blow out. He put the chart on the table for Brian to see and pointed to an area equidistant between

Land's End and Brest. 'We'll hold here for a while. There's no rush to get anywhere, is there?'

'No, not at all,' Brian said. 'What are our docking arrangements at Port Casablanca?

'There are no restrictions at the moment, so we can land whenever, as long as we inform port services—Marsa Maroc—a couple of hours beforehand.'

'Fine,' Brian said, 'Let's aim for sometime tomorrow. We could all do with some chill-out time. What's the weather like if we go a bit further out?'

Nick lifted the chart and said, 'If we make a broad circle into the Celtic Sea, it's going to be clear.'

'Let's do that.'

Forty-eight hours later and in the morning sun, Pru gently rolled off the lounger on the top deck and made her way down the spiral staircase and into the lounge. They were moored off the Moroccan coast, just north of Casablanca; the sun was too hot, and while it felt good for her to relax up there for a while, the saloon was cool. Looking out, the sky was an unnatural deep blue and clear of any cloud over a calm, even bluer North Atlantic Ocean, and the *Magna* was perfectly still. She saw Brian on his laptop under the awning of the forward deck, scanning through the online news reports. Brian looked up to see her emerge through the glass sliding doors in a chiffon top and shorts.

'Coffee?' she asked. 'I seem to have cracked the use of the coffee machine if nothing else.'

'Please,' he said, smiling at her. 'That would be nice.'

She went back into the lounge as Nick came out.

They exchanged good mornings.

'Do you want a coffee, Nick? I'm just making one.'

'Thanks.'

Nick sat down opposite Brian.

'Right, I've verified that all our previous links have now been close-looped,' Nick said 'No association from either business, Banfield or ours, has any connections outside the existing framework that can be traced back. The only thing Mark and I are working on now is the format and protocol platform for any ongoing software programmes that we develop. The existing modified file extension platform is quite unique to us, and if we continued with it, there would be a remote possibility that some smart hacker could trace it back to source.'

'Good, I've just been looking to see what is breaking in Bournemouth. Other than an incident on the pier, there's nothing so far.'

'What have they got on that?' Nick asked.

'Just that the old Reef Cafe on the pier front was the subject of a suspected random shooting whereby the front window was shattered. No one was hurt.'

'That's good, right?'

'Maybe. Seems a little too low-key for my liking. That wasn't a .22 air rifle shot; it buried itself three inches into the concrete wall.'

'But you didn't leave anything behind?'

'No, but I have no idea what the police would get off CCTV. We mingled a while with the crowd outside, but it depends where the cameras are as to whether they could see us before we emerged.

'I'm sure it'll be fine' Nick said.

Brian looked out towards the coast, 'I could do with getting into town sometime,' he said, 'to verify my accounts are in order. What have you two done about your financials?'

'We set everything up some time ago; it was only a matter of closing existing ones down. Which is why we were delayed getting to the boat on Tuesday. All sorted though.'

'Good.'

Pru came through with coffees and sat alongside Brian.

'Fancy a trip to Casablanca today?' Brian asked.

'Sure. Sounds exotic.' It would be the first time they would have a chance to discuss their bizarre situation alone.

An hour later, Harry took the *Magna* in closer to shore and a little further south, just off El Jadida, where there was a small marina. He launched the dinghy off the back, and Brian and Pru boarded.

'Do you want me to take you in?' Harry asked.

'No, we'll be fine, thanks.'

Monte Carlo, El Jadida certainly was not. It resembled a rundown canal marina in the north of England, but it had free four-hour mooring, which suited them, as the smaller the footprint they left, the better.

After landing and securing the dinghy to a free mooring position, they searched for somewhere that looked remotely English. They settled on a place with street tables and chairs outside the Hotel L'Iglesia, where, to their dismay, an old Moroccan-looking lady appeared with a notepad. As it turned out, she had a smattering of English, which was good enough for them to order two coffees and establish where the nearest bank was. While they were on a roll, they also ordered a taxi for twelve o'clock, which would give them an hour to get some money exchanged to pay the dear old soul.

The coffee was black and rich and came with an assortment of small, hard biscuits which resembled ginger nuts in texture and bourbon in colour and taste.

Brian left Pru outside the hotel finishing her coffee while he made his way to the bank using the old lady's directions scribbled on a napkin.

It took him less than twenty minutes to acquire the equivalent of five hundred pounds in local currency, which turned out to be over six thousand Moroccan dirham. They had another coffee while they waited for the taxi. It arrived at twelve on the dot, a run-down Renault of some indistinguishable model. Its driver, an obvious friend of their Moroccan host, exchanged pleasantries, which probably included the fact that his fare was English so international charges would probably be accepted.

It turned out to be a forty-five-minute ride to the Sheraton Hotel in Casablanca, where the PO box station was located in the basement.

Any ideas of Casablanca being either romantic or exotic soon vanished as they made their way across the heavily industrialized port area. The only thing that set it apart from the likes of Liverpool and Merseyside was the palm tree–lined main streets and the blazing sunshine.

The driver pulled up outside the hotel and, after a short while, established that the fare was a thousand dirham. A little negotiation brought it down to eight hundred, which Brian handed over.

The Sheraton was a five-star hotel, which was not immediately obvious from the outside but was something else from the minute one walked through the revolving doors. Its plain exterior facade had been replaced with ornate black-and-white marble floors and large decorative pillars; walls adorned with very dark, almost black, hardwood accessories; and glass—glass everywhere, casting incredible reflections, creating a mind-blowing visual effect that took the breath away.

'Wow,' Pru said with her mouth open as she tried to take the whole scene in. 'I wasn't expecting that.'

'No, neither was I. Perhaps this explains the five-hundred-pound-a-year price tag on the PO box.'

'Christ, what do you pay on the Caymans account?'

'You don't want to know,' he said, walking towards a sign marked 'Tören'.

They went to the front desk to asked about the PO box site, where one of five elegantly dressed receptionists directed them to the lift and basement. In the fully mirrored lift, subtle Moroccan music played underneath the automated voice presumably informing them on which floor they were arriving at, or passing by. The basement was two floors below ground and also housed access to the car park.

Brian used one of the two keys to allow admission to the secure area, where only one person was allowed access at any one time. The other key was for the box—box 2277.

He removed the contents and slid it into his inside pocket, locked the box, and left the secure area.

Pru, waiting outside, felt uncomfortable and somewhat vulnerable while Brian was locked in the chamber. As Brian emerged, he grabbed her hand, and they moved back to the lift and pressed the call button. The display on the panel showed it to be on the ground floor, and it took but a few moments to reach the basement. The outer doors shuddered slightly as it arrived, whistling air through the gaps as it did so. The doors slid open, and they entered the lift as a short, long-haired Asian man exited, brushing past Pru too closely for her liking. He caught Pru's eye, furtively, as the lift door closed.

Back in the expansive foyer area of the hotel, they decided that they would check out the paperwork over a cold beer in the bar.

The fully glazed bar overlooked a large courtyard and pool surrounded by many empty sun loungers with parasols.

He took the envelopes from his pocket and opened the first, which was from one of the three banks. It contained credit and debit cards and an introductory letter. In another was his PIN. All three banks had sent cards, but only two PINs had arrived so far.

Pru could see it was all bank-related stuff. 'Is it all okay?' she asked.

'Yes, just one PIN missing, so I may have to come back at another time.'

'What do *I* do for money? Not that I have a need for it right now, but I'm sure I will soon.'

'Now I have this lot, we can go online and make them joint.'

They finished their beers and left the bar. Back at reception, Brian asked for a taxi.

'Certainly, sir,' the receptionist said, 'and can I ask where you need to go?'

'El Jadida.'

'Perfect, please give me a minute.'

They sat down on one of the long, studded couches, and as they did so, Pru was caught by the sense that they were being watched by someone just outside the bar area. The guy from the basement with the long hair was sitting with his chin in his hand, looking across directly at them, but he immediately averted his gaze when he saw Pru look back.

'Can we get out of here?' she said to Brian.

'Why?'

'The man sat over there'—she directed her eyes in his direction—'is watching us. He also came out of the lift as we entered it from the basement.'

'Are you sure?'

'I'm sure he's the guy from the car park, if that's what you mean.'

As Brian looked across at the man, he got up and walked out of the hotel.

CHAPTER 26

◇◇◇◇◇◇◇◇◇◇◇◇◇

The flight from Southampton was delayed for forty minutes because of a handling dispute. That gave Kevin and me some time to go through his other findings on Hillingdon's file.

Kevin found his way to the executive lounge that his Virgin card gave us access to and ordered coffees. We sat on bar stools, he unpacked his laptop, and we both plugged our phone chargers to it.

He pulled up the folder with the seven jpegs and opened up file number four. He turned the screen to face me and pointed to the heading at the top right-hand corner: 'Pacific Fabrinet (Pac-Fab-PR)'.

He looked at me as if this should mean something.

'Sorry,' I said, shrugging my shoulders.

'"Pacific Fabrinet PR" is the name of my business in Puerto Rico. As far as I'm aware, it's a unique name. The "PR" is "Puerto Rico", but there are no other divisions to my knowledge. And look.' He pulled up an email. 'I requested this from my PA earlier.'

It was headed 'End of year turnover Pac-Fab-PR 2018. Bottom line £15,849,112.50'. He pulled his calculator from his case, added up April to September's figures, and showed me the calculator: £8,003,249.50. He then turned back to the laptop screen and scrolled down to line ten. Sure enough, there it was: £8,003,249.50.

We then looked through the other six files, not really knowing what we were looking for but just checking line ten. They were all reasonable turnover figures for small to medium-size businesses—innocuous, understated, not likely to draw attention. But all were being piggybacked and used to clean millions of pounds of, presumably, dirty money.

My eye was caught as I scanned across the second file in the list that we had been looking at earlier—the name at the top: IN-Need. It hadn't struck me earlier, but Joe's girlfriend, Steph, said she worked for, as I understood it, a company called 'Indeed.' Had I misheard? Could this in fact be IN-Need? I didn't have Steph's number to confirm, but I decided I'd get Joanne on it.

Lost in thought, I didn't hear the message over the PA, but Kevin said, 'That's us.' The flight information panel across from us displayed that gate G2 was now open.

I finished my cold coffee, and we collected our things and moved towards the departure gate.

I could see that Kevin was uncomfortable. It had been a long time, if ever, since he had travelled economy class; and with two stopovers, it was going to be quite a trial for him.

We got settled in our seats, and I called Joanne before we got under way.

'Hi, Greg. You've gone rogue, I hear.'

'Yeah, something like that. Listen, could you check on Pat's brother for me? You will have to tread gently; he's a little defensive about Pat getting hurt on my account. Can you find out the name of the credit company he and his girlfriend work for and text me the details?'

'Sure. Can I ask why?'

'It may be linked in some way to the Hillingdon files.'

'Okay, will do. How long are you going to be off the grid?'

'I guess as long as it takes.'

'Can you also ask Chris to get the fraud squad to look at the company names listed at the top of each of those files. See if they can sequester their accounts. This is really big, Jo; be careful.'

'Look after yourselves,' she said with a note of concern in her voice, and she ended the call.

We seemed to be held in a queue on the apron leading to the runway, in which there were several planes in front of us.

The captain, with an Eastern European accent, came over the speaker to apologize for the evening's delay and explained that the dispute had put all flight plans in a bit of a mess but we should be on the runway within ten minutes.

A flight attendant then informed us that all electronic equipment should be put into flight mode for the duration of the flight.

I opened up the settings on my phone, and Kevin did the same just as my phone buzzed with a received message from Jo. It simply read, 'IN-Need branch launched in Bournemouth this month. Company established 2016, Bristol Street Birmingham under the name of "Street UK Loans".'

Just before I turned it off and locked it into flight mode, I replied: 'Can you get their accounts for April to September 2019? And ask Chris to keep an eye on Pat's brother, Joe, and Stephanie; they may be in danger - TNX.'

I looked at Kevin. 'It is "IN-Need", not "Indeed".'

CHAPTER 27

<><><><><><><><><><>

When Anni finally got through to her brother, he was, as expected, apoplectic.

'Where are you, Anni?' Bryant barked.

'I'm with Jan at the den.'

'Why?'

'I'm going through CCT footage with Mikka and Dessi, trying to find them.'

'Any luck? Because let's face it, that's what you're fucking hoping for. Is Petrov with you?'

'No. Listen, Bry, we don't need Petrov; he'll just cause a bigger mess that we'll have to clear up.'

'Do you have any idea just what sort of mess that Cain and his fucking Abel can stir up? Those two need to be removed and lost for good before they have the opportunity to give any credence to the file.'

'Jan, look!' Anni called urgently across the room. 'Wind that back,' she said to Mikka.

'What, what?' said Bryant in her ear.

'Hold on,' Anni said.

Jan came over, and the team scrutinized Mikka's screen.

'That's them,' Janek said, pointing to the screen.

'Where are they?' Bryant yelled.

Anni looked at the timeline on the screen and put the phone to her ear. 'They went into a phone shop in Bournemouth town centre yesterday evening, 6.27 p.m.'

'Yesterday—great,' Bryant shot back with dismay.

'We can follow them now, though,' Anni said almost apologetically.

Janek was immediately on his phone, looking at Mikka's screen.

'Smart Shop, Old Christchurch Road,' he snapped into his burner. 'Yes, it's a phone and PC repair outfit.' He listened for a few moments and then finished off in Ukrainian. Looking at Anni, he said, 'Let me know where they go from there' as he snatched his leather jacket off the back of a chair. 'This is the green phone,' he said, holding it up. 'You have the details, Mikka; call me if you see anything else.'

CHAPTER 28

◇◇◇◇◇◇◇◇◇◇◇◇◇◇

Steph had spent the morning fielding enquiries as best she could and contacting clients with appointments and making new arrangements for them where possible. Joe left a message to say that he would be in before lunch, which hadn't satisfied Billy, who had already rang twice. He became more agitated than normal when Stephanie suggested he might like to come in and cover. This, it would appear, was not on the cards.

Joe walked in just after eleven looking pale and worn, but he managed a smile when he saw Steph.

'You okay?' he said.

'Yeah, how is she?'

He shrugged. 'Just time, I guess.'

She grabbed his hand. 'Billy is still on your case,' she said as they both walked into his office and sat down. 'Did you think about asking that that detective, Greg, to contact Billy?'

'Thought about it,' he said. 'In fact I had a missed call earlier and a voice message to contact a Detective Joanne Dawson with respect to Pat. Suppose I'd better check that out first.' He pulled his phone from his back pocket and scrolled through his missed calls. He was just about to make the call when a couple walked in. They strode up to the office with obvious intent and identified themselves as Detectives Joanne Dawson and Phil Green.

Joe looked down at his phone screen, cleared down the contact page with J. Dawson CID, and clicked it to off.

They all sat down around Joe's conference table.

'What's this about?' Joe asked.

Joanne looked at him. 'I think you know DCI Greg Richards; he is heading up the case we are currently working on, which may have some connection to this place.' She gazed around.

'In what way?' Joe asked. 'What case?'

'Possible fraud, maybe money laundering; we're not sure at this stage, but the people involved appear to have few reservations about employing violence to protect their scheme. Greg is concerned for your safety.'

They both looked at Joanne, horror-struck.

'How does any of this concern us?' Steph said. 'We just work here.'

'We know,' Phil said. 'We realize you have only just started here, but we think there has been something going on for some time, long before you joined the IN-Need organization. Tell me about the other people in the business.'

'Well,' Joe said, 'we really only know one, and that's this Billy character. He's, like, the boss, I guess. He seems to know the ins and outs of the company; he was the one who took me through my induction here on the first day. I think all the training that I went through before that was done via a third party. It was pretty generic, and apart from the last half a day, which was directed specifically at running this office and was conducted by …' Joe thought for a moment. 'Can't remember his name … Jim someone, I think. Sorry, I might have his name in my notes at home.'

'That's fine; don't worry about it,' Joanne said. 'Tell me a bit more about Billy.'

'Well, he comes in here a couple of times a week, sometimes brings clients. When he does, he insists on taking over my office.'

Steph said, 'He was weird when he came in a couple of days ago—in a right mood.'

'To be fair, he's never in a good mood,' Joe said, 'but he was certainly agitated that day over something.'

'When was that, exactly?' Phil asked.

Joe leant over and pulled his diary out of his drawer.

'Actually, he was so unsettled he left his notepad here.' Joe put it on the desk in front of Phil as he looked through his diary. 'Ten thirty Monday, I had to take my appointment in the open office. Oh, Billy's business card.' Joe pulled it from the front of his diary.

Phil slid the notebook and card towards him with his fingernail. After pulling plastic gloves from his pocket and slipping them on, he opened it.

It was a simple lined pad; all previous pages had been torn out. He flicked through. There were what looked like phone numbers on the back page, but other than that it was empty. He read the card. Joanne offered an evidence bag from her jacket pocket, and Phil slid them in.

'I've handled that,' Joe said with some concern in his voice.

Joanne looked up at him. 'Don't worry; we'll sort that. I think in the meantime, to be safe, you should shut up here and come with us to the station. We can get all this down on paper and make sure you are kept secure until we know a little more of just how, or if, Billy has any involvement. We'll get SOCO in here; they will probably want the hard drive from your computer.

'Can I just take a note of the mobile number on the back of the card? He is my only line of contact,' Joe said.

'Sure.' Phil showed it to Joe through the evidence bag. 'Don't make contact until we have cleared him. Would you be okay for me to put a tap on your phone? That way we can keep a track on anything coming in.'

'I guess so.'

Phil, looking at the notepad in the evidence bag, said, 'Do you empty the bins, or do you have cleaners come in?

'Cleaners come in every other night,' Steph said. She got up and went to her desk and returned with a card. 'This is them,' she said, handing it over to Phil.

∽∾∽

Billy, on his way to pick up the notepad, saw the couple walk in ahead of him, and his police response mechanism was twitching off the scale. He sidled into the cafe opposite and took up a seat at the window and ordered coffee. He couldn't see clearly into Joe's office, but it was quite obvious that these two were conducting the interview and not the other way around. Also, Stephanie was seated with them. *No reason for that*, he thought.

He called Anni. It went to voicemail.

CHAPTER 29

◇◇◇◇◇◇◇◇◇◇◇◇◇

The stopover at Heathrow was nearly two hours and made us wonder why we hadn't driven there in the first place, but we finally convinced ourselves that parking and booking in would have taken considerably longer. And it gave us chance to check emails and so forth.

I had a reply from Joanne; it read, 'IN-Need accounts April–September - £3,112,065.22.'

I showed it to Kevin, and he set up his laptop.

I also had a message from Chris to say that Pat was out of ICU and they had a lead on the baseball bat. It had been bought in Camden last week; fortunately it was a new model, and only two of that type had been sold. However, one was bought by a regular for his grandson and the other had been paid for in cash, so no trail. They did get a description from the owner, which they were following up on. Another interesting point was that they had traced the serial numbers on the gas canisters at the Tithe to a hardware shop, also in Camden. They were talking to the Met with respect to known criminal gangs in the area, and apparently there was no shortage of those. He ended his mail by asking us to be careful.

Kevin turned the laptop to face me. Line ten read '£3,112,065.22.'

Benfield and Pacific Fabrinet might have been a coincidence; a third, IN-Need, was not.

I messaged Chris back with what we now knew of the scam and asked for him to check on the other company names listed in the Hillingdon files. I also requested, knowing it was a big ask, that he keep me updated on Jet. I added the vet's phone number.

We headed to a menswear outlet to look for a couple of heavy coats. Kevin, being Kevin, dragged me into Burberry. I found a nice duffel coat which I winced at the price of. Kevin approved and grabbed one of a different colour and a couple of scarves.

After this we had a further hop to Moscow and a three-hour stopover before we were to land at eleven o'clock tomorrow morning at Spilve Airport, Riga. All the time, I had the two girls on my mind and hoped against hope that they were still okay.

The flight to Moscow was on time and uneventful, which was more than could be said about the last leg to Riga. This was delayed by a technical issue with the 747-8, a fifteen-year-old plane that I would prefer it not to have technical issues with. And, having finally got off the ground fifty minutes behind schedule, and before we had left Moscow airspace, an elderly gentleman towards the front of the plane was taken ill to the point that the captain decided to return to Moscow to drop him off. All in all, we lost four hours and finally dropped into Spilve at two thirty in the afternoon, somewhat the worse for wear but very glad of the heavy overcoats.

The airport is sited to the left of the River Daugarva and north of Riga and looks like something conjured up out of the Russian revolution. Kevin hired a BMW 5 series from Hertz, and within forty minutes of landing we were on the road in a BMW 528, heading in the general direction of Riga.

We decided to get as near to the Zunds dock as the place *White Angel* was sighted two days prior. While Kevin negotiated his way around some intricate one-way systems, I was looking on Google for somewhere to stay.

'There is a hotel directly opposite Zunds', I said, 'called Radisson Blu Daugava, or something like that.'

'Okay,' Kevin said. 'See if we can get a reservation. How's your Latvian?'

'Shit, I hadn't given that a thought.'

'They may speak English,' he said. I put the location into satnav— eventually, having found the English icon, which was helpful, as it directed us correctly around the city and their undistinguishable road signs. Once on track, it was in fact only fifteen minutes to the hotel. I called the number listed, which was answered almost immediately by what I can describe only as a short blast of grunts.

'Hi,' I said, 'Do you speak English?'

A guttural sound came back which I could just about decipher as 'A little.'

Okay, I thought, *we're in with a chance at least.* 'Do you have any rooms available?' I asked.

Silence. I heard some mumbling in the background, and after several moments a woman's voice came back.

'Can I help, please?'

'Oh, hi, I would like to book two rooms today if possible.'

'We are only having one today. Two tomorrow.'

'Okay,' I said, 'we will take that please.' *I don't mind sleeping in a chair if I have to*, I think.

'How you pay?'

'We have credit cards.'

'No cards.'

I looked at Kevin. 'They don't take cards.'

'I have dollars or sterling with me,' he said.

'Will you accept UK pounds or US dollars?' I said back to the phone.

'Dollars.'

'Fine, we will be with you shortly.'

The line went dead.

It was less than five minutes before we rolled into the large open space that was obviously the hotel car park.

The reception was a minimalist expanse of marble, but by all accounts it was quite a fashionable hotel, sporting a spa, gym, and swimming pool.

The guy on reception was, I'm guessing, my first Latvian encounter, and he took one look at us and disappeared into the office behind.

A few minutes later, a very attractive young woman, whom I would guess was about twenty-five, appeared, dressed in a pristine white blouse and short black skirt. I recognized her voice as my second encounter. Her badge pronounced her as Erika Radisson, so she was in some way related to the hotel owner.

Face to face and with a few additional hand gestures, she was not nearly as abrupt as she seemed to be over the phone.

She apologized for having only the one room, but it was a suite in the main building, and she motioned with her arms to show that this was the main building as opposed to the many annexes that seemed to run off it.

We agreed, and though the price was two hundred dollars a night as opposed to the eighty euros advertised, I'm guessing the latter would have been for the annex rooms. Either way Kevin was fine with it, and a young lad appeared in reception, gathered up our bags, and beckoned that we follow him.

The lift took us to the second floor, where the lad opened the door to room 302. He walked in ahead of us with a big smile, put the bags down, and a waved of his arms as if showing off his wares. It was a nice room with one king-size and two divan beds and a view over the docks and river, albeit somewhat industrial. But we weren't here for the view. The lad headed for the door, and Kevin pushed a ten-dollar bill into his hand. The sight of the beds was tempting; I didn't think either of us had managed more than the odd cat nap over the last twenty-four hours, but I wanted to see if we could track down the port authority tapes to see what else we could glean.

I texted the team just to let them know we had arrived and where we were staying.

Back in reception, the old guy rushed off to get Erika for me. He came back and, pointing to a lounger in the foyer, said, 'Sit please. Erika minutes.'

I took that to mean Erika would be down presently.

A short while later, she rushed in through the main entrance door.

'Sorry, something wrong?'

'No, no,' I said. 'We were wondering whether you know where we can find the Rigan Port authority building.'

I realized as I was saying this, and her expression confirmed it, that this would not have come up in basic English language training.

Kevin was on his phone and had pulled it up on Google.

He showed the phone to Erika.

'Ah, Rīgas Pasažieru osta,' she said. 'Ja, Ja. Over side of river. Come, come.' She walked to the main entrance door and onto the grass outside and pointed to a bridge over the river to our right.

'Akmens tils—bridge,' she said, pointing over the bridge and then swinging her arm left.

As we looked left, I recognized the ramp and railing running along the dock directly in front of us from the video where the girls were extracted from the *White Angel*. We were closer than I expected.

I dragged my attention back. 'Over the bridge,' I said.

'Ja, follow road, side of water.' She now pointed off to the far left. 'White home,' she said, exaggerating her pointing.

I thought I had it. 'Over the bridge and follow that path.' I also pointed. 'The white building over there?'

'Ja, ja.'

'Thank you,' I said with a slight bow. I have no idea where that came from.

She nodded and walked back to the hotel.

We set off in the direction indicated, and after fifteen minutes or so we entered the building with a sign bearing an English translation: 'Freeport of Riga.'

The three occupants all looked as though they had come out of the same mould: six-feet tall, shaven heads, and muscular—the archetypal Eastern European bouncer type. They were, as it turned out, anything but. Their English was good, and they were convivial. We introduced ourselves as off-duty UK police searching for the two ladies who were being held on the *White Angel*, one of them being a detective with the UK police department, and the other, her sister.

They were Hugo, Ellis, and Oliver. Two of them, Oliver and Ellis, were on shift when they received the bulletin about the *White Angel*, and Hugo remembered the video being sent to the UK several hours later. The boat left Riga without posting a route, so there was no idea where it might have headed.

We enquired whether there was any more video showing where the two girls might have gone, or at least in which direction they were taken?

They were very clear that all video was of the local docks only. They had no jurisdiction outside this area, and other than the fact that they went left along the dock after leaving the vessel, they had no other official footage.

'Official?' I said.

Hugo looked at Oliver, who nodded.

'We do have an elevated site view camera which does actually extend outside our perimeter, which, as it happens, was scanning in the general area of the Zunds dock at the time.' Hugo went over to the monitor desk and keyed in the recording time and camera. What appeared on the screen was a wide-angle view of the Zunds dock, scanning slowly from left to right. As it scanned, the *White Angel* came slowly into view. This was a much clearer image of the vessel, and as the camera proceeded on and the whole boat, albeit in the distance, came into view, the four individuals, Aleysha and Maya included, were hustled off the back and along the footpath.

'Can you zoom in on this?' I asked.

'Of course.' Hugo held down a key with an up arrow while using the joystick to move around the screen and keep our subjects in view.

I saw Aleysha struggling with her captor, and at one point she was swung around by him and ended up on the floor, looking precisely in the direction of the camera.

'Can you freeze that?' Kevin said.

Hugo backed the tape up slightly and pressed the pause button.

'Still fighting,' Kevin said, looking at me.

'I know,' I said with a sigh.

It was absolute confirmation of their identities.

We continued watching as Hugo moved the video on. They walked up to the hotel that we were now booked into, and I hoped against hope that they would go in, but no such luck. They walked on past and disappeared between it and the bridge entrance we walked over earlier, just as the camera scanned on and past where they would be heading.

'That's all we have, I'm afraid,' Ellis said. 'And when it scans round again, they're gone. However, my brother-in-law is a sergeant in the *Policija;* he may be able to help.'

They got the fact that we were working on our own, without UK authority, and sympathized with our position and would assist in any way they could. All three handed over business cards, and we offered ours. It was now four-thirty, and Ellis was on shift until six, but he said he would be happy to talk to his brother-in-law that evening.

While we both hated the fact that more hours were passing, we also concluded that a few hours of shut-eye would do us no harm.

We thanked them and made our way back to the hotel.

On the way back, my phone pinged. It was Robin Grant. The message just said, 'Call me.'

I showed it to Kevin, and he said, 'They will just want to haul you in. I would ignore it.'

'He may have news about their team coming in.'

'Maybe! Your call.'

I decided to make contact when we were back in the room.

On the coffee table in the suite was a bottle of vodka and a jug of water. I am not a fan of vodka, but we were cold, and it certainly helped in that department. I punched in Robin's number.

'Hi, Robin. Any news?'

'Where are you? That's a continental ring I just got.'

I realized Chris hadn't told him.

'Have you had the go-ahead for your team in Lithuania?'

'They are wrapping things up there now, going through a debrief and reviewing current operations. All being well, they should be operational in Riga by tomorrow night. Listen, you had a message on your old phone.'

'Yeah?'

'It's official; there is a ransom for the girls. The message came from the same phone that Aleysha sent her message to you from.'

Apparently the ransom was quite simple: all evidence, hard and otherwise, of the Banfield file in exchange for one of the girls. The other was to be held over until this can be verified.

'To allow them time to withdraw, clean up their illicit act, and disappear, more like,' Kevin said.

'I agree.'

Ellis had left us a message to meet with him and his brother-in-law at the Chat Cafe at eight thirty. He left directions; from the map on Google, it looked like a short walk from the hotel.

We confirmed this with Erika before we set out. She looked at Kevin's phone and verified we had the right place, and her expression suggested it to be a less-than-savoury area, but with an almost imperceptible smile, she obviously thought that's what we might be looking for.

She was right. the Chat Cafe was a greasy spoon on the very extremes of a recently built and expansive mall where, at this point, the money had obviously run out. It was a pick-up joint on the edge of Riga's red-light district and, I guess, a place where uniformed officers were not seen as out of place.

They were sitting in the window, and both got up to shake hands as we walked in. Ellis introduced his brother-in-law as Gordie, another mountain of a man bursting out of his uniform, the lapels of which notified me that he was a sergeant.

His English was thankfully as good as Ellis's, and he informed us that his boss had had contact with a DSI Bowman yesterday, who had informed him that we were heading over to look for a fellow officer. Gordie had been instructed to assist as long as it didn't compromise anything else they were working on.

I expressed my gratitude, and we spent the next hour over vodka and ice, outlining the case, the girl's abduction, their relationship to Kevin, and how it looked as though their operation could likely impact many businesses here in Latvia, and certainly in the UK, as well as Kevin's company in Puerto Rico. And finally there was the ransom demand.

Gordie was silent while we went through this, and when it looked as though we had finished, he spread his enormous hands on the table and said, 'Right, the *White Angel* is not new to us.' He had a deep, rich voice with an attractive accent. 'One of the men taking your girls off the boat is known to the department. He was the captain of the vessel two years ago when we boarded as part of a drugs sweep. It was clean. But Maris Provofz and his associate Krzysztof Kin run a textile company here in Riga, and we have long suspected it to be a front for something; and given its location, we would assume it to be drugs. But the vessel was not only clean during the sweep; we had dogs in, and there have never been drugs on that boat. That said, all our surveillance has not picked up anything illegal, either going in or coming out. We gained a warrant to search the property four months ago on the back of suspected illegal migrant workers, but it came up blank.'

'What is the name of the company?' Kevin asked.

'Elevation Textiles,' Gordie said.

'I recognize that name,' Kevin said, pulling out his laptop.

'How big is this outfit?' I asked.

'They employ about thirty staff here in Riga.'

Kevin scanned through the Hillingdon files.

He got to file seven. 'Bingo, Elevation Textiles.' He ran his finger down to line ten. 'Turnover of eight million euros—sound about right?' he said, looking at Gordie.

'I wouldn't really know,' he said, 'But it seems reasonable.'

'Or ...' Kevin did some mental arithmetic. 'One hundred thirteen million?'

'No, that is very unlikely,' Gordie said, and Ellis agreed.

'What do we know about their operation?' I asked.

'Well, they not only supply to Latvia and Lithuania but also to a multitude of market traders and private fashion houses. All direct sales, no Internet activity that we have been able to establish. They have a fleet of around fifteen vans that are out seven days a week.'

'Have you ever pulled over one of these vans when it was on a return run?' I asked.

Gordie looked at me, and as the clouds cleared, he came to realize that this was a cash operation and that the drugs, or whatever, probably never get to Riga. 'No, but I think we should,' he said.

'Do they manufacture here in Riga, or is it pure distribution?'

'No, there has been textile manufacturing in Riga for over a hundred years. The Wari Audums factory was established after the last war and just produced children's clothes. It changed hands six years ago when a consortium bought it up along with a couple of smaller outfits that had good logistical links to the trade. It was renamed Elevation Textiles, and Provofz and Kin head it up, but all the original staff still run it. It has diversified now and supplies bolts of cloth to other producers, as well as finished garments. If we take these two shady characters out of the equation, it is generally considered a good employer.'

'Where is the factory?' I asked.

'No more than twenty minutes' walk away,' Ellis said. 'There's also a warehouse the other side of the river, about five minutes from your hotel.'

Kevin and I looked at each other and then at our watches. It was gone ten o'clock. 'Where is the warehouse?' Kevin said.

'It's on the Kapsula,' Ellis replied.

Kevin pulled up a map of Riga on Google.

'Show me,' he said.

They both looked at the map and zoomed in on an outcrop of land that jutted into the river about a quarter of a mile left of the hotel.

'There.' Gordie pointed. 'But you can't just break in if that's what you are thinking.'

It was in the opposite direction to where the men had taken the girls from the boat. Had it been the other way, it would have been exactly what I was thinking.

'Are there any other properties that are associated with these two guys that could be considered as a safe house?'

'Look,' Gordie said, 'You will have to leave this with me; I'll check this out in the morning. Two years ago, they had a flat in the centre of town, but that area has been redeveloped. I don't know if they have a residence here any more.'

We drank more vodka and watched a number of scantily clad young ladies come in, look around, see Gordie, and leave.

'You said they have fifteen vans, which means there must be at least fifteen drivers. That's a lot of people to keep quiet,' I said.

'Unless they are on both payrolls,' Kevin said.

I could see Gordie thinking something over.

'What?' I said.

'Maybe nothing, but last year there was a suspicious death of one of them. He was involved in … what you call … an RTA in Utena, Lithuania. A hire car was driven off the road into a truck-sized rock. The car burnt out and killed the single occupant, but there was always a suspicion that the fire was staged. The source of the fire was from the rear, which sounds plausible, as that's where the fuel tank is, but normally in these instances any fire emanates from the point of major damage—in or around the engine in this case. Also, there was no real reason that anyone could establish as to why he had hired a car. It was suggested that he may have had a mistress in Utena, but nothing was ever confirmed. His wife vehemently dismissed this theory but strangely didn't pursue it.'

'Maybe she was paid off too,' I said.

'Or threatened,' Gordie suggested. 'I need to look into reopening this case. I will take it up with my boss tomorrow.'

'And,' Kevin said, 'please look up any possible properties where they could be holding the girls.'

Before we left, I asked Ellis whether there had been any further news on the *White Angel*. There hadn't been, but he said he'd keep an eye out for me. What I didn't want was for it to redock and take the girls off again. Right now, with the ransom in place, I felt that they were relatively safe; they had their reasons to keep them alive—certainly up to the point they got what they wanted anyway—and we knew where they were to within a few square miles. I wanted to keep it that way.

We said our goodbyes and agreed to meet up again tomorrow. I was hoping we could do so early in the day, but Gordie said it was probably unlikely that he would have any free time until the evening. We exchanged phone numbers, and he promised to ring as soon as he could.

It was too late to call Chris when we got back to the hotel, so I sent a text to the team to update them on the day's events.

CHAPTER 30

Anni picked up the agitated voice message from Billy Conro. It said only, 'We have a problem with the credit shop in Bournemouth. Call me back.'

He answered on the first ring.

'What is it?' Anni asked. She hadn't heard from Billy in a while.

'The police have been to the shop and taken Joe and Steph,' he said.

'What do you mean they've taken them?'

'They shut up shop early and left with two plain-clothed rozzers'

'Well? There's nothing to connect us is there? You cleared the computer, right?'

'Yes, but I may have left my notepad; there's nothing in it, but it will have my prints on.'

'Fuck! Will we never get a break on this,' she said to no one in particular.

'Sorry, Anni.' There was a long pause.

'Okay, look, we'll take you offline and clear your ID. I'd put you in the Tithe, but that's now been compromised, so we will have to use Canderlay at Lower Upton. I'll send you the details.'

'Okay. Thanks, Anni. I'll get cleared out this evening.'

'Do it now; they could be on to you at any time.'

'Will do. Thanks again, Anni.'

Anni ended the call and rang Janek.

'Hi,' Janek answered.

'Billy Conro—You know him?'

'Yes, he's a tosser.'

'He's also a loose end. He'll be at his place, Beach View, Cliff Road, Cranford Cliffs today, or Canderlay from tomorrow. Any news on Cain and Cole?'

'Working on it right now. At this rate, you'd better transfer some more cash.'

'Okay.'

'Where's Bryant?' he asked.

'He flew out to see Filip in Prague this morning.'

'More loose ends?'

'Hopefully not,' Anni said.

He ended the call, and she felt deflated and disheartened.

She looked out of her fifteenth-story office window across the Thames, wondering where it had all gone wrong. It had been so easy when it was just her and Bryant. It had even been fun. Where had that gone?

She picked up her phone and called Tia.

'Where are you?'

'In town,' Tia said.

'Can I see you?'

'Sure. My place?'

'That would be nice.'

Anni grabbed a coat and left immediately.

Tia's apartment was just off Piccadilly, close enough to her roots in Chinatown but far enough away to isolate herself from the Triad gang leaders that she had been associated with since her youth. Anni was never quite sure whether her attraction with Tia was rooted in love, lust, fear, or just fascination with her lifestyle, which was unorthodox to say the least.

Anni had called on Tia numerous times as a fixer, a banker, and, more recently, a shoulder to cry on, metaphorically. She had never asked for anything in return. Her advice, when it came, came without compromise: 'This is the problem; here is the solution.'

'Leave it with me,' she would say.

'Oh my God, Anni, what's up?' she said as she opened the double doors to her apartment, pulling her in and putting an arm around her. They spent the next couple of hours going over the events of the last few days, those that Tia wasn't aware of, before ending up on the super king bed, where Anni's troubles vanished, at least for a while.

∽※∾

Anni woke up from a deep, relaxing sleep, the air conditioning chilling beads of sweat on her back. Tia was still naked at the bar, fixing a cocktail, with her phone tucked in her shoulder, talking quietly in Cantonese slang. Anni recognized some of the phrases and knew this was the language of the Triads. *God she is beautiful*, she thought. Her fears returned but were muted in Tia's presence. Tia turned to face Anni and said into the phone, 'Listen; I must go.' She then put the phone back on the counter.

'How you feeling, sweetie?'

'Better, thanks,' Anni said with some reservation.

'Well, what we need to do today is get your affairs in order and regain some perspective. You can stay here until we can tie down some of the detail and get some direction for you. Where is Bryant?' she asked.

'He's in Prague, trying to close off any leaks in that direction.'

'It's too late for that. The authorities will have already collected all the base data that they need to pursue internationally. It's time to cut and run, Anni.'

Anni's eyes gave away her horror at the thought. 'Bryant will never do that; you know he won't.'

'Yes, I do know that, and he'll take you down with him. That's why, for once in your life, you have either got to confront him or let him go.' She went across to a printer under the deck facing out onto the canal basin and pulled off three printed sheets.

'But he's my brother.'

'I have many brothers,' Tia said. 'Some I have lost; others are lost to me. There comes a time in your life when you must be selfish and think of number one, to the detriment of everything and everybody else. In this case, it will probably include me, and now is your time.' She handed over the sheets to Anni.

'I can't lose you, Tia; I can't.' Looking down at the flight reservation, she could feel the colour drain from her face.

'We'll see. Get dressed, or we seriously won't achieve anything today,' Tia said with a wicked smile—a very unique smile that Anni loved, with a slight twist to the edge of her mouth caused by the pull of a pronounced scar under her chin.

After a very strong black coffee, Anni reluctantly called her brother. It rang five times before he answered.

'Bryant?' she said.

'Yes. Look, Anni, I'm kinda tied up here just at the moment; can I get back to you?'

'I'm going home, Bry.'

'Okay, I'll catch up later.'

'No, I'm going home. To Yantien. Tia's made the arrangement; I'm on a flight this evening.'

'Shit, Anni,' he said way too loud, and he then looked around at the stern faces gathered at the makeshift boardroom table. He tried to moderate his tone.

'Look.' He lowered his voice to a virtual whisper. 'We'll work this out. Tia doesn't understand what's at stake.'

'I think she does, and that's why I'm going before it blows up in our faces. And Bry, I want you to do the same, please.'

Bryant stormed away from the table with one hand held up in apology to the group. 'Excuse me just for a minute.' His anger was barely under control.

'Look, Anni, this isn't something you just walk away from; you know that. We have people—uncompromising people. I have eight of them sat around a table here in Prague, and there are others, who will be left with blood on their hands. And they are not the sort to turn the other cheek.'

He realized he was talking to a dead phone. 'Fuck you, Anni.'

He hit redial to call the last received number. He got a long buzz and then nothing.

⁂

Anni looked at Tia, startled, as she watched her phone that Tia had just grabbed from her hand head out of the fifth-floor window and into the canal. 'What did you do that for?' she yelled. 'Fuck, Tia! Why? Why?'

'He would have talked you round, Anni,' she said flatly. 'This is your one chance to get out of this in one piece, and an opportunity—a *good* opportunity—to forge a new life. Ultimately wherever you like. When you get to Yantien, your cousin Sum Chan will have a new identity. It's a blank page for you, Anni—*you*, not you with someone else calling the shots, but just *you*. And maybe, just maybe, I might join you sometime in the future.'

Anni collapsed on the sofa, the reality of what she was about to do suddenly hitting her straight between the eyes. She hadn't cried since she was a kid and her big brother left to join the army. She cried now. Tia joined her on the sofa, wrapping her in her arms.

Anni looked up at her. 'Will you come with me?' she said, almost as a plea.

'Not now, but we'll see.'

Later that evening, after Anni was well on her way, Tia's phone rang. It was Bryant.

'Tia, where's Anni?' Bryant's voice was full of outrage.

'She's gone, Bryant, and hopefully, for her, you won't see her again.'

'What have you done, you stupid bitch? You have no idea, do you? No one can just disappear in today's world. Fifteen years ago it was possible, but not now. They will find her, Tia!'

'They won't be looking for her, will they? None of these problems fall at Anni's door; they are squarely at yours. All the contracts that you have in place with these characters, which I warned you against five years ago, are in your name. Anni is only a co-partner in Omnicamp, a legal marketing organization that you have corrupted. There are no documents that link her to file 2277.'

'Oh yes there are! There are agreements that she signed with the software guys that set it all up!'

'There are no such documents,' Tia said.

'There are; they are logged in the company archives.'

'There are no such documents ... any more.'

Tia closed her phone, transferred all her contacts to a new phone, and tossed the old one to join Anni's in the canal.

CHAPTER 31

◇◇◇◇◇◇◇◇◇◇◇◇◇

Back at the station, Chris was laying out a group of photographs in conference room 3. He looked up as Joanne and James knocked. Chris waved them in, and they gathered around.

Joanne pointed to one photograph of a bloodied Asian man. 'This is Khalid Memshabin.' She pointed to another. 'And this is his son, Hassain. They front a tech phone repair shop in Old Christchurch Road here in Bournemouth.'

Chris looked up. 'Yes, we know them; they are the main protagonist in our MEMS case that Greg and Aleysha were working on.'

'Coincidence?' James said.

'Possible but unlikely. What do we have from the crime scene?'

Joanne opened a Manila folder. 'Well, the place was well and truly turned over, and Khalid was tortured. Two broken fingers and a shot to the upper thigh, which bled a lot before the fatal wound, a bullet to the temple. Hassain had a single shot to the throat; no way of knowing whether this was before or after his father's demise. Nothing from forensics yet, but we do have CCTV from across the road.' Joanne turned to the wall-mounted monitor and clicked the remote, inserted a USB drive, and hit play. 'These two entered at sixteen twenty-five on Wednesday.'

The image, though at distance, clearly showed two hooded individuals entering the phone repair shop. Both wore gloves and seemed to be making an effort to ensure their backs were to the cameras, as if they were aware of them. The timeline showed them in the shop for eighteen minutes.

'Can we zoom in on any of this?' Chris said.

'I'm waiting for a file from forensics that will enable us to manipulate it on the video suite.'

Chris picked up the phone and hit a speed dial number. 'Who are you dealing with?' he said to Joanne with his hand over the receiver.

'Charlotte Price.'

'Hi, this is DS Bowden. Can I talk to Charlotte, please?'

There was a pause. Phil flicked through the documents in the folder. 'I see there's a bank of computers in the back room. I assume SOCO have them?'

'Yes,' Joanne said, 'but the hard drives have been removed.'

'Oh, Hi. Charlotte. Any progress of the CCTV from Old Christchurch Road? ... Excellent, can you send it across—electronically please.' He looked at Joanne. 'Write this down please, Jo: 88709543. Thanks Charlotte, that's great.'

He put the phone down. Joanne left the room with the reference number and returned a few minutes later and pulled up the CCTV on the video suite. With the console, she was able to move around the image, highlight, and enlarge.

Chris said, 'I want to see the section as they enter the shop.'

Joanne drove to the specific timeline and zoomed in as the first hood opened the door and just for a fraction of a second looked down the street in the direction of the camera.

'Go back and freeze that frame and send it to Charlotte and ask her to see if face recognition can pick anything up.' He nodded to Jo to carry on.

The screen animated, and when both were inside, the Open sign was switched to Closed.

'Okay, that's a positive; these are our guys wanted for the murder of the Memshabins.'

Get as much info as you can from this CCTV and forensics Jo, and we'll call the team back later.'

'Any news from Greg?' James asked.

'Just further confirmation that there is some sort of money laundering going on centred around Banfield and their subsidiaries. Also, there is a credit shop in town that is in some way connected, and we have a detail keeping the two current employees safe.'

'And what about MI5?' James continued.

'Orders are being prepared to move the Lithuania team to Riga; we are supplying them with all the info we have.'

As he was saying this, the phone rang, and it never ceased to amaze Chris how often events cross over by sheer chance.

He picked the phone up and pressed 'loud speak'. It was Robin Grant, informing him that part of the Lithuanian team was being redirected to another operation. Only two of the original group would be heading to Riga.

James pushed his chair back violently. 'For Christ's sake!' he said, and he left the conference room.

CHAPTER 32

◇◇◇◇◇◇◇◇◇◇◇◇◇

Six hours later

'Nothing on face recognition yet,' Joanne said, 'but they are going to try again later when they get image enhancement back from the lab. And, unsurprisingly, no useful fingerprints. So far, the computers, without hard drives, are not yielding anything. They are also checking the buffer memory on the printer. They will get back to me if anything comes up from this.'

'Okay, thanks for that; keep on at them please,' Chris said. 'Do we know where James is?

'He left the station this morning,' Phil replied. 'Didn't respond to this meeting message.'

'Strange. Can you get hold of him later, Jo, please?'

'Sure. Should we be worried?'

'I don't think so. Just track him down, will you.'

'So there has been a text message on Greg's old phone.' Chris proceeded to explain the contents and that MI5 were looking to trace its origins. 'They don't know that Greg and Kevin are in Riga yet, but I will have to inform them of this soon if we all want to keep our jobs. Other than knowing where they are, I have nothing more from them unless they've been in touch with either of you.'

Both shook their heads.

Chris stood up and went over to the whiteboards. 'Right, so what we have so far.' He looked across at the photographs and the associated notes and began to write in marker on a clear screen.

'We can now positively link the Neville Hillingdon hit-and-run to the file that he accidentally uncovered. Aleysha and Maya's abduction was a result of Maya's relationship with Hillingdon. Greg very nearly fell victim to a plot at the Cottage at Thorney Hill because he was associated with Aleysha. Banfield Marketing, while a legitimate company, along with God knows how many others, are having their finances massaged to presumably hide illicit drug money.' He wrote 'Yet to be proved' in brackets on the screen.

'We now have a possible link to two other potentially missing persons. One Jeremy Caine and one Pam Cole, who also work at Banfield. Caine is described as a quiet, insular person but has been reported as not turning up to work as expected by a concerned colleague and had not responded to phone messages with respect to meetings he had arranged. Cole, on the other hand, was registered as missing by a close friend who phoned her on Monday. She did not answer, but according to this friend, Kerry Walpole, she always gets back to her as soon as she can.'

'That, then, may or may not be connected to the deaths of Khalid and Hassain Memshabin. Anything from ballistics on this case?' he said, looking at Joanne.

'Not yet, sir, but I have Greg's MEMS files I'm going through to see if there are any associations with Banfield,' she answered.

'Good. The notebook from the IN-Need shop has identified the prints on both it and the business card as belonging to the card holder, one William Conro, known affectionately as Billy. He is in the system: 2008 on drugs trafficking; received two years at her majesty's pleasure. He is now employed by an international marketing organization in the city, Omnicamp, as a financial consultant. We have the fraud squad looking into him.

'Then there is this shot fired at the cafe on the pier. It's difficult not to imagine that this is also in some way connected.

'There are a couple of CCTV cameras from the vicinity, and their footage is being evaluated. Hopefully we will get something tomorrow.' He downed the last of another cold coffee and continued. 'Robin Grant will be back here in the morning, so I would like everything pulled together for then, please. He will be updating us on the team going into Riga, and hopefully we will have something beneficial from Greg before I drop the bombshell as to where he is.' Chris scanned over the boards. 'Anything I've missed? he asked.

Phil said, 'I've extended our stop-and-seize order on the *White Angel* to encompass all ports and shipping within five hundred miles of Riga, but nothing so far.'

'Thanks, put that on the board, will you, Phil, and keep me informed, please. One more thing while we are updating the board: the shoe print of what we believe to be the assailant at Alderney Hospital is'—Chris looked at his memo pad—'an Under Armour Junior Ripple GS training shoe, sold almost exclusively online and very common, so no lead there, but it is a size five and a half junior fit, so quite a small foot.' He shrugged. 'For what that's worth.'

Joanne's phone buzzed, and she looked down at the screen. 'They have a photofit for one of the guys at the phone shop. They are sending it over shortly.'

CHAPTER 33

◇◇◇◇◇◇◇◇◇◇◇◇

'He probably just fancied you; these Moroccans are hot-blooded.'

Pru looked at him. 'Seriously?' she said. 'It could be many things, but that is the most unlikely.'

'I don't know; I fancy you.'

'Well thank the lord for that; I would be totally fucked if you didn't, now wouldn't I?'

'I don't think he looked dangerous.'

'Just how does someone look dangerous?' she said cynically.

Let's find a street cafe where we can see if he re-emerges.'

Brian cancelled the taxi, and they left the hotel and walked south in the general direction of town. But before they came across a cafe, they stumbled into a row of dusty red Peugeots. Passing the first one in line, the driver got out and rushed to open the rear passenger door and invited them in.

'Taxi sir, madame,' he said in clipped, well-practised English.

Brian had a thought. 'Let's take it to the next village or town. That way we can establish if we are being followed. I really don't want to lead anyone back to the boat.'

'How could anyone know we are here?' Pru said.

'I don't think they do, but I would rather err on the side of caution.'

They nodded to the driver and got in. The air inside was thick with tobacco smoke and alcohol.

Brian managed to point on the driver's satnav to a place that looked to be about five miles south of their present position, marked Hay Hassani, which the driver acknowledges with an enthusiastic pat to his chest. 'My home. Very good.'

Brian spent the relatively short journey with his arm around Pru, looking back to see whether they were being followed. *Certainly nothing obvious*, he thought.

In Hay Hassani, they thanked the driver and handed over two hundred dirham. He didn't offer change but thanked them politely.

Walking away from the main street, they found what they were looking for—a cafe bar with a good view in both directions. One way in, one way out. They ordered another couple of cold beers and settled down in a window seat, Brian watching up the street, Pru watching down.

Brian was aware that Pru was tense again, her nerves on edge as she looked out, scared of what she might see—scared that three days in, they had already been rumbled.

Twenty minutes later and there were no signs of their short, long-haired Asian, and they felt comfortable about leaving the bar. Brian left a hundred on the table, and they exited the cafe.

Back on the main street, they looked for a taxi to return them to Jadidda. They now had only thirty minutes to get back to the boat before their free mooring ran out. Not knowing what the regulations were about overstaying, they were keen to be on their way and to reach the relative safety of the *Magna*.

Was it by coincidence or design that the driver that brought them to Hassani was still where they left him?

He smiled as he saw them crossing the road.

Pointing at the road opposite, he said, 'My home.'

They both smiled cautiously.

'Jadidda?' Brian asked.

'Of course.' He looked at his watch. 'Half hour—six hundred.'

Brian agreed, and they both got in. They again had their breath taken away by the reek of smoke, now tinged with a whiff of cheap perfume. The latter proved to be from a bottle of Moroccan Myrrh aftershave, which rattled around on the dashboard all the way back to Jadidda.

Rounding the small harbour wall, they could see the dinghy still moored where it had been left. As they moved nearer, they saw there was no restriction ticket—no warden waiting to pounce either. They both breathed a sigh of relief and virtually ran to it.

The outboard started without missing a beat, and as far as they could see there was no one taking any notice of them.

It took only five minutes after leaving the little harbour, and sounding the horn as they pulled close to the *Magna*, Gary appeared on the aft deck and helped them back on board.

'How'd it go?' he said.

'We'll talk about it in a bit,' Brian replied. 'Right now I think we both need to freshen up.'

Half an hour later, Gary, up on the control deck, was preparing to get the *Magna* under way. They both sat in the lounge, with the rest of the crew around them, explaining their encounter at the hotel.

Nick got up. 'I need to check something out,' he said, and he went down to the office.

He came back a few minutes later with an electronic gadget in his hand.

'What's that?' Brian asked.

'A frequency monitor. We've had some, albeit minor, interference this afternoon on the Skype screens; and thinking about it now, it began when you returned.'

'Meaning?' Pru said.

'Maybe you picked something up.'

Brian sat up. 'What, like a bug?'

'Possibly. Worth checking out' He flicked the start switch on the monitor, and it immediately bust into life.

'Shit,' Pru said.

'Ignore that.' Nick pressed another button. 'That's just a self-test routine.'

It settled down to a low beep. But as he swept around, the tone changed and the LED indicator lights flashed between amber and green.

'We should have a look in your cabins,' Nick said, walking towards Pru's room.

It went solid amber as he approached and red when he entered the room. Moving around the room, the tone became high-pitched, and the red LED flashed intermittently as he aimed it at Pru's wash box in the corner.

'My jacket's in there,' she said, and she went over to retrieve it from the chest. She laid it on the bed and watched the monitor. 'Shit, shit, shit.'

'Get us under way Gary!' Brian barked.

He left with Mark in tow.

Nick went over the jacket and found the device on a barbed clip that had been inserted just above the hem at hip height. It was no more than three millimetres in diameter, encapsulated in a clear epoxy bubble, making it almost invisible.

'The guy in the lift,' Brian suggested.

'Hang on, Gary!' Nick shouted. Then, looking at Brian, he said, 'Let me take the dinghy out with this, and I'll plant it somewhere. It might give us some time to put space between us.'

They all agreed, and Nick went off with the device.

'How the fuck have they got on to us?' This was more of a statement from Mark than a question.

Nick had noticed earlier in the day that a small cruiser with a large bird emblem on the mainsail was anchored just a short way off. Their occupants had set off in a dinghy for the town just after noon. As the dinghy was still missing, he assumed they had yet to return. Pulling along on the seaward side, he called out to anyone aboard. There was no response. He pushed the barbed clip into one of the handrail ropes and left.

Before the ding was fully locked home, the *Magna*'s engines were being wound up. Nick got on board, and he and Mark secured it in place.

Brian and Gary agreed to set sail in the general direction of the Canary Iles and ask Nick to disable the transponder.

☾ﾟﾟﾟﾟﾟﾟ☽

Ten hours later, they dropped into a mooring alongside other similar vessels on the Puerto Tenerife at Santa Cruz. The *Magna* did not look out of place; there were far more exclusive, more modern crafts along the extensive dock front. Brian had decided that this would be a good place to hold up for a while and see whether anything from their Casablanca experience transpired.

Pru had been jittery ever since the emergence of the bug, but landing here at Tenerife seemed to have settled her a little.

They had gone ashore to find somewhere for breakfast and, making their way towards town, came across La Pandorga, which offered a full English that turned out to be exceptional. Brian had activated two of the credit cards and checked them out by paying for breakfast with one and withdrawing cash from an ATM with the other. He also contacted the third to redirect the PIN. They found a bar in town and sat with a coffee, discussing the future and how it might look—how they were going to cope. By the time they were heading back to the yacht, nothing had really been resolved, but they had a better understanding of their position and, more importantly, their limited options, which Pru was slowly coming to terms with.

Back on the *Magna*, Nick met them as they came on board.

'We have picked up a message from the Moroccan coastal authority that a vessel, *El Condor*, has been destroyed in an explosion outside Casablanca harbour.'

'Was that the boat?' Brian asked.

'Fairly sure it was; I never got a look at the name, but there was an image of a bird on the mainsail.'

'Any mention of casualties?'

'No,' Nick said

'Okay. Well, keep an ear open. It could be good news for us.'

Pru had a different viewpoint as she pushed past them both. 'Innocent people may well have died on our account!' she said as she stomped up the corridor and slammed and locked her cabin door.

'She could well be right; that doesn't sit well.' Brian said to Nick. 'We'll stay here for a day or so.'

CHAPTER 34

◇◇◇◇◇◇◇◇◇◇◇◇

Though apparently quite cosy by Eastern European standards, the suite got cold at night. I had little sleep, and what I did have was broken and restless, so I was up before six. I had a text message from Chris to call him. Thinking it a little early, I made myself a coffee, trying not to disturb Kevin. His laptop was open on the occasional table and I wondered if I would be able to get on to my emails, thinking it easier to type with as keyboard than with fingers on my phone. The screen was open but in sleep mode, so there was no need to sign in, and I didn't think he would mind. I was, however, somewhat taken aback when I hit the enter key to wake it up and find a Google page spring up with a full-size picture of a Glock 42.

'What the …!'

'Just seeing what's what,' Kevin said as he sat up in bed.

'What do you mean what's what? Get that idea out of your head now,' I said.

'I have. The only place I can find to buy one is Walmart, and *they* are in short supply in Riga.'

I heard my phone buzz on the bedside table. It was Chris repeating his previous message.

I hit the dial button and walked back to the table.

'Morning. What's new?' I said.

He sounded a little fraught—tired, I felt—but his first thought was to let me know that Jet's procedures had all gone well and the vet felt he would make a good recovery over the next couple of weeks. He then went through their briefing from the previous evening. I had no love for the Memshabins or their associates but (a) I didn't wish them dead, and (b), that blew any links we may have had to the bigger pond that these guys were just paddling in.

'Joe and Stephanie, from IN-Need,' Chris went on. 'We checked out their boss, William Conro—Billy. He owns a rather large and very imposing property up on Cranford Cliffs. Our guys visited him last night. Not going to be enjoying the impressive views, I'm afraid. He was shot through the throat.'

I sighed in disbelief, the image of the Glock-42 appearing in my mind's eye. 'Have you had a chance to look at the other accounts in the file?' I asked.

'Yes, and I think you're right; they are all individually, and to them unknowingly, part of a massive fraud ring, but we are not doing anything with it at the moment. We don't want them to know what we suspect and put the girls in any further danger. While they still think they have a bargaining chip, they should be safe.

'I agree. Anything from the spooks?'

'Robin Grant is coming in this morning. As I understand it, there is a two-man team heading your way sometime today, but I won't have anything more on that until he arrives. I will need to tell him about you and Kevin.'

'Two-man team?' I said. 'Pushing out all the stops then. We have international drugs, fraud, and kidnapping of an officer and a civilian, and the best they can do is a two-man team? Shit, there must be something really fucking serious going down somewhere else. I can't wait to hear about it.' I was about to end the call before I said something I might regret, and I think Chris sensed this.

'I know; hold on,' he said. 'As little as it may be, we need all the help we can get, and they have access to way more intelligence than we do, and it just may be what we need to get the girls back. What have *you* got?'

I could tell he wanted to keep me on the phone, allow me time to calm down. And his use of 'We need all the help we can get' told me that he was fully supporting me.

'I need something to tell Robin to soften the blow when I tell him where you are,' he said.

I took a deep breath; Kevin came over and put my coffee on the table and sat down. He cleared the picture of the Glock from his screen and shut the laptop.

'We met with a couple of port authority guys yesterday, and a police sergeant who was a cousin of one of them joined us last night. They know of the *White Angel* and have had suspicions that it, and a company called ...' I looked at Kevin.

'Elevation Textiles,' Kevin said.

'Elevation Textiles—they are in association with suspected drug smuggling. That company incidentally is also in the Hillingdon file, but they have never been able to prove anything. They have a factory and a warehouse here in Riga, but given their location and the CCTV footage of the girls being taken from the boat, the port's camera shows them being taken in the opposite direction to either. We don't believe that they have been taken there. Gordie, the police sergeant, is looking into any other properties they may own, and we hope to meet up again this evening.'

Chris wanted to know the details of the factory, the warehouse, and the names of those involved, which I said I would send by email. I knew this was for Robin's benefit, and I certainly didn't want to make things difficult for Chris, so Kevin and I got everything down and sent off before going down for breakfast.

I was surprised to see the breakfast room virtually full when we arrived, with a mixture of obvious dockworkers and suits.

We were shown to a table by a new face—young, probably late teens. But unlike in the UK for someone of that age, she had an engaging smile and an understanding that we were foreign. We had many pleases and thank-yous, some even in the right context. Her badge pronounced her as 'Silvee', and she handed us each a menu.

'Tea, coffee?' she asked. We both agreed on tea. She nodded with more thank-yous and disappeared.

Just about the only thing with contents that we recognized on the handwritten menu was called 'svētdienas vēlās brokastisa'. This was followed by a list of unpronounceable items with 'Danish bacon' amongst them. We both decided this sounded like a safe bet and pointed to this when Silvee returned with our *black* tea.

'Sundea Broonch,' she said, delighted with her attempt at English, and we both gave a thumbs up. Neither of us decided to tackle hand gestures suggesting milk, so we took the tea without.

When we returned from serving ourselves to the juice and cereals from the buffet, Erika was waiting at our table.

'I have now two rooms if you like,' she said.

We looked at each other, shrugged, and told her that we were okay with the room we had, and we thanked her. She smiled and headed back to reception.

Kevin's phone rang, and looking at the screen, he said, 'I need to take this.' He got up and followed Erika towards the reception area.

CHAPTER 35

<<<<<<<<<<<<<<<<<<

'Where the fuck is James!' Chris shouted across the incident room.

'We don't know,' Joanne said, 'but he's not at home. His phone is, though; we had a uniformed officer break in twenty minutes ago, and his mobile and radio are on his bedside table. No car keys, no car, no sign of any struggle, and definitely no James.'

'Shit. What's going on? Is he missing or the subject of another abduction?'

'CCTV from the parking area outside his flat has apparently been inoperative for months. The landlord was informed several weeks ago, but there has been no response to the residents' committee.'

'Any other CCTV that we can pull in?' Chris asked.

'We're looking into it, guv. By the way, one of the assailants from the phone shop—the lab have come up with face-rec on him. He is Janek Dvroak—has history in Chez special forces. He's also been linked to organized crime in London, thought to be a gun for hire, but there's never been sufficient proof to take him down.' Joanne looked at her notes. 'Believed to have a property in Camden, but if he has, it is not registered in his name.'

'Put his face out on our national person of interest page. Let's see if we can tie him down,' Chris said. 'There's a lot going on in Camden; I'd like to get a look at where he lives.'

Robin and an assistant had been shown to conference room one, and Chris was in two minds as to whether he should mention James's absence to them.

Chris led Joanne and Phillipa, a new recruit to the team, into the conference room.

Robin was standing in front of a whiteboard, jotting down notes.

He turned around and, without any formalities, introduced Helen, who he said would be his liaison on this case. They all sat around the oval table, and Robin pushed cards from Helen and himself to the others, saying, 'These are our new contact details. Helen is to be copied in on all correspondence. Now tell me about your man DCI Richards?'

Chris pulled an awkward face. 'Yes, well, I'm afraid he's taken it upon himself to pursue this matter personally, along with Mr. Goodwin, DC Coombs's cousin. They are in Riga and have made contact with the port authorities and the local police.'

'We know. And it's not helpful. I hope you made that clear to your DCI. It's hard enough for our guys without any loose cannons with personal ties to muddy the waters. There is no place for emotion in circumstances like this; it must be cold, calculated, and precise. Throwing untrained personnel into the mix can completely fuck it up; you should know that. Can you recall them, or at least get them to a place where they can have zero effect?'

Chris considered this for a moment. "I tell you what, I'll look at that when I know what plans you have in place,' Chris said, feeling somewhat put out by being told what to do on his own patch. 'Greg is unlikely to back off just because he is told to; he's a policeman, not a soldier. Also, I would have thought having a "highly qualified DCI" in the field of operation could be a valuable asset, particularly when you currently only have two team members, no?'

'Okay, I shouldn't have used the term "untrained",' Robin acquiesced.

'But without them being integrated, logistically and strategically, they could screw the campaign up before it gets off the ground.'

'Then we should keep them informed operationally. We can direct and use them as eyes on the ground. You couldn't have two more motivated individuals at your disposal. And, incidentally, the cousin has proved to be a very effective intelligence gatherer.'

There was silence in the room for what seemed like an age; the atmosphere was thick, both sides waiting for a crack.

It came when Robin stood up, looked directly at Helen, and said, 'All right, open secure communications with DCI Richards'.

He then directed his attention to the rest of the group. 'We have a briefing with the team in four hours. I want us all to convene back here then. There's a comms crew on its way to set this room up, in'—he looked at his watch—'forty-five minutes. We should have audio and visuals before the briefing. In the meantime, I would like it if all relevant information related to Riga and the *White Angel* can be assembled in here. I also need you all to read and sign the Official Secrets Act document that Helen will issue shortly.' To Helen he said, 'Please ensure that the two remotes get copies.'

'They will be on the SIM,' she said.

He nodded acknowledgment and, looking at Chris, continued. 'Is there another room Helen and I can use?'

'Sure, and thank you,' Chris said, getting up and leading them out.

'Let's hope we don't all live to regret it.'

'By the way,' Chris said as he walked them down the corridor, 'and at this point I don't know if it's relevant, but I have a missing officer.'

'From the Blue Rabbit team?' Robin asked.

'Yes, he left the office yesterday.' He continued to fill him in on the details. 'We have an APB out, and we're trying to get a fix on his car, but in all honesty, we have nothing to go on as to direction.'

'We'll have to leave that until something comes in and assume there is no connection until we know differently. We can't get distracted, but keep me informed,' Robin said.

CHAPTER 36

◇◇◇◇◇◇◇◇◇◇◇◇◇

Kevin returned from the foyer sliding his phone into his back pocket.

'You okay?' I asked as he sat down.

'Yes, fine; few problems back at the factory.'

I had no reason to question this, but by my basic reckoning, it was 2.00 a.m. in Puerto Rico. 'That's an early call,' I said.

'Yes, I know. Simona is the best PA I've had; she's never off duty, and apart from some snags at the factory, apparently Westline Investments—read "Bodican"—have informed our solicitors that due to the issues being reported over the Tithe cottage, they are removing their interest and sending a contract retraction within the next twenty-four hours.'

'That's' interesting,' I said.

'Yes, and they want access to recover the telecommunication equipment.'

'Even more interesting'

That aside, I do have a few business calls to make after breakfast.'

'That's fine. I'll do a recce of Elevation Textiles, see what comes up. Okay if I take the car? It might be easier for a stake-out.'

'Sure, can you get a camera with a decent lens while you're out; I think it might come in handy. You can put it on my Amex card; I'll sort it in a bit.'

Breakfast was hearty and, barring the expanse of cabbage chutney, was on the whole very tasty.

Back in the room, Kevin gave me his business credit card and PIN. 'If they don't accept it, draw cash from an ATM.'

'How much are you happy to spend?' I asked.

'Whatever you think. Listen, my whole adult life I have spent money on trivia—on so-called pleasures. This is the first time I feel I have a proper use for it, and I am more than content spending whatever it takes to get those two girls back. And, by the way, I'm also very glad that you share my passion.'

I grabbed my duffel coat and car keys and confirmed with Kevin the factory site on Google maps on my phone before heading out.

The BMW was fully frosted up and took several minutes before the heater, on full blast, had any effect. I reluctantly used the Amex card to scrape a good clear patch on the front screen.

I had to drive several miles before I could access a road that crossed the river.

Parking just off a main square in the centre of town, I walked around for a while before I came across a general store with a section loaded with camera equipment. I was able to point to a Cannon digital SLR set that included a telephoto lens and carry case.

I apologized to the assistant for being English and tried to ask how much the set was.

He wrote down on a piece of paper '€3,350.00'.

I showed the Amex card, and he gestured for me to give it to him.

'Seventy euros more,' he said.

We agreed on €4,400.

I was in the shop for another fifteen minutes while he waited to see the transaction clear to his pending account.

He smiled for the first time as he handed over the card and the carry case. I thanked him and left the shop.

The factory was in a heavily industrialized area, busy with large and small wagons alike. Health and safety had obviously not reached this part of the world yet, as forklift trucks criss-crossed each other at speed with absolutely no consideration for foot traffic.

I managed to park the BMW about a hundred yards riverside of the Elevation Textiles loading bay.

It was over an hour later before the first van, an unmarked grey Nissan that had seen better days, pulled up to the shutter doors, which immediately rolled back, and the van drove in. Just enough time for me to run off a dozen shots. My hour-and-a-half wait had not been totally wasted.

Fifteen minutes later, the same van emerged, and I was able, after looking at the images on the camera, to establish that it had gone out with a different driver.

Over the next hour or so I edited a couple of the shots to focus on the two drivers' faces and forwarded them to Gordie.

I got a message straight back to let me know that they didn't have facial recognition but he would get one of his aides to compare it to their mug shot catalogue. Also, he was going to get off shift at three o'clock and asked whether we could meet up at his station, 9 Matīsa iela.

I checked the satnav; it was less than ten minutes away from where I was located. I decided to contact Kevin and see how he was getting on, but before I got a chance to do so, I got a call from an unknown number with UK codes.

I answered, and a very English voice informed me that she was Helen Carter and that she was Robin Grant's liaison officer.

'Okay,' I said.

'You are to be integrated with the special forces team that has been deployed to Riga. As such, we need to establish secure lines of communication. A special SIM card has been sent to your hotel and will be with you this evening. There is to be a briefing this afternoon which we will bring you up to speed with later, when you have the SIM installed. Also on the SIM is an official secrets document which both of you will need to read fully and sign. Instructions on how to make contact will be sent to you separately via a new email address that has been established purely for this operation. To log on to this, go to https/—'

'Hold on,' I say, 'I need to write this down.'

'I'll send it in a text which will be automatically deleted within five minutes. Do not write anything down; commit it to memory,' she said.

'*I hope it's a short code,*' I said, thinking I'd take a screen shot just to be on the safe side.

'It will be. It will also have an embedded file that disables your camera.'

Shit, I thought, *do they also study telepathy in MI5?* 'Fine,' I said. 'When will you send it? I'm on a self-imposed stake-out at the moment.'

'Text this number when you are prepared.' The line went dead.

'Bye then,' I mouthed.

In the meantime, two vans had arrived at the loading bay, and the first had been ushered straight in, as before. I got the camera prepared as an individual ran out from the loading bay towards the driver of the second van like a wild, unchained Alsatian, mouthing off something with exaggerated arm and hand gestures that indicated that he was not happy about him being there.

I clattered off more shots of the vans and of the irate character, zooming in on both him and the rear door—the lock in particular, which wouldn't have looked out of place on a safe door. There were two mortice-type keyholes and a solid brass handle.

The second van was ushered out of the bay and drove off back past me. I lowered the camera and made as if I were making a phone call as the driver looked directly at me. He was young—maybe twenty. Probably a newbie.

I rang Kevin to ask what he was up to. He was walking around the perimeter of the warehouse on Kapsula.

'Nothing happening here at all,' he said. 'How about you?'

I explained about the call from Helen Carter and what was going on at the factory.

'Do you have your laptop?' I asked.

'Yes, why?'

I may want to download some of these photographs; I also need it to activate the SIM back at the hotel. Gordie wants us to see him at the station at three o'clock. I'll pick you up if you like.'

'Is it at Matīsa Street?' Kevin asked.

'Yes,' I said.

'I've got time to walk; I'll see you there.'

'Okay.' I dropped the phone on the passenger seat and picked up the camera again. The shutter doors were opening, and the first van pulled out, and I could confirm again it was a different driver.

CHAPTER 37

◇◇◇◇◇◇◇◇◇◇◇◇

Chris and Joanne entered Conference Room 1, which Chris thought now looked like a compact version of the NASA space centre. Three technicians were surrounded by a bank of monitors pulling up various images from who knows where. One central large screen was currently blank. The boardroom table had been removed, and half a dozen chairs had been placed at the back of the room. Robin was conversing with the technicians and verifying that they would have access to CCTV in and around Riga. Helen Carter was in one of the chairs at the back, working on her laptop. She looked up at Chris and gave an automated smile; he and Joanne sat down alongside her.

Robin turned around and flicked a remote at the large screen, and it came alive with a map.

'Good afternoon.' He turned back from the screen to face the assembled group. 'Well, first up, we have had further communication on DCI Richards's old phone from the abductors. The first exchange is to take place at Ventspils heliport on the north-eastern coast of Latvia tomorrow, further details to follow. This is a two-and-a-half-hour drive from Riga. Our team has instruction to set up a remote base there using local force for intel. Your DCI's old phone is being operated from somewhere around Prague. We have the Czech intelligence agency trying to get a fix on it now.'

Turning back to the main screen, Robin said, 'This is Riga's main centre.' He moved the on-screen pointer around. 'The hotel where DCI Richards and co. are staying ... And this is the port headquarters. And down on this monitor here is a live feed from the port's roving camera. The monitor shows a slow-scanning image from high up, covering a large area of the Riga dock in real time. We have been given authority by port officials to access control of this scanning camera, and within the hour we will have communication with an operative in their control room. These others are currently showing images from various CCTV feeds around the city. We have access from here to sixty-five live cameras. Our team are tying up with the local police and the Latvian special task unit out at Vedazimes.' His pointer on the large screen moves out south-east of the centre. 'Here ... We have some intelligence on Messrs Maris Provofz and Krzysztof Kin from our UK database as having an association to a drug cartel running out of Tunisia. The Tunisian authorities planned a raid on a warehouse in Borj el-Khadra on the Tunisia–Libya border in 2017.' The map changed, and pointer went to the southernmost point of Tunisia. 'It was destroyed hours before the raid.' The map was replaced with a photograph of a burned-out building. 'No one claimed responsibility, but as there were civilian casualties, the Americans were blamed, even though they had no interest in the area at all. It was believed that the proceeds from this cartel were feeding the so-called Islamic State terrorists. Provofz and Kin were in the vicinity at the time, and radio chatter picked up by our agents in Algeria immediately after the explosion had voice recognition of them both arranging dispatch of fifteen vehicles to a location in Libya, which neither we nor the Tunisians had jurisdiction over.

'These guys, and there are several others who we believe could be involved with this racket, rarely take prisoners, and it is mind-boggling as to why they have in this instance.'

Chris flicked through some papers he had on his lap, opening the report from face-rec on the phone shop. 'Could Janek Dvroak be one of these other individuals?' he asked.

Robin nodded. 'Yes,' he said. 'He's a communications expert. It was thought at the time that he intercepted the details of the Tunisian raid. Why?'

'Two other employees of Banfield have gone off the radar. We believe they acquired new identities from a local group called the Memshabins. Two of *them* were killed by Dvorak and an associate two days ago.'

'Any trace of the missing persons?' Helen Carter asked.

'Not as yet,' Joanne said. 'All the information in the way of hard drives et cetera from the shop had been removed. Forensics have got some partial information from the printer buffer, but all we have is a Christian name, which may or may not be relevant … Prudence.'

'Okay, that's fairly unusual; we'll see what comes up from lost identities,' Helen said.

One of the technicians turned round to Robin and said, 'We have a live feed from blue team on monitor three, sir.'

Chris, who had been stunned with what had been put together so far by special forces, looked at monitor three and was surprised to see a young man with shaved head and casual shirt drinking a mug of what appeared to be coffee. That was not at all what he expected—that being a team in full combat uniform, waiting for the order to go. *Maybe a little premature*, he thought on reflection.

'Afternoon, sir.' A clear, rich, well-educated voice came through the speaker.

'Commander, what do you have so far?' Robin asked.

'Okay, well the task force here has given us some good information to go on with respect to the individuals named in the report. We have an expected location for Kin and Provofz tomorrow evening, twenty hundred hours at Barents restaurant. Apparently they are signing a deal to supply textile to Estonia.'

'Are they thought to be in Riga now?' Robin asked.

'Don't think so; the word is that they are expected in the port area tomorrow afternoon.'

'On the *White Angel*?' Chris asked.

'Sorry, commander,' Robin butted in. 'I should have introduced you to the squad here. This is Superintendent Chris Bowden and his team.' He presented them by name and rank but faltered at Phillipa. Looking at her, he said, 'Sorry, we haven't …'

'DC Phillipa Gowen,' she said.

Robin continued. 'Helen you know, and I have Gerald, Bill, and Peter here on keyboards.' Turning round, he said, 'And that's Commander John Wright and his wingman, Major Ron Holland.'

Another face moved into view on monitor three. 'Hi there,' the major said, and he moved out of view again.

'Does this lot have clearance?' the commander said.

'I have signed OSAs here,' Robin replied. 'There is also a DCI on the ground in Riga who may be able to assist with some local intelligence. He is not cleared yet but, all being well, will be by this evening.'

This provoked a disgruntled groan from both the commander and the major. 'I'll need a face-to-face with him as soon as possible.'

'He also has the sisters' cousin in tow,' Robin said.

'For fuck's sake, sir, we can't operate like that! Two captives we have to liberate, while babysitting two others.'

'I know, but they're there now; we'll have to work around it.'

'Please register my objection in your report sir.'

'Noted,' Robin said.

'Anyway,' the commander continued, 'The *White Angel* is scheduled into port tomorrow, so I would expect Kin and company to be aboard. Interestingly though, Thames House have been looking into the *White Angel*, and they are fast coming to the conclusion that there is a duplicate vessel out there, registered with the same name or similar. It is believed that there is a clean vessel that docks at various ports around the Baltic and North African coasts, appearing to promote suspicious activity.'

'How do you mean "suspicious"?' Chris asked.

'Well, offloading at odd hours, like three o'clock in the morning; carrying pallet loads of flour, textile rolls, and the like, which turn out to be flour and textile rolls, with paperwork that verifies their final destination; or it is registered as "just carrying foreign visitors". It has been boarded seven times in the last eighteen months by drug- and people-trafficking enforcement agencies. In every event, it has been given a clean bill of health. It was inspected twice in Algiers over the last six months.

'But looking more closely at its docking records, it reappears at ports it simply wouldn't have had the time to get to. It is thought that this second vessel could be the one carrying contraband, but it never gets picked up, as it is now on the authorities' clean list.

'That aside, we plan to get eyes and ears on Kin and Provofz at Barents and plant a bug if we can. With the team here, we will follow him and any associates to their locations here in Riga. One of them will undoubtedly make contact with the girls, and we will formulate an extraction plan from there.'

'Do we have surveillance set up at Ventspils yet?' Robin asked.

The major's face moved into view on the screen and said, 'The task force here have been in touch with the airport commissioner and have a liaison meeting at fifteen hundred tomorrow sir. I'll report back on that later.'

'Can you get all the details of these two non-coms so we know what we are dealing with?' the major asked. Chris was in half a mind to dispute his tone but thought better of it.

'Helen here, major. We will have comms set up this evening with DCI Richards; I'll send his file over now. Goodwin is, I'm afraid, an unknown—some unauthorized intelligence-gathering for the local force in Puerto Rico, but that's all we have. Sorry.'

'Roger that.'

'Okay, thanks. Anything else from anybody?' Robin looked around the room, and when no responses came, he wrapped up the meeting.

Back in his office with Phil, Joanne and Phillipa, they were all a little taken aback by the speed and breadth of the operation, not to say greatly impressed with the intelligence and technology being brought to bear.

'Has Greg or Kevin been in touch with any of you?' Chris asked.

They all confirmed that neither of them had.

'Helen has said that we should avoid any contact, at least until she has a signed OSA document from them both.'

They all nodded in agreement as Helen knocked at the door and poked her head around.

'Excuse me,' she said. 'Robin and I are staying at the Strand Hotel in Boscombe, but we are available twenty-four seven.'

'We are here for anything you need,' Chris said. 'Whatever time.'

'Likewise,' Phil said, and Joanne and Phillipa agreed.

'Thanks,' Helen said, and she left.

CHAPTER 38

◇◇◇◇◇◇◇◇◇◇◇◇◇◇◇

Matīsa Station was part of long, dark industrial-looking brick boulevard, very old, Soviet Russian in style, with no frills. I met Kevin outside. The fully red-bricked entrance led into a dimly lit reception area. Faded cream tiles adorned walls and ceiling, and a heavy steel cage separated it from the duty sergeant and his steel desk. I approached the cage and asked for Gordie. He looked up and wrote something down.

'viņš drīz būs lejā,' he said.

'English?' I ventured.

'Zel—Padon kuntz. Will be here shortly,' he said with a very thick accent.

Gordie appeared a few minutes later, unlatched the cage, shook our hands vigorously, and invited us through. We were shown into a small office on the first floor that overlooked the industrial boulevard, with bars at the windows. If it wasn't, it certainly felt like a jail cell, and I sensed the irony of the likes of Gordie putting villains away only to end up in a cell himself. I supposed at least he could go home at night.

'Okay, we have some activity here. Your government is now involved with ours on this matter, so you have already ... how you say ... ruffled feathers.'

'We're sorry about that,' I said.

'No, no problem; we are used to it. It's normally Russia who ruffle the feathers, and they are not so polite. Sorry, would you like coffee?'

'Please,' we both said, and he left the office.

'What was the warehouse like?' I asked Kevin.

'Literally that. There was no one there at all. I looked through the reception door window, and it's just an open space—no offices, no outbuildings. Partially racked out and about half full of what I would expect to be rolls of cloth.'

'Okay, so we can write that off as a location, along with the factory. It's too busy to hide the girls, but there is definitely something dodgy going on there,' I said.

Gordie returned with three coffees, very black, and sporting an aroma that could make one's eyes water.

'My boss would join us,' Gordie said, 'but he has no English, so I will debrief later—if that okay with you?'

'Of course,' I said. 'Did you get anything on Kin and Provofz?'

'They have rarely been here in Riga together, but recently, on a couple of occasions, they have booked into the Opera Hotel in the centre of the city. Just about the most expensive we have to offer. Only ever for one night, and they are both booked in this evening—again for just the one night.'

'Is the *White Angel* scheduled into port?' Kevin asked.

'Yes, twenty hundred hours today.'

'Can we arrange for it to be watched, with a view to holding if there is any danger that the girls are to be extricated?' I asked.

'This is something that I will have to clear with my boss, but personally, under the circumstances, I would see this as essential. I will check and get back to you later.'

I asked Kevin to set up his laptop; I wanted to see whether any of the images of the guys I had from the factory struck any chords with Gordie. I removed the SD card from the camera and plugged it into the slot on computer.

Kevin pulled up the images and turned the screen round so that we could all see. Going through each one, Gordie shook his head, saying he would like his boss to go through them, when suddenly he pointed to the young lad that got turned away.

'That is Petrov—Petrov Gorvel,' he said, looking at me as though it should mean something.

'He is the son of the man who was killed in the car accident in Utena, Lithuania, I told you about. I'm not even convinced he is old enough to hold a licence.'

We all sat and thought about it for a while, letting it sink in. Several scenarios came to mind: hormonal teenager pissed off with parents rats on his dad and is offered a job as payment, son of a dead employee is offered a lucrative job as compensation, son is made to work for dad's employer as a means to keep him quiet and protect the mother. Or none of the above. Whatever, it seemed very strange.

'I will ask if we can have him checked out,' Gordie said. 'Can you send the photos to this address?' He wrote his email down on a notepad and tore it off. 'Thanks,' he said, handing it to Kevin. 'Can you hang on for a minute while I check Petrov out?'

'Sure,' I said.

'More coffee?' he asked from the doorway.

I was not sure I'd come down from the last one yet, but I said, 'Why not.'

Kevin declined.

A few minutes later, a young female officer entered with my coffee. She had a broad, friendly smile as she put the mug down. I recognized the aroma, but this time my senses were not offended.

Kevin sent the images to Gordie's address.

'See the door catches on the vans?' I said. 'I wouldn't mind betting that the driver has one key and the other is a key the recipient holds so it can only be opened either at the factory or its final destination.'

I agreed; however, it was overkill for van full of cloth.

Gordie returned and said they would be looking into young Petrov. He was eighteen and held only a pre-test licence.

We chatted around the issues with Elevation Textile, but I was thinking all the time that this was not the problem I wanted to focus on.

'We need to get back to the hotel and update the guys back in the UK,' I said. Kevin shut the laptop, and we made to leave. The cell door opened and was filled with a uniform, and another mountain of a man walked in with his hand outstretched.

'My boss, Chief Bravof,' Gordie said, immediately standing to attention. I got up and took the offered hand, which mine disappeared into. He nodded and grunted a little awkwardly and then turned to Gordie and said something in Latvian. After several minutes, he looked at both Kevin and me, nodded again, and left.

'The van Petrov was driving today has been sighted twice at the Opera

Hotel in the last few days. It was reported by hotel staff on Tuesday as causing an obstruction to waste bin removal in the underground carpark, where an argument between the driver and hotel maintenance ensued. The licence plate was entered onto the hotel's restricted access file, and when it reappeared earlier today, it was refused access. Chief Bravof has issued a warrant to have the vehicle picked up.'

Suddenly my mind was racing, and I could see Kevin was thinking the same. *It might be a long shot, but what if the van was used to bring the girls to the hotel, where they were to be held until the exchange had been formulated? What if the van went today to pick them up and move them to a location more suited to Ventsplis heliport?*

'We need to get to the hotel,' I said, thinking I probably should not have said that out loud.

Gordie stood up. 'Look, you have no jurisdiction here; we will take control of this, and we will keep you fully informed. If anything happens to you, or you commit an illegal act on Latvian soil, you will have no protection from the law. If this were between the three of us, we could do something undercover. My government and yours have eyes on us now. That is no longer an option.'

'I understand,' I said, realizing we—that is, Kevin and I—need to work out a plan. 'Will you go to the hotel now?' I asked.

'I need to agree a strategy with Chief Bravof, but I'm sure a visit to the hotel will be in there.'

Good, I thought, *this will give us enough time to check out our theory first.* We got up and thanked Gordie for his time and agreed to keep in touch.

Back in the car, we confirmed that we thought there was a possibility that the girls were being held at the Opera Hotel.

'Put it in satnav,' I said.

CHAPTER 39

◇◇◇◇◇◇◇◇◇◇◇◇◇

We parked in a side street just around the corner from the hotel entrance. I was just about to get out when Kevin pushed a Glock 42 into my hand.

'Kevin, what the fuck? We can't do this.'

'Just in case,' he said. 'They hide well in these duffel coats.'

'And what if we get frisked?'

'Why would we?'

'Shit, Kevin.' I shook my head in disbelief. 'What experience have you had with firearms?'

'Weapon of choice by the Puerto Rican police, and yes, I have used one before … admittedly only on a firing range.'

'I can't believe I'm doing this; it goes against everything I've ever done.'

'When have you ever been in a situation like this, Greg?' he asked.

I was lost for words but tucked it into my inside pocket.

The reception area in the hotel was vast and very Westernized. As we walked towards the concierge, I was aware I had no idea how to frame the question I wanted to ask without it sounding ridiculous: 'Is there a room that has been occupied by a group including two women?' *There are probably hundreds*, I surmised.

The concierge smiled as he saw us approach, and I apologized for being a foreigner, but as it turned out he was another Latvian whose second language was English.

I tried to explain that we were police from the UK looking for two women who we feared may be being held against their will, possibly in this hotel, and that they would have been here for two to three days without leaving the room.

I could see his concern at my explanation, and I asked myself whether I would believe this, were it presented to me in his position. Probably not.

He said, 'I don't think I can help without authority, sir.'

I tried a different approach, saying that one of the women was a fellow officer.

He shrugged an apology.

Kevin tapped my shoulder, and I turned round to see Gordie and two other officers striding across the foyer towards us.

'Shit, that was quick.' The steel lump I felt resting against my left breast made me feel very uncomfortable.

'We can't work together if I can't trust you, DCI Richards.'

'I'm sorry,' I said, putting my hands up. 'Just trying to—'

'I know exactly what you are "just trying" to do, and you can't. I thought I made that clear. Please take a seat over there.' He pointed away from the concierge's desk.

The hotel manager was called, and they had been in discussion for some minutes when Gordie walked over.

'There's a suite on the third floor occupied by a so-called family of four. All meals have been taken in the room. I would say it is the most suspicious booking. My officers are taking details of the alleged occupants and will run them through the database later. In the meantime, we will take a look. You are welcome to observe only. No intervention. I must have your agreement, or you stay here.'

'Okay, Gordie. Look, I'm sorry. I really didn't think you would get the go-ahead this quickly,' I said.

He nodded, and we, along with the hotel manager, made our way to the lift while the other two officers took the stairs.

Outside room 3166, Gordie knocked at the door and signalled to the manager to unlock it. The two officers had Heckler & Koch semi-automatics drawn.

Gordie shouted something, and the two officers rushed in, also shouting. 'Wait here,' he said to us. I could hear them going from room to room, but there was no evidence of any other voices. From an adrenalin high, my deflation was physical. After a few minutes, Gordie came out into the hall and shook his head. 'No one here.' He said something to the manager, who headed off down the corridor. 'You can come in; we want to lock up in case anyone returns. You can look around to see if there are any indications that your ladies have been here. Avoid touching anything, please.'

I made my way across the suite to the bathroom—the one place that sets women apart from men. There was nothing in the way of toiletries other than the hotel stock of shower gel, shampoo, and conditioner. However, around the shower drain were some hairs, long and fair. I called Gordie, and he pulled out a pair of gloves and an evidence bag from his side pocket and gathered some of the hair into the bag.

Kevin moved out onto the balcony and collapsed on his haunches, his head in his hands. 'I thought we had them,' he said as I joined him. 'It gets to something when the only thing I'm grateful for is that they are still alive.'

'I know,' I said. 'But we're one step closer, and I don't believe that they are aware we are on to them. Hopefully they'll slip up sooner rather than later.'

'Gordie, what CCTV does the hotel have?' I asked.

He came out to us. 'I have asked the manager to gather all the tapes for the last three days, but the footage only covers the lobby, car park entrance, and exit. I doubt the girls would have been brought through the lobby.'

I agreed but asked whether we could look at the car park footage for today.

'Let's go down and see.' He talked into his radio, which I learned connected him to a lookout on the landing, to confirm there was no one on the way up.

Back at reception, we were crowded into a small security office behind the baggage store. Hotel security were operating the VCR and were speeding back from the current time and stopping whenever a vehicle exited the barrier. Four of us scrutinized each vehicle, not really knowing what we were looking for. Then, ten cars back and only thirty-five minutes prior, a grey Nissan came into view, and Kevin said to hold that frame. He dragged out his laptop and pulled up the images I had taken earlier. As he was flicking through, I realized what he thinks he may have seen.

'There,' he said. 'The "unchained Alsatian" from the factory.' We all looked at the screen and agreed he was one of the same.

'Did your boss get a chance to look through any of these?' I asked Gordie.

'Not before we left, no, but let me call him now, and I'll put out a warrant on that Nissan registration.'

I took a mental note of the registration for future reference.

'Listen, Gordie, I really do need to tie up with my contacts in the UK. Will you call me if anything comes up?'

'Of course,' he said. 'But no more tricks!'

'Sure, and thanks'

Kevin and I walked out onto the street but were immediately aware that we had company.

'Keep walking,' a well-built Caucasian male on Kevin's side said. 'So which one of you is DCI Richards?'

'And who the fuck are you?' I said, turning to face the one on my side, and I was immediately aware of something that felt like an iron bar across my back, ensuring my forward-facing progress.

'You must be the DCI then. We are the special forces team sent to free your colleagues and whose crime patch you are trampling all over. Now, move towards that black saloon across the street and get in the back seats of the car behind.'

Strangely enough, we did so without any further questions.

Once inside, he said, 'I'm Commander White, and this is Major Holland.'

The commander drove off, and I plucked up courage to ask where we were going.

'Your hotel. We can't discuss anything until you have clearance, and that won't happen until we have a signed OSA registered with HQ— something you should have done several hours ago before you decided to go vigilante.'

White drove without the aid of satnav or any other directions and parked in the spot I'd vacated earlier.

Inside the hotel, I picked up a registered package that had been left at reception and gave it to the commander.

In our suite, Kevin handed over his laptop and password to the major, who plugged a dongle into a USB port and spent the next twenty minutes downloading files.

'Your phone,' he said to me, and he took it, flipped it apart, and swapped the SIM. He entered the codes from the website and, after a few minutes, handed it back.

'You now have access only to the numbers listed. It, along with this laptop, is now fully secure and will be monitored constantly for traffic and location.'

I clicked the home button and saw all my normal apps.

'That's a virtual screen; none of your apps are operational. Only the date app, top left, is functional, and that sets off an alarm beacon only to be used in absolute emergencies. You must tap it three times in succession to activate it. Other than that, you can call or leave messages to the numbers listed, and you will receive calls as normal. That's it. Now'—he turned Kevin's screen towards us and removed the dongle—'read this, both of you. It's just like the terms and conditions with any contract, except these rules will be applied to the letter, and there is no get-out clause, so treat it seriously.'

I remember scanning this, or a document similar, when I was at police college, never for one minute thinking it would be applied to me.

'Before we move away from my phone,' I said, 'Can you clear Gordie's number? He might be useful with local knowledge.' After a short explanation as to who Gordie was, and his assistance so far, the major took my phone, keyed in something, and showed me the screen. 'This number?'

'Yes,' I said. He clicked close and handed me my phone back.

Reading and rereading several sections of the OSA took us the best part of twenty minutes, after which the commander presented us with an electronic pad that we signed and applied our fingerprints and facial rec to.

By the time we finished a coffee, the authorization came through.

'First off,' the commander said, 'this is a very abnormal situation for us. We operate as a close-knit team, relying on each other totally. We are not used to, or good at, integrating non-combatant members. That being said, whilst we have a lot of help in the way of numbers from the Special Task Unit here, and the local police force, we have so far had little useful intel that we didn't already know.'

'So … you can call me John.'

'And I'm Ron.'

There was a comedy element, and it wasn't lost on any of us.

With this out of the way, the atmosphere was noticeably more relaxed.

'So what did you get from the Opera Hotel?' John asked me.

'We are fairly sure the girls were held captive for the last few days in room 3116. There were hairs in the shower which I believe belong to one or both sisters. Sergeant Gordie'—I pulled his card from my wallet—'Vaordski, has them as evidence. Aleysha's DNA will be on file.'

Ron picked up his radio and called into HQ and asked for Miss Coombs' DNA to be sent to his panel. Whatever that is.

'We also have a registration for a Nissan that we think may have carried the girls from the hotel this afternoon, along with the driver that, again, the local force might know.' I wrote the registration number down from memory, and Kevin pulled up the image of 'Alsatian man.'

'Well, you have been busy.'

John asked whether Gordie had good English, and I told him it was probably better than mine. He called Gordie's number from his card. He introduced himself and asked to have the DNA from the hair as soon as possible, suggesting that he could get express clearance via the Latvian government if needed.

He also asked whether he had any details of the driver of the Nissan leaving the hotel. John pressed a button on his phone to record and asked Gordie to send the file to his phone. I could hear Gordie but couldn't make anything out. John ended the call.

'He said he will get the DNA within the hour. The driver is Janek Dvroak, has been linked here in Riga with both Kin and Provofz. We know them all; we have our own file on these three, but Gordie will send theirs over shortly. We are dealing with some very unsavoury characters here, and we shouldn't underestimate their capacity for violence. They are likely to be armed, so I need you two in an advisory role only. Understood?'

We both nodded and left it at that. I was half inclined to mention the fact that we were both carrying but decided against it. Considering the level of trouble I was already in, I thought one more misdemeanour was going to make little difference.

Ron received a message through his headset.

'The LSTF are in location around the heliport,' he said to John. 'They want us to check it out.'

John told us to stay put and to keep them informed on anything we got from Gordie and his team.

They gathered their things, saying that we would catch up later, and they left.

Kevin and I looked at each other.

'I'm not staying here,' Kevin said.

'We have no car,' I replied.

'It's a half hour walk away,' he said. 'Let's go.'

The restaurant was in full flow as we passed, and I popped in and gathered some fruit and wrapped biscuits, realizing we hadn't had anything since breakfast.

Crossing the bridge over the river, I got a call from Gordie.

'The Nissan has been reported abandoned at Kandava by a shop owner. It's on the main road to Ventspils,' he said.

'How far is that from the Opera Hotel?'

'An hour and a half'

'Shit, we are two hours away then,' I said.

'I'll have a patrol car there shortly to secure the scene, and I'll be on my way in a while, so see you there?'

'Any intel on the occupants?' I asked.

'Not as yet, no.'

'Okay, we'll see you later.'

I had the same feeling now that I'd had when heading to Corf Castle days ago. Too late to the party to have any positive affect.

We jogged as best we could back into town and were grateful to find the car was still where we had left it, unclamped and without a parking ticket. We clambered in, and Kevin drove while I put Kandava into the satnav. Sure enough, our ETA was eighty minutes.

I called John to let him know about the Nissan and that we were going to follow it up with Gordie. I think he felt we were okay dealing with traffic and just asked to be kept informed.

On the E22 to Kandava, I realized just how comfortable Kevin and I had become in each other's company, reliving events in totally different times associated with Aleysha and Maya. I learned that Maya's preferred distance from Kevin stemmed from an incident on a family holiday in a Spanish villa when they were all young adolescents. There were six adults and eight teenagers ranging from thirteen to seventeen years old. Kevin and two of his mates were the oldest, Aleysha was sixteen, and Maya fifteen. After a pool party that went on late into the evening, Maya had retreated to her room that she shared with Aleysha on the ground floor and showered. While she was in the shower, the three boys moved a table so that they could stand on it and see into Maya's shower. When she realized, she threw a bar of soap at the window, which caught Kevin square in the eye—a fitting punishment which left him with a black eye for the remaining three days of the holiday. Those three days were excruciating for both Kevin and Maya. The incident was embarrassing for Maya, who never mentioned it—not even to Aleysha, as far as Kevin knew. And Kevin could never acknowledge the shame he felt either in front of his mates or to Maya. She had treated him with contempt ever since, and there had never been the occasion for him to make amends when he was able to broach the subject in later life.

'An untreated running sore,' he said with some sadness.

Just outside Kandava, I contacted Gordie for directions. He had just arrived at the scene and guided us in.

As we pulled up a few yards behind the Nissan, my heart was thumping in my chest. I could see in my mind's eye the girls being dragged unceremoniously from the vehicle. But to where? Barring a rundown cafe and the general store whose owner had reported the car because it had been left with the rear passenger door open and an occupant had absconded with an apple, there was nothing. The village was a further half a mile; why stop here?

Gordie strolled over. 'I have a forensic team on the way,' he said. 'There is a blood smear on the rear passenger window and what look like good fingerprints.'

'Did the shop owner see anything?' I ask.

'He was aware of a car pulling up just ahead of the bus but didn't see anything. His daughter, who is only seven, apparently ran out to see if anyone was going to come into the shop as she normally does. She ran back and called to Daddy that the lady had stolen an apple from the display and had run away.'

Kevin, looking inside the Nissan, said, 'Could she describe them?'

'Just that the lady was blonde and pretty, and that she didn't notice anyone else.'

'Okay, that narrows it down,' I said. 'Did she say where they went?'

'She didn't, but by the time she and her dad emerged back outside, the woman had gone, presumably on the bus. This is not a normal bus stop, but the drivers will stop if a passenger asks. I suspect the Nissan driver pulled the bus over with a view to losing any trace there may be on his vehicle.'

'Do we have a registered owner?' Kevin asked.

'Yes, a Ms Gelda Voklof. We haven't been able to trace her yet. There's no one at her flat in Riga; we suspect the car to be stolen.'

The hairs prickled on the back of my neck. 'Has anyone gone into the flat?' I asked.

'She may be at work or something,' Gordie said. 'We don't like breaking and entering without good cause. A suspected unreported stolen car is not a good enough cause.'

'You know what these guys are capable of, right?'

Gordie's radio crackled to life, and he walked away.

Looking around the Nissan, we found was nothing other than the smear that was giving any clues.

'Look,' Kevin said, 'I want to go back to the port and keep an eye out for the *White Angel*. How about you stay with Gordie and see where this goes?'

I was okay with that. I was as nervous as Kevin that they may use the *Angel* as an escape hatch.

Gordie returned. 'Bus drivers have to fill out an incident report when they get back to the depot,' he said. 'The driver of the bus on this route reported that two guys were, in his words, forcibly escorting a fair-skinned young woman with a foreign accent off the bus at Pope.'

'Where's that?' I asked. 'And when?'

'Half an hour from here, and two hours ago. Also, the DNA from the hair in the hotel shower is positive for Aleysha Coombs.'

Just the one woman stuck in my brain. I explained to Gordie that Kevin wanted to return to the port and asked whether it would be okay if I were to tag along with him.

He agreed and said that his boss had agreed that when the *White Angel* docked, our guys would keep an eye on it. Kevin took the car back in the direction of Riga, and we headed for Pope in the fading daylight.

En route, Ron called me and asked about the outcome with the Nissan. I brought him up to date and asked how things were going at Ventspil. He said they had it well set up with security cameras and live feeds to their tablet. They were on the way back to Riga now for their liaison with Kin and Provofz at Barents. John did say he would see whether he could get anything from the task force on Pope, and likely safe houses there.

I felt we were fast running out of useful time today, and Gordie confirmed this after our second pass around the small hamlet of Pope, suggesting that it was probably time to get back. There was nothing that looked out of the ordinary. Gordie had not received any information about potential drug activity in Pope, and I was sure he had a family to get home to, so just after eight we were back on the E22 to Riga.

CHAPTER 40

◇◇◇◇◇◇◇◇◇◇◇◇◇

Kevin parked in the Riga Port Authority car park and was immediately approached by an official waving his hand for him to move on. He got out of the car, at which point the official pulled his jacket back to reveal his weapon, unclipped it from its holster, and put his hand around it. Kevin put up both hands and said, 'Hugo, Ellis, Oliver?'

At this the guard took his hand off the gun and said something undistinguishable.

'English,' Kevin said.

'Wait here,' the guard managed to say as he spoke into his radio. There was a short two-way conversation after which he indicated that Kevin should follow him. They went into the Freeport building that Kevin and I had been in yesterday. Only Ellis was on duty, and he got up from his seat to welcome Kevin. 'Sorry, just me tonight; I have the night shift. Your boat is just docking.' He pointed to where the floodlights were glowing back over Zunds dock. 'We have Policija undercover in the area.'

'Okay, that's good. You might like to send in sniffer dogs before they ship out.'

'It's been cleared before,' Ellis said.

'Yes, I know; I'm just saying it might be worth a recheck.'

Ellis looked at Kevin questioningly.

'Just saying,' Kevin repeated, thinking that he wasn't really sure how much he was allowed to reveal of what John had said earlier.

Kevin asked whether it would be okay if he sauntered over in the general direction of Zunds. Ellis said something to the official still standing in the doorway, who shrugged, which Kevin took as a reluctant agreement.

'I'll come with you,' Ellis said. 'Just let me redirect everything to my phone.'

Ellis grabbed some small binoculars. 'Night vision,' he said.

As they crossed over the Akmens Tils bridge in front of our hotel, they could see two figures on the rear deck of the *White Angel*. Not wanting to raise suspicion, they walked off the bridge in the opposite direction. From the other side of the bridge, and through its arch, they could just see the rear of the vessel. Ellis put the glasses to his eyes.

From behind, Kevin was aware of someone approaching. He tapped Ellis on the shoulder, and he turned round to come face-to-face with what Kevin could only describe as a tramp. *A junkie*, he surmised, *probably after a quick fix*. They exchanged words, and he turned out to be one of the undercover cops. They spoke for a few moments, and then Ellis introduced Kevin to detective Bolg, who said hello in English and asked about his involvement. Kevin explained that the two abducted girls were his cousins and that he wished to help in any way he could to free them from their captors. Bolg's words came out as 'good', and 'you're welcome', but his expression and body language said something completely different.

'Please stay out of the way; we don't want you harmed,' he said.

Kevin turned to Ellis and pointed up at the hotel 'That window up there is our room. We could get a good vantage point from there.'

Bolg became agitated and said, 'You go now.'

Ellis looked through the bridge to see the two were leaving the *White Angel*.

'Okay, you go to your room,' he said. 'I need to get back.'

Kevin went into the lobby of the hotel and disappeared into the shadows of the stairwell, where he could see clearly along the towpath through the picture window. Shortly the two figures came into view, and Kevin was able to get sight of both. *If people can have a gangster look*, Kevin thought, *they certainly have it*.

At that moment, his phone buzzed in his back pocket and made him jump. Pulling it out and turning back towards reception, he could see Erika hurrying in his direction.

'Are you okay, Mr Goodwin?' she said.

'Yes, I'm fine. Excuse me,' he said, putting his mobile to his ear. 'Hi, Greg, how's it going?'

'Where are you?' I ask.

'At the hotel with eyes on the *Angel*. Do you have photo ID of the Kin and Provofz? I think they have just left the *Angel*.'

'Are you following?'

'They have undercover cops on the ground, and I have been instructed to stay out of the way. What are your plans?'

'I'm on the way back with Gordie; I'll see if John can send images across to your computer. Should be back in about half an hour. See you then.'

I touched the speed dial for John. He answered with an abrupt tone 'What.'

I told him that Kevin believed that Kin and Provofz had just left the *White Angel*. He informed me in no uncertain terms that they had and that he knew about it. Their contacts had eyes on them and were keeping them informed minute by minute.

'Please find a bar and get drunk or something,' John said, and he ended the call.

'Like that's going to happen,' I said to myself.

'What?' Gordie asked.

'Nothing, just talking to myself. Do you mind dropping me back at the hotel?'

He smiled as if it were a given.

Gordie pulled the patrol car into the car park at the back of the hotel. I thanked him and said we'd probably catch up in the morning.

Back in our room, Kevin was looking at pictures he had taken of the two characters as they walked away down the towpath.

'Not very useful,' he said. 'But look.' He pulled up some other pictures of the *Angel*. 'I ran this video for around ten minutes just before you got back. I think there are only two other crew members on the craft.'

'That seems doubtful on a vessel that size,' I said.

'I agree, but there is no one on the bridge, and you can see straight through the lounge areas on both levels ... unless they have crew in their cabins, which seems a little unlikely at this time of day.'

'Perhaps we should take a stroll and have a look,' Kevin said.

'Well, I'm certainly not just going to sit here twiddling my thumbs; that's not what we came all this way to achieve,' I said.

We donned our duffel coats.

It was bitterly cold, and a breeze was running down the river, making it even worse. On the walk, we surmised what we thought might be going on. By all accounts, only one of the girls was being held captive in Pope, which meant the other could be back on the *White Angel*, or heading for it either today or tomorrow. As we passed the *Angel*, the two crew were on the rear deck, smoking and drinking vodka. We nodded to them as we passed, but there was no reaction—just a fixed stare. I muted my phone before we left the hotel, and I was aware of it vibrating in my trouser pocket. It was John.

'Are you in any position to get a view of the *White Angel*? We have the task force in position at Ventspil, and the undercover crew are following Provofz and Kin into town. We would just like eyes on the boat if you can. And report any movement.'

'We are on the towpath just north of the *Angel* now. There looks to be a bar about a hundred yards ahead. We'll take up residence there. I'll get back to you.'

'Roger that.'

It was very much a dockers' bar, but there were a couple of tables outside—we assumed for smokers. However, when Kevin went in to get drinks, smoke billowed out around the door as he opened it.

He was back too quickly to have ordered.

'Waiter service,' he said.

'How did you figure that out?'

'Mainly hand signals.'

Right now I was wishing we had brought the camera; the telephoto lens would have been an asset. We could make out the two guys still sat out on the rear deck, and the bottle of vodka was being hit quite hard—to combat the cold, we suspected.

A scrawny fellow with a scrawny beard and bad teeth strolled over to our table.

'Ja.'

With two fingers in the air, Kevin said, 'Divi alus.'

I looked at him. 'What?'

'Ja,' the waiter said, and he walked away.

Kevin showed me his phone screen. 'Good old Google,' he said.

'What do you think you have ordered?' I asked.

'Two beers, I hope.'

This was confirmed a few minutes later when Scrawny returned with two jugs of brown frothing liquid that passed well as beer.

After about an hour and another jug of beer, the two guys on the *Angel* were well into their next bottle of vodka when a third person joined them from somewhere, presumably below deck, pulled up a stool, lit a cigarette, and helped himself to a drink, which he slugged straight back and replaced with an immediate refill. They chatted for a while, and the third man got up and left the boat, heading back in the direction of the hotel.

I moved around the back of the bar as if to go to the gents, just in case we were being watched, and called John.

'Yes,' he answered abruptly.

'There are, as far as we can tell, three guys on the *Angel*, one of which has just left, heading in the direction of town.' Peering around the corner of the building, I could see him still on the towpath, closing on our hotel. I let John know this.

'Is there any way one of you could follow without raising suspicion?' he said.

'Possibly; I'll let you know.'

By the time I got back to Kevin, our man was turning onto the bridge over the river.

'John wants me to follow him,' I said to Kevin. 'I'm going to the front of the bar and down the road that is running parallel to the towpath but behind the brick wall. That'll put me back at the hotel, out of sight of the *White Angel* until I hit the bridge. Can you text me as to which way off the bridge he goes? I'll have lost sight of him by then.'

'Sure. Be careful,' Kevin said.

CHAPTER 41

◇◇◇◇◇◇◇◇◇◇◇◇◇

Ron was established at the restaurant well in advance of the scheduled time with Jenna, one of the English-speaking undercover agents; they were acting as a couple on a date.

John called in a sound check from his car parked down the street, and two of Gordie's sergeants were in a first-floor flat opposite with video and directional sound equipment aimed at Barents' front window.

Back in Bournemouth, Robin, Chris, and Joanne were in the temporary control room along with the technicians. Additional sound checks with John, Ron and the rest of the crew in Riga had been verified. Video feeds from outside the restaurant, the streets around it, and the roving camera at the port, which was now fixed on the *White Angel*, were all clearly displayed on the various monitors. The third man from the *Angel* had been picked up on this camera but had disappeared into a dark camera area on the other side of the bridge. Greg's phone message to John was in text form in a dialogue box in the corner of the large screen, and he, too, had been on video crossing the bridge. Kevin's text message telling Greg that the third man had turned right after leaving the bridge was also displayed under Greg's phone message.

Ron had established, from a sly look at the booking screen when they came in, that there was only one table booked for four people at eight o'clock, and he had managed to get a table that was directly behind and in the window. He was also able to instruct the guys on the cameras which table they would be expected at.

At five minutes to eight, two gentlemen in suits and carrying briefcases arrived at the booking desk and were directed to the reserved table.

Kin and Provofz arrived ten minutes later. Their loose leather jackets could be hiding anything from a Kalashnikov to a bazooka. But as they approached the table, they removed them and placed them over the backs of the chairs. No bazooka. The other two got up with a semi-bow and shook hands. There were no obvious weapons.

After introductions were made and drinks had arrived, Jenna pulled out a small tablet from her handbag, and began to type in English. She and Ron then looked at it as though they were checking out holiday destinations. What she was actually doing was translating what she was getting from her earpiece, which was an audio feed from the directional mic across the street.

Most of the conversation was related to Kin's willingness to supply upwards of a thousand twenty-five-kilo bolts of Turkish fabric. They referred to a catalogue that one of the suits pulled from his briefcase. By the time the main course was completed, they appeared to have an agreement on quantity, type, and stock holding.

There then followed a discussion on payment terms, which Jenna struggled to hear, as their voices were notably lowered, but what she did get was '... discounted secured cash payments deferred by one delivery.' From this they understood it to mean that a delivery would be made and paid for in cash on the next delivery, which would include a discount on the first—of how much she was unable to establish, but they knew they may be able to get more from the recording. There had been nothing so far on why Ron and his team were here.

At this point, a scruffy individual entered the restaurant. While none of the staff were looking, he sidled up to the first table by the window, where two girls were sitting. He said something to the girls, and they both put up their hands and waved him away. He was then at the table of four, touching his baseball cap and in a pleading gesture saying something to Provofz. Kin rose from the table and shouted some Latvian obscenity as the tramp stumbled backwards, grabbing the back of Provofz's chair to prevent him falling over. He grumbled something as he made his way out of the restaurant.

Ron confirmed to his chest mic that the bug had been planted under the lapel of Provofz's jacket.

Robin came back to verify that they had active audio from it and that they were working on filters and levels to clean it up as much as possible. One of the techies also confirmed that they had location as well.

'I would have preferred it to have been on Kin; I think he is the lead,' Ron said quietly into his mic. 'But it wasn't practical.'

He and Jenna continued referring to the tablet, and the four resumed discussions in lowered voices.

The audio from the bug was then relayed to the team in the restaurant.

John returned to the car and stripped off his baseball cap, wig, and beard and discarded them, along with the raincoat. He wired up and asked Ron whether any suspicions had been raised, and he got confirmation that all was well.

Jenna pushed the tablet in front of Ron. 'Look,' she said.

'Provofz: "We need to finish. We have another meeting in twenty minutes with Janek."'

Alarm bells rang, as Ron was under the impression from Gordie and Greg that it was Janek Dvroak who had driven the Nissan and was now in Pope with a possible hostage.

'John,' Ron said quietly to his chest mic, 'this could be who Greg is watching. If so, we need to warn him. Dvorak's reputation is for no warning shots and no loose ends.'

'Roger that,' John said.

CHAPTER 42

Having run around the outside Luntz dock, now somewhat out of breath and thinking that I really needed to get back to circuit training, the bridge was, as expected, devoid of my quarry. But as I walked up the steps, my phone pinged; a text told me he had turned right after leaving the bridge. I set my phone to silent, and as I approached the opposite end of the bridge, looking right over the railings, the path, bathed in a yellow wintry light from sodium lamps, swept slowly left, and I could see a good four hundred yards. Halfway between me and the point at which the path disappeared to hedges on both sides was my mark. Pulling the hood of my duffel coat up, I ventured into a slow but silent jog to narrow the gap. This made me acutely aware of the heavy object bouncing up and down in my inside pocket; to be fair, I was quite thankful for its presence.

At about a hundred yards, I slowed to a brisk walk, and the third man was entering the covered hedge area, which, after another fifty yards, gave way to an avenue of low trees. The sodium lights were being replaced now with white streetlights, but these were well distanced apart. The silhouette of my mark had something familiar about its posture and gait, but I couldn't put my finger on it.

I felt my phone vibrate, and although it was on silent, the buzzing seemed to break through the thick evening air the way it does at a church service when inadvertently left on silent but not switched off as requested.

I looked ahead, spotting no noticeable signs that the third man had picked anything up.

It was a message from John: 'Be aware if you are still following the male from the Angel; it could be Janek Dvroak. He is extremely dangerous. Do not approach under any circumstances. We will tie up with you shortly.'

Janek Dvroak, I thought. *The probable—no, definite—killer of the*

Memshabins. That's where I've seen him before, in the video outside their shop. I looked up from my phone. The path was clear through to the shopping mall on the edge of the dock, some three hundred yards away. *Fuck.* I suddenly felt very exposed. I had no idea where he went, and there were, by now, many dark hiding places where he could be lying in wait. I put the phone to my ear and made as if talking to my wife, using quite loud, excited vocal gestures whilst looking straight ahead and down at the path. Strangely, I actually imagined I was talking to Cat, and I envisaged her responses. I walked on in this fashion for about two or three minutes and came upon a couple of benches, one facing the river and the other with its back to it, where I sat and continued my virtual conversation. There was something mildly therapeutic about this activity, and I wondered why I'd never done it before. I was now able to sit back and look around in apparent obscurity, as though my mind were elsewhere, and to some extent it was.

There were no moving shadows, and no noises beyond that of a distant dog barking and the low motor hum from a boat moored behind me. I continued laughing into my phone, thinking about some of the antics Cat and I would get up to on holiday or with Jet at the beach. It really was an easy conversation and undoubtedly released some of the tension I was feeling. My hand vibrated. It was another message from John. I looked at it as though I had just received a photo from Cat and smiled, forcing a slight chuckle.

'Do you have eyes on?' it said.

'Hold on,' I said out loud. 'I have a photo to show you.' I typed back, 'No, lost him five minutes ago.'

'Stay where you are. Provofz and Kin are heading in your direction, ETA ten minutes. We will be following.'

I put my phone back to my ear and continued to reminisce with Cat while looking aimlessly around.

Back twenty yards towards the bridge was an alley between two old netting huts with what looked like abandoned warehousing abutted up behind. I got up from the bench, still immersed in my virtual discussion with Cat, and ambled along the tow path in that general direction.

Looking out over the river, I casually leant back on one of the small birch trees that put me opposite the alley, and while pretending to look at another imaginary picture on my phone, I turned in the direction of the alley. Halfway between the entrance and a brick wall across the far end where the warehouse presumably started was a set of steps on the left-hand side leading up to, I guessed, a doorway. Out of the corner of my eye I saw a discarded cigarette end flicked from the top of the steps and the fading glow of a door being shut. Odds were it was him, but I had no point of reference—nothing to confirm it.

I decided to take up position back on the outfacing bench, construct a drunken pose, and wait to see who turned up. I texted John to let him know my whereabouts and my suspicions as to where Dvroak, if indeed it was him, may be.

Less than five minutes later, and completely unaware of his presence, I was tapped on the shoulder by the undercover cop Kevin had spoken to earlier. After I jumped from the bench as though I'd just been shot, he casually walked around and sat down.

'Sit,' he said. 'I'm Bolg. You must be the DCI; your colleagues are coming this way.' He looked at my duffel coat. 'Not a very convincing disguise.'

'No, I was not expecting to need one.'

I tried to explain as best I could about the possible third man and the alley.

'We need to move away from here then,' he said. 'This looks too obvious. You head back towards Zunds. I can make myself look scarce around here.'

I wasn't happy about this, but I got his point; spooking them at this stage could be catastrophic. So I moved away down the tow path to the verge of the hedged area, where I tucked into a thicket. Though I had an impaired view, I could see the entrance to the alley, and I saw Bolg behind the covered railings of an empty moored boat.

A few minutes later, two heavyset individuals came into view. They were scanning as they went and slowed down on approach to the alley. They virtually walked backwards into the alley and disappeared.

Kevin texted to say that three crew had returned to the *Angel*; two of them were in the bar, and the other had joined from further up the river. All three were on the bridge of the *Angel*, which was now lit up as though they were preparing for departure.

I forwarded this text to John, who came back again with 'Roger that.'

CHAPTER 43

The pressure in the control room at the station was intense. The technicians were skipping between cameras to do their level best to keep Kin and Provofz in the shot and update the team on the ground of anything that might be useful. Rupert had been on the phone almost constantly with his Latvian counterpart, and Chris, Phil, and Jo watched the main screen, which was currently showing the location of the bug that Provofz was carrying. It also showed a ping from Greg's phone that right now was virtually on top of the bug.

The texts from both Kevin and Greg continued to scroll down on the left-hand side.

Another text from Kevin to Greg appeared under the last: 'The two guys from rear deck are leaving the Angel and coming in your direction.'

This was immediately forwarded from Greg to John.

Joanne texted Greg to warn him of what had just come in and was immediately embarrassed to see her text appear on the screen in front of her.

Chris looked at her in sympathy but realized she was probably going to get some strife from Rupert.

Rupert looked up at the screen. 'For fuck's sake, Jo, don't be stupid; your phone is not encrypted.'

Jo suddenly wished the floor would open up. 'Sorry, sir,' she said.

Rupert, shaking his head, reopened the mic to John and put on a headset. 'John, what's your status? ... I know ... yes ... she's one of the team here, mate; sorry, it won't happen again ... Yes, yes I've logged it ... Okay, John, I've got it.' He glared at Joanne, who got up and left the room.

At this point, one of the small monitors that had remained blank stuttered into life. Rupert took off the headset and sat in front of it. A young blonde-haired woman appeared on the screen. 'Hi, Rupe. Bad news, I'm afraid. Thames House have just picked up a radio message that we believe emanated from the *White Angel* north of Riga. It read, "Possible Rigan police involvement, bring forward to 00.00." Which obviously means that they are now on high alert.'

'Okay, we are closing in on a location in the dock area, but we are fairly sure one of our hostages is held somewhere in a village called Pope. Can you get satellite coverage of any outlying buildings? I don't think they would be held up anywhere central. Our problem now is that Pope is close to two hours away from the team's current position.'

'I'll see what I can do.' The screen went blank.

Rupert looked directly at Chris and, switching his gaze between him and Jo, said, 'Sorry Chris, but this is not a game. The team is about to go into an area they have no intel on. Not surprising that John is working on a short fuse; the last thing he needs is his own side throwing a curveball. Add to that, that they have a coalition of three operatives going in; their only ace in the hole is that of surprise. Three on three, they should always come out on top, but potentially there are another two opposition heading into the arena, which skews our advantage.'

'I do understand,' Chris said. 'We are a close family here too. I'm sure Joanne had no intention to upset any plans. She'll be devastated.'

'Yeah, well, I'll let you tell John that. Look, go and get her back; we need all the eyes we have on these monitors.'

Phil left and returned shortly with Joanne in tow.

'Sorry, sir,' Joanne repeated to both Chris and Rupert.

Rupert nodded an acknowledgment, and Chris winked. She sat down in front of the bank of monitors and gathered her composure.

One thing you learn early at police college is to put any failures immediately behind you. Learn and move on; if failures fester, they will affect future performance.

One of the technicians flicked the combined sound switch to speakers. The room came alive with at least three voice sources. John was heard saying that he needed the two incoming neutralized before they proceeded. Another voice with an accent called for Bolg to provide backup, and there was acknowledgment of that.

CHAPTER 44

◇◇◇◇◇◇◇◇◇◇◇◇◇

I could hear footsteps coming from the other end of the hedged area and hunkered down well into the undergrowth. About thirty yards short of my position, they veered right through a gap in the hedge and disappeared. I surfaced from my hiding place and ventured out to the edge of the path, still securing some cover. I immediately texted John to say that the two guys from the *Angel* had turned off the path about three hundred yards before the alley. I got no response this time but felt a vibrated pulse to indicate the text had been seen.

I suddenly became aware of a commotion building behind me and saw three dark figures run into the alley and Bolg moving across the green from his previous position on the boat. The three disappeared up the alley while Bolg stayed in wait at the entrance.

⟨ↂↂↂ⟩

Chris watched as texts and phone messages continued down the screen as the operation moved to a critical stage. One of the monitors previously showing a street view flashed into active life with a live stream from John's headcam. Chris thought it looked uncannily like a scene from *Call of Duty* as John ran down the alley and up the steps. Tension in the control room was tangible, with everybody leaning forward in anticipation, hopeful of seeing one or both girls safe.

From the left of John's camera, someone, presumably Ron, volleyed a ram into the door lock handle, which splintered, and the door flew open, flooding the camera with white light. For a few seconds there were no visuals but just the intimidating shouts from what sounded like an army of intruders. The camera came back to life, and a smoke stream spiralled down a long corridor, followed by a bright light, taking the camera out again. Then came a loud explosion.

Joanne noticed that the Provofz bug and Greg's phone pinged virtually together on the large screen but began to separate as Greg moved away from the alley.

∽◉∽

Less than a minute later, I heard shouting followed by an explosion from, I'm guessing, a flash-bang. To my relief, I heard no shots fired; but shortly after, I heard a disturbance back along the path in the direction of the bridge. The two guys from the *Angel* burst back through the hedge, dragging a limp body, which I was convinced was Maya.

'Stop—armed police!' I yelled, dragging out the Glock and waving it in their general direction, untangling myself from the undergrowth.

Maya fell to the ground as they both dropped her, turned around in unison, and unloaded several rounds of suppressed automatic fire down the pathway. I crumple back into the hedgerow. Fortunately for me they had a streetlamp directly in front of them, and I can only assume I was still well hidden in the shadows of the hedge, as the shots passed by and buried themselves in the path further down towards the alley. I also heard what sounded like a single shot some way off, and not silenced, which seemed to come from behind my assailants.

I recovered myself from a near foetal position, waiting for the pain of further shots, and looked out to see the two figures turn back to the bundle on the floor.

In a single move, they gathered Maya up and proceeded to run, with her feet barely touching the ground. She flopped like a rag doll, but I could detect some resistive movement from her. I was running now, down the path towards the sodium lights, and as I broke out of the hedged area, I could see them, two hundred yards, maybe less, ahead. I had the Glock firmly planted in my right hand. I realized I hadn't released the safety lock earlier. Always good to be prepared! I lifted my arm in their direction, aware that there was no way I could fire at this range, but I shouted out any way and fired a shot high in the air. They slowed to a walk. The hulk on the left of Maya put his arm around her back and took the weight while the other turned round in my direction. I piled left and took some cover

224

from one of the sodium lamp pedestals as I saw muzzle fire. The man was shooting from the hip. Lumps of turf and stones exploded around me, and I heard him shout something.

I moved out, and in my head I was screaming, '*Give me a safe shot!*' But they were all but in line down the path. The one who had fired spun round and fired one last blast, and I heard the click of the firing pin in an empty chamber. Turning back, he quickly caught up and resumed running, with Maya slung between them. I followed, but I was aware that they still had one loaded automatic, so I dodged from lamppost to tree. I speed-dialled Kevin to warn him, but there was no answer.

'Fuck, Kevin, they're heading in your direction.' I hit the button again. Still nothing. Because of my deviation, I was losing ground. Maya's feet were now dragging heavily along the path as they rattled up the steps of the bridge. Once on the bridge, I lost sight but knew I could make up ground, and I ran as fast as I could to the bridge entrance. I looked behind in hopes of seeing the extraction crew, but there was nothing. I called John.

'Not now, Greg.'

'Maya's being dragged back to the *Angel*,' I managed to say between grabbing gasps of air. I heard him shout about grips and ties, and the line went dead.

ᏬᎲᏑ

Virtually everyone in the room stood up together as Greg's phone message came over the loudspeaker.

'John, did you get that?' Rupert said.

'Affirmative, but we need to secure this scene; we have two heavily armed assailants neutralized, but there may be others.'

'There are,' Rupert said aggressively, 'and they are getting away with one of your targets. Wrap it up!'

ᏬᎲᏑ

Clearing the steps on the dock side of the bridge and looking through the railings, they were coming up on the *Angel*. There was no sign of Kevin. In the distance I could just see the bar, and there was no one outside. I felt, along with other emotions, agitation build up inside me, thinking he was

225

probably getting another beer, practising his Latvian. By the time I was across the covered part of the bridge and to the steps on the far side, they had disappeared aboard the boat. I was surprised not to hear her engines roar, but I could also see that her mooring ropes were still in place over the dock bollards. This gave me hope, and I ploughed on in the shadow of, and against, the wall on the left-hand side that I had skirted earlier, in an almost crouched position, as I was now very exposed. Other than some bales of rope and mooring bollards, there was nothing to hide behind. As I approached the *Angel*, I could hear raised foreign voices, demanding in tone, and I envisaged them being directed at an almost unconscious Maya.

I looked around for any sort of support, but there was none. *God only knows where Kevin is.* Hitting the call button to Kevin for the third time produced his voice message. *Why would he turn his phone off? Unless he is also in trouble.* I couldn't process that now, so I pushed on.

I ventured gingerly onto the gangplank. Fortunately, a vessel this size was not going to be affected in any way by my weight, and I padded onto the rear deck noiselessly. There was still a half bottle of vodka on the low-level table, and the urge to take some Dutch courage was almost overpowering. Instead I passed it by and moved cautiously towards the voices. The sound was immediately in front of me, and as I looked through the porthole window in the lounge door, I saw the heads of the two thugs who had walked on with Maya bobbing around aggressively.

I crept up to the door, which would be latched in transit but was swinging slightly with the natural rock of the boat, allowing me glimpses of the interior. To my absolute shock, I saw Kevin on the opposite side of the lounge with his back to a spiral staircase leading to the upper deck and bridge, holding a blonde guy in a white shirt round the neck with a Glock pointed at his temple. I pushed the door slightly, with my Glock extended, and saw Maya, who was now just about supporting her own weight, but she was being held in the same position as White Shirt, with an automatic stuck in her kidneys.

The next few seconds passed by as though in slow motion.

Firstly, Kevin caught a glimpse of me through the now partially open lounge door. His microexpression was picked up by the guy holding Maya, who threw her to the floor and swung round the Heckler & Koch and pointed it my direction. A gunshot went off from across the room, and

White Shirt fell to the floor. Kevin, unaware that we had one empty semi-automatic, was in full flight across the lounge as he fired twice into the guy facing me. My mind was flying, trying to work out whether he had had the time or chance to replace the magazine. I decided he hadn't, and I was immediately rewarded by a repeat of the sound I had picked up earlier, just before he collapsed in a heap in front of me. I focused my weapon on gorilla number two, who raised his weapon in the direction of Maya, who was now prostrate on the floor of the lounge.

Kevin's attention, as was mine, was then fully on the remaining target. Up close, a giant of a man, expressionless, he looked me defiantly, straight in the eye, and I could sense his finger on the trigger, his weapon aimed directly at Maya. I put two shots centre core, and Kevin, still running forward, sent another two in the same general direction. The gorilla stumbled backwards and wrapped himself around the spiral staircase, but not before a short blast was released from his automatic. Kevin's selfless run ended in a dive that encapsulated Maya almost completely, and he caught the remaining 9mm shot destined for Maya's back through his upper left shoulder. The target was still scrabbling, now on the floor, trying to bring his weapon round in our direction. He took two more to the chest from my Glock and sprawled out on his back. There was silence for a second as I took in the situation. That silence was immediately shattered by another three rounds from the doorway. Bolg, in classic firing pose, took out White Shirt, who had managed to grab the Heckler & Koch from the floor.

Kevin, moaning and writhing in agony, rolled off Maya and leant himself up against a lounge bench. I knelt down and gathered Maya in my arms. Her tense body was wired and shaking. She first looked at me, completely dazed and in shock, and then at Kevin. I felt some of the tension leave her body and laid her on one of the sofas.

Kevin, through gritted teeth, said there were two others tied up on the bridge. 'I shot out the control panel, hoping it would render the *Angel* dead in the water, so to speak,' he said. His head flopped back on the bench seat, blood now seeping through his duffel coat.

'Don't worry, buddy; we'll get you sorted out,' I said, more in hope than belief.

Just then the commander burst in, weapon raised, followed by Ron in the same pose. Taking in the scene, they holstered their weapons, called for paramedics, and moved towards Kevin, him being the one looking the most in need of attention.

'There are two others still on the bridge,' I said to Ron. 'Kevin has tied them up, but I haven't checked.'

Ron nodded across at Bolg, pointed to the stairway, and headed off with him in tow.

John injected Kevin with something, and his head rolled into an almost upright position. He shone a light into both eyes and then peeled back his coat to reveal a blood-soaked jumper, which he cut open with a knife. He stuffed a small wadding tube, the size of a tampon, into the wound. Kevin shuddered as the pain shot through him, and John asked me to keep my hand on the wadding until the paramedics arrived. He got up and checked on the others. After he confirmed all three were dead, he proceeded up the spiral stairs.

Maya was still taking it all in; tears were running down her cheeks, and her shoulders rocked in rhythm with a gentle sob, borne out of relief as much as anything else. Kevin grabbed my hand with more strength than I thought he had in him. 'Greg, go and get Aleysha for me; I can hold this damn thing in. Nothing is going to happen to Maya now. The BMW is in the hotel car park.' He handed me the key. 'And … I don't think they will be taking her to the airport; it's too clumsy, and they are not stupid. There is a marina at Ventspil, and it would be far easier for them to get a clean getaway from there, particularly in a vessel with a faulty transponder.'

'The other *White Angel*?' I asked.

'Probably. Now go, before action man gets back.'

He awkwardly gathered his Glock from the floor and reached into his coat pocket with his good arm, pulled out two magazines and a box of .38 shells, and stuffed them in mine. With that, he let his head lean back.

I moved across to hold Maya's hand and look at her. Some colour was returning, but she still looked vacant and lost. My heart went out to her, and I hated the thought of leaving her, but I realized she had overheard Kevin. She squeezed my hand. 'Go; I'll be fine,' she said.

I kissed her on the cheek and exited the lounge.

Looking back from the tow path, I could see that the three guys were still on the bridge.

The BMW was frozen up again, but I had no time to wait for the heater to do its stuff, so the Amex card came out again, and I scratched a peephole in the front screen and set off.

I knew my way to the E22 and drove there as fast as I could. It was a little disorientating driving at speed with impaired visibility on streets that may or may not be icy, and on the right-hand side of the road. I was also very conscious that my left hand was sticky from Kevin's blood, which felt uncomfortable on the wheel. Once on the E22, I checked the POI in the satnav for boating. There it was—Ventspil Osta. I only hoped that Kevin was right. It had just gone 11.00, and my ETA was 12.39. By all accounts, I would be thirty-nine minutes too late.

I called Gordie and hoped he had not gone to bed yet.

'Ja.'

'Gordi, it's Greg. Sorry it's so late; do you have any patrols around Ventspil?'

'We have a couple on shift close by. I have one patrolling around Pope for any suspicious activity.'

'We think they may be extracting via the marina at Ventspil. Can you get one of them to check out for a vessel similar to, or the same as, the *White Angel*?'

'It's a free dock there,' he said, 'there are no port regulations. "Pay as you go", I think you call it in the UK, so no records.'

'That makes sense,' I said. 'I'll be there in under an hour; I might like some backup if that's at all possible.'

'I'll get one of my team to the marina. Unfortunately, both officers out there have limited English. I'll set up a relay between us, where they contact me, and I'll forward to you.'

'Thanks, Gordie, that's kind of you.'

'It's okay. I'm not sleepy anyway, but I will put the vodka away.'

The E22 was thankfully reasonably straight and quiet, and I was making good time. Even though the voice in my head was telling me to relax, the tension in my shoulders was coalescing into a physical ache and was in danger of impacting my concentration. I flashed past the general store at Kandava at just short of 150 kph.

The map in the centre dash console went black for a moment and was replaced with a large phone symbol and a muffled ringtone. It was John calling me.

I press the off-hook button on the steering wheel and eased my foot off the accelerator a little.

'Where do you think you're going?' he barked.

'We—that is, Kevin and I—think Aleysha is going to be removed by boat, possibly on the other *Angel* from the marina at Ventspil, not the airport.'

'And you were going to share this with me when?'

'Sorry, but we are running out of time, and I don't have to jump through hoops like you do to put a plan together and coordinate a team. I'm thirty-five minutes away, according to the satnav, which means I'll make it in half that time if you get off the phone.'

'A team plan is how we keep everyone safe,' he said with a degree of sarcasm. 'We're on our way. Please keep me informed, Greg.'

I pressed the on-hook button on the steering wheel, and the screen reverted to the map, showing I had fifty kilometres to go. It was 11.55. By my reckoning, I'd be there at a quarter past twelve. I could only hope that they would be late and that somewhere between here and there *I* would formulate a plan—ironically the very thing that John would have already had in place by now.

CHAPTER 45

◇◇◇◇◇◇◇◇◇◇◇◇◇◇

'Greg?'

'Yes, Gordi.' He was on hands-free, so I assumed he was heading to Ventspil. 'What do we have?'

'There *is* an Amels-55 anchored just outside the marina, but there are any number of other vessels moored up. My man on the dockside has swapped his patrol car for his own and is parked up just outside the main entrance.'

'He knows what he's looking for?' I said.

'Yes, men with at least one, probably reluctant women.'

'Definitely just the one woman; Maya is now secured. Is he alone? These men are dangerous.'

'He is right now, but he will be joined shortly by my other officer, and they are armed. How is Maya?'

'She'll be fine, very shook up. What car am I looking for, and your officer's names?'

'It's a cream Citroën. Jan is there now; Petor will be joining him.'

'Thanks again, Gordie. I should be there within the next ten minutes, if you can let your officers know.'

I called John and filled him in about the Amels-55 and the backup we had on the dock side. He was never going to sound impressed, but at least he was not biting my head off.

It was 12.08 as I entered the outskirts of Ventspil, and Gordie called me again.

'Put 48 Krona iela in to your satnav,' he said. 'You'll see the Citroën in the lay-by at the end of the service road. My guys have just reported that a dinghy has been launched from the Amels. Where are you?'

'Just coming through the town,' I said, fiddling with the satnav. I got the address in, and I was less than a kilometre away.

'A couple of minutes,' I said. 'Is a BMW going to stick out?' I asked.

'Stick out? Sorry … explain?'

'Will it look out of place here in Ventspil?'

'Oh, no, there are a few expensive yachts that moor there rather than suffer the congestion of Riga. Their owners will have executive cars.'

'Okay, thanks. I think I can see the Citroën up ahead.' I crossed a railway line embedded into the tarmac—remnants of an earlier time when this port was more active, I suspected—and switched off the headlights as I coasted quietly towards the lay-by.

Inside the Citroën were two individuals: the driver had binoculars directed through the gap in the harbour walls of the marina; the other was looking straight at me.

I looked right, towards the harbour entrance, and If I hadn't known better, I would have said it was the *White Angel* out there in the ghostly glow emitting from the marina tower lights.

Pulling up in front of the Citroën, I avoid flashing my lights in favour of a raised hand to the windscreen. The passenger nodded, and I got out and walked across. The driver put down the binoculars, got out, and offered me his hand.

'Jan,' he said, and he pointed with his other hand towards his colleague in the car. 'Petor.'

'Pleased to meet you, and thanks for your help,' I said, doubting they understood.

'Good,' Petor said from inside the car, and he indicates for us to get in.

'Your hand?' Jan said. Looking at my blood-soaked left hand.

I rocked my head. Under the circumstances, it was way too long a story to tell, so I settled on waving my hands to suggest it was nothing. 'It's okay,' I said, and Jan leant across and took out a box of baby wipes from the glove compartment and passed them back.

The wet towels did the trick, and from the odd word and pointing gestures from the two of them, I got that the orange dinghy tied up three pontoons across from us was the one from the *Angel*. There were two men in dark trousers, overcoats, and what looked like trilbies from where we sat, with their collars pulled up against the cold wind. Jan offered me the binoculars, which brought them into focus, and I got a good look at both their faces—no one I recognized. But I did feel relief that, by all accounts, they hadn't yet got Aleysha away.

'I'm going to walk along the dock front,' I said, passing back the wipes and making a walking motion with my finger and pointing to my chest.

'We follow,' Jan said. I nodded, smiled, and peeled myself out of the back of the Citroën. The two individuals from the dinghy were loitering at the end of the pontoon, smoking, and looking around. There were plenty of dark alleys and doorways along this rear section of the dock, so remaining hidden at this stage was no real problem for the three of us. I wanted to get a good triangulated formation around the marina entrance so that we could at least try to cover all eventualities. I pointed to what looked like a concrete bus shelter on the other side of the main entrance, with raised barriers attached that look as though they had not been in use for many years. I let them know that that was where I was heading; that Jan should remain here on the left-hand point, just short of the entrance; and that Petor should take a position the other side of the booth on the centre reservation, between the incoming and outgoing marina roads.

From my vantage point, I could see the street leading away in both directions. There was no traffic and only one other car visible, parked on the brow of the hill to my right. I had a clear view through a hole in the back of the shelter to the pontoon. The two guys out there were simply pacing around to keep warm. A blue glow lit up one of their faces—a message or a call on his mobile, I suspected.

Whatever it was that lit them up, the 'Blues Brothers' on the pontoon were suddenly agitated and began to walk towards the marina entrance slowly but deliberately, scanning as they went.

I felt my phone vibrate and looked down to see a black screen with just 'John calling' on it in small text. I placed it to my ear.

'Can you talk?'

'Quietly,' I said.

'We have just intercepted a call from the Rigan peninsula, about ten miles from your current location. It was in Russian and simply said, "first parcel catastrophic. Second parcel on its way 1245."'

I looked at my watch; it was now 12.35. 'Where are you?' I asked in a whisper.

'At best we are thirty minutes away. What have you got?'

'Two men on the dockside heading our way slowly with a dinghy ready to head back to the *White Angel*-2. I have two armed officers, and we have the marina entrance covered. Covered for what, I'm not entirely sure.'

'I gather from Kevin that you are armed?'

'Yes,' I said somewhat sheepishly—not knowing why, given the current circumstances.

'Be careful; it's been three years since you had any firearms training.'

'I'm hoping it won't be necessary.'

'If you can hold things up or delay proceeding until we get there, that would be for the best.'

I got a flash of inspiration at the word 'delay'. What if I could get to their dinghy and achieve what Kevin did with *White Angel*-1?

Closing the phone, I signalled to Petor that I was going to go around the back of this section of the marina, behind the row of wooden huts, which would put me two pontoons further up from the dinghy. I could work my way back from there in the shadow of the huts.

I moved silently away from the shelter, and as I did so, I hear a car door close some way off behind me. I hoped Petor or Jan had that covered.

I rounded the end of the walkway and looked from the shadows down the row of pontoons, and there, twenty yards down, was the orange motor launch, which was much larger than it had looked from my previous viewing point. A further thirty yards or so were the Blues Brothers, still looking edgy while facing the marina entrance, but still looking left and right. They seemed to have stopped well short of the entrance as though in wait for further instructions.

I moved down towards the dinghy wishing I had John's knife, as this would have been the silent way to scuttle the craft. Even with a silencer (which I didn't have), the Glock would still be heard above the wind gusting across the harbour. Without one, it was going to wake the neighbourhood. Another option came to mind—I could untie it and push it out, hoping it didn't get drawn back in by the light swell. A motor noise coming from my right caught my attention, and I looked out towards the harbour entrance to see a large fishing vessel passing the end of the pontoon. For a minute I debated calling out, but I immediately dismissed it. The single occupant was not looking in my direction, and I couldn't see such an action providing anything other than further confusion.

Decision made, I decided to untie the dinghy and walk it as quietly as I could to the far end of the pontoon and let it go into the open area of the marina. Creeping up and staying low, I reached the dinghy. From there I could crouch down under the cover of the craft while I untied the front from its mooring hitch. Once I had it free, I realized it was a lot heavier than I had anticipated. In reality, this was not a four-man dinghy that would be used for transporting fishermen to and from their vessel, but a centre-console rigid inflatable with inboard motor and capacity for at least eight passengers—or, more likely, contraband. Just moving it away from the edge, from my current position, was an effort. Moving it twenty yards to the end of the pontoon from a crouching position was going to be a mammoth task. Looking over the bow, I saw they were still there, looking away from me. As I gingerly and silently untied the rear mooring, I could see where Jan was, but by all accounts, he was invisible. I decided I was going to have to haul it, which was not going to be achievable unless I stood. I did so with slow, deliberate caution. Thankfully, there were no creaking pontoon boards. Also, there was no key in the ignition of the centre console—another option scuppered.

Progress along the pontoon was painfully slow, and I managed to get about halfway before a wave from the swell of the passing launch flowed in and swung the dirigible out, causing a clockwise motion that sent the rear section thudding into the side of the decking. The Blues Brothers both turned round, and I dropped back into the cover of the boat. But I was too late; suppressed shots were fired high over my head, presumably in avoidance of the vessel. I heard them running along the dockside. I could ill afford for them to get too close. If they reached the end of the pontoon, I would have no cover at all. Flicking the safety off the Glock in my right-hand pocket and levelling it over the bow of the dinghy, I fired a round low and between them, splintering planking directly in front of them. They drew up to a halt as I ducked below the bow. Right now I had more cover than they did, and my cover was their get-away vehicle, which I was sure they were not in a hurry to scuttle. I fired off another couple of warning shots, which sent them scurrying for cover.

In my peripheral vision, I saw headlights coming down the road on the far side of the marina. The Blues Brothers were now in the shadows of the fisherman's huts but still visible to me. Looking right, towards the entrance, I saw a silhouette of someone moving up the dock, also in the shadow of the first huts. This was neither Jan or Petor, but his outline and movements looked familiar. *Gordie?* The car, a Nissan, pulled into the marina entrance and parked equidistant between the marina barrier and the two goons hiding in the shadows.

At this point I didn't want to raise any alarm that might cause them to turn around and drive out. However, events took a turn that was out of my control, as the two suits dived out of cover, waving their arm at the vehicle.

The driver got out cautiously, and I could hear shouting between them. He proceeded to get back in. Three shots rang out, and the left-hand side of the Nissan collapsed as two of the tyres were taken out by Petor, who was also shouting. I saw an H&K levelled in Petor's direction from the leading Blues Brother. I had no choice and fired two aimed shots. He crumpled to the ground, and the weapon spun away. The second turned round to face me. He obviously had no further concern for the dinghy and released a burst of fire in my direction. I felt a searing burning sensation in my left upper thigh as I dived back behind the dinghy and realized it was now drifting away from the edge of the pontoon. I made a lunge for it as another burst ripped through the rubber outer shell, releasing a blast of compressed air. I managed to scrabble on board and wrap myself around the back side of the centre console. My thinking was that the inboard motor, located under this raised portion, might give some protection—up to the point, that is, when it sank, of course.

A third extended report from the H&K splintered the fibreglass of the bow section, sending a violent shudder through the boat. I became aware of water gushing in around my hip. I was also trying to block out the pain from my opposite thigh. At this point I had no idea what I was dealing with here, but barring the pain, my leg was working okay. Two more shots embedded themselves forward of my position, and then I heard the click of another empty weapon. Taking my chance, I grabbed the second Glock from my other pocket and released the safety. I then knelt with both arms extended and sent two 9mm bullets in his direction. Both met their target, in the upper right and upper left chest, flinging him brutally backwards into the shadows of the wooden huts like an oversize puppet with its strings cut.

The Nissan's engine revved violently, and I was aware of a single shot having been fired somewhere around the entrance. My overriding concern was that Aleysha was probably in the thick of it, and I worried for her safety, but my lunge on to what was left of the dirigible pushed it even further from the pontoon, and jumping back was no longer an option. As it was quite obviously sinking and I was already soaked, I took to the water and dragged myself, with difficulty, up onto the boardwalk. My left leg, though operational, was going into spasms with the pain, and I was walking towards the dock as though being tasered every other step.

The Nissan was in full retreat in reverse, but because all of the tyres barring one were now deflated, it buried itself in the front wall of the first hut. The front passenger door was flung open, and the silhouette hiding there immediately dashed out, kicking the passenger door shut with such force that the glass shattered. He grabbed the rear passenger door, swung it wide, and leant in, and I saw my first glimpse of Aleysha's profile. He grabbed her and unceremoniously dragged her out of the vehicle.

Jan was closing on the back of the Nissan, and I saw his weapon raised. A flash appeared from the muzzle as the rear window exploded and blood was sprayed on the front windscreen from inside. Aleysha was bundled to the ground by her assailant, and they both disappeared from my view behind the passenger door. I was now less than ten crippling yards from the vehicle, and the two guys in the front seats, having ducked when the window blew in, now swung round with their weapons, moving towards Jan and Aleysha.

There was no time to think. The driver had moved further around the 180-degree arc he needed to travel to line up with Aleysha rather than the passenger, so I fired the Glock in my right hand, which was aimed at the driver, low of the windscreen, ensuring any deflection by the glass would only move the bullet from chest to head, and not head to roof. My left hand let off two shots in the general direction, but my right realigned on the passenger. *Goodnight.* The inside of the Nissan became a very unpleasant place to be in less than a couple of seconds. I raced over, as best I could, to where Aleysha was being shielded against the rear wheel of the Nissan. Her cover looked up and around cautiously before getting to his knees, and I realized the familiar silhouette to be that of DI James Powel. *How... when ...*

I fell to my knees and grabbed them both, pulled them towards me, and hugged them as I have never hugged anyone in my life. We were all sobbing for what seemed like minutes when Aleysha finally said, 'Can someone get this bloody cable tie from my wrists?' To hear her voice again aroused so many emotions inside me, which I'm sure were compounded by the comedown from the adrenalin high and the loss—looking at the pool that was developing on the ground to my left side—of blood. Collapsing back against the Nissan, Jan walked around the vehicle and quickly checked the inside before kneeling beside me and opening my coat.

'You not okay?' he said, looking at my blood-soaked trousers and pressing his hand hard in the general area of the wound.

Petor walked across on his phone, calling for the paramedics. He pulled out a knife from his belt and freed Aleysha from her ties. She and James then stood up. She turned towards him; gave him a very long, intense hug; and said, 'Thank you. Thank you so much, James.' She then came and sat down on the other side of me.

'So what have you been up to while I've been away? Can't leave you for a minute, can I,' she said, running her finger along the scab on my chin.

'You're one to talk; you look a wreck,' I replied.

She smiled. 'Let me do that,' she said to Jan, replacing his hand with hers.

I could feel her probing to find the entry point, and I juddered violently when she found it. A few seconds later, she also found the exit.

'That's good,' she said.

'Doesn't feel so good.'

'Well, at least it saves time later digging around looking for it.'

CHAPTER 46

◇◇◇◇◇◇◇◇◇◇◇◇◇

Maya woke feeling fuzzy, but the fear that had gripped her for the past days, which seemed like weeks, had subsided. The room was bright but furnished in comfortably warm colours. Looking around, she saw there was a jug of water and a tumbler on the side stand. She sat up, leaning on her elbow, and poured herself a glass.

'Aleysha!' she whispered to herself. Where was Aleysha? She hadn't seen her since they were moved to the dock house. How had Greg managed to find her, and what the hell was Kevin doing there? Her memory of the previous evening was blurred, but she clearly remembered someone, and it must have been Kevin, lunging on top of her, and feeling the shudder in his body as a gun exploded above her.

The door opened, and a nurse came in rolling a machine in front of her. She smiled on seeing her awake.

'Good day, Maya. Or do you say Miya?'

'May-a, but it is spelt M-eye-a,' she said.

A brief look of confusion came back from the nurse, as this probably didn't compute in basic English-to-Latvian translation.

'How are you feeling?'

'How's Mr. Goodwin?' Maya asked, ignoring the question.

'Oh, Mr Kevin is in intensive care at the moment, but his operation went well, I believe.'

'Can I see him?'

'Not yet, but ask your consultant when she comes; she will be here soon.'

The nurse piped Maya up to a machine which showed her heart rate, blood pressure, temperature, and oxygen levels to be normal. She noted the readings down in a file and clipped it to the side of an X-ray light box on the wall.

'Who can I speak to about what happened?' Maya asked the nurse.

'You need to talk to your consultant first; I will tell her you are not sleeping.'

'Thanks.'

With that she left the room and closed the door.

Maya was left trying to recall the events leading up to her being dragged back on to the yacht she had been hauled off of days earlier.

She remembered being locked in a room when they first arrived at the dock house, and her screaming and banging on the door for Aleysha. There was an abrupt response when the door burst open and one of the thugs growled something at her, slapped her across the face, and pushed her face down on the bed. With his knee in her back, he injected her in the buttocks with something. The next thing she could recall was hearing explosions, maybe gunfire. She seemed to be lying on the ground, a tarmac path, and was then dragged between two men across a bridge.

She recollected that the gangplank to the boat was too narrow for the three of them, and she was pushed ahead, barely able to keep her balance. Adrenalin was probably the only thing keeping her upright. As they continued to push her through the saloon doors to the lounge, she saw someone holding what she remembered to be a crewman, an arm round his neck and a gun pushed to his head. At that point, she was unaware of his identity. Only when he spoke to say to the two guys behind her that the boat was disabled and they should put down their weapons and that an armed response was on its way did she realize, with astonishment, who it was.

But before his sentence was complete, she was grabbed around the neck herself and felt a searing pain in her lower back as what she guessed to be a gun was pushed into her kidneys.

The door opened again, and a young woman in uniform entered.

'Miss Coombs, I'm Dr Vernon,' she said with a mild American accent. 'How are you feeling? You have had a rather bad experience, I understand'?

'Yes, but I don't feel bad—physically anyway.' She could feel she had an involuntary tremor throughout her body, and it reverberated in her voice.

'Right. Do you feel okay to answer some questions? There are people outside who are desperate to talk to you, but I need to be sure you are up to it.'

'Yes, I'm fine. Let's get on with it, can we?'

What followed was twenty minutes of multiple-choice questions to establish what level of trauma the events of the last few days had inflicted on her. By the end, she was remarkably calm, and the shaking had subsided, though in reality whether the effects of the chlorzoxazone administered by paramedics at the dock had fully worn off was up for debate. Either way, the doctor agreed that, barring being a little dehydrated, she was in good health. The doctor told her to relax, to have something to eat, and to drink plenty of water.

'When can I see Mr Goodwin,' she asked, 'and Aleysha?'

'He is still suffering the effects of the anesthetic, so maybe later this evening.' She left as another nurse entered with a tray of vegetable soup and another jug of water.

The soup was probably the first thing to pass her lips since they left the Opera Hotel and was delightful.

The door opened slightly, and Maya looked up to see her sister standing there. The tray was flung to the floor along with the empty soup bowl, beaker, and jug of water as she bounded off the bed and they both fell into each other's arms. They were silent for quite some time, immersing themselves in the deep relief that they were now allowing themselves to feel.

'Did you know Greg and Kevin were here?' Maya asked as they both settled on the edge of the bed.

'Not until last night. Do you remember James Powell?' Aleysha said.

'Wasn't he the detective that got you into all that trouble some time ago?'

'I may have to rethink that. James dragged me out that old Nissan while Greg and some local bobbies proceeded with a gunfight at the O.K. Corral. They wiped out three of the thugs that were at the dock house, along with another two goons who were waiting to take me to god knows where.'

They hugged again as the realization that they had survived what they had been through hit them.

'Seems like we both have some re-evaluation to do. Kevin saved my life, for sure, and I haven't spoken to him for eight years, all over a childish prank.'

'I think, among a lot of other things, this has taught me some salutary life lessons,' Aleysha said.

'I agree,' Maya said. 'Where is Greg, by the way?'

'He's in a ward two down from Kevin. he took a bullet to the leg. Straight through, so he'll be fine. He's sleeping it off at the moment. The surgeon finished sewing him up around six o'clock this morning.'

They looked at each other as only siblings can.

'We made it, Aley.'

'I know; it was touch and go there for a while, sis.'

They embraced each other and cried freely before relaxing back on the bed.

CHAPTER 47

◇◇◇◇◇◇◇◇◇◇◇◇◇

I came round feeling numb from the waist down and a little thick in the head, with a nurse checking my blood pressure.

'Mr. Richards, welcome back,' she said with a very thick Latvian accent. 'Doctor with you shortly.'

'Thanks,' I answered. She wound the pipework and blood pressure cuff around the machine and left.

'Hi, buddy,' I heard a disembodied voice say from the other side of the room.

'James.' I smiled widely, and he got up from the chair, pulling it close to the bed.

'This is a story I want to hear,' I said.

'Me too. How are you feeling?'

'Absolutely fine down to my waist. I can't feel anything from there on, so I'm hoping that's good. How did you get over here—and more to the point, why? Isn't it bad enough that one of us puts his career and life on the line?'

'Really, I don't know what I was thinking other than that it appeared to me we were getting a very diluted effort from the home office and I thought you just might need some help. I also didn't want you to feel responsible for me, so it was my decision to take a low profile. My nav case—the little box of illegal tricks that you lot take the piss out of—allowed me to track and get a digital response from not only your new phone but your old one as well. Although that went dead in Prague two days ago, but not before I saw the ransom message about the swap at Ventspil. I was never convinced about an extraction by air, so the marina was my first choice. But I could also track your movements. I carried on driving around Pope long after you left last night, but I could have confirmed that the Nissan must have moved on or been garaged, because I think I covered every residential property in the village.'

'It would have been nice to know you had my back,' I said.

'I know, and it was my intention to make contact at the marina anyway, but you had already made your way up the pontoon, and I was concerned about alerting the two goons. I managed to let the two officers know that I was friendly and would position myself inside the marina in the shadows of the first hut. I didn't know at that stage that I would be the only one present without a weapon, and that World War Three was about to break out. I did see, after the Nissan turned up, that you were drawing fire from them, although I didn't appreciate at the time that you were hit. I also saw Aleysha in the back of the Nissan as it ploughed into the woodwork less than ten feet away, so I grabbed my opportunity to drag her away with the intention of running behind the car in the general direction of the two officers. It scared the shit out of me when the rear window burst in and I could see the two in the front seats, covered in blood, looking like zombies, swinging around with sub-machine guns heading our way. My only thought then was to keep Aleysha and myself as low as possible to reduce their firing angle. That was just before Hopalong Cassidy burst onto the scene and blew their brains all over the inside of the Nissan. Nice work, by the way.'

'Probably not how I envisaged the encounter going, but to be fair, I had had a similar clash earlier, on the *White Angel* in Riga.'

'So I hear,' James said. 'You and Kevin, regular Crockett and Tubbs. By the way, the two Glocks have been impounded by the special ops team. I think one of them is waiting to talk to you. I said I would let them know when you were awake.'

'Okay, thanks. I guess I'd better face the music.'

'Not sure they can complain too much; after all, mission accomplished I would say.'

'We have left a bit of a bloodbath behind us, though.'

'All bad guys, mate,' he said with a wry smile.

'How's Kevin? Do you know?' I asked.

'He's going to be fine. He's out of intensive care but was still asleep when I looked in earlier.'

'Thanks, James, for everything. You know you won't be able to claim any of this on expenses, right?'

'It's been worth it; believe me.'

'Who knows you're over here?'

'Officially, no one, but I imagine Jo suspects. She would have been down in the den and noticed my nav case missing. Whether she would mention it, I don't know.'

'How *are* the girls?'

'Still suffering the effects of shock, I think, but they will be fine. They both fell asleep in Maya's room. Best thing for them right now.'

'I'll tell the guy outside in fatigues that you are awake, shall I?'

'Sure, and thanks again, mate'

James left, and I suddenly felt tired.

Ron knocked on the door and walked in; apparently John had already been called away to another hotspot.

'Well, aren't you the hero of the day?'

'I don't feel so heroic at the moment,' I said.

'Well, probably wasn't how we would have done it, and we would have liked to keep some of the bad guys alive, but to be fair, I think all the lost ones were foot soldiers, barring Maris Provofz, and quite honestly, the world's a better place without him. That isn't to say that we condone vigilantes acquiring illegal firearms and using them ad hoc on foreign soil.'

'Right, I won't do it again, sir,' I said. *Christ, I hope I never have cause to,* I thought.

'I have the Glocks, and they are now registered to us on our equipment log. As far as anyone else outside this room is concerned, you, Powell, and Coombs were part of our undercover extraction team. That makes us look good and keeps you legal. Understood?'

I nod. 'Sure.'

'We have arrangements in place to get you all back to the UK tomorrow night. Direct RAF flight from Ventspil to Southampton. Takeoff twenty ten, arrive twenty-three fifty. No first or business class, I'm afraid, but there will be temporary bunks for you and Kevin if you need them.'

'Thanks,' I said.

'Off the record'—Ron looks around the room as though expecting someone else to be there—'It was a pleasure to sort of work alongside you—even if technically, as it turned out, it was only in a support and clear-up capacity. Had you been younger, I would have suggested you consider yourself for the service. However, look after yourself, Greg.'

'Thanks, but never in a million years.'

He smiled, we shook hands, and he left.

I must have dozed off after this encounter, probably from relief that we hadn't caused an international incident and that it looked as if no one was going to be held accountable for any misdemeanours we may have been party to. The next thing I was aware of was a gentle hand on my shoulder. I opened my eyes to see my fresh-faced partner.

'Okay, you look better than the last time I saw you,' I said, 'although I have just woken up.'

'Piss off, Richards, before I stick my finger back in your bullet hole.'

'Good to see you too.'

'How are you?'

I tried to sit up, but I was no longer numb from the waist down and felt a searing pain through my thigh.

'Okay, the anaesthetic has obviously worn off,' I said, 'but good. How about you?'

'I have been trying to write it all down, but to be honest, I'm still finding it harrowing, particularly when I think of Maya and how it could have turned out.'

'I know, but it didn't, because we have an excellent team. To be honest, it's become more like a family over the last week.'

'I have a lot to thank James for,' she said. 'And probably to apologize for as well.'

'You know he came out here on his own, don't you? I didn't know he was here until I saw him with you on the dock.'

'I haven't had a chance to talk with him yet. Apparently, according to Kevin, he left to go and see some guy called Gordie. Wanted to tie up some loose ends before we head back.'

'Gordie is a local police sergeant who helped us locate you and supplied a lot of good background intelligence that the special forces, both ours and the Latvians', used to identify the felons. There was a lot at stake for both sides here. That file that Maya's boyfriend unearthed identified billions of dollars of laundered drug money connected to a ruthless organization who we now know have no qualms about disposing of people who get in their way. Father and son Menshabins? They were gunned down in their attempt to shut down other interested parties involved with their organization—people in the know who could put the operation in jeopardy. You and Maya were kept alive as a bargaining chip, although Kevin thinks there is something deeper that may relate back to his parents and your relationship with them. Currently we know their operation extends from Northern Europe to South America, but it is probably much wider. We believe that Banfield, Kevin's company in Puerto Rico, and a company called Elevation Textiles here in Riga, along with a finance house in Bournemouth, are just the tip of the iceberg. We also think the Tithe cottage is in some way bound in as well. Your contract on that has been terminated. Oh, and by the way, the scab on my chin and my funky haircut are thanks to a home-made bomb that was set in the Tithe shed and nearly took my head off.'

'What! At the cottage?

'Yes. It's going to need some work, I'm afraid.'

'Bloody hell, Greg! I'm not worried about that, but shit, this was just something we stumbled on. No idea all this was going on in and around Bournemouth. Wow!'

'How are Kevin and Maya?' I asked.

She looked dazed from these revelations and said almost absently, 'Making up for lost time, I think.' Staring across the room at nothing in particular, she shook her head as if to wash these thoughts away. 'Yes, sorry, Kevin was talking to her about the events at Mayako Hospital in Japan. Not something I wished to revisit, so, I left them to it. Thought I should come and see if you were awake.'

'So good to see you Aley; you can't imagine.'

'Really, you think? There were times when I wasn't sure I'd see the light of day again, let alone friends and colleagues. I didn't know about the ransom so couldn't figure why they hadn't disposed of us. God knows it would have been easy enough.'

'Yes, sorry … thoughtless'

'No not at all, but seeing you, Kevin, and James coming to our rescue …' She filled up, and I grabbed her and held her close for only the second time in six years.

'How can people be so evil?' she said between sobs.

'I don't know, but what I do know is that we are not going to let this shit bug us for the rest of our lives. We will fix it, and we will come out stronger and more determined to root out the bad guys. That's what we do, Aley.'

'I know.' She wiped her face with her hands. 'You want a coffee?'

'Dream on; we need something much stronger.'

CHAPTER 48

◇◇◇◇◇◇◇◇◇◇◇◇◇

It had been a very late night, and at 7.00 a.m. Chris walked into a deserted incident room. He phoned through to Robin Grant, not really knowing what to expect. After a preliminary debrief, he expressed mixed emotions at a successful assignment, but at the cost of a massive clear-up operation, and with a lot of unanswered questions about the Bournemouth CID involvement.

'An inquiry into who knew what, who did what, and why would undoubtedly follow,' Robin said. 'The upside for all parties is that they have, at the same time, thwarted a major drug and money laundering operation with worldwide tentacles. Three Eastern Europeans have been arrested for illegal firearms possession from the dock house in Riga, including one Janek Dvroak, wanted in at least three other countries on various charges including attempted murder and money laundering. Intelligence on the *White Angels* proved positive, and both have been seized by the Latvian drug enforcement and contraband authority.'

Chris started to relax a little as Robin continued. 'Elevation Textiles were raided at first light this morning by Gordie and his team, and all assets seized and operations halted, pending further investigation. And we *will* do what we can to show your, may I say in hindsight, *exceptional* team in as good a light as possible.'

'Thanks, Robin'

The call ended, and Chris put the phone down, rocked back in his chair, and sighed.

Joanne appeared at the coffee machine and called across. 'Coffee, guv?'

'Yeah, I'll have it with a shot of brandy, please.'

'Sorry, the pods with brandy have all gone.' She smiled.

Looking fresher than she deserved to look, she walked into his office with the coffees.

Chris looked up at her as she entered. 'Did you know James was out there?'

'I didn't know, but it doesn't surprise me. His nav case was missing from the den. That's the only thing that might have suggested he was at least trying to keep in contact with Greg.'

'Could you mention it next time, please?'

'You think there's going to be a next time, guv?'

'I sincerely hope not. Exciting as it may have been at times, the worry for Aleysha and her sister and other team members was not worth it.'

'Not to mention the paperwork coming our way off the back of it,' Joanne said. 'When will they be back?'

'A while, I guess. They won't release Kevin or Greg from hospital for a couple of days at least. Can you start processing the incident reports and log everything off the whiteboards and screens. There are a number of issues that will come off the back of this: the situation with the Tithe cottage, the Menshabins, and the apparent murder of William "Billy" Conro.'

'Will do,' she said.

'Phil will be in around ten; get him on board as well. Thanks, Jo.'

Joanne left the office and took her coffee to her desk. She tapped the password to open up the CID screen and finished the coffee while waiting for it to load.

The flashing amber signal at the bottom left of the screen informed her that she had unopened email. Clicking on it, she saw she had three emails in bold. Two informed her that she had training days next month, and the third was from Greg. Attached was a photograph of him and James relaxing on his hospital bed, with the caption 'Don't know what all the fuss is about.'

She quickly typed back, 'What fuss? Have I missed something?'

CHAPTER 49

〰〰〰〰〰〰〰

We were to be flown home on an A400M Atlas troop carrier, feeling like we were being smuggled out of a communist state country under the cover of darkness. The aircraft was on the outskirts of the airfield, and we were driven in two armed jeeps, under armed guard, through a gateway in the perimeter fence.

There to meet us before we were ushered aboard were Gordie, Jan, and Petor.

Gordie walked up to me and shook the free hand that was not holding on to a crutch. 'You are welcome any time, Greg. my guys say they have never had so much excitement in such a short space of time. I hope you get well soon.'

'Thanks, Gordie, and thanks for all your help; I hope we haven't caused too much trouble—read: paperwork.'

Ignoring that, he turned to the girls, standing back, and said, 'So this is what it was all about. Okay, I understand now. Well worth the effort. Good job, guys. Oh, Ellis and the others send their best wishes.'

Jan and Petor shook my hand, nodded, and smiled.

James offered his hand and said, 'Without these two, I don't know where we would be.'

I agreed.

Gordie said, 'They are good at their job. They are going to have to be with the amount of work you have left us to do. We currently have six people in our jails connected to Elevation Textiles, and I think that will be something that rolls on and on.'

'Sorry,' I said.

'Not at all. Riga is committed to putting the past behind us. Clearing

251

out the old regime with its inherent corruption is our goal. From our point of view, it's just a pity it took a foreigner to unearth it.'

'I'm very happy for you to take the credit; it was not what we were here for,' I said, looking at the girls.

We briefly shook hands again as an RAF officer was becoming increasingly impatient to get us on board.

The girls said their thank-yous and we walked—or, in my case, waddled—up the cargo bay platform.

There were two cots laid out on one side of the transporter and well-padded seats with full harness seat belts down the other. We all sat, Kevin alongside Maya, and Aleysha with James. I was on the end nearest the bay door as it slowly clamped shut, and we were underway. After about half an hour of mulling over the events of the week and looking down the row of what I could now call very close friends, I felt incredibly grateful to all involved at the outcome. So I succumbed to the horizontal position of the cot and fell asleep. It felt good to be heading home.

CHAPTER 50

◇◇◇◇◇◇◇◇◇◇◇◇◇

Several weeks later

I had done a lot of sitting around over recent weeks and had watched the Autumn leaves turn and fall. My leg was getting better by the day, and I could see that Kevin, though still in a lot of pain, was becoming restless to get home. However, his consultant was nevertheless unhappy about him flying long-haul. He spent virtually all his time on the phone, and I knew this was to do with his business back in Puerto Rico.

Aleysha and I were finally being allowed back to work next week, and to be honest we were not sure whether we were looking forward to it or not. Jet was almost back to his old self, now walking and running at about a fifteen-degree angle. His shaved patches were still quite obvious, but that aside, there were no physical signs of his trauma other than cowering whenever approached by anyone he was unfamiliar with.

Pat recovered well after being brought out of her coma and, according to her doctors, would have no lasting side effects. Right now she was partially deaf in one ear and suffering recurring headaches, both of which the doctors assured her would subside within a few weeks. She was convalescing at home and spending a lot of time walking with Jet and Lucy. They had become firm friends, as indeed we all had. Pat and I met up at the Aruba bar just off Bournemouth Pier for a drink a week ago, and we were joined by her brother Joe and, I think I can be sure now, girlfriend Stephanie. IN-Need, as a group, were under administration, but Joe and Steph were looking to make an offer for the single premises in Bournemouth if they could secure the client base.

Neville Hillingdon was still in hospital but was improving with the help of Maya and Aleysha. His coma had left him with no recollection of either the accident or events leading up to it. His last memory was of him and Maya enjoying an Indian takeaway at a desk in his office, oblivious of the events about to unfold.

Maya had drip fed him with titbits of the last few weeks, but he was experiencing short bouts of depression, and she'd been concerned about overloading him. I had seen him several times on the ward, and he seemed a really nice guy. In Aleysha's words, he was the best that Maya had attracted so far. He was expected to be allowed home within the next few days, once he'd mastered the art of walking up and down stairs on crutches.

Repairs to the cottage were to begin in four weeks' time at a cost of over £45,000. But Kevin had negotiated some major structural improvements and got the insurance company to agree to pay 85 per cent. Everyone seemed very happy with that, but its future with respect to ownership appeared to be up for debate. A revaluation, after the rebuild, was put at £1.5 million, and Kevin was happy for that to be split equally between the girls. Kevin had also offered to invest that for them and could guarantee an annual return of forty thousand each, which was the part up for debate—but I felt that would not be for long.

⚬ᴍᴍᴏ

Back in the Virgin lounge at Heathrow, Maya, and Aleysha, and I settled into the easy chairs looking out over runway one. Kevin, the only one with a flight bag, looked relieved to be on his way home as he joined us and pulled up a chair, and then winced with the pain from his shoulder.

However, looks can be deceptive.

'You know, if it weren't for the fact that I have responsibilities to a lot of people back home,' he said, 'I think I would stay. I'm going to miss you all.'

'And the weather?' I asked.

'Okay, there is that. If it weren't for the responsibilities and the weather.'

'And the attractive Puerto Rican ladies,' Maya said wryly.

He sighed. 'The responsibilities, weather, and ladies. Yes,' he said dreamily. 'Oh, the ladies.'

We all smiled and agreed that he wouldn't be staying this side of the Atlantic anytime soon, but that we would miss him too. It had been quite a journey we had all been on, and it had affected us all in one way or another.

Three vodka martinis and one bottled beer arrived on a tray escorted by one of the model-like Virgin hostesses, who also produced four lunchtime menus.

We had about an hour before Kevin had to board, so we all ordered some light snacks—except Kevin, who ordered the all-day Virgin breakfast.

'I won't see one of these for a long time,' he said.

The decision had been taken to sell the Tithe, and Kevin asked the girls collectively to keep him informed and said he would let them know about the investments just as soon as the arrangements had been made. At his insistence, and much to the girls' vigorous objections, Kevin said he would set the investments up with his money until the release of monies from the cottage, which, along with their existing benefits from the Tithe from previous years, would give them both the freedom to choose what they wanted to do. He also added that if any of us needed anything, he was there and could be here within twenty-four hours.

We hadn't really had a lot of time to talk about what was happening in Puerto Rico. My impression was that he either didn't want to discuss it or there were real problems. If it were the latter, I would have expected him to raise the issue.

As it turns out, there *were* a lot of problems, but he had been consumed with trying to sort them out.

'Sorry,' he said, 'But the issues back at the factory have taken their toll. It turns out that my right-hand man—or should I say woman, Simona—was tied into the scam. She was keeping two sets of books; she was arranging deals with these so-called textile suppliers. I am very sad about it. I've known Simona for five years. She came with great references and has lived up to them all. So right now she is in a Puerto Rican jail, the thought of which has kept me awake at night. And she will stay there, pending an enquiry which will not even get to the top of the judiciary pile until I get back and start proceedings. In addition, all barring two of my suppliers have disappeared. I have fifty plus staff that I have had to restrict to standard eight-hour days. Half of them, as of last week, have no productive work until I can get new suppliers on board.'

'Eight-hour day—doesn't sound so bad,' I said.

'They expect to work ten or even twelve hours. They are hard workers, good workers, and I pay them well above the average, but it is still subsistence. Which accounts for why I have had no complaints from any of them so far. Currently I'm covering half the salary bill personally. Hence, among all other things, my need to get back as soon as possible.'

More vodka martinis were consumed before the Virgin hostess approached Kevin to let him know that boarding would be in five minutes.

We all hugged and said our sincere goodbyes, and I, for one, was very sad to see him go. We all had a great deal to thank him for.

We stayed in the lounge and watched him board, waving as he walked up the stairway and into the Airbus A380.

I checked at the desk to see whether we owed anything for our drinks and snacks, but as expected, it had already been dealt with.

The drive back to Bournemouth was sombre, made more so as within twenty minutes of leaving Heathrow, Aleysha in the front and Maya, spread out on the back seat, were asleep—a result of the vodka martinis, I suspect.

CHAPTER 51

◇◇◇◇◇◇◇◇◇◇◇◇◇◇◇

Two months later

Aleysha and I were in conference room 1, tying up the loose ends of the MEMS case. There was one file that we left to one side which was associated with the new identities that it would appear Poppa Menshabin had arranged for the two missing Benfield employees. This was still open and held an interest for us both; at some point in time, we would look into closing this.

Aleysha's phone buzzed.

'It's Kevin,' she said looking at me, laying the phone down between us and touching the loud-speak button. A photograph of Kevin with his arm in a sling flashed up on her screen.

'Hi, Kevin, how you doin'?' she said. 'I have Greg here on loudspeaker.'

'Great, thanks. You guys okay?'

'Hi, Kev, good to hear you. How's your shoulder?'

'Mate, I get slight twinges now and again, but really, it's fine. Listen, I'm coming over to London next week; I really need to see you guys.'

'Sure, when?' Aleysha asked.

'Well, I'm landing Wednesday, but I have some business to deal with in Stoke Newington on Thursday. Perhaps we could catch up on Friday?'

'Yeah. How long are you over here for?' I asked.

'Don't know yet; the weather's not been that good, and the Puerto Rican women are losing their looks.'

'Great, shall we come to you, or you to us?'

'I thought I'd book into that hotel you and I stayed in at Bournemouth. Derby Lodge or something.'

'Derby Manor,' I said. 'I'll book it; how many nights.'

'Three for starters; we'll see where we go from there. See if you can get the suite on the top floor. Thanks.'

'That's great. Can't wait to see you again,' Aleysha said.

'Dare I ask how Pacific Fabrinet is doing,' I said.

'It's now MAleycoomb Textiles, and it is starting to turn around. But listen, we'll talk about that next week. Really looking forward to seeing you all.'

He disconnected, and the photo disappeared.

The new name wasn't lost on either of us.

'Wow,' Aleysha said. 'What do you think that was all about.'

'Don't know. Don't care. It will be just great to see him again,' I said.

'He knows that the cottage is up for auction Tuesday week; maybe he wants to see how it goes,' she said.

'Perhaps he wants to see it before it goes? That would tie in with a three-day stay.'

'I sent him photographs of the before and after. It looks really good now it's finished,' she said. 'The builders have done a remarkable job. How about we take a drive out this evening?'

'I would like that,' I replied.

'Jet can have a run around the garden,' she said.

We agreed for Aley to come over to mine, as it's sort of on the way, for around six-thirty, and take my car from there to the cottage. Jet is happy in the back of the Focus.

'Maybe take in a meal on the way home,' I suggested.

'There's a new place in town I would quite like to try.'

'That's it then.'

We cleared the files away, completed the outstanding paperwork, and headed off home.

⁂

The cottage was spectacular. The double-width garage extended well past where the shed used to be, with four fold-back mahogany doors, topped with a beautiful dark grey slate roof that had been blended into the ornately finished existing thatch perfectly.

I had mixed emotions as Aleysha turned the key in the new matching mahogany front door. How I felt when I was here last rushed back when

I walked through the hall and into the conservatory. It was a physical sensation in my chest—the same desperation I felt at the time when I was searching for clues as to Aleysha's whereabouts, mixed with the gratitude that it was now all over.

A completely different emotion hit me as we ventured out onto the patio. I shook my head, the hairs on the back of my neck prickled, and I found my hand brushing across the scar on my chin.

'Are you okay?' Aleysha asked.

'Just reliving my last visit.'

'Sorry, this was probably not a good idea.'

'No, I'm fine, really. It's wonderful, Aley. Are you sure you're doing the right thing in selling it?'

We sat on the patio steps. 'Yes, I'm sure. Much as I have always loved it, and the alterations are fabulous, I could never have envisaged actually living here, even if I could have afforded it. I'm more of an apartment-in-town person than a cottage-in-the-country person.'

I knew what she meant. We scanned the rear of the property, where there was a new, larger, utility room, running along two thirds of the back of the garage, fully equipped with washers and dryers. The last third was taken up with a brick-built shed, complete with large stable-type door.

Aleysha took my hand in hers and turned towards me.

'I'm so sorry for what happened to you here. Let's go.'

She locked the conservatory door, and I walked back past the kitchen. In the darkness of the hallway, I was aware of a light flashing on the phone display. 'I can't believe this has been left in.' I said.

'I think there is some issue over ownership; the agents are looking into it, but it probably still belongs to Bodican.

'What's this flashing light mean?' I asked.

Aleysha walked over and hits one of the buttons.

'Message for the occupant: Please ensure that there will be someone resident in the property on 14 March, as there will be an engineer on site at 10.30 a.m. to remove the phone equipment. Thank you.'

'We should have this taken out. Our special electronics ops division just may be able to get something useful out of it.'

'I agree,' she said. 'It's the fourteenth tomorrow.'

I rang Chris and let him know, and he agreed to send a comms engineer as soon as, and for a plainclothes officer to act as the resident.

I'm not sorry to leave the Tithe and am very happy to be supping a half of lager in the Plough on the way back.

'So where are we going?' I asked.

'Casa GourMex. It's Mexican,' she said.

I look down at Jet. 'Sorry, mate, you're going to have to go home.'

CHAPTER 52

◇◇◇◇◇◇◇◇◇◇◇◇◇

Kevin was happy to make his own way to Bournemouth, and we agreed to meet up at the Brasserie Blanc, a French Raymond Blanc restaurant with a large covered outdoor seating area overlooking the English Channel.

Gazing out to sea, we had a clear blue sky, and a light refreshing breeze was fluttering the pure white canvas awnings. Aley, Maya, and I were early and well into a bottle of Côtes du Rhône when I looked around, hearing heavy footsteps heading in our direction, and saw the recognizable figure of Kevin striding up along the wooden boards towards us with a broad smile. Aley was immediately on her feet and rushed up to embrace him, and Maya was not far behind. I stood up and realized he was not alone. There was a very beautiful olive-skinned lady three or four paces behind, who pulled up short when Kevin was engulfed by his cousins. Walking around the threesome, I extended my hand in her direction, and she grasped it gently.

'I'm Greg,' I said, 'and in there somewhere are Kevin's cousins Maya and Aleysha.'

Her light, crisp voice has an accent that would melt hearts. 'Yes I know,' she said. 'Believe me, I have heard an awful lot about you all.'

Kevin turned around, still holding Aleysha's and Maya's hands in his. 'Let me introduce you,' he said, freeing himself from the girls and putting his arm around the stranger. 'This is Simona.'

Our expressions must have given something subconscious away.

'Yes,' he said, 'the same Simona that we talked about before. It has taken a long time to sort things out, but that is a story for another time. I need a drink.' He looked down at our table. 'And not red wine.'

He called a waiter over and ordered a jug of French 75. He explained as we all sat. 'A marriage of champagne, gin, lemon juice, and zest.' He and Simona looked and smiled at each other. 'Something I have been introduced to recently.'

After feasting on Brixham crab, boeuf bourguignon, a Moroccan mezze platter, and confit duck leg, we all felt stuffed and spoilt, and we moved to the inside lounge to relax.

Simona was delightful, as quietly confident as she was attractive; and if introducing her to us all was the purpose of the visit, that would have been all great by me. However, as the afternoon turned to evening, the real purpose started to emerge.

'Our adventure,' he said, 'has highlighted events happening around the world that are destroying lives. Just as one example, and I have unearthed several over the last few weeks, Simona's family—and I mean her whole family—have lived the past four years in fear for their lives, reliant on Simona and her brother, who works in the same capacity at a textile recycling plant in Bayamon, Puerto Rico, assigning deals to either pre-allocated, bogus, or illegal suppliers and running a hidden set of accounts. There were two attempts on Simona's life in jail, which were, in all honesty, probably only foiled because of my and Simona's previous involvement with the security services there. I have moved her family from Rio Piedras to Condado, near our factory, with new identities and new jobs in the hope of protecting them.

'The police departments across Puerto are now running these corrupt outfits and their associates to ground. To be honest, we may have taken the heart out of the organization in Puerto Rico, but that is a very small cog in a very large gearbox.'

'What are you saying, Kev?' I asked, not sure where this was going.

'Bear with me. Right now we have the factory running on an even keel. Our meeting yesterday in Stoke Newington was very good for us. We have struck an exclusive deal with Afrique Fabrics to supply new and innovative materials and designs, which will bring us into profitability again before the end of the year—not like it was, but that's okay; at least now I know any profit is fully clean. I have a new CEO in place, and Simona here is bringing the finance director up to speed, which will release us from the day-to-day running of the business. I want to get to the core of this organization and cut it out ... and I would like you to join me.'

This last remark was directed at me, which had taken me aback somewhat.

Aleysha piped up. 'You're not leaving me out!'

'No of course not—nor you, Maya, if you want.'

'Hold up a minute,' I said, 'We can't just go chasing a cartel all over the world when (a) we don't know who we are chasing, (b) we don't know where they are based, and (c) we have no authority.'

'Maybe not, and I'll cover the authority angle later, but I have a very good place to start. I believe my parents were sucked into this in Asia maybe ten or twelve years ago. I think the Tithe and other places like it were set up as safe houses when they needed to hide away important individuals when things got too hot, keeping them securely connected to their networks while arrangements were made to relocate them. I have a lot of contacts now in Japan and South Korea, and I believe that is where the epicentre is.'

'Great, Triads and would-be Genghis Kahn-ites. Oh and (d), by the way,' I said, 'we have no means of funding it.'

Simona leaned down, picked up her clutch bag, and pulled out an envelope marked 'Cuartel de la Policía de Puerto Rico'. She extracted a folded letter and handed it to Kevin.

'I will translate,' he said.

'It will be easier if I do that,' Simona said, taking the letter back.

'And it will sound so much better,' I added.

She smiled, Kevin agreed, and we all sat back.

'"To Mr Kevin Coombs,

'"Due to our combined efforts across the whole of Puerto Rico between police and port authorities, government agencies, and Mr Kevin to close down and bring to justice the parties involved with the illegal drug trafficking and money ..."' She stopped and smiled. 'Sorry, no real word for "laundering"; "washing" is as near as we get.' She continued. '"... money laundering brought to the attention of the authorities by Mr Kevin. We believe great progress has been made over the previous few months to eradicate this with upwards of thirty-five individuals placed in custody and as many as eight illegal businesses closed. Many checks and balances have now been put in place to ensure Puerto Rico remains as free as possible from this cancer.

"'As a result, a fund has been set up from the proceeds recovered so far and, as of writing this, stands at $47.5 million and rising. After reimbursement to those genuine workers who have lost their jobs during this phase, 50 per cent of the remaining fund will be returned to the Puerto Rican citizens in tax reforms; the remaining 50 per cent is to be put at the disposal of Mr Kevin to fund the ongoing fight against this activity here in Puerto Rico and wherever else Mr Kevin feels fit. The authorities here and the US State Department have sanctioned that Mr Kevin set up an exploratory team to collect intelligence and report findings of such activity. His team will receive support wherever possible from local law enforcement authorities in all countries that the United States have friendly agreements with. Checks will be put in place to ensure that there is no conflict between the fund and MAleycoomb Textiles; to this end, Mr Kevin has agreed to step down from the board of directors of said company while maintaining a controlling share. Contracts will be put in place to formalize this in due course.'"

She placed the letter on the low table in front of us and said, 'Signed by Pedro Rossello, Commander in Chief and Mayor, Puerto Rico; and Michael Pomero, Secretary of State, United States of America.'

We remained silent for what seemed like an age, all of us mulling over our own, probably very different, views as to where this could lead.

Aleysha was the first to break. 'Okay, not at all what I expected this trip of yours to yield.' She looked straight at me 'What do you think?'

Kevin said, 'Look, this isn't something we can all decide over a few drinks; I know that. But there are other things you should probably be aware of as to where this whole thing is going.

'The US is keen to assist because they know most of the drugs and drug money are filtered into the mainland through the likes of Puerto, Cuba, Panama, et cetera. We can have a significant effect without them putting their heads above the parapet, and it's self-funded, so no cost to the US taxpayer. As far as they are concerned, this is a win-win. We'—and he holds Simona's hand—'are heading over to Riga next week. Chief Bravof, Gordie's boss, has arranged for a meeting with a Latvian presidential aid, along with British and US embassy officials, to discuss a similar arrangement. According to Gordie, whom I spoke with a couple of weeks ago, they have impounded cocaine and cannabis worth millions, and cash to the tune of fifty-six million euros, not including the two impounded *White Angels*—which, by the way, though are both marked as the *White Angel*, the one that the girls were abducted on, and effectively the dirty one, is registered as the *Dark Angel*. Rather poignant, really.'

He continued. 'Though Latvia and surrounding states are still a long way from democracy, and I know from my discussion with Gordie they have concerns that a number of government officials may well be connected in some way to this ring, they are essentially very keen, if only at this stage, to be seen to be making the right moves to eradicate corruption. I think it will be baby steps, but we know there is a lot of good intelligence to be gained in Latvia—Intelligence that I hope will lead us to the dissolution of this evil cartel, that has put Simona, Aley, and Maya through hell and continues to do the same to others.'

He refers to a notepad as though having lost his way for a minute. He then sighs. 'We are not likely to get the same immediate response out of the UK. It's a far more bureaucratic and stuffy organization, with rules and regulations on top of rules and regulations. Okay, it's going to take longer, but I think we can make inroads if we lead by results and show what we can achieve elsewhere with a dedicated team and a single agenda. Our future presentations will include past successes.'

There was another brief silence as we took in the scope of what Kevin and Simona had put together in such a short time.

'Look,' I said, 'What you have achieved is remarkable, but you're right; this isn't something to jump into without careful consideration of all the implications. You have obviously thought this through, but I do wonder whether emotion is your prime driving force. I think we all need to sleep on this. This is life-changing in every respect. How about we all catch up at the manor tomorrow evening, say six o'clock.'

'You're right,' Kevin said. 'My initial reaction was driven out of fear— fear for the girls, then by the wrongdoing that Simona had been put through, and after that I saw the cloud that her family had had to live under. And yes, I was angry. Yes, it did drive me to obsession. But I think that over the past few weeks, some degree of normality has returned; I can now be more objective, look at the bigger picture. My position, albeit lowly in Puerto Rico, has enabled me to make contact with people who can make a difference and who are prepared to listen to my proposals and back them, as has been shown by this letter. I agree that whoever wants to be involved needs to enter with his or her eyes open, and to that end you all need some time for consideration to allow what's at stake to be absorbed. I'm putting no pressure on anyone. Simona here has come on board because of her commitment to do right by the people that this syndicate has wronged. But if she wants out, that's fine too; there are no contracts being put together here, just an agreement to do the right thing wherever possible to bring the perpetrators to justice.'

Looking around at the three of us, Kevin said, 'I didn't mean to provoke such a solemn mood among us.'

'Thoughtful, I think, not solemn,' I said. 'You show a passion that I know we would all like to possess, and maybe we will, but there's a lot to take in.'

We finished our warm, flat drinks and all agreed to meet up tomorrow.

'Do you need a lift to the manor?' Aleysha asked Kevin.

'No, we have a hire car, thanks.'

We said our goodbyes, and I drove Maya and Aleysha home in virtual silence, all lost in our own thoughts. I had a few that kept coming back, such as the phone system at the Tithe, with reference to what Kevin said about safe houses and the need to keep in close contact with their network. I felt that might explain the over-specified phone system and the satellite dish in the roof space. I also couldn't get away from the two missing Banfield employees being implicated but probably missing of their own accord. As part of or to get away from the syndicate? That's a question I kept asking myself. And on balance I was coming down in favour of the former, in which case they could be an asset. *I'm thinking as though I've already agreed to change my life. What would Catherine say?*

CHAPTER 53

◇◇◇◇◇◇◇◇◇◇◇◇◇

Friday was normally quiet—a day I put aside to do paperwork and catch up on deferred emails. I let Chris know I was going to be doing this from home today.

Believing I would get more done was wishful thinking, as I couldn't get my mind away from Kevin's proposal. I deliberately didn't contact Aley, as I was sure she would be going through the same dilemma and didn't want to have any influence on her decision. However, at ten thirty, she rang.

'I haven't slept a wink,' she said.

'No, me neither.'

'I think we need to sit down together and compile a list of pros and cons—questions that we have answers to and those that we don't.

'I agree,' I said. 'Do you want to come over?'

'Sure, I'll be over lunchtime.' I heard Maya say in the background, 'Me too.'

'Yes, all three of us,' I said.

I had several cups of coffee but couldn't focus on anything else, so I went out and took Jet for a walk, hoping the fresh air might help. It didn't, but when I returned, Pat and Lucy were waiting outside my door.

'We thought *we* could do that?' Lucy said.

'I know. Sorry, I needed some fresh air to clear my head, but it hasn't worked. Come in. Do you want a coffee or something?'

Pat, who had had long hair before the incident, which necessitated most of its removal, was developing a bob, but it was still spiky on top where her head had to be shaved.

'How are you feeling?' I said to her.

'Good. I haven't had a headache in three days, and according to the

267

audio doctor, I have about 75 per cent of my hearing back. Quite honestly, if that's all I suffer from this, I consider myself very lucky. Can I have tea, please?'

'Me too,' Lucy said, petting Jet.

'How are Joe and Stephanie?' I asked Pat.

'They're good; they have managed to arrange finance for the business, but the administrators are trying to negotiate a price for the client base—which they are holding out for at the moment, as they don't see this having any value to anyone else. And at ten thousand, they think it is too steep.'

'I agree; they should stand their ground.'

I put the teas down on the kitchen table.

'Listen, if you two want to take Jet off, that's fine. I have a meeting in half an hour. Not sure whether we'll have it here or down the King's Head.'

'King's Head sounds favourite,' Lucy said.

Pat sat down at the kitchen table and pulled her tea towards her, and I could see she was pondering something.

'What is it, Pat?' I asked.

'I don't know; I've been getting visions—flashbacks really. I'm sure you don't want to talk about this now.'

'Go on,' I said, pulling up a chair.

'Chris has let me look through some of the Hillingdon / Blue Rabbit case files while I've been home, and something the doctor who was attacked at the hospital said brought something back. That afternoon when I was here, I heard the knock on the door, never even considering looking through the peephole, which was stupid. The minute I turned the latch, the door burst open with such force that I was immediately knocked to the floor. They were both wearing masks, but the short one—the woman, we all presume—stood over me just before I heard the other one say something like "Teeagow". I looked up to see Jet skidding on the floor to get purchase, with his teeth bared. But I think I saw a scar on her chin under her mask. The next thing I heard was a short yelp from Jet, and then everything goes blank. The thing is, *Gŏu* is "dog" in Chinese. So it could have been him warning her about Jet. Tia may be her name. Now Janek Dvorak keeps coming up in the case file, and I remember when I was stationed at the met in 2017 and the Kamid Hussain case fell apart. Everyone knew it was Dvorak who had beaten him with a baseball bat before shooting him, but when you take away the eyewitnesses, which is what happened, we only ever had circumstantial evidence. The point is, Dvorak had a close association with one Tia Chien Tu, who sported a scar under her chin, believed to be from an altercation with a Triad boss. But I still might have dreamt it, Greg.'

'I don't think so,' I said. But at the same time, I was thinking, *This could just be another small piece of the ever-expanding puzzle.* 'Thanks, Pat. this could well be important in the long run. Right now I don't know where this investigation is going.'

We finished our tea, and they gathered Jet's lead and some biscuits and left.

I called Aley and suggested we meet at the King's Head instead. They were happy with that, and half an hour later I was seated outside in the pub garden with a refreshing lager and a head full of questions. The girls were fashionably late and agreed on a bottle of Pinot Grigio. We were obviously not working today.

Within just a few minutes, we had aired a number of concerns.

Maya wanted to count herself out even though she knew she would probably have regrets later, but she felt she had a commitment to Neville. Also, Banfield was being renamed and restructured, and she believed there would be some exciting opportunities there. Aleysha's concerns were for her sister, but Maya insisted she doesn't want that to be an issue. Mine were for Jet, and there had to be some serious number-crunching done.

We went around the issues over several beers and wines. Some things seemed less of an obstacle with the aid of alcohol, while others only got worse.

At three o'clock, Aleysha's phone rang. 'It's Kevin,' she said, putting it to her ear. '... Yes, sure ... I'll see ... Okay then ... Thanks.' She put her phone down on the table.

'He would like to go the Tithe—asked if you would come with us?'

'I'll take a rain check on that if you don't mind,' I said. 'We'll catch up later.'

'We'll see you at the manor at six?'

'Will do.'

Kevin and Simona were in the conservatory at the back of the manor when we arrived, and they both got up and greeted us warmly.

Kevin had arranged a bottle of Champagne, and there were trays of canapés on the glass table.

After the pleasantries, we all sat down businesslike and put our concerns on the table. Kevin listened with both thoughtfulness and interest before he launched into his proposal and how, if we wanted, we could fit into it.

'Okay, there will be three arms to this team,' he said, 'intelligence, legwork and business expansion. I can see Aleysha supported by myself and Greg, chasing down leads, tracking the money, or whatever on paper, the Internet and via the Dark Web. Greg and I will follow up on these, checking for authenticity and relevance. In the initial instance, the focus would be on the syndicate we have personal ties to, but in the long term, this will be expanded to include other corrupt organizations where drugs, money laundering, or people-trafficking are involved. For us to function, there always has to be a money angle that we can exploit, for it to be self-funding. We must be able to give back to those who have been harmed or damaged in any way by the organizations we aim to bring to justice. For us to stay safe, we need to be anonymous, work in the shadows ... Sorry, I'm talking as though you are all on board here. You are our dream team.' He looked at Simona. 'But we are committed to taking this forward, one way or another. It will just be slower and harder without you.'

He continued. 'Because we want to be a single-issue team, we will need other countries, other authorities, and other business interests to sign up. This is where I could see you, if you wanted to, Maya, playing a significant role alongside Simona. Presentations and promotional literature will need to be professionally put together to pitch our programme. You have the skills to do this, Maya, and Simona has the story line to base it on. Approximately 90 per cent of your time can be spent here in Bournemouth, with a small outfit, preparing for the 10 per cent away from home, where you and Simona pitch your proposals.'

Maya smiled. I felt she could see herself in this role.

'Of course, there are many obstacles we will need to address. For one, most will have to be conducted in a foreign language, but I'm sure there must be ways around that.'

Maya nodded. She'd had to do that in the past for Banfield.

'How are we to be underwritten?' I asked.

'For me to say that you don't need to worry about that sounds way too glib,' Kevin said, 'but in all honesty, the fund from Puerto Rico alone will cover us all for the next five years, and I know we will get something similar out of Latvia. And, okay, if the worst happens and we can't get any additional funding, we wrap it up five years from now knowing we gave it our best shot. And whatever happens, we will have helped countless individuals in the process. But shall we eat? I have a table booked in the restaurant here. As I recall, it was excellent last time.' He looked at me.

⟨⟩

Sitting back, having finished a meal that I was sure none of us would recall in the future, I couldn't believe how far we had all come. As I surveyed those around the table warmly, the conversation, which prior to sitting down here had been very one-sided, was now all-encompassing, everyone having his or her say with enthusiasm and vigour. Kevin, and I assume Simona, had thought of everything. They had a clear vision—a vision that they would like us to be part of. As a bit of an outsider, I felt privileged to be included, and just a little excited. I found myself talking in my head to Catherine again. She would want to help the helpless—that I know for sure.

As the evening drew on and the restaurant emptied, I thought that all of Kevin and Simona's efforts needed a conclusion, one way or the other, from us.

'So,' I said, 'How do we do this? With a show of hands? Or a simple yes-no?'

Aleysha immediately raised her hand and said, 'Yes.'

Maya followed 'Yes.'

'Then it's unanimous,' I said. 'When do we start?'

ABOUT THE AUTHOR

◇◇◇◇◇◇◇◇◇◇◇◇◇◇

Paul A Cooper was born 1952 in Solihull, Birmingham, UK, an unspoiled only child of Doreen and Alan Cooper. (He added the 'unspoiled' bit)

Having been brought up in Kenilworth, Cooper moved to Warwick in the early seventies and has now settled in Leamington Spa. He first had the intention of writing a book in his late twenties, long before computers, spell check, or five children. After about thirty handwritten foolscap pages, the project was abandoned, never to see the light of day again.

Now entering retirement and looking for a hobby that can constructively fill a space previously occupied by full-time employment, Cooper finds that writing works well as that hobby and is an unexpected pleasure.

Printed and bound by CPI Group (UK) Ltd, Croydon, CR0 4YY